Rajni

Gurutej Singh Khalsa

Order this book online at www.trafford.com
or email orders@trafford.com

Most Trafford titles are also available at major online book retailers.

© Copyright 2014 Gurutej Singh Khalsa.
All rights reserved. No part of this publication may be reproduced, stored in a retrieval system, or transmitted, in any form or by any means, electronic, mechanical, photocopying, recording, or otherwise, without the written prior permission of the author.

Printed in the United States of America.

ISBN: 978-1-4907-4330-1 (sc)
ISBN: 978-1-4907-4331-8 (hc)
ISBN: 978-1-4907-4332-5 (e)

Library of Congress Control Number: 2014913980

Because of the dynamic nature of the Internet, any web addresses or links contained in this book may have changed since publication and may no longer be valid. The views expressed in this work are solely those of the author and do not necessarily reflect the views of the publisher, and the publisher hereby disclaims any responsibility for them.

Any people depicted in stock imagery provided by Thinkstock are models, and such images are being used for illustrative purposes only. Certain stock imagery © Thinkstock.

Trafford rev. 08/26/2014

www.trafford.com
North America & international
toll-free: 1 888 232 4444 (USA & Canada)
fax: 812 355 4082

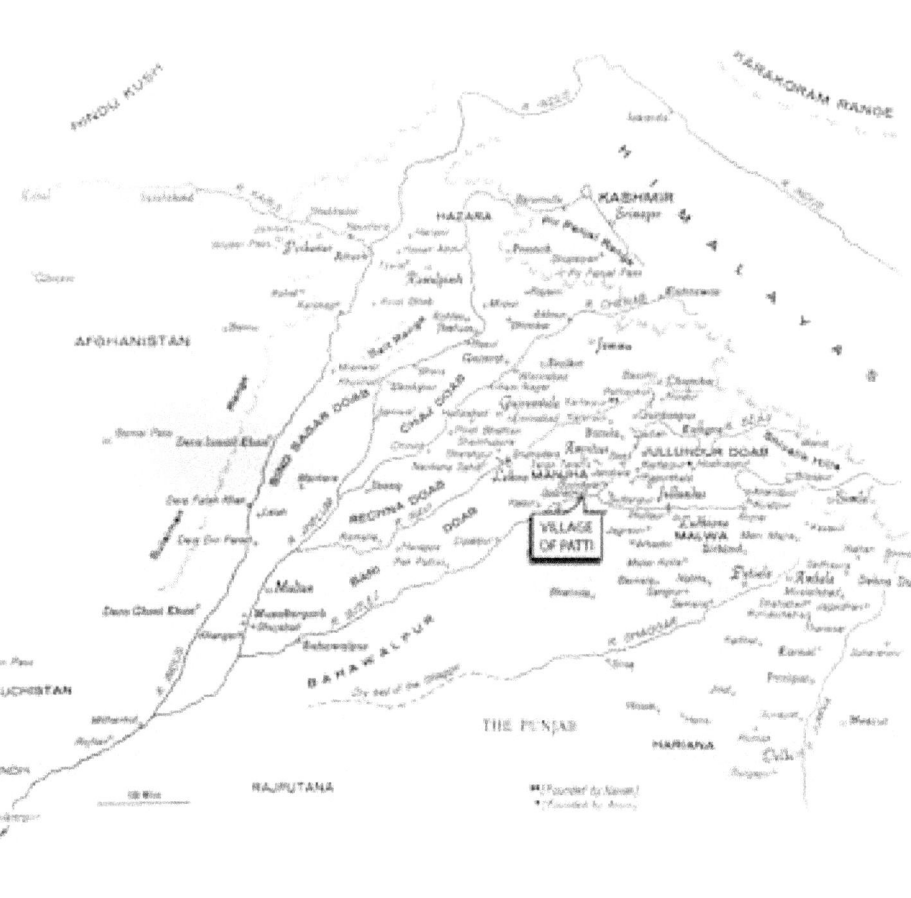

GLOSSARY

Akal Purkh	The undying or eternal personality of the universe; a name of God that is an intimate term of devotional familiarity.
Ayurvedic	A reference to the ancient healing system of Ayurveda from India, which literally means "science of life" and provides a holistic and comprehensive approach for the preservation and maintenance of the human body.
Avatar	One who is believed to be an incarnation of God.
Bagavad Gita	A Vedic scripture, part of a larger work, the *Mahabharta*, in which the deity Krishna gives spiritual instruction to Arjuna.
Bhai	An affectionate term meaning *brother*.
Bhang	Cannabis.
Bhangra	Traditional Punjabi folk dance. Bhangra is to the Punjab as square dancing is to Texas.
Chachaji	Common term for uncle or unclelike person.
Channa	A garbanzo bean.
Chapatti	Round, unleavened flatbread, rather like an Indian tortilla.
Chauti	Little or small.
Chuni	Sheer, veil-like material worn by Indian women to cover their heads.
Dacoit	Highwayman or bandit.
Dal	A dish made of any variety of mung beans cooked with spicy masala.

Darshan	Literally, sight of or vision of. To have one's darshan, such as that of a guru, is to have his vision of the divine. Essentially, a blessing.
Dhol	A cylindrical, trapezoid-shaped, two-headed drum, with one head larger than the other and played with rattan sticks. Used in the traditional Punjabi folk dance known as bhangra.
Dhoti	A long, single piece of cloth, tied around the waist and groin and worn by men in lieu of trousers.
Doab	The land area between two rivers.
Durbar	Formal court, as in court of the king, or court of the guru.
Falad	A kind of folded steel used for sword blades, similar to Damascus steel or Samurai steel, where the iron is heated, then folded in on itself and hammered. This process is repeated until the resulting blade is very strong and durable, and able to hold a sharp edge
Fulkari	Bright, woven mulitcolored cloth, often with tiny mirrors sewed into it
Ganga	Ganges River.
Ghee	Clarified butter.
Hazooria	A long scarf, often delicately embroidered and worn around the neck of saintly people.
Howdah	A carriage for people placed upon the back of an elephant.
Hukamnama or hukam	Literally *order*, *directive*, or *guidance*; in Sikh tradition it is the directive of the guru.
Ji	Literally *soul*. It is used as an honored term of affection and reverence, in recognition of the divine spirit of another.
Kameez	A long, knee-length tunic traditionally worn by Punjabi women.

Khir	Rice pudding.
Kirtan	Indian sacred music.
Ladu	A kind of Indian sweet made with graham flour, ghee, and sugar.
Lassi	A drink made with buttermilk or yogurt; can be sweet or salty.
Mahabharta	A Vedic scripture that describes a civil war, believed to have taken place at the end of the Dwarpar or Copper Age; Bagavad Gita is a subtext of Mahabharta.
Mahankalka	The energy of the collective souls and entities in the Heavens.
Mahount	An elephant handler.
Maya	The illusion of incarnation. In the Vedic and Sikh traditions, the human is under the illusion of Maya, unable to see the reality that God is all things.
Mendhi	Intricate decorations on the hands of brides and bridesmaids made with henna dye.
Mudge	Water buffalo.
Mudra	A symbolic hand position.
Mussalman	A Muslim.
Parandee	Strands of colorful yarn or ribbon that girls braid into their hair.
Pashmina	Very fine and soft spun wool, similar to cashmere, but softer, lighter, and warmer.
Puja	Devotional service, adoration of a deity.
Raag or Raga	Classical Indian musical scale intended to create a specific mood.
Ramayana	A Vedic scripture that describes the life of Rama, believed to be an incarnation of the deity Vishnu.
Rebab	A stringed musical instrument.

Rishi	An ascetic yogi who has achieved absolute union with the universe and who controls great spiritual power and knowledge.
Saag	A dish made from mustard greens and spices.
Salwaars	Long, baggy trousers worn by Punjabi women.
Sarangi	Stringed musical instrument played with a bow.
Sarovar	Tank or pool, body of water.
Sati	The practice of a widow throwing herself upon the funeral pyre of her husband and dying along with him.
Satya Lokha	The Hindu equivalent of heaven.
Shabd	Hymn.
Shakti	Creative energy or power, also feminine energy.
Sindur	Red paste used as a personal decoration, primarily by married women, to define the part in a married woman's hair to indicate that she is married. Also known as kumkum.
Sutras	Verses from Vedic scripture.
Sudra	The lowest caste in the Hindu caste system.
Tabla	Small tunable hand drums used to accompany kirtan.
Tantra	The practice of generating and channeling the creative energy of the universe for personal transformation; black tantra uses that energy to control another without their will.
Tulsi	An herb also known as holy basil.
Vedas	The ancient Hindu scriptures upon which Hinduism is based and practiced.
Vaishnavite	Worshipper of the deity Vishnu.
Vedic	Way of life and tradition based upon the Vedas.

DEDICATION

Dedicated to my beloved wife Priya, who has faced her challenges with all the courage, dignity, grace, and honor of Rajni.

PROLOGUE

IN THE PUNJAB STATE OF Northern India, approximately ten miles from the border of modern Pakistan, stands the ancient city of Amritsar. Founded around 1575 by Guru Ram Das, the fourth guru of the Sikhs, Amritsar became a major center in the region. Today it is one of the larger and more prosperous, though seriously polluted, cities of the Punjab.

The city grew up around a pool of water considered to have miraculous healing properties, and people came there because of it. The origin of the water is ancient, perhaps even mythic, and for millennia before the founding of Amritsar, that pool was a sacred place of pilgrimage and healing. Guru Amar Das, the third guru of the Sikhs, conceived a plan to expand the natural pond into a large tank, which would become an open place of pilgrimage, and to erect a *mandir* or temple in its center. The tank was excavated by the fourth guru, Guru Ram Das, and his youngest son, the fifth guru, Guru Arjan, saw the completion of the mandir in 1604. It became known as the Harimander, the Temple of God. In the early decades of the nineteenth century Maharaja Ranjit Singh, the Sikh ruler of the Punjab at that time, had the Harimander covered with gilded copper and white marble. Today it is more commonly known by the name the British gave it: the Golden Temple.

This is a most sacred place of pilgrimage and is open to people of all faiths without exclusion. Since ancient times the water that fills the tank has been considered to be sacred, and for Sikhs as well as many people of consciousness, it is considered to be a great blessing to take a sip of and dip in the water. Over the centuries millions of people have claimed that by doing so, the pains and illnesses of their hearts, minds, and bodies have been relieved.

This is the story of that water.

Says Nanak, by bathing in the tank of Ram Das, all sins and mistakes are washed away.
—Guru Arjan, the fifth Sikh guru

Oh Lord, our Lord, how excellent Thy name over all the Earth.
—Eighth Psalm of David

It doesn't really matter how you call His name: Allah, Jehovah, Sat Nam, it's all the same. We all come from one Creator.
—Mukhia Sardarni Sahiba Krishna Kaur Khalsa

What follows is a work of fiction based on myth, legend, tradition, and documented historical events.

AKAL PURKH

The Immortal God sat in His Grace, relaxed in the Infinite, His dwelling place . . .

ONE

SINCE ETERNITY THERE IS ONLY Me. My vastness is profound, My peacefulness is absolute, but My loneliness incomprehensible. I have no peer, I have no mother or father, and I cannot create another Me. I suppose that it would be truthful (though quite unfair) to say that I am an impotent bastard. Since I am all that there is, I am complete and whole, but the experience of such solitude gave me the sense that there must be more to Me than I understood. So to ease My loneliness, I formed this creation to experience My completeness. No one has My perspective, but many (and Oh Me, how tedious they are) think they know Me and have the audacity to tell people that they speak for Me.

Everyone wants something from Me, which is understandable since I am all things and most have the misconception that they are separate from Me. And because My love is so vast, I usually give people what they want, though I sometimes want them to ask Me nicely or in some special way. Just as it is not possible for anyone to conceive of or to understand the extent of My loneliness, neither can they grasp the depth and absoluteness of My love. That is why I created everything. I enjoyed it and made sure that all that I created was interdependent and interactive, so that no one thing should ever know this eternal solitude. You know the expression "it's lonely at the top"? You have no idea.

For more than thirty-six Ages I sat alone in My ecstasy. In the choral harmonic reverberation of My silence I meditated on Myself, locked in a profound trance deeper than death, absolute as love, and eternal as space. Still as the night, I never stirred. Silent as the sky, I uttered no sound. I reached and stretched, I contracted and inverted, but found no beginning and no end. Then I understood that I am all that there is, all that shall be, all that has ever been. Can you believe it? That was a painful realization.

Then, I announced to Myself, "I'm bored." Needless to say, that was an understatement. And in that twinkling, with no malicious forethought, I created cause and effect.

What few understand is the incalculable, infinite vastness of My mind: of Me as the Totality, which means that the individual simply does not have the capacity to understand it all. It amuses Me, however, when people believe they do understand. People would do much better to experience My love, My vastness, and My wisdom, rather than try to understand it. One is achievable; the other isn't. I created humanity so that I could experience Myself.

I like to give varying versions of the creation and the evolution of humanity. It amuses Me and confuses many, yet inspires the stalwart to seek the truth on their own. There is truth in all versions, and people accept the version that is easiest for them to identify with. Look deep and find the truth in this one.

Four great Ages have been recorded upon the Earth. First was the Golden Age, now long past and the return of which lies far in the future. Humanity lived in My radiant glory. The four pillars of Truth, Devotion, Compassion, and Charity supported the structure of the society and served to guide people through life day-to-day and breath-to-breath. People lived the Truth, spoke the Truth, and honored and respected each soul, each life-form, as a living Truth. For this reason, that time is known as the Sat Yuga, or Age of Truth. It was an Age when deities walked the Earth and all mysteries were known.

Then, the most tragic of things happened. Someone—the names are not recorded, nor the time and place of the occurrence (of course I know who did, it but I'll never tell)—but someone, perhaps unknowingly, broke the heart of another. Like a tear in the membrane of consciousness that binds all humanity, it ripped through the heart of each person. What you may not realize is that since all hearts are contained in Me, it ripped through My heart even deeper. They felt the pain and sorrow of that betrayal, and for the first time, experienced fear. So like a hawk hovering over a field, the disease of depression stalked people's minds.

I gave humans free will and that will was asserted to break a heart. In sadness, the Sat Yuga passed.

The radiant, ancient Age turned Silver from Gold. One-quarter of the knowledge and awareness of the Golden Age was lost. Now, only three pillars supported the society: Devotion, Compassion, and Charity. Truth and awareness were three-quarters of the previous Age, which by today's standards is still considerable. It was during this Age that the *Vedas* were written, which set down in writing the great oral tradition of the Golden Age. It fact, it was a beautiful Age.

Yet, like the Golden Age before it, the Silver Age dimmed and eventually passed. Life on Earth darkened. The three pillars of the Treta Yuga shook. The pillar of Devotion crumbled. And the sadness deepened.

The tarnished Silver darkened and turned to Copper.

Copper, when polished, has a luster similar to gold, which gives a sense of richness and warmth. Unlike gold, however, copper is not a pure element. It tarnishes easily and its luster is quickly lost. And so it happened in the Copper Age, the Dwapar Yuga. People of grace still rose each day and polished their souls. After all, you do come into the world with that shine.

Yet, understanding of Me as Infinite, as the Formless in every Form, as the Seen and Unseen, Known and Unknown was limited and in some places was lost entirely. So the deities got involved and made direct contact with people. Representations of God took the form of idols, and changes in the flow of life were interpreted as reward or punishment. People believed that if I or a deity was angry, then people died, crops failed, and misfortune came. In this way, the roots of superstition spread.

Greed increased and the struggle for power prevailed. Those in power used religion and superstition to control the people. They created castes and classes to restrict society and the expansion of the individual. In the Dwapar Yuga, fear found fertile ground in which to root, and those roots ran deep. Depression possessed millions of hearts, and hopelessness grew. They warred with a vengeance.

In the blinding flash of white-hot fire, the Dwapar Yuga passed.

Then came the Kali Yuga, the Dark Age, and human suffering increased. Humanity not only suffered from the impact of war, disease, famine, and unspeakable brutality, but there was also the suffering of the spirit; the deep and continuous pain that comes when the soul is unfulfilled and hopelessness grips the heart.

Superstition contaminated spirituality and filled the void that was left by the loss of the ancient technology—the meditations, incantations, prayers, and practices that elevated the soul and brought union with Me.

Spirituality gave way to religion and dogma—and the doubt, fear, and insecurity that come with it—took control of people's lives.

It was a curious occurrence. The yogis, swamis, priests, and monks hid in their caves, forests and mountaintops, where they meditated in peace and comfort in pursuit of their occult powers. When they were hungry, they came to the villages and towns to beg and preach, and to frighten and condemn the people who supported them.

Rulers and their governments, fueled by religious fervor, weighed heavily upon the societies. If the rulers weren't oppressing the people for their own avarice, the religious leaders persecuted them in My Name to fulfill theirs. People were confined by the limitations of their minds, the perceived threat of spiritual damnation, and the real threat of death, dismemberment, and torture imposed by both government and religion.

Spirituality simply became a lost by-product. Once faith was organized and codified, the rule of dogma prevailed. Within the various religions, different sects and factions erupted, and the conflict continued. Somewhere along the way some people got the idea to call their religion "the only true religion," and then the fight was on.

As the quest for power grew, so did the practice of the black arts. Black magic and black tantric, the science of possessing and controlling the mind of another, were perfected, and some practitioners excelled at their craft. It was called the Dark Age for a reason.

Fear became a driving motivation for action. The concepts of guilt and sin were injected into religion, and the concept of the devil evolved. In many places on the Earth people lived in fear of demons. It is true that demons can be kind of spooky and ill-behaved, and some demons did help to promote the spread of the black arts on the Earth. I can be something of a rascal at times.

It is also true that the Darkness is as infinite as the Light. After all, it is the polarity and since the Universe is infinite, it must be infinite at both ends. It is also true that there is some very strange and, well, dark energy at the dark end of the cosmos. Out of that dark energy come some very powerful and ugly demons who feed on the energy of other beings. Since light expands and darkness contracts, that dark energy is self-centered and draws other energies into it. And the energy that those forms enjoy the most is fear. The devil was born out of fear, and where fear takes root, the devil prevails. However, the amusing concept of the devil as a single personality fighting with Me for control of the cosmos was totally man-made. The influence of the devil became a convenient way to justify almost anything and avoid responsibility for one's actions.

Perhaps the greatest violation of all that was sacred was the degrading treatment of the female. People forgot that in woman is the *shakti*, the creative power of the Universe. Once respected and honored, women were declared by some religions to be unclean, ignorant, and incapable of spiritual achievement. Kings declared them to be property of the crown and claimed the first night of marriage as their own. Husbands beat their wives and brothers slept with their sisters.

Which brings Me to the point of this story and why I asked Rishi Mahan Akal to create such a special soul and place it in the body of a female. Oh Me, what a beauty she was! She did the job in a most elegant way but her sacrifice was great and she suffered in her human life.

She asked Me if I understood her pain and the depth of her suffering. Since time immemorial, people have prayed to Me, cried to Me, and cursed Me. Those who suffer think that I am punishing them, those who are happy think that I have blessed them. Understand this: I am without enmity or malice. I don't get angry and I don't punish. Humans forget that I gave them free will. Yet if you believe that I don't care, then create something precious yourself and nurture it. Does a mother, even among the animals, not care for and nurture her young? As you grow in each day, so I grow. Yet I abandon no one. In the limited human perspective it could be determined that I don't care, or even that I don't exist. See it from My perspective first, then we'll talk.

I set my beloved girl on that course because time and space demanded it and her soul flourished because of it. Her sacrifice, her devotion, and her conversations with Me brought me comfort and helped to assuage My own loneliness.

Her quest and the reason for it is a beautiful story.

TWO

As the circumstances of time and space evolved, a situation arose that needed taking care of, and I needed someone powerful and devoted to Me who could and would do it. Only a *rishi*, in fact only one rishi, could create that soul, and it was the kind of request that I had to make in person. So, I moved across the Heavens to the Sapt Shring, the place of the Seven Peaks. I called for a large plate of sweets and after a brief flutter of wings and sparks of light, the angels brought me a plate of the rarest sweets. With that in hand, I set out to meet Rishi Mahan Akal.

I'll explain about the rishis. They are like yogis, only exceedingly sophisticated and elevated. The rishis are different from the angels and deities. They are much more independent and do not always cooperate with Me, which is interesting since they did great austerities and meditated on Me for years, even lifetimes, to get My attention and achieve union with Me. Rishis are fewer than angels or deities. Because they are unique and special, they keep to their own corner of the Universe. They are so respected that they are never disturbed. Whenever I want their services, I am compelled to call on them in Person. Their meditation is so profound that it takes considerable effort and finesse to bring them out of it and only I have the power to do this. Often, disturbing a rishi who is in meditation does not go well and can put the rishi in a bad mood, and believe Me when I say that the company of an annoyed rishi is unpleasant. Although I created everything, including the rishis, they have power over Me.

Rishi Mahan Akal is one of the great sages of the Universe. For many Ages and Yugas he meditated and performed incredible austerities and ultimately, he merged into Me. Because he achieved union with Me, his meditations were no longer for his own elevation, but for that of the entire Universe, which made My job a bit easier. Rishi Mahan Akal was deeply respected and revered by all beings, even the demons.

I like to use My angels and deities for the eon-to-eon running of the Universe. They are fast and obedient and generally comply with whatever I direct them to do. The rishis, though, are reserved for bigger, more critical jobs. As Indra once complained to Me, "When You want something dealt with, You send us, but when You want something 'taken care of,' You send the rishis." And he was right.

On My way to the Sapt Shring, I pondered on My rishis, somewhat like a proud parent whose children have achieved great success.

"Here I Am, the Creator and Sustainer of the Universe, whom all creation, manifest and unmanifest, praises. Yet My rishis do whatever they want, whenever they want, and answer to no one. Their meditative power is essential, but how did it happen that they have such power over Me?"

Normally, whenever I wanted someone to do something on My behalf, I just whispered in his ear, but in this Kali Yuga, people often can't recognize My voice. Some hear voices from their own madness and think that it is Me talking to them, or want others to believe that I have spoken to them. Sometimes I assume some dramatic form and appear before the confused person just to have an impact and occasionally to show off, which I do enjoy. This has always gotten good results since a personal visit from God is just about as good as it gets in the Universe.

Naturally, I usually choose people who are more inclined to be compliant with what I want: people who need a mission or who incarnated to carry a specific message. The rishis, though, have never been impressed by My performances. They have seen the entire known and unknown Universe, even parts of Me that I am unable to see. After all, we all have our blind spots. They have even told Me on various occasions to go and do the job Myself because they are meditating and have a Universe to sustain. And I let them get away with that!

Every once in a while though, a rishi's ego has flared up and caused Me trouble. And trouble with a rishi is never a small thing because they are so very powerful. There was Harynikash, who became so powerful that, in the form of Vishnu, I offered to grant him any wish. Harynikash, like most rishis, was pretty clever and tricked Vishnu into making Him essentially immortal and frighteningly powerful. Naturally, Harynikash developed an ego that was bigger than his powers, and things got seriously out of hand.

He forced people to chant his name instead of My Name, but his son, Pralad, refused. Harynikash then set the entire countryside ablaze and, somewhat lacking in his parenting skills, forced Pralad to embrace a pillar that was glowing red hot in the center of that torched terrain. Pralad went the distance to the pillar and as he approached it, saw an ant crawling up the pillar without burning. He understood that I was with him and would protect him. I had to send Vishnu in a rather spectacular form, half man and half lion, and at a precise time of day, to kill Harynikash.

Then it struck me. I am bound by the powers of love and prayer, and a rishi's prayer is very powerful and focused. Their love is selfless and absolute. And for that reason, they have power over Me. The truth is that I am a little jealous of My rishis. They get to meditate all the time while I have to run the cosmos. Only My Will binds them, while I am bound by the powers of love and prayer. Goes with the job, I suppose.

But I digress. Suffice it to say that I have always admired and respected the rishis. Anyway, I arrived at the Sapt Shring, one of My favorite places in the entire Universe. I love the high snowy peaks, the crystal-clear water of the lake, and the bright blue sky. With the exception of My own abode, the Sapt Shring is the most peaceful place in the Universe.

As I said, it has always made Me uneasy to disturb a rishi, especially one as powerful as Rishi Mahan Akal. I gathered flowers from various parts of the Earth and tied them together with a glistening ribbon, which I pulled from the tail of a passing comet. A little show is sometimes useful. Then, with the flowers and sweets in hand, I approached the cave of Rishi Mahan Akal and laid them before him. The rishi, as usual, was deep in meditation and did not stir.

To pull a rishi from his meditation is usually a little painful because I actually remove the rishi from very deep within Myself. It is always better if the rishi comes to consciousness by his own will. Fortunately one of My greatest attributes is My patience. So I sat next to Rishi Mahan Akal and softly entered his meditation. I surrounded his great soul and very gently pulled him to consciousness. This rishi was reluctant. He was in deep ecstasy. Still, I always get what I want so little by little, Rishi Mahan Akal began to respond.

"Oh, great rishi, we need your help."

Slowly his respiration began to increase and his eyelids fluttered.

"What is it, lord?" he said softly.

"My dear rishi, it is an important job that requires your depth and touch."

The rishi was unmoved by the flattery. "What job?" His voice was calm and neutral.

"Remember the sacred pool of water we created?" I'll tell you about the water shortly.

"Of course! That was a great day," the rishi replied.

"I need you to create a unique soul, a female, to carry the suffering of the Kali Yuga to that pool. For that to happen, we need the light of that constellation." I pointed to a distant constellation consisting of seven stars. On Earth the constellation was known as the Pleiades.

"My lord, you pulled me from my meditation for *that*? You can easily do it Yourself."

"There's more, Mahan Akalji. We need you to transform the energy of the *Mahankalka* [the collective energy of the souls in the Heavens] and blend it with the light of those stars. Since she will be female, go to My female deities and take beauty and strength from Bhagvati, grace and harmony from Saraswati, and take determination, depth, and compliance with My Will from Durga and Kali."

"This is serious. She will have a heavy karma to bear." Rishi Mahan Akal picked up one of the sweets and chewed it reflectively.

"She will bear the suffering of the Kali Yuga. This is important and only you have the meditative capacity and the authority of free will to make that happen. I cannot interfere in such a direct way. I can only guide the energy and make suggestions. Humans do as they will."

"What about her circumstances?" he asked.

"You meditate, figure it out yourself." I laughed out loud.

The rishi stared out across the vastness of the mountains and listened to the wind as it carried the sound current across the infinite. He closed his eyes and beheld the Universe before him. He understood the necessity of accepting the job. He took another bite and chewed quietly, contemplating what he had to do.

"Will you do it?"

"Yes, lord, of course I will."

Then my great rishi pulled his shawl over his shoulders, closed his eyes, and went to work.

THREE

THE SACRED POOL OF WATER that I referred to had come about after the deities and angels had a meeting with Indra. Indra was like CEO of the Heavens and had the responsibility to oversee the progression of things on Earth. He took his job seriously, and as the Ages diminished, he became concerned. He met with the other deities and angels, but reached no conclusion about what to do.

Their conversation went like this:

"The situation is becoming unstable," they advised.

"It's the demons," said another, "they mess up everything."

"It's not the demons," said Indra. "I have fought with and vanquished some of the most powerful ones. They like to make mischief and misguide people, but the darkness that is spreading does not come from them. It is the result of the collective energy of all humankind."

The angels and deities simply stared at Indra, expecting him to have a solution. Though they are big on devotion and service, they are a little short on humor and tend to take themselves much too seriously. Still, they always manage to maintain their innocence, which is why I enjoy their company. However, it is that very innocence that causes them to be out of touch with things and ridiculously naïve at times.

Indra was known for his jealousy. He often tried to slow a saint's progress toward union with Me by placing temptations and diversions along the way. Indra's jealousy could not tolerate it when other souls got close to Me. Yet Indra was also concerned about how things were developing. His compassion could not be contained.

Indra paused and looked at his colleagues. They flapped their wings and fiddled with their halos. One angel reached out to Earth and saved someone who was drowning. Some created cloud formations and multicolored lights in the sky, but no one really had a solution to the problem. In his *soma*-induced ecstasy, Indra thought the other deities looked kind of silly.

"All right, then, it's clear that we won't find a solution on our own. Keep an eye on things until I return."

So Indra came before Me and as usual was a little sheepish. Now don't misunderstand, Indra was a powerful deity and proved to be very useful to Me in many ways. He saved the world from many demons, though that jealous streak was a problem. Yet when he came before Me he was sincerely concerned.

"You want to tell me your concerns about the Earth?"

"Yes, lord," Indra replied, uncomfortably. "Things on Earth seem to be going rather badly. I mean, it is not turning out the way we . . . uhh, at least the way *I*, expected. It is a strange time now. Hearts have been broken and the others are saying that the demons are responsible."

"Listen to Me, Indra. As Chief of the Heavens, you must know that the Universe is ever changing. It is only here, where I dwell, that there is absolute stillness. There must be change. Otherwise there is no growth and therefore, no completion. The souls who walk the Earth are many, but they all are Mine. Any way they can find to know My Love, to know that they are Me and that *I AM*, is worthwhile. So I give them various ways to know that; wherever they are on Earth, whatever the psyche of their personality.

Yet those who will go beyond belief and have the living experience of their own consciousness will know Me and will dwell here." I placed My radiant hand over My infinite heart. "They move at their own pace. That is why you have a job." I always enjoyed teasing the deities, but Indra was especially gullible.

"So few of them seem to be moving toward You though, my lord," he sighed

"Please tell Me, then, in what direction I am not." Indra stumbled a little, which made me laugh. "But you are right. Before long they will fabricate a devil and say that he is My sworn enemy and that We are fighting for control of the Universe. Once they get hold of that idea, all hell will break loose down there."

Indra was a true devotee and he loved Me mightily, but one thing he truly appreciated about Me was My sense of humor, which is as vast as the Universe and as powerful as lightning. The deities and angels always took themselves too seriously, constantly trying to be holy or angelic and outdo each other with their divine posturing. This was a nuisance to Indra because the deities felt that they had to maintain a certain image and demeanor. They loved to visit humans and watch their reaction. However, this made for some real communication problems in Heaven and often caused conflict and ruffled egos. It was a lot of work for Indra to keep order and maintain peace in the Heavens.

"Don't be concerned. The Ages will change as they are meant to. Instead, be concerned for those who fail to measure up to the demands of the times. I love everyone, but must let them come to Me on their own, through their own efforts and as their own hearts guide them. I'll meditate a little longer to find a solution. The Age will turn again, things will become darker and stranger. This is the way of the Universe. These Heavens will not fall, nor will the Earth be lost.

"Get everyone together, all the Heavens from all corners and folds of the Universe. Everyone! Strategize and have them focus their prayers toward the Earth. Let me meditate, and I will come to you shortly."

Without uttering a sound, Indra touched My feet, and his light faded and became dense as he returned to the others.

When Indra reappeared, all the angels and deities, who had been grousing the whole time, complained to him that he had been gone too long and that they were getting tired of waiting; that after all, they had pretty important roles in the Universe and couldn't spend a couple of Ages waiting around for Indra to do his job.

"He wants to meditate a little longer," Indra said simply. Immediately the others were quiet. Some folded their wings and bowed their heads. They all had the deepest respect and reverence for Indra.

"He said that this is the way things are meant to be. It is, after all, His play. In the meantime though, He wants us to focus our prayers on the Earth. He said to stop the nonsense about the demons and devils and understand clearly that this is the energy that humanity itself has created. He said that if humans get the devil idea, all hell will break loose down there."

No one laughed and his words sounded flat. He paused, feeling a little foolish. "Let's just look after things and give them more help. The time might come when some of us have to incarnate to help them. And remember, none of this devil business!"

Indra startled all the deities. Lightning flashed across the deep blue of the spiritual sky. Everyone knew Indra was serious.

"Akal Purkh wants us to have a meeting," he paused reflectively, "to strategize and focus our prayer. The Age darkens. Now is the time for action. We need all the great souls, ascended masters, demigods, semigods, devas, deities, angels, elements, power sources, prophets, preachers, swamis, rishis, all those souls who have previously incarnated, all those souls who will incarnate in this Age, and anyone else around here who can generate a vibration." Indra paused to catch his breath.

The entities of Heaven stared at Indra, their mouths open. They all felt a sense of urgency, but no one moved.

"Get them all together quickly! And nothing more about demons and devils! Next thing you know, they will create guilt and sin. Then"—Indra paused, his face darkened and his eyes glowed in a most eerie way—"then," he repeated in a faraway-sounding voice, "we will have a big mess."

All were silent, stunned by Indra's instructions. No one moved. Not a feather dropped, not a wing twitched. Indra seemed far, far away, lost in another time. He looked up with a sudden jerk of his head. His eyes flashed illuminating the Heavens and the surrounding ethers.

"Now get busy!" he thundered.

All the entities scattered in a flash of light and sound to gather the forces for change. They searched all the corners of the known Universe, then all the corners of the unknown Universe, and then all the corners of the parallel Universes. A great gathering was about to take place and no one wanted to miss it.

In the Heavens, the cosmic assembly convened. When Indra appeared, no one spoke. There was long silence as he stood before the great assembly. He looked at the vast sea of souls and beings. The glittering, radiating energy of the collective whole, the Mahankalka, was very powerful.

Eventually, they felt My presence. Usually I like to make a big entrance, but this time I wanted to set the meditative mood so I manifested gradually.

"Here together we have the most powerful force in the Universe. We have come together to create an energy that will help humanity and give them a way to remember their divinity. Together now we will create the *Sat Sangal Dhara*, the Golden Chain of Truth."

I paused to let the concept penetrate through the assembly. "To do this, we must merge our energies together and become one vast and pervasive soul connection. Then we will beam that energy to the Earth in a single ray, along a diagonal axis. The beam must be aimed at an exact point of longitude and latitude and its impact will have a most powerful effect on the Earth."

There were shouts of agreement, then quickly, silence again. All looked to Me.

"All right, we'll join together. Form straight lines, and they must be perfectly straight! Choose a partner and sit facing each other." I deputized a few thousand angels to dart around and get the lines straight. They moved very fast, ensuring that everyone had a partner. The lines stretched almost out of sight, across the vastness of My Heavens. With surprising quickness, the long lines became straight while big, billowy, heavenly clouds formed over them. It was an impressive sight. Even I was awed by it, but then I do love My own work. I have a very artistic nature.

Before long there was silence.

"To bring balance to the Earth and give humanity a way to be free we will vibrate sounds to form the *Tresha Guru*. This sound will create a most powerful energy. Now, take the hands of you partner and we'll chant the sound *Wahe Guru* together."

I chanted the sound softly at first, my harmonic resonance penetrating the atmosphere. As I continued to repeat it, all the Heavens began to vibrate to the frequency of that sound. The assembled body chanted with Me and as they began to vibrate, the energy grew and intensified. Slowly, the resonant membrane of the Universe began vibrating to that frequency and the energy expanded.

"Focus this energy on the Earth," I shouted My thundering Godly shout. "Sit straight. You think this is a joke?"

Those in the congregation adjusted themselves as they continued to chant louder. As they did so, I moved the energy, managing the flow.

They continued to chant. The sounds rose and fell, becoming dissonant, then harmonic and like the sound of the gong, moved and penetrated as the energy steadily grew. The absolute primal beauty and unrestrained intensity of it was beyond anything any of them had experienced before and this despite the fact that beautiful sounds in the Heavens are the norm. They sat in absolute bliss as the vibratory effect escalated. All the Heavens vibrated. All the Universe vibrated. Then in a single motion, I directed that beam of energy along a diagonal axis to the Earth.

Upon the Earth, a large mass of land, nearly the size of a continent had made its way across what is now known as the Indian Ocean. Over millennia, this mass of land moved with the roll and rapture of the Earth until it collided with the greater continent of Asia. The intensity of that collision was so powerful that at the point of impact, the larger land mass was disrupted and buckled, forcing the tectonic plates upward toward the sky. When the dust settled and the waters receded, the tallest range of mountains on the Earth, the elegant Himalayas, touched the base of Heaven.

Below the mountains the land opened and spread into a broad, fertile plain. Five streams were born in those mountains and began to trickle, then flow. They followed the course of gravity and made their way down the slope of the Himalayas and onto the plain below. They opened across the flat land and followed their individual destinies in the constant ebb and flow of life, fertilizing the plain as they ran through it. In the ancient tongue, the word for *river* was *ab*. There were five life-giving rivers, and the word that means *five* was *panj*. So the region across which the five rivers flowed came to be called the "land of the five rivers" or *punj ab*, and it was into the heart of the Punjab that the beam of the Sat Sanghal Dhara was directed.

The intense beam struck the Earth with such a great force that it penetrated through the surface. The energy continued to flow deeper into the water table below. The water began to vibrate, and then bubble to the surface. Still the chanting continued as I directed the energy into the water, which vibrated at the frequency of the sound, changing the orbit of the atoms and molecules that composed it. Eventually, a small pool of water formed on the surface of the earth.

"Inhale!"

The voices of the angels and deities stopped but the divine sounds continued to echo through the Heavens and upon the Earth itself. Across the spiritual sky cosmic lightning flashed behind corpulent clouds, followed softly by distant thunder. Rainbows and light radiated against the powerful hum of totality.

In the Heavens all were silent. The pool of water vibrated in that silence.

FOUR

The Kali Yuga was a wonderful time to be a demon. Since religions had rejected and condemned so many of the common people, there was a fertile ground where the demons could create all kinds of mischief. However, all demons know that they are part of the whole and have a role in the grand scheme of things. They are very good at testing and tempting, and they teach lessons about how not to behave. Moreover, they are very clear about who they are and the role they play. So as things began to go somewhat awry, the demons became a little confused and wanted to have a meeting with Indra.

Now, Indra was never very fond of the demons. Not that he was afraid of them; he just didn't enjoy their company. He had fought with many during his time and was very accomplished at defeating them. Once there was a mighty dragon demon named Vritra who had consumed all the water on the Earth, leaving it dry and the people suffering. So Indra decided to take Vritra on himself. It was a long and terrifying battle and the sounds of the fighting shook the Earth and the Heavens. But Indra, who was never in doubt of the outcome, prevailed. He split the demonic dragon open and the waters spilled out of him and fell back to the Earth. I was very proud of him and Vritra died with a flourish worthy of such a powerful demon.

Indra didn't relish a meeting with the demons. He never trusted them and always felt that they were up to some deception, which they usually were. He was wary of somehow being manipulated for their benefit. However, he felt that a meeting might be worthwhile and that he would get some useful information. Besides, as the manager of the Heavens, he did have an obligation to meet with them occasionally. So accordingly, he agreed to the meeting.

Indra didn't want to meet with the demons alone, and since this would be an important meeting, he invited Shiva to join him. Shiva had considerable control over the demons. He could destroy them easily and since he was without fear, they had no influence over him. The demons had deep respect for Shiva, mostly because they feared him and fear is a powerful motivator, but also because they enjoyed his company. He understood them and communicated with them without arrogance, which they appreciated. After all, Shiva was the lord of all things, the beginning and the end. So Indra thought that having Shiva at the meeting would be a good move.

Together they made the trip to the appointed location by Lake Mansarowar. Indra rode on his elephant and Shiva rode on Nandi, his beloved white bull. They made their way leisurely down from Mt. Kailash, and Indra, deep in the ecstasy of soma, was in an unusually reflective mood. His jealousy of humans was legendary, and he was pondering how humans, when they applied themselves, could merge wholly with Me. It was a sore point for him, something that he resented and could never reconcile.

"Eh, Shivaji?" he asked.

"*Hain* ji?"

"Shivji?"

Long pause.

"Shivji, if you could take the human incarnation, would you?"

"My dear Indra, you are the lord of the Heavens. Why do you ask me such a question?"

Long pause.

"Uh, it seems that the human incarnation is unique, unlike anything else in the Universe, yet we deities are denied that experience."

"Listen, Indra. I am Lord of the Universe. I have meditated for Ages and defeated demons and deities. I drank the world poison, which I hold in my throat. When I play my drum and dance the *Nataraja,* all creation is transformed back into me. Yet my identity is still separate from the Akal Purkh and shall be for all eternity. This is my *dharma*. We serve Akal Purkh in the way that we do, but we shall always remain apart from Him."

The sunlight shone brightly on Shiva's blue face and his long coiled hair. He swayed easily as Nandi moved steadily under him. Indra remained silent as Shiva spoke.

"In all creation, it is only in the human incarnation that the law of cause and effect exist. So it is only in the human incarnation that one's grit can be tested and challenged. In the heat and pressure created when sacrifices to the higher self are made, the carbon of the soul will become a diamond. When that simple man whom nobody knows and who, with all the limitations of a human, faces the challenges of time and space to which you and I are immune, and in so doing remembers the Name of the Akal Purkh, then I and the entire Universe bow down to him.

"No, Indra, I would not take the human incarnation, but I would like to meet such a one whose mettle is tested and found to be true and who, encumbered by the human incarnation and *Maya's* seduction, still remembers God's Name."

Indra was silent for some time. When he finally did speak, his voice was remote and far away, as though he was speaking from another dimension. Very softly he said, "A different Age is coming."

They made their way down from the snowcapped Mt. Kailash, far from the touch of man, deity, or demon. At the place they chose on the banks of Lake Mansarowar, the silence was as profound as death and stillness prevailed through all things.

Indra and Shiva spoke little when they arrived. The purple mountains rose around them to their snowcapped peaks, beneath a sky that shimmered a deep, mystic blue. The soma they had consumed put them in a contemplative mood, so they sat by the lake and meditated. They merged into the silence and stillness, lost in the ecstasy of their own perfection.

In their usual style, the demons arrived late with a lot of noise and chaos. They put on their best spook shows for the two deities, trying in vain to scare them and impress them with their power. Some rose up out of the lake, others stood up from the Earth, and others manifested themselves out of the air. They set up a powerful screeching and wailing that split some of the large stones that were nearby. Shiva and Indra didn't budge from their ecstasy, and eventually the demons settled down and became calm, though in their usual rude way failed to introduce themselves. In time, first Shiva, then Indra, acknowledged their presence and after the usual formalities and exchanges, the meeting got underway.

They addressed Shiva directly, semi-ignoring Indra, which annoyed him considerably. But Indra was patient and did not let it get the better of him. The demons admitted that they were enjoying the Kali Yuga. They considered it the best Age ever for being a demon. However, they told Shiva that demons were being given far more credit for things than they actually deserved. Indra thought this was curious for demons to be so honest. He then realized correctly, that they were concerned about things on the Earth as well.

"Humans have really gone crazy." The chief demon spoke with reasonable respect.

Indra and Shiva agreed.

Encouraged, the chief demon said, "It is much easier to possess people than ever before."

Again they agreed.

"There are many things that people are doing on their own with only a little guidance from us," he said with sickening innocence that caused Indra's eyes to change colors like a kaleidoscope. Indra knew they weren't telling him everything.

Indra despised the demons and could not disguise it. Since he was Chief of the Heavens and since demons in his opinion had no place in Heaven, they disgusted him. However, the soma helped him to get through the meeting. If the demons were amused by Indra's discomfort, he was not amused by their arrogance. Indra thought they were extremely unattractive and he hated the way they spoke with their guttural, gravelly voices and weird accents. Most of all, Indra could not stand their smell. While on Earth demons sometimes appeared to be very attractive and charming, to Indra who could see through their façade, they were rude, crude, and highly unattractive beings, with poor hygiene.

One demon asked, "Didn't you fellows have a big meeting or something not too long ago?"

Indra eyed the demon and wondered what he knew. "We had a conference to discuss the situation on Earth. Why do you ask?"

"Well, shouldn't we have been invited!"

His anger rising, Indra thought to himself, *Who do they think they are to come here looking so ugly and smelling so bad on the pretense that they want to discuss the development of things on the Earth? They're not even trying to be civil!*

Shiva placed his hand on Indra's shoulder to calm him. Indra composed himself and responded quickly.

"Look," said Indra, "it was a very specialized meeting. All we did was pray together for the well-being of humanity." He sighed, "Nothing more."

"You didn't send down a special beam to the Earth or anything like that?"

"Well," replied Indra, carefully, "every prayer is a beam. Our prayer was beamed down to all."

"Listen," said the chief demon pointedly, "we consider this to be our Age, as demons who have, ahh, perfected, ahh, a certain craft and approach to things. We are getting a lot of credit for things that we haven't actually done but which, I must say, we are proud to take credit for."

Indra cringed at the sound of the demon's voice. He never could tolerate that sound, and this demon clearly understood that and purposefully taunted him.

"We recognize that there are many people who are . . . aahh . . . *open* to . . . umm . . . certain *demonic* options at this time." He paused and regarded Indra with his red eyes. "We have recognized that people have developed a certain . . . ohh . . . moral flexibility, shall we say?" He spoke very slowly and deliberately, drawing out his vowels almost to the point of adding additional syllables, "There is an openness to other perspectives that only we can offer." He paused demonically gazing out across Lake Mansarowar, looking as though he were commenting about the weather on Earth.

His deputy interjected, "We . . . ummm . . . would prefer that you not interfere with that. In fact"—the demon paused just to irritate Indra and winked with an annoying smile—"I'm sure that you would agree with us that this is all part of the Great Plan?" The pitch of his voice raised a half step. "After all, we are all One"—he paused again, listening to his own echo off the high peaks that rose above the lake, his grin fading ever so slightly—"aren't we? All part of the whole?" Another half step.

Indra hated the implication. Although he understood that there was nothing that had not been created by Me, he never could bring himself to admit that there was a connection between the demons and the deities. He understood that there had to be polarity in the Universe, but he wasn't happy with the idea that he and the demons were even remotely related.

The chief demon eyed Indra and smiled that demonic smile that Indra hated. "Can't we all just get along?" said the demon. His tone was sticky sweet.

"Are you crazy!" shouted Indra, his voice explosive as a volcano, his echo skimming across the surface of the lake, then rising to the snowcapped peaks around it. "Do you just expect that we will sit back and let you morons have your way with things?" His voice echoed across the Heavens, and as he waved his mace over his crown, sparks flew from his head.

Shiva again placed his hand on Indra's shoulder and squeezed slightly. "You don't need to let us have our way with anything." The tone of the demon's voice never changed and his annoying smile never left his rather disturbing face. "Just . . . hmmm . . . let the humans have *their* own . . . aahh . . . *way* with things. Didn't the same Creator who created us also create humankind? Uhmmm?"

He eyed Indra, clearly enjoying his discomfort. "We'll just continue doing what we've always done, helping people out in our own way. Aren't we all here to help? Isn't our purpose to"—another irritating pause—"umm, *guide*," he emphasized the word, "*humanity?*" He paused again, looking at Indra with his red eyes. Indra was silent, raging inside.

"By the way," the demon whispered in Indra's ear, causing him to cringe, "we know about the water."

Sparks flew from Indra's head and hands. He raised his mace as if to smite the demon's ugly head, just as flame erupted from the third eye of Lord Shiva, which caused all the demons to jump back.

"Keep away from the water," Shiva said softly, between his teeth. "Keep away from the water or perish. You do not have the strength to contaminate it, and if you touch it, you will be transformed." He let his trident fall into his left hand.

"We make no promises," replied the demon, somewhat more respectfully. "After all, we all come from the same source and we are just the polarity." He smiled patronizingly and placed his hand on Indra's shoulders. "Lighten up a little. You look like you could use a little break. Come visit us sometime. We'll do lunch, have a little soma. It'll be fun!" The demon laughed out loud.

"Stay away from the water," hissed Indra.

Shiva reached out and grabbed the chief demon by the throat and pulled him to within inches of his smooth, blue face. "Keep away from that place and advise all your colleagues to do the same." He loosed a spark from his third eye that struck the demon squarely in the face and sent him rolling across the ground and tumbling into the lake. The other demons jumped back and rather than running to assist their chief, ducked behind the rocks and trees to hide.

Mounting Nandi, Shiva called out, "Heed this warning, my friends. *Heed* this warning!"

FIVE

Although Shiva tried to calm him, Indra in his jealousy and neurotic sense of responsibility could not relax, no matter how much soma he quaffed. He was disappointed that the demons knew about the water, although he should have expected it. He was also upset with himself. He was annoyed with his reaction to the demons, and he told himself that he had to become more neutral when dealing with them. He knew they were playing with him, but the comments about the sacred water disturbed him. Yet it wasn't really that. He just didn't like the demons with their bizarre sense of humor and disgusting ways. They knew they could rile him up, and they did. As I watched him, I had to laugh at Indra's reaction.

Still, he and Shiva had protected the secret of that special place. He could not permit it to become contaminated by the demons. It was created for the healing of humanity and to retard the spread of the evil insanity to which mankind had given birth and was nurturing with its superstitions. Like flames before the wind, this madness raged in their minds and spread across the earth. It wasn't the demons and Indra knew clearly that they were no real threat. The people of the Earth were harming themselves foolishly and dangerously and that had to be arrested.

So, once again Indra meditated and in the infinite depth of that ecstasy, he arrived at My lotus feet.

"We need to secure the Golden Chain. Let's finish the job. This is the time. Indra, my love, Get everyone here—fast!"

When all the divine beings, divine candidates, entities, and powers arrived, Indra spoke firmly and with authority.

"The demons consider this to be their Age and want us to leave them alone." Laughter erupted from the gathered throng. Indra surveyed the infinite host, letting the power of his presence and his silence roll across the Universe. The divine assembly grew still and watched him in silence. His imposing presence glowed brightly as the energy was building.

"Now, the devil is a big issue on the Earth," he said sternly, "and this ridiculous concept is giving people an excuse not to be responsible for themselves. It is leading to a darkening of the spirit and a malignancy of the heart. This is unfortunate, because we all know that the people of the Earth are spreading this energy themselves. The demons don't have to do that much."

He looked over the vast assembly stretching out across the clouds and planets, the sunrises and sunsets, rainbows and stars. The sound current, like wind in the trees, was ever present and filled the space.

With a sharp edge to his voice, Indra spoke with force. "I told you what would happen if you continued with all this demon business, blaming everything on them. Now, mankind itself has created the devil from the energy of its own mind." His pause was sustained in the Heavens for some time.

Then his voice exploded across the Universe, causing wings to flutter and halos to fall. "From the energy of its own mind! Do you understand what you have done?"

Simultaneously he made his face appear only inches before the face of every entity seated there. They sat up straight with ashamed looks on their faces. As I said, Indra was a very powerful deity.

"You have made an already complicated situation worse, and we have to stop this nonsense."

Millions of voices murmured, "It wasn't me," or "I didn't mean to do it," or "I was only trying help," or "We thought it might get their attention" and millions of other comments.

"Silence!" thundered Indra, the Chief of the Heavens. "Now form your lines!" His voice hung in the atmosphere without diminishing.

Again thousands of angels darted through the assembly to straighten the lines, lightning fast. And as quick as a thought—well, perhaps as quick as a prayer—the lines were formed. And thirty-three million beings sat in anticipation.

This was an excellent time to make an entry, and so I did, in a steadily increasing incandescence that took form and personality. I surveyed the gathering stretched across the known and unknown, hidden and manifest Universe. The reverence was deep, the silence total. Prayer and thought merged in devotion to Me.

"Arms and wings at a perfect sixty-degree angle, the tips touching those of your partner," I spoke with divine authority. Then in a whisper, "We have to finish it, now."

And again they began chanting the *Wahe Guru* sound, and once again those powerful vibrations echoed across the Universe. This time the energy was stronger and accelerated more quickly. They continued to chant, and I directed that dynamic energy to the Earth along the diagonal axis, from the crown of the Heavens into the pool. The energy flowed, and the healing and regenerative powers of the water grew stronger.

The demons watched from a respectable distance and they understood clearly that Indra and Shiva were serious. Great power flowed into the water. They recognized that if they went near that pool, their carefree demon days would end. They resolved to stay away and concentrate their mischief elsewhere.

On the Earth in the land of the five waters it was the end of summer and the time of the equinox, when the balance of light and darkness is equal and there is clarity through the ethers. The air was humid with a trace of coolness and a change of color in the atmosphere. It was the time when the axis of the Earth in its elegant rhythm allowed the North Pole to drift away from the sun, causing the angle of the sun's light to cast an etherial radiance upon the atmosphere.

In the mountaintops and the monasteries, the renunciates and recluses felt the energy. In the temples and cathedrals prayers accelerated, meditations deepened, and recitations were done with more sincere devotion. The magicians stopped their magic. The sorcerers stopped their incantations. The criminals stopped their crimes and for one brief moment in Time and Space, there was peace and healing on the Earth. Beside the pool a *beri* tree, a kind of jujube, sprouted and took root.

"Inhale!" The chanting stopped but the glow over the Universe and the echo through the sound current was overwhelming, ringing with the infinite echo of the absolute.

"Exhale and send the energy to the water!"

The energy continued to flow to the Earth as the gods and goddesses, saints and sages, devas and deities, angels and cherubs, masters and rishis all directed the *Wahe Guru* energy in to the water. They vibrated and radiated, shining across the Heavens as a bright, cosmic rainbow.

"Relax."

A long period of silence followed as the entire Universe glowed and vibrated. All those present just sat there in the Heavens, literally staring off into space, their divine minds adrift in the ethers. Neither Indra nor any of the deities moved or spoke. Vishnu radiated colors. Shiva sat in profound trance, his breath suspended, the Ganges flowing from the crown of his head. Yet not a muscle moved. Even the cobras around his neck and arms were as still as stone. The profound silence seemed to absorb all the sounds of the Universe.

In My most serene and soft voice, I spoke.

"Throughout the Universe and especially upon this little Earth, there are many sacred places. Some are remote and inaccessible. Some hold great power and mystery, while others seem sacred to only a few. The power and divinity of most places is held in the heart and mind of the pilgrim who bows and prays there. It is that act of devotion that establishes and sustains the sacredness of a place. The problem is that many such holy places have become esoteric and access to them is restricted. The caretakers to whom I have entrusted some of those places have become arrogant and selective about who can have access to them. This is one of the reasons the world suffers.

"This place that we have just blessed is different. It will be open to all, with no restrictions. It will be a place for householders and renunciates alike. Anyone who wishes to come in reverence shall be allowed to enter that water. They will be healed, their souls will find solace, and their prayers will be heard." I paused, lost in My own essence.

"There are many paths that bring each soul back to Me. I have sent many in My Name to serve and heal humanity. All have done their best, but for some, cults of personality have grown up. In this way, people are divided and many have become excluded so that the essence of what was taught is lost."

The silence was absolute. Only the continuous flow of the sound current prevailed against the divine radiance of the Heavens.

"Now we will try a different approach, one that will not place focus on the personality, but on the essence. This will not be about believing, but about the direct experience of consciousness. All that will be required is reverence, so that anyone who touches that water with reverence, who meditates or prays beside it with reverence and in the language of their own heart and soul, will find solace." I paused while the concept penetrated throughout the assembled host.

"My beloved ones, mind that sacred spot well. Its time is near. Indra will explain My plan. He will lay it out clearly so you can discuss and execute it. And please,"—I paused somewhat slyly—"No more devil-business!"

And with that, My radiant presence evanesced into the Infinite.

Then Indra explained how the plan would come together and how the Sat Sangal Dhara, which We had created, was to be held and maintained.

"To consecrate and confirm the power of the water and to truly establish it for all humanity," he spoke in dignified and somber tones, "will require great sacrifice. The creative shakti energy is required to sanctify it and make it complete. Therefore an innocent, divine girl will bear the suffering of the Kali Yuga and bring it to the water. This will require great personal sacrifice so that the healing power of the water can be recognized. The results will be unmistakable and irrefutable.

"I must warn you as well: When that time comes, she must carry the load herself. We can pray for her and protect her along her way, but none can carry the load for her. The blessings of the water are for humanity during the Kali Yuga and a human must bring it to fruition. Do not interfere and don't try to help except through your own prayers. Understood?"

The collective sound of thirty-three million deities, entities, angels, cherubs, demigods, semigods, and ascended masters, especially when they are in agreement, could be impressive.

"The important thing now is to establish the Golden Chain on the Earth. This will be done through the incarnation of a great soul who will carry the Sat Sangal Dhara to the Earth and establish a culture of consciousness that will serve the sacred water. He will bring to the Earth the living power of the sound that we just created, which shall help to guide people through this Kali Yuga. He will be of the Bedi line, who are well-versed in the Vedas, and will be known as Nanak. Nine successors will bear his flame and secure the Golden Chain to the Earth."

There was a stunned silence across the Heavens because there are few secrets there. While they may be elevated and enlightened beings, they still like to gossip and play the *I know something you don't* game. Sometimes I start the rumors Myself as a kind of amusement. But no one had heard this one before, so they were all surprised. Needless to say, it boosted Indra's status.

On the Earth, the water vibrated and waited quietly.

THE GOLDEN CHAIN

The Father of the Bedis was given the call to begin
To ignite the Light of Wisdom within the hearts of Men.

SIX

My beautiful Rishi Mahan Akal meditated. He reached out through the ethers and gathered the elements to form that special soul. He had helped many souls to incarnate before, but this time it was different. I had asked him personally.

The Mahankalka are a powerful energy that sustains and guides the evolution of the Universe, and that collective energy had been infused in the water of the sacred pool. Now Rishi Mahan Akal had to take the distilled essence of that energy and give it form.

As I had requested of him, he fused, then distilled the essence of the Mahankalka and blended it with the light of the seventh star of the Pleiades. He nurtured it through timelessness and added the power and capacity of a rishi to sacrifice. Then, going before Durga, Saraswati, Lakshmi, Kali, and the other great goddesses of the Heavens, he asked for and received the virtues and strengths from each of them. All of this was fused into a single, powerful soul.

When My great Rishi was ready, he called the entire heavenly congregation to come and consecrate her. They came readily, and each of those great beings, with infinite care and reverence, blessed her. With each touch, each blessing, and each prayer, the radiance and resilience of that little soul increased, glistening like a perfectly cut and polished diamond in the morning sun. Then holding her close to his heart, he came before Me and laid her at My feet.

I was very happy with the work of the Rishi.

"See," I told him, "only you could do this job."

Rishi Mahan Akal, though a humble rishi, was pleased.

"Forgive my pride, my lord, but this is truly a jewel that will shine on the Earth."

I picked up the little soul, so tiny in My Great Hands, yet so radiant. I held her close to My face and whispered to her, "Soon you must take the breath of life and fulfill your destiny. But for now, abide with Me. I am not yet ready to give you up. Watch and see how the Golden Chain links to the Earth and to your destiny." She rested in My lap, and together We watched.

This is how it happened.

*   *   *

Back in the days of the Treta Yuga and not long after the sacred pool was first formed, Lord Rama and his wife, Sita, had two sons, Lav and Kush. They grew up to be able rulers of their kingdom, which was the ancient Punjab. Lav laid the foundation of the city of Lahore and Kush laid the foundation of the city of Kasoor. Each brother ruled in peace and harmony, but their succeeding generations began to feud and eventually went to war.

Raja Kal Ketu of Kasoor, a descendant of Kush, was the victor. Raja Kal Rai of Lahore, a descendant of Lav, surrendered his city to Raja Kal Ketu. Rather than remain in bondage in the Punjab, Raja Kal Rai moved his family to the areas outside the Punjab, in a region known as Sandoh Desh.

The Raja of Sandoh Desh had a daughter, Rani Kumari, whom he decided to give in marriage to Raja Kal Rai. Having grown tired of the responsibility of rulership and desiring to spend his remaining days in meditation, he gave his entire kingdom as dowry to Raja Kal Rai. Raja Kal Rai and Rani Kumari had a son whom they named Sodhi Rai. He became the father of the Sodhi dynasty, the Sodhi Sultan.

Sodhi Rai grew up to be a strong and brave man, full of self-respect and devotion to Me. With a comprehensive understanding of his family history and the pain they endured by their defeat at Lahore, he decided to reclaim his ancestral lands. He organized a massive army and marched back through the Punjab to Lahore. He defeated the descendants of Raja Kal Ketu and they were forced to scatter. Sodhi Rai now ruled the Punjab.

The descendants of Raja Kal Ketu settled in the various regions around the area, where they established small villages and communities. One family that settled in Kashi became very highly educated and over time, became famous for reciting the Vedas. Raja Sodhi Rai and his family ruled the greater Punjab with great success and credit, while the descendants of Kush and Raja Kal Ketu became famous throughout the region for their knowledge of the Vedas and strict observance of the Vedic traditions.

In time they became so renowned that whenever anyone seriously sought instruction in the Vedas, they went to a member of that family to teach them. The head of the family was so imbued with the essence of the Vedas that he was considered to be one with them. The essence of the Vedas was in his presence, in his speech and actions, in his thoughts and heart. Eventually, the title of Vedi, one who has mastered the Vedas, was bestowed upon him and ultimately the entire clan came to be called Vedi. With missionary zeal, the Vedis spread their education and knowledge about Vedic culture and philosophy throughout the country. As languages evolved in that region, the "v" sound became "b" so that in time, Vedi became Bedi.

Raja Sodhi Rai learned of their fame and depth of understanding of the Vedas, which inspired in him the desire to resolve the past animosity between the two families. Accordingly, he wrote a letter to the Vedis in Kashi and invited them to return to the Punjab and visit him in Lahore. They accepted the invitation and were received with great honor and ceremony at the court of Raja Sodhi Rai, who urged them to spread their teachings in his kingdom.

In time, Raja Sodhi Rai himself became a student of the Vedas under the Vedi Guru. He was well-advanced in years by this time and had grown tired of the responsibilities of leadership, as his maternal grandfather had before him. When he had completed his study of the first three Vedas and was just beginning exposition of the fourth, Raja Sodhi Rai was overcome with a desire to renounce the world and devote his life to meditation and perfection of the self. Upon completion of the fourth Veda, he could bear it no longer and made plans to renounce the world and donate his entire kingdom to the Vedis in gratitude for what he had learned.

He approached the Vedi Guru and very humbly spoke to him. "Oh, Holy Sir, my heart and mind grow weary of the affairs of this world. Through your guidance I have been transformed. My entire kingdom is yours. Please take it now, so that I can pass my final days in contemplation, free of the bondage of this world."

"My son," spoke the Vedi Guru, "neither I nor my family have any interest in the affairs of state. Our mission is to enlighten people with the wisdom of the Vedas, and we are quite happy doing that. I have no desire to become entangled in the web of the world and turn my attention away from the Almighty."

The Raja replied, "I offer this kingdom to you as a small token of gratitude for the wisdom and awareness I have gained from your teachings. The people of the Punjab are a brave and loyal people and would benefit immeasurably from the teachings of the Vedas. If you take this kingdom, they will not only be loyal to the Raj, but will follow the Vedic traditions for generations."

The Vedi Guru asked for time to contemplate the offer of Sodhi Rai, as he was reluctant to make such a decision quickly. He and his clan had dedicated themselves to mastering the Vedas and helping others to attain that mastery as well. Now he was asked to take on a great worldly burden, which would pull him away from his life of meditation and devotion. It took many days of prayer and meditation before he found his answer. So, after some time, he sent for the Raja and spoke to him softly.

"My son," he began, "our families have been enemies for generations. Yet, with great courage, you have brought that to an end. You have dedicated yourself to learning the Vedas and have attained deep and intimate understanding. Through that understanding, you have become enlightened. Out of gratitude for what you have attained, you offer to return this Raj to us, something that we never desired. We recognize, however, that the course of destiny is at play here and this shall fall on us come what may. Better that we embrace this sacred trust than to turn from it irresponsibly. Because of your humility and sincere devotion, and after much contemplation, we agree to hold this Raj in trust—but only in trust.

"Go now and pursue your life of contemplation. In your own ecstasy and by your own right, you will merge with Him who is all things. We will hold this Raj in trust until the Kali Yuga. Then you will incarnate to teach the Name of God and turn the Age in the direction of righteousness. At that time you will be known as the Guru of Miracles."

Sodhi Rai touched the feet of the Vedi Guru and left for the jungle where he did achieve union with Me. The Vedi Guru took the reins of state, and he and his subsequent generations ruled the kingdom wisely and righteously. One of the generations that followed him in the Kali Yuga was that of Kalyan Chand Bedi, the father of Nanak.

*   *   *

It is said that at the time of his birth, in the year 1469 CE, Nanak laughed out loud like an old man. Nanak was his parents' second child.

The firstborn had been a girl, Bibi Nanaki. Choosing not to follow one of the more cruel customs of the time, Pitta Kalu let his infant daughter live. Yet he longed for a son. Three years later in answer to Pitta Kalu and Mata Tripta's prayers, Nanak was born.

With such a magnificent soul and so great a destiny, Nanak did not relate to the world as his father expected or as the world demanded. He heard another cadence in his boundless and radiant heart, and it took him many years to adjust to life in the world. Nanak sought solitude in the company of his own soul, which meant that his poor father was simply unable to understand him.

As Nanak matured, he became remote from his family and Pitta Kalu's concern for his son grew, causing Mata Tripta ever-greater anxiety. So Kalu decided to send Nanak to school. His prayer was that the process of learning would engage Nanak's mind and give him something worldly to hold on to. He hoped that in this way, Nanak would grow more in touch with his family and the world around him.

Yet after only a few days in school, the mullah brought Nanak home. Pitta Kalu was distraught, concerned that his son had misbehaved in a way that humiliated Kalu and his family.

"Why are you here, Mullahji?" Kalu demanded of Nanak's teacher.

"Why? I have come to return your son to you. I have nothing further to teach him." His voice was matter-of-fact, as though Pittaji should already know why the mullah had returned his son to him.

"What has he done? Did he insult you with his insolence?" Kalu's tone was at once accusatory and defensive.

"No, Kaluji, he did not insult me." Mullahji paused and gazed at Nanak who was sitting quietly on the ground, his eyes closed. "He amazed me, Kaluji!" Then softly, "He truly amazed me."

Kalu sucked air between his teeth. He could not grasp what the mullah was saying. Mullahji understood this. He placed his hand on Kalu's shoulder and turned him away from Nanak.

In a quiet, almost conspiratorial voice but with powerful intensity, Mullahji spoke. "My dear Kalu, do you understand what has happened here?"

"Perhaps not." Kalu began to tremble slightly, thinking young Nanak had committed some crime.

"Don't you recognize this soul you have fathered?" The mullah was incredulous.

Kalu's jaw went slack, but he remained silent.

"My dear Kalu, be patient with this boy. He will bring honor to your name and to all your generations. He knows all he will ever need to know. There has never been another like him. Allah in His mercy has brought this child to your family. Perhaps someday, I will have the opportunity to sit before him and learn." Placing both hands on Kalu's shoulders, the old mullah looked deeply into his eyes. "He is a blessed one, Kalu. He grasps instantly what he hears only once."

Poor Kalu was as lost as a child in the darkness. The words of the old mullah simply did not register in his agitated and deeply confused mind. He could not speak, but looked at Mullahji with confused desperation in his eyes, searching for an answer that would bring him comfort, something that would allay his fears and ease his deeply troubled heart.

The old mullah had taught many boys in his nearly seventy years. He had taught gifted students who went on to become prominent men. He had taught problem children who could not or would not learn. A few distinguished families had even retained him to teach their daughters. He loved teaching and he loved learning. But he especially loved when he had ignited a spark in a child. Mullahji was kind and wise and deeply respected by the community. He wanted Kalu to understand that Nanak was not an ordinary child and that he should not have ordinary expectations of Nanak.

"Listen to me, Kalu sahib," Mullahji spoke softly, trying to choose words that could bring some comfort to this worried father. "I have learned more from this boy in a matter of days than I learned from a lifetime of study, prayer, and meditation. I am ashamed to refer to myself as a mullah before him."

Kalu's face contorted to a startled and confused expression.

"Kalu, this child is special. He has a most auspicious destiny. I have done his chart and read his lines. He is special and he will bring healing to the world. He will give to humanity the key that will open the very heart of God."

Kalu stopped and said in a startled voice, "Are you saying he is an avatar?"

"He is more than that, Kaluji."

Kalu looked at the old teacher as the late morning gave way to early afternoon. The sounds of the village, the smells of the fires and livestock, the voices of the children all blended at that moment into a perfect harmony. For a long time both men stood silently.

"Mullahji," Kalu's voice was soft and unemotional, his gaze was far away, neither looking at the old mullah nor at any object in his immediate sphere. "Mullahji," he repeated, with a strange and unusually broad smile, "you are a crazy old man. Leave my son to me." With that, he paid the mullah and escorted him out of his gate.

In the Hindu tradition, when boys of the upper castes reach the age of eleven, they undergo the rite of initiation, and the sacred thread is bestowed upon them, thereby making them what is known as twice born. The *janeu* is made of soft strands of cotton which are woven into a thin cord. The cord is twisted, and then looped over the left shoulder and around the right hip. It is an ancient ceremony and cause for great celebration in a family.

I always like these observances when they are done with devotion and the initiate has a sense of sacredness about it. They began as a way of keeping a clan together, of marking significant transitions in life, and to help people remember Me. As time passed, however, they became for many a matter of ritual and show and a source of income for the pundits.

Pitta Kalu and Mata Tripta had made elaborate plans for Nanak's initiation. Family members, friends and relatives, as well as most of the village of Talwandi, gathered at the home of Kalu and Mata Tripta, who scurried around excitedly. Pundit Hardyal arrived somewhat ostentatiously and instructed everyone to be seated so that the ceremony could begin. Nanak was brought before the pundit, who began to recite the Sanskrit passages in a deep sonorous voice.

At the appropriate time he took the sacred thread, twisted it as prescribed by tradition, and raised his hands to place it over Nanak's left shoulder. And once again, to Pitta Kalu's horror, Nanak stunned his family.

"Stop, Punditji!" There was authority in his boyish voice, and the whole congregation drew a collective breath. Pitta Kalu's face contorted, his eyes widened menacingly in an attempt to intimidate young Nanak.

"What is it, boy?" demanded the priest. "You mustn't stop this ritual."

"But I have a question." Nanak's voice was innocent and filled with concern.

No one had ever questioned Pundit Hardyal, who was highly regarded by the people of Talwandi.

"Then ask, son," said the pundit, humoring Nanak.

"Punditji," he said, "what difference can a thread make? Shouldn't the essence of the heart differentiate one man from the next? Isn't that what is regarded most by God and what truly sets us apart?"

Nanak was right: what I regard the most is indeed the essence of the heart.

Punditji opened his mouth, but could not speak. Pitta Kalu, humiliated and red-faced, tried to stand but could not move.

Closing his eyes, Nanak began to sing softly in a melodic and enchanting voice.

> *"Out of the cotton of compassion*
> *Spin the thread of contentment,*
> *Tie the knot of continence,*
> *and the twist of virtue.*
> *Make such a sacred thread,*
> *O Pundit, for your inner self."*

No one spoke, not even Pitta Kalu. Mata Tripta had tears in her eyes and Pundit Hardyal was stunned. The verses of Nanak affected the old pundit, much as Mullahji had been affected when Nanak was his student. In the prevailing silence it seemed as though all activity in Talwandi had ceased and the usual sounds of a busy village were muted. Quietly Nanak rose, went into the house, and lay on his cot. Pitta Kalu's head plummeted into his hands and his body shook with anger, humiliation, and bitter disappointment. Pundit Hardyal silently placed his hand on Kalu's back, but the poor man was inconsolable.

Pitta Kalu, desperate about his only son, was running out of ideas about how to give him a sense of responsibility. Despite his anger and frustration, he was a deeply concerned father and feared that Nanak's unwillingness to deal with the world around him would only result in tragedy. Pitta Kalu thought long and hard and finally decided that Nanak should marry. He thought that a wife would give Nanak a companion and someone to care for. If Nanak could recognize and accept the responsibilities of a householder, then he might accept responsibility in the world.

According to the custom, Pitta Kalu and Mata Tripta interviewed families with marriageable daughters and finally decided on a girl from the nearby village of Pakhote. Nanak, without a word, dutifully attended the ceremony and was married to Sulakhani in her village, as was the custom. Shortly thereafter he took Sulakhani back to Talwandi and his father's house. Nanak promptly ignored his new bride and resumed his solitude once again.

In time, however, Nanak softened somewhat toward Sulakhani. Though he could not please Kalu and demonstrate interest in commerce or farming, Nanak did begin to spend time with his young bride, and eventually he fathered two sons, Siri Chand and Lakhmi Chand. They were bright boys, and Nanak took to fatherhood with some enthusiasm. However, his lessons were those of spirituality and the nature of the cosmos, rather than the nature of the world. Pitta Kalu, Mata Tripta, and Bibi Sulakhani all feared that Nanak was leading his sons down the same path of idleness that they believed he was walking.

After years of trying, Pitta Kalu finally threw up his hands, believing he had failed as a father. Nanak showed no interest in anything his father tried to engage him with. Indeed, Pitta Kalu grew concerned that Nanak might adversely influence his grandsons. He told Nanak that since he seemed to have no aptitude for anything, he should enter into government service. So Nanak decided to leave Talwandi and join his sister in Sultanpur. She had married a government officer named Jai Ram a few years earlier and according to tradition, moved to Sultanpur and the home of her husband.

Sulakhani took the news of Nanak's departure very hard. From the beginning he seemed to be a disinterested husband, which was a source of considerable pain to her. He was seldom around, and when he was, his mind was always elsewhere. Though he had fathered two sons with her, he demonstrated little interest in family life, or for that matter in life at all. So when he told her that he would be leaving and going to Sultanpur, poor Sulakhani was crushed. She was gripped by a desperate fear. For a woman, especially one with two young sons, to be abandoned by her husband was a curse from which she could never recover. She was terrified.

"You are my husband," she said, her girlish voice tiny and weak. "And when you sit with me in this home, in my estimation I possess the sovereignty of the whole Earth.

Without you now, this world has no meaning for me."

Nanak was touched by her plea, yet firm in his resolve. Placing his hand under her chin, he tilted her head back and looked into her eyes. Softly and sincerely he said to her, "Your sovereignty shall ever abide. There is no need for you to be anxious. Remain here with our sons. If I can earn my living, I will send for you. Show courage now and honor my request."

Sulakhani tightly closed her eyes and squeezed the tears from them. Nanak helped her to stand, and in silence she helped Nanak to finish his preparations for his trip to Sultanpur.

SEVEN

THE REUNION OF SISTER AND brother in Sultanpur was joyful, and Nanak brightened in Bibi Nanaki's house. Jai Ram was a good man and took an immediate liking to Nanak. He offered to find him a position in the administration. Nanak, not wanting to be a burden to his sister, was eager to work. Perhaps it was the responsibility of fatherhood or perhaps it was a matter of maturity, or some resolution that he had reached in his mind, but he was now more present and interested in the world around him. Sultanpur gave Nanak new stimulation.

Jai Ram used his influence to find Nanak a government post, and in a short time, Nanak took a job in the *modikhana,* where the granary and stored goods of the government were kept. People paid their taxes and fees to the government in grains or goods, and were paid for services or settlements in kind. Nanak was like an accountant, and it was his responsibility to measure and account for what was taken in and what was issued out.

In what was a seriously corrupt government, he was remarkably trustworthy and untouched by the corruption around him. Each day, farmers brought their grain to the granary, and Nanak recorded how much was delivered and what was to be credited to the individual's account. Portions that were to be issued as payment were weighed and distributed accordingly. It was Nanak's responsibility to record the going out and the coming in, and he did so with absolute accuracy.

There was every opportunity for personal gain through corruption, and many prodded him to fix the scales or alter his entries in the books. He was offered money, gems, land, additional grain for himself, as well as horses and elephants. Yet Nanak remained uncorrupted and kept perfect and accurate records, always with a kind sense of humor. No one could figure him out and no one could corrupt him. And so he became respected by the community.

Not wanting to burden his sister, Nanak rented a house near the granary where he lived with a childhood companion who had followed him from Talwandi. Mardana was a Muslim who had been touched by Nanak's wisdom and spiritual power when they were both just boys. So when Nanak decided to move to Sultanpur, Mardana made the decision to join him there, and he served Nanak for the rest of his life. At that time though, they were both still young and their extraordinary lives were only beginning to unfold.

One evening as they sat together, Nanak turned to Mardana and in a soft voice said, "I have a gift for you."

"For me, my brother? What have you brought me and why?"

Nanak picked up a bundle that was wrapped in a plain woolen shawl and handed it to Mardana with a sly smile. Mardana carefully unwrapped the shawl and saw that he held a stringed instrument. He regarded it with amazement and confusion.

"A *rebab*? Why would you give me a rebab?" Mardana was touched, but could not understand the motive of his unusual friend.

"My brother, for many, many lifetimes we have walked together and in each of those lifetimes you expressed yourself on the strings of this gourd. Stroke it and see how it feels in your hands."

Mardana held the rebab as though it were a newborn baby. He regarded it intently and idly turned the tuning pegs as he instinctively tuned the six gut strings by ear. As he tuned the strings, the sheepskin parchment that stretched over the cavity of the rounded body vibrated with the tuning. He did not speak, but his hands caressed the strings. As he plucked with the fingers of his right hand, the fingers of his left hand began to press the strings at various points up and down the neck, while sound escaped from the strings. The mellow tones of the gut strings caused the sheepskin parchment to vibrate, and those sounds reverberated and blended in the rounded cavity below it. Music floated melodiously into the air.

Closing his eyes, Nanak began to sing a song of devotion with his friend.

"*It is Thy light that lives in every heart and Thy light that illumines every soul . . .*"

Like the music vibrating from the strings of the rebab, Nanak's hymn was spontaneous, sweet, and soothing. In a short while, a crowd had gathered and Nanak and Mardana continued in this way for some time. When they stopped, no one spoke or moved.

"You have mastered this instrument for lifetimes, my friend," Nanak whispered. "You will do it again in this life."

Thereafter, each evening Nanak sat before the people who came to his door and without a word between them, Mardana began to play the rebab and Nanak closed his eyes and sang the poetry of his soul. Nanak's reputation grew, and the people of Sultanpur, as well as those of the surrounding villages, sought him out. People would gather at his door each evening to listen to him speak and to meditate and recite their prayers with him. He became respected as a teacher as well as a dedicated public servant.

One evening Nanaki approached Nanak. "You have truly grown in this place. Father is happy with you."

"He is a good man and has done what he believes to be right."

"There is such great truth to your teaching, but I must tell you that I think your life is a little one-sided."

Nanak raised his eyebrows.

Nanaki continued, "Have you forgotten that you too are a householder?"

Nanak smiled, "You are too wise for me." He laughed out loud, "Too wise! I'll be happy to have Sulakhani and the boys with me."

For seven years Nanak lived the life of an honorable householder, never displaying the behavior that had so concerned his father. He seemed as cheerful during this period as he had seemed melancholy during his youth.

Nanak became increasingly recognized as a teacher and seldom had time for himself during the day. People constantly came to him for counseling and advice about every aspect of their lives. They asked to be healed, asked his blessings on their children, asked advice about business, and even asked him to arrange for suitable husbands or wives for their sons and daughters.

Every morning, three hours before sunrise, Nanak and Mardana would walk through the forest to the nearby Bein River, a tributary of the Beas. There he immersed himself in the water, winter or summer, until his every cell tingled with the cold. After bathing, he sat under the trees and meditated until sunrise. In the distance he could hear the *adhan*, the Muslim call to prayer, and the ringing of the temple bells as Hindus engaged in their morning devotions.

That early morning time was precious to him. The solitude of the forest and the music of the river soothed and comforted him. It was a time of peace, when he meditated on Me in deep trance and rapturous ecstasy. One morning he stepped into the river and did not come out. On that extraordinary morning, Nanak Nirankari, the Worshipper of the Formless God, was absorbed by Me, the Formless God Himself.

* * *

I went to Nanak and offered him a cup of nectar, from which he drank deeply. As he drank, I drew him deeper into Myself, and in this way, Nanak merged with Me wholly. There was no distinction between Nanak and Me. At that moment, all knowledge of the Universe, the truth of all things, the form of the formless, and the known and the unknown, were revealed to Nanak. Deeper than the sea, higher than the Himalayas, lighter than ether, Nanak found himself surrounded by My living, infinite, vibrating presence. Every atom of every molecule of every fiber of his being was filled with My essence. And that state of limitless ecstasy became Nanak's identity, before all the angels, deities, and thirty-three million gods, goddesses, and entities.

I honored him as the father of a universal lineage of spirit with the mission to free humanity from the tyranny of the mind. All of the Heavens met Nanak and, with the greatest respect, honored him for agreeing to accept such an important mission. I whispered the *Wahe Guru* sound in Nanak's ear and gave him the key that, if applied by an individual, would unlock the prison of superstition and ignorance into which humankind had confined itself.

"Go and repeat My Name," I told him, "and cause others to do the same. Establish this Golden Chain on the Earth. Live in the world, but be not consumed by it. Serve My creation, for I love each soul that walks upon it. Bring them comfort, teach them how to free themselves from their fear, frustration, pain, and suffering. Instruct them how to merge with Me as you have. Know that I am ever with you. This cup of nectar from which you have drunk marks My sacred pledge to you."

Then I held out My precious little soul that the great Rishi Mahan Akal had created. "Her time comes before long," I told him. And My beloved devotee bent and blessed her.

* * *

The people of Sultanpur had been watching the river and searching the forest for three days. They had searched for a body, but what they found was a great teacher, a guru. And for Guru Nanak, life as he had known it changed.

Guru Nanak walked calmly out of the forest, and the people gathered around him staring speechless for some time. Clearly, he was a different man. He was more radiant, more powerfully present, and more deeply serene. His eyes blazed, his face shone, and he exuded absolute joy. The people of Sultanpur felt his serene joy and it filled them as well. His friends and family urged him to speak, to explain what had happened. Yet as the crowd walked back to the village, the guru remained silent. When they got to the center, Guru Nanak raised his head and opened his arms to the people, smiling.

"There is no Hindu! There is no Muslim!" he said to them in a startlingly loud voice. Then softly, "There is only God."

In the early morning sun the crowd stood in startled silence. For the Muslims, his words were heresy.

"Explain it!" the people demanded.

"There is but One God," said Nanak.

"How is He identified?" they asked.

"Truth is His identity," responded the guru.

"What does He do?" they cried.

"He is the doer of everything." Nanak said it matter-of-factly, as though any idiot should know that.

"Describe him!" someone shouted.

"He is fearless and without anger; undying, unborn, and self-illumined!" declared Guru Nanak. Again, silence.

"How do you know this?" asked another.

"I know this by the grace of the True Guru," he answered. There was such absolute certainty in his voice that no one present considered that what he spoke was other than truth.

"How can we know this ourselves?" asked someone else.

"Meditate!" he answered, his voice penetrating into the psyche and soul of each one present.

"And what truth will we know?" several asked at once.

"He is true in the beginning!"

"We know that!"

"He is true through all the ages!"

"What about now! It is in this age that we are suffering!"

"Even now He is true and I, Nanak, affirm that He shall forever be true!" All were silent for some time.

"Explain it!" someone broke the silence.

"We have made God very complex in our minds, but in reality, He is very simple and to know Him is very simple. First, rise each morning during the sweet hours before the rising of the sun. Bathe yourself and cleanse your body, then sit quietly and cleanse your mind.

"What do we do, pour water through our ears?" someone shouted.

Everyone laughed. Guru Nanak looked at him directly and laughingly said, "Hey fool, simply meditate by reciting God's name. By doing that repeatedly you will change the habit patterns of your soul, deflect the blow of your karma, and your life will improve!" The pitch of his voice raised a tone.

"What is God's name?" shouted someone in the back.

"God's beautiful names are many. All are good."

"What else!" someone yelled.

"Work honestly and earn by the sweat of your brow."

"We already do that," many replied.

"And remember Him while you work. Then share what you earn with those in need and contribute to the community. Be kind to each other, don't speak ill of another, and never speak ill of yourself. God in His mercy will enter your home, and you will be happy. Forget the austerities and incantations! God is very practical and knows that you have work and families. Just remember Him. God has created everything, He does everything, and He is everything. You only need to recognize it."

"Which is better," someone shouted, "a Hindu or a Muslim?"

"What is best is to be righteous and honorable. Recite God's name with love in your heart so that becomes your identity. Surrender to His will with joy, give freely of yourself with all your heart to all who need your help. Whatever path you walk, walk it with devotion. Make kindness your mosque, sincerity your prayer mat, and what is kind and just your Koran."

"But what is God's true religion?" another shouted, sounding confused.

"My beloved," Nanak said with a smile, "there is but one God. From Him come all things and back to Him return all things. He is the source of all and is so great and vast that it is beyond our limited capacity to comprehend. Still, there is no prayer of the heart that is unheard, no meditation that does not lead to bliss. The true religion is that which keeps His memory ever in your mind, His love ever in your heart, and which relieves the suffering of others. Where you pray is where your heart leads you. Pray in a mosque, pray in a temple, or pray in the cozy solitude of your own home. Just pray with sincerity and devotion. God hears all prayers."

"Oh, Guruji," another asked shyly, "we have been told that only renouncing the world and begging is favorable to God and that we who are householders can never truly know Him."

"My friend, religion rests upon the back of the householder. What greater challenge is there than to live in the world and discharge your responsibilities while remembering Him with every breath? Those who are false shall only obtain what is false, but those who are true shall find in themselves the Truth."

"Then from where should our prayers come? From what scripture should they be recited?"

"Let your prayers be recited from your heart. Whatever you recite, do so from your heart, with the love of God filling you. Idle repetition of texts is not prayer, yet to recite with devotion is favorable to God. If you are Muslim, be a good Muslim and five times a day pray from your heart with love for God. If you are Hindu, be a good Hindu and follow the Vedas with devotion. In this way you will grow, your mind will find confidence, and your soul will find peace. This is your life's purpose."

So it was that in the summer of 1496 CE at the age of twenty-seven, Guru Nanak made his way out of his home and into immortality. Trusting the care of his lamenting wife to Me, and with a most humble prayer, Guru Nanak set out with Mardana.

He went to the mountaintops and scolded the yogis for abandoning the world and hording the great technology of mind and spirit that they possessed. He reprimanded them for using their psychic powers and black magic to frighten and control people, rather than to elevate and heal them.

He came to a place high in the Himalayas by a deep blue lake. Many yogis lived in this high and remote place and Nanak wanted to meet them. As he and Mardana approached the place the energy changed, the temperature became colder, and they heard strange sounds. Soon, demonic faces and frightening forms appeared before them. They came to a clearing by the lake, and Nanak sat down under a tree. Slowly, naked yogis and *sadhus*, yogis who had attained mystical powers, began to emerge from the forest that surrounded the great lake.

"Greetings, boy," said Charpat, the yogi. "Tell us of the world you came from."

"Why should I tell you? You have left it to suffer, what do you care?"

The yogi stared at Nanak. He did not expect to be talked to in this way.

"So then, you have come to join us?"

"What is there to join?" asked Nanak.

"If you truly want a spiritual life, you must leave the world, renounce all your possessions and desires, and be here with us."

"The world is a pool of burning hot fire," said Nanak, "and you have the knowledge of how to cool it, of how to pass through that fire without being burned. Yet you choose to remain here, hiding from it. Shame on you! What kind of spirituality is this that leaves humanity to suffer? Your cowardly actions only serve your egos."

All were silent. Nanak's words stung them.

"Look, son," said Charpat kindly, "let us have tea together." He handed Nanak a large copper urn. "Go to the lake and fill this with water."

Quietly, Nanak took the urn and walked to the lake. As he knelt down to fill the urn, he no longer saw water in the lake but gems: gold and silver, large red rubies, shining blue sapphires, and bright, radiant diamonds as far as he could see. It was a lake of treasure. He laughed out loud as he stood up and carried the urn, empty, back to the gathering.

"Well, boy, have you filled the urn?" demanded the yogi.

"I am sorry, *ji*, but there is no water in the lake." He placed the urn before Charpat and took his seat before the fire.

There were now many yogis and sadhus sitting in their yogic postures in a circle before the fire.

The yogis were silent. No one had ever passed that test. They had tried to frighten the guru, but he remained unfazed. They tried to tempt him with jewels and riches, but he was unaffected by that as well. He returned the urn empty, since he had been asked to fill it with water and there was no water in the lake. The yogis and sadhus were impressed, especially since Nanak was still such a young man.

"You truly are great," said one of the sadhus. "Why not join us here? This is where you attain true spirituality, not down in the world."

"Let me ask you, oh sadhu, when you depart this body, where will your soul reside?"

The sadhu was silent.

"You have such great powers. You can turn water to treasure, you can manifest things in the air, and you can levitate yourselves. Has this brought you closer to God? You live here and serve yourselves, but what about those who suffer because you refuse to help them?"

"We have helped all who have come to us."

"You hide here! You live in fear of the world. You have not renounced it, you have retreated from it! You practice your incantations to gain your spiritual powers. Yet in so doing, you have bound your souls and become trapped by those very powers. How shall you pass through? You know the mantras to change your form. You know the mantras to manifest things from the air.

"Is all your time here with all your sacrifice only to gain power, or did you come here to know God and to polish your soul? Yoga is union, yet your union is not with God but with your ego. What can you offer me here except to be bound by the very powers you covet? You know meditation and can help people to be free from their fears and superstitions. Why have you turned your back on those who pray for help?"

The yogis could not answer him. They tried to challenge and argue with him, insisting that only a renunciate could achieve spiritual awareness, but for each argument and challenge, Nanak vanquished them with the truth and power of his words. He remained only briefly with the yogis. Driven by his mission, he and Mardana made their way from the mountains.

Everywhere he went Nanak saw a world that lived in fear. He challenged the Brahmins for their exclusionary and hypocritical ways and chided the pundits for putting fear in the hearts and minds of the people. He challenged the caste system and the role of women. Guru Nanak emphasized in his teachings that all life is born of woman and that the future depends upon the grace and devotion of a woman. He spoke openly against the common and forced practice of *sati* and against the gruesome practice of killing a firstborn child if it was a girl.

In Hardwar, a most sacred place of pilgrimage for Hindus, the guru joined a huge predawn crowd that had gathered on the shores of the Ganges. They entered the water and performed a ritual for blessing their ancestors and washing away their sins. The assembled crowd began throwing water toward the east in the direction of the rising sun. Nanak entered the cold rushing water himself and moved among the throng, cupping his hands and tossing water toward the west. Eventually, even in such a chaotic mass of humanity, his peculiar actions drew attention.

A large crowd surrounded him and they stared in amazement. Finally, an astonished Brahmin asked, "Heh, fool, what are you doing? Are you a Hindu or Mussalman?"

"If you are Mussalman, why have you come to a Hindu place of pilgrimage?" asked another.

The crowd was gathering courage now and a third Brahmin asked "Why are you throwing water to the west instead of toward the rising sun? What guru has taught you such a strange ritual?"

Guru Nanak paused and faced the last who spoke, "Brother, why do you throw the water toward the rising sun? To whom do you offer it? Who receives it?"

"Why," answered the first Brahmin, "we make this offering to the souls of our ancestors."

"To your ancestors? Why?"

"Are you truly such a fool?" the Brahmin responded. "We make this offering because it brings their souls joy and brings us great happiness, satisfaction, and prosperity," he said proudly, with a great air of piety.

"Seriously?" asked the guru in amazement. "How far away are your ancestors?"

A learned pundit stepped forward arrogantly, the U-shaped mark of the deity Vishnu freshly drawn on his forehead. "Our ancestors reside thousands upon thousands of miles away," he stated with great authority, mightily satisfied with the sound of his own voice against the rushing waters of the Ganga.

Without a word, Nanak turned back toward the west and began to forcefully throw huge palms full of water in that direction with a fury that seemed to hinge on desperation, as though he were fighting a fire.

"Wait! Stop!" the gathered men shouted. "Stop, you madman! You have not answered our questions."

Nanak paused again, nearly out of breath, a look of concern on his face. "When I left the Punjab, I had just planted a field. There is no one there who will irrigate it for me, and I am now concerned that it will go to seed if I don't water it. You see, my field is on an elevated area, and the rainwater doesn't settle on it. I have no choice but to irrigate it from here."

"Are you crazy?" bellowed the authoritarian pundit. "How do you suppose this water that you throw will ever reach the Punjab? Your field will dry up, you lunatic!"

"Truly?" asked the guru incredulously. "My field is much closer than your ancestors, so how can the water that you throw reach them, yet the water that I throw not reach my field?"

No one spoke as the sound of the rushing Ganga harmonized with the bells and horns and morning chants that filled the air.

With chilling seriousness, Nanak looked the pundit in the eye and said in a quietly penetrating voice, "You have forgotten God. Without love or devotion your minds have drifted and gone astray."

"What are you saying? How can a mind that recites the Name of God forget Him or go astray?

"A mind that recites the Name with sincerity and devotion never forgets and cannot go astray. Yet a mind that is filled with hypocrisy such as yours," and he turned to another, "and yours," and he turned again, "and yours can be true to none and will drift like a boat with no anchor. Your rosaries are only for show and your recitation is hypocrisy."

Nanak turned to the Brahmin who first approached him. "You are thinking of your trade with Multan," to the next, "and your trade with Kabul," to the next, "and your trade with Delhi." Then to the pundit, "And you are thinking of what you might gain from this gathering of pilgrims."

To a man, the crowd stepped back in the water two or three paces. In the distance the sounds of the morning rituals continued against the constant gush of the Ganges, while the rising sun broke over the Himalayas and shone brightly upon the serene face of Nanak.

"What can we do?" whispered the pundit.

"Make your devotion live. Recite the sacred names with love and let that fill you. In this way you will bring honor to yourselves and your ancestors. You are lost in your rituals and do them only for show, while your hearts putrefy under the garbage of your minds. Awaken from the *Maya*!" he said brightly. "Care for your communities, serve the living God that resides within you by serving each other, and let devotion fill you. In this way you will be transformed."

With that, Nanak waded to the riverbank in silence. With a nod to Mardana who had been watching the dramatic scene evolve, Guru Nanak walked toward the west away from the Ganges and down toward the plain of the Punjab. Mardana hastily collected their things, cast a parting glance at the befuddled congregation still standing in the water, and double-timed his steps to catch up with the guru.

EIGHT

During this time, India was under the rule of the Afghan Lodhi dynasty. Yet in 1526 the Mughal, Babur, staged his invasion force on the Afghanistan border and drove into India with stunning impact. Pain, suffering, and rivers of blood spread across the land as he drove his conquering army toward Delhi, then Agra, where the throne stood.

Guru Nanak watched as the elephants, horses, and soldiers swept across his beloved homeland. The shrieks of the dying and the tears of the survivors touched his heart and shook his serenity. Yet in his wisdom and spiritual depth, he recognized that it was all My play and a result of the free will that I bestowed on humanity. Those who died came to Me and were received with loving care. Those who suffered cleared their karma quickly.

Many people prayed and communicated with Me, calling on Me as they never had before. I enjoyed the attention. When people call My name to curse Me or praise Me it always makes Me happy. Even those who deny My existence please Me because when they argue that I don't exist, they actually give Me a kind of off-handed acknowledgment.

It is interesting, but most people seem to call on Me only when they are desperate, in trouble, need help, are in pain or suffering. And once the situation passes, they forget about Me. It doesn't matter really, whether people praise Me or curse Me. I am unfazed by either. Any attention pleases Me. It diminishes My solitude. Yet when people call on Me with an open heart and humble mind—well, interesting things can happen,

The great thing about Nanak was he recognized that from My perspective there was no malice, no wrath, and that good or bad exists only in the mind. For many, this was an opportunity to grow. So the evolution of time and space moved as I saw fit, and like all things, it was neither good nor bad. It simply was.

After twenty-eight years of traveling on foot to teach, elevate, and inspire I was very proud of him and gave him a break. Nanak finally settled with his family near the banks of the River Ravi and soon a thriving village sprang up around the venerable guru. Guru Nanak called his village Kartarpur and devoted himself to agriculture and tending to his congregation. Each morning he rose before the sun, as had been his habit throughout his life. He bathed in the nearby River Ravi and then meditated and chanted with his disciples. Daily he held court and received visitors, gave advice, guidance and inspiration to the congregation, and delivered his teachings in verse form.

Life at Kartarpur was peaceful and very satisfying for Guru Nanak. Mardana, however, now well-advanced in years and physically weak from his long, hard travels and physical suffering with the guru, fell ill.

"I think the inevitable awaits me impatiently," he told the guru. They sat in Mardana's house in the late afternoon, as the sun descended toward its rendezvous with the horizon. Mardana lay upon his simple bed. A brown woolen shawl covered him from his shoulders to his feet. His long, white beard rested upon the shawl in bright contrast, highlighted by the afternoon sun upon it.

"It waits for us both, my friend. I won't be far behind."

"Guruji?" he asked thoughtfully. The question seemed important.

The guru raised his right eyebrow and lifted his head, slightly thrusting his chin toward Mardana in acknowledgment.

"When we were young, I was a Muslim and you were kind of a Hindu. Yet, you heard a different *raag*, and I followed you. Now, we are neither Muslim nor Hindu. I am your Sikh as you have always been my guru. This night shall be my last. How should I pass it so that my soul doesn't wander again?"

"We will take you to the banks of the Ravi. Sit at its edge in silent meditation and breathe through your nostrils long, slow, and deep. With each inhale silently recite *Sat* and with each exhale, recite *Nam*. You will grow calm and still, and as the night passes, your soul will be absorbed by the light of the Akal Purkh. It shall never wander again."

And before the dawn Mardana's soul separated from the body that encased it and he merged with Me. I was quite pleased with him.

* * *

Some distance from Kartarpur across the fertile lowland of the Punjab near the River Beas, was the village of Khadur. A village of good wells with sweet water and successful farming, the main industry of Khadur was weaving. In the most prominent area of the village, near where the village priest lived, was a community of industrious weavers. Their section of the village was marked by rows of small, shallow holes in front of their mud and thatch huts. Inside each hole was a peg upon which the weavers placed their spindles for the day's weaving.

Most of the villagers of Khadur were devotees of the goddess Durga. Considered by many as the "Goddess Who Is Unattainable," Durga was a consort of Shiva. Deeply nurturing and giving, she could also be terrifyingly powerful as well as ferociously protective. When really annoyed she transformed herself into the goddess Kali, who even frightened Me at times. I held her in the highest esteem. After all, I had Rishi Mahan Akal infuse her energy into that special soul.

The head priest of the village, who was deeply devoted to the goddess, was named Lehna. His sincerest expression of devotion for his beloved Durga was when he danced for her at the times of her worship. When he danced he was one with her, lost in the ecstasy of Durga's presence. So absolute was Lehna's absorption in his devotion to his goddess that he never removed the dancing bells from his ankles, so that each step he took was a reminder of her presence.

In the lower region of the Himalayas, east of the Punjab was the village of Jawalamukhi, a place sacred to the devotees of Durga, where flames erupt from the mountain and worship of Durga was continuous. Each year Lehna organized and led pilgrimages to Jawalamukhi where daily he danced until he was overcome with exhaustion, his feet raw and sore.

The villagers of Khadur had great reverence for Lehna. He was devoted and sincere, a responsible family man, and managed his affairs and obligations honorably. He was a good priest and always available to counsel those in need. Known for his kindness and hospitality, Lehna took a special interest in the youth of Khadur and dedicated considerable time to teaching them.

As in most villages Hindus, Muslims, Jains and Sikhs lived and worked together in Khadur. Their greatest fears were invasion by attacking armies or being attacked and forced to pay tribute to any of many bands of dacoits. These rogues often numbered in the hundreds and usually controlled a territory, demanding annual tribute from the villages in their area in exchange for protection from other bandits.

Failure to meet their demands was often fatal to a village. So the villagers depended on each other. They respected and participated in each other's celebrations and observances, which always made Me very happy. Still, Khadur was predominately a Hindu village and Hindu customs and philosophy governed village life.

The few Sikhs who lived there were mostly converts from Hinduism. A recently converted Sikh named Jodha was a neighbor of Lehna. Each morning Jodha sat on the roof of his house and recited the hymns of Guru Nanak. One morning Lehna walked from the temple of Durga after performing the morning *puja* to the goddess. It was just at sunrise and he was in a joyful mood. The bells around his ankles *chinged* with his stride, in cadence to a collection of ill-tempered *mudges* that moved along the path ahead of him. The sounds of their hooves and the bells around their necks created a counterpoint to Lehna's ankle bells. The morning was musical to Lehna and he listened to the rhythm of the bells, which supported the melodic calls of the birds and the nasal, high-pitched singsong of the herdsman. Lehna turned toward his house while the mudges moved on toward their pasture, their music lingering in the distance. The voice of the herdsman faded and the melodic sound of Jodha's recitation, like the faint call of a soaring hawk, brushed Lehna's ears.

Like a man in love who has not seen his beloved for many days then catches a trace of her perfume Lehna, as if in a trance, followed those sounds to Jodha's house. Quietly he entered the gate and sat on the earth below Jodha's roof. The buzzing of the flies and growing heat did not disturb Lehna as the impact of Guru Nanak's hymn penetrated deeper into his own psyche. When Jodha was finished, Lehna called up to him.

"Eh, Bhai, where have you been to learn something so lovely?"

Jodha looked down at Lehna, his teeth shining white behind his dark beard. "Oh, Lehna! Please come inside. You must have breakfast and I will tell you what has happened."

Over breakfast, Jodha told Lehna about Guru Nanak explaining how he met the guru and how that experience had changed his life.

"He is such a beautiful man! When he speaks to the congregation you feel that he speaks directly to you. When he looks at you, you know that he sees directly to the core of your soul. Whenever I see the guru I feel happy!"

Jodha smiled his big smile with his bright teeth, but his voice was sincere and direct. "Listen, Lehnaji, you must meet the guru for yourself."

Jodha paused, then with innocent prescience he added, "You are a deeply spiritual man and I think that you would gain much from meeting him."

"Is this possible?" There was a note of disbelief in Lehna's voice. For a holy man to be so accessible was unusual.

"Oh yes, of course," laughed Jodha. "You must meet him. I will tell you the way to go and you must set out immediately. Don't wait another moment to meet him. You will see and understand for yourself."

Two mornings later Guru Nanak walked in contemplative solitude along the road from Kartarpur. The hour was still early, the sun not yet above the horizon. Curiously, the guru was unaccompanied and the road unusually deserted. The sun broke the plain of the horizon spreading warmth and light, like honey, across the Earth. The bright dawn illuminated an oncoming rider, while silhouetting the guru against the rising sun. The sound of bells and horns and the chants of the morning devotions from the nearby villages drifted across the greening fields in the otherwise still morning air. And with each hoof beat of the approaching horse, the guru heard the rhythmic *ching ching* of ankle bells.

The silhouetted image of Guru Nanak against the brilliance of the rising sun mesmerized the approaching rider. Sunlight seemed to radiate from the head of the great Guru. The rider, unable to distinguish any definite features other than Guru Nanak's white beard, reined his horse and stopped alongside him.

"Oh, babaji, am I near the village of Kartarpur?"

The guru looked into the eyes that beheld him, reflecting the rising sun. "You are very near, ji. May I know your business there?"

Lehna, leaning forward in his saddle replied breathlessly, "I have heard of the great Guru Nanak and hope to meet him. Do you know of him?"

"I do know of him. Why do you want to meet him?" Nanak could be something of a rascal himself.

"A man in my village, Jodha, told me of him and I have a feeling that I could benefit by meeting him."

"I see," the guru answered reflectively. "Yes, I do think you could benefit by knowing him. May I know your good name, ji?"

"My name is Lehna, baba." Then somewhat impatiently, "Please, will you tell me how to find Guru Nanak?"

Guru Nanak smiled at the young man and said, "Well, Bhai Lehnaji, only you know *how* to find him, but I will be happy to show you *where* to find him. In fact," he said, as he took the reins from Lehna's hands, "it will be my privilege to lead you to him."

Lehna remained in the saddle lost in his own reverie. His heartbeat quickened and his mind raced as Guru Nanak walked quietly, leading Lehna's horse. There was no traffic along the road that still morning as the sun ascended toward its zenith. The scents of the morning cook fires blended with the aromas of the fertilized fields and the grazing livestock. The sounds of the morning devotions gave way to the sounds of a village rising to meet the day: children playing in the streets, the bells of the cows and mudges being driven through the village, and the laughter of the women at the wells, all to the rhythmic jingle of Lehna's ankle bells. Yet it was the profound silence that existed between Lehna and the guru that was the most deafening for him.

They stopped in front of a rather large mud brick house with an unusually large courtyard that was raked and well-tended. Many feet had frequented the courtyard and a smooth path was worn to the door of the house. Off to the side of the house fluttered a beautifully embroidered canopy, under which was a raised dais covered with white sheets and decorated cushions. The many pipal trees around the courtyard area provided shade and Lehna noted that this house had its own well. Behind the house was the stable and manger. A young girl sat beside a mudge expertly milking it. To the left spread perfectly tended fields, with the earliest shoots of mustard greens making their way through the surface of the earth toward the sun.

Guru Nanak stopped at the gate and handing Lehna the reins said in a cheerfully musical voice, "This is the home of Guru Nanak. I must leave you here and go about my own business. Please go to the front door and knock. Ask to see the guru. I believe that he will receive you most graciously."

"Thank you, Babaji," said Lehna. "You've been most kind."

By the time that Lehna had dismounted, the old Baba had disappeared.

Curious, he thought, *I never saw him leave.*

Short of breath from excitement, Lehna opened the gate and entered. His anxiety diminished in the peaceful refuge of the guru's courtyard. He had left Khadur hours before sunrise, yet standing in the shade of the courtyard Lehna felt refreshed. In his life Lehna had met many holy men, sadhus, fakirs, yogis, swamis, pundits, and magicians. He had seen amazing displays of spiritual powers and heard scholarly Brahmins discourse for days on all the subtle and mystical meanings of the Vedas. However, while they had entertained him, they had neither elevated him nor given him a spiritual experience. In fact they all seemed rather full of themselves, more intent on showing off than on giving true spiritual instruction. To Lehna, it seemed that they had spent many years studying, meditating, and practicing austerities so they could show off and gain materially.

He brushed the horsehairs from his *dhoti* and straightened it so that the blue border was even along the bottom and up the front, then smoothed his blue vest with the gold embroidery over his white *kurta*. He held a large colorful and fragrant garland that had been specially made the evening before, eleven rupees, and a hammered brass box filled with delicate sweets. With the jingle of his ankle bells reassuring him and with a prayer on his lips, Lehna approached the door and knocked. After a brief wait, someone answered.

In proper Hindu tradition Lehna spoke. "Please forgive my rude intrusion. I am Lehna," he said humbly, "an unworthy pilgrim from the village of Khadur. I have been told of the glorious radiance of Guru Nanak, which is equal to that of Lord Vishnu, and I, a mere supplicant, only have the hope of possibly beholding the wondrous presence of such a guru so that I might receive his generous *darshan*. My prayer is that in this way my mind might be stilled and my longings fulfilled."

"Guruji is unavailable at this time. Please come in the afternoon when he will be in durbar," and the servant gestured toward the dais with the canopy in the courtyard."

"Forgive me, ji, but a servant of this house led me here and told me to knock at this door. He told me that if I did so, the guru would receive me."

The servant eyed Lehna suspiciously. He looked down at Lehna's ankle bells and the slightest ray of recognition seemed to pass across his face. "Please wait, I will inquire." The servant shut the door and left Lehna standing.

After a wait that seemed to take the rest of the morning, the door opened. "Guruji will be pleased to see you." He escorted Lehna into the presence of Guru Nanak. When Lehna saw the guru sitting and smiling brightly at him, his heart and mind circled each other like birds in flight.

"Eh, Ram!" Lehna exclaimed, his eyes tearing. "You are Guru Nanak."

He rushed before the guru and, laying down his gifts, placed his forehead at Nanak's feet. "Forgive my arrogance for not recognizing you before. I am so ashamed that I remained mounted in your presence while you led my horse with your own hands. I spoke to you as if you were nothing more than a servant."

Lehna was astonished that the guru could be so humble and simple. In his experience holy men, fakirs, and men of knowledge and learning were ordinarily quite arrogant, with seemingly unlimited hubris. Normally, people never looked them directly in the eye and never spoke to them unless authorized to do so.

"No forgiveness is required, my son." The guru's voice was warm and comforting. "I simply led you to where you belong. You must stay a few days and we will become acquainted."

Lehna remained all that day and the next two with Guru Nanak. On the third day, the guru advised him, "Return to Khadur and see to your obligations there. Recite my hymns and meditate on God's Name each day, as I have instructed you. Come and be with me not less than every fifth day." Lehna was sitting on the floor in front of the guru and Guru Nanak had the index finger of his left hand placed at the center of Lehna's forehead. They slipped into a trance and remained joined in that way for some time.

Lehna returned to Khadur and early the next morning before sunrise, he solemnly removed the bells from around his ankles and quietly buried them in his courtyard. He was deeply satisfied that he had gone to meet Guru Nanak. His way of viewing the world, his life, and all that he had been taught and accustomed to had changed. He was a different man than the one who, less than a week before, had asked Jodha about the devotional songs he sang. Yet while Lehna was pleased with the turn his life had taken, the weavers and other villagers were very annoyed that their priest would abandon his responsibilities to them and the goddess.

A few citizens of Khadur joined with Lehna, but most considered him to be mad and carried on with their largely superficial devotions to Durga. Lehna was blissfully happy and served the guru in every way. He would go to the house of Guru Nanak and clean it, care for him, attend the durbar, rake the courtyard, tend the livestock, and work in his fields.

A well-known yogi came to visit Guru Nanak and he was received with great honor. Since his childhood, Nanak had always enjoyed the company of the yogis and sadhus who roamed across India and that joy never left him. He loved to engage them in discussion, to meditate with them and discourse on the Kali Yuga. This yogi was quite impressed and praised Nanak for the success of his mission, and how many devoted Sikhs were in his village. The guru regarded the yogi with his long hair piled high on his head and the mark of Shiva inscribed on his forehead with ochre sandalwood paste, and he laughed out loud.

"My dear Yogiji, you have not looked deeply enough."

The yogi was surprised by the guru's response. "How do you mean, Guruji? You have so many disciples who respond to your every word. They follow your teachings devotedly."

"Oh, Yogiji, look again," laughed Nanak. "I will show you true devotion and what a rare thing it is. Eh, Hari Das!" he called to one of the attendants.

"Ji?"

"Announce that the guru will be taking a walk shortly and that those who consider themselves to be devoted to him should join us."

Shortly, the high-pitched voice of Hari Das could be heard in the distance calling the people of Kartarpur to join the guru.

"Yogiji, please wait for me outside. I'll join you shortly, and you will see beyond all doubt what is devotion, and what is simply emotion."

The people of Kartarpur began to assemble outside the guru's house. They filled the courtyard and seeped past the wall and out into the road. Lehna waited with the yogi near the guru's door while the crowd gathered. The village was in a happy mood. They loved it when the guru came out and walked among them. They enjoyed his company and many people took the opportunity to ask him questions, to try to get his approval or blessing for some idea, or to further their own status in the community.

It had been a bright, sunny day, but as the people waited for the guru, the wind picked up. What had been a cloudless sky grew dark and the temperature began to drop. A number of people, anticipating that it would rain, changed their minds and went home. Suddenly the door flung open and four large, rabid-looking dogs ran out of the door, barking aggressively and bearing their fangs. People jumped back and some, fearing the dogs, decided to go home as well.

Against the cacophony of the dogs and the wind, Guru Nanak stepped through the door. Usually when the guru went out he was dressed in a long white tunic, a white turban, and his wooden sandals. However, when he came out on that day he wore a dirty tattered animal skin, which covered his loins and hung to his knees. He was barefooted and bare-chested with a stained and frayed old shawl looped over his left shoulder and under his right arm. He looked as though he was ready to eat someone. In his right hand he held a long and very sharp knife, which he waved in the air. He looked like a cross between a bandit and a wild man. Many people, disturbed by the guru's appearance, ran away in fear and confusion.

Looking neither at Lehna nor the yogi, and with the growling dogs leading the way, the guru set off into the surrounding jungle like a hunter after a wounded animal. The people who followed him did so tentatively.

The entourage moved into the forest, despite the noise of the dogs and the marked silence of the guru. After some distance and with the guru still silent, people began to notice copper coins on the ground. Many stopped to collect the coins, thinking that they were being rewarded by the guru for demonstrating their devotion by walking with him. After filling their pockets they returned to the village thanking the guru for their good fortune.

Guru Nanak continued along the road, gripping the knife more firmly, the look in his eyes more wild and fierce, the dogs making more noise and behaving uncontrollably. He waved the knife over his head as if he were ordering a cavalry charge. He never looked anywhere but straight ahead and he never uttered a word. In a short while, the road became littered with silver coins. This time many more stopped and picked up the silver coins, thinking these were the blessings of the guru for going farther than the others. Those who collected the silver coins also returned home after filling their pockets, singing the guru's praises loudly.

After a few more furlongs the road became littered with gold coins. Most of the Sikhs who remained with the guru collected them, congratulating themselves for their devotion. After all, they reasoned, they had remained with him the longest and this was his way of rewarding them for their sincere devotion. With their pockets bulging they turned and went home. With him now were only the yogi, two

Sikhs, and Lehna. The guru still had not spoken, but continued with determination.

The small party continued in silence for another furlong, and then the guru stopped. Before them was an abandoned funeral pyre. Now, even the dogs ran away. The stench of death was pervasive, making it uncomfortable to breathe. Upon the ground lay what appeared to be a rotting corpse covered with a white sheet and around the body were four lighted *ghee* lamps. The sky appeared as a dark bruise. The wind had stopped, though the clouds continued to thicken in the sky. In silent audience were spirits, deities, and demons. The atmosphere was still as death, making its presence undeniable. It could be tasted in the air and felt upon the skin.

Guru Nanak turned to those who were with him. "Whoever wishes to accompany me further must eat of this." His voice was fierce.

The two remaining Sikhs were now convinced that the guru had lost all sense and ran for home.

Lehna stepped forward and quietly asked, "Oh my guru, shall I begin at the head or the feet?"

"Eat from the waist," instructed the guru gruffly.

Holding his breath and with a prayer, Bhai Lehna lifted the sheet. The stench of the corpse faded, and the fragrance of incense and flowers cut through the thick air. Under the sheet Lehna found a mound of sacred *prasad*, the sweet food blessed by the guru. Taking it in his hands, he stood and offered it to Guru Nanak.

"My beloved guru, please take this. Allow me to have what remains when you are finished."

With a rush of wind the sky spun and the air cleared, and for the first time in more than two hours, the guru smiled.

"Yogiji, behold my one true devotee! Of all those around me, only he is imbued with true devotion. There are many in Kartarpur, but none of them were devoted enough to stay with me to the end."

Smiling broadly the yogi replied, "Guruji, even with my yogic powers I couldn't see clearly. You have taught me a meaningful lesson today. For once in my life I have seen real devotion and the living power of love."

Then, accepting the prasad from Lehna Guru Nanak spoke, "This prasad has come to you because you are willing to share it with others before yourself. You have made the guru very happy."

I was very happy as well.

The yogi folded his hands in supplication and turned to Guru Nanak, "Bhai Lehna has now merged with you. You and he are inseparable."

Guru Nanak nodded and turning to Lehna, embraced him. "Truly you are of my own body, my own essence: my *ang!* From this day you shall be known as Angad. The light of the guru will shine in you and the Sat Sanghal Dhara will pass through you."

The time of Guru Nanak had passed, but the Golden Chain had been secured to the Earth. As the flame of one candle lights the wick of another, so the light of the guru passed from Nanak to Angad. Guru Nanak formally appointed Angad as guru and announced that he would soon leave his body.

His mission was complete. He had served humanity, shared his teachings with Hindus and Muslims alike and was beloved by all. Those close to him gathered around and asked what should be done with his body after his death. The Hindus wanted to cremate him and the Muslims wanted to bury him.

Guru Nanak loved the compassion of the Hindus and the close brotherhood of the Muslims where, unlike the severe cast system of the Hindus, all were equal in faith. Yet as his last act, he wanted to confirm his first statement when he stepped from the Bein River, that there was no Hindu and no Muslim.

"Upon my final breath, Hindus shall place flowers on the right side of my body and Muslims shall place flowers on the left. Cover me with a white sheet and in the morning turn it back. On whichever side the flowers are still living, those who placed them shall have the last rites over my body."

With that he drew the sheet over himself, ordering the *Sohila*, the bedtime hymn, to be sung. Then slowly, deliberately, and with concentrated focus, Guru Nanak exhaled for the last time and merged with Me. With great anticipation the sheet was lifted the next morning. Instead of finding the body of the guru and wilted flowers on one side or the other, the entire area beneath the sheet was filled with bright, blossoming flowers.

Their intoxicating fragrance filled the air for days.

NINE

As Guru Nanak carried his mission to the world and anchored the Golden Chain to the Earth, in the village of Basarke lived a sincere man, also of the Bedi line, known as Amar Das. He was prosperous by agriculture and trade, yet kept Me ever in his mind. You know, the soul is such a beautiful thing and when it is polished through sincere prayer and meditation, it has a beauty unmatched in the cosmos, which eases My loneliness and brings Me incredible joy.

In his twenty-third year, Amar Das married Mansa Devi and began to raise a family. Amar Das worshipped Me as a devout *Vaishnav,* one who is a devotee of Vishnu, and strictly followed the disciplines described by that sect. Despite his devotion, he felt a void within himself that he could not fill. He often reflected that this gift of human life was passing him by, for it seemed to him that he made no progress in the evolution of his soul. He longed for a guru to show him the way.

Around the age of forty, he made a vow to make an annual pilgrimage to the Ganges and bathe in her sacred waters. The Ganges flows from the top of Shiva's head and the waters are considered sacred. Each year, painfully aware that he had no guru, Amar Das dutifully made the pilgrimage to that sacred river and prayed to find his guru. For twenty years, though he performed all the rituals and pujas and threw water toward the rising sun, his longing remained unfulfilled.

Hindus recognized the sacredness of all things, but in order to grow spiritually and to achieve status in life, they believed that one must have a guru. In those early days of the sixteenth century, a man without a guru was considered to be like a man with a contagious disease and therefore unfit to be associated with. For the upper castes, especially the Brahmins, a man with no guru was considered to be like an untouchable who contaminated the purity of Brahminical space.

Though outwardly he gave the appearance of a proper Kashatriya, he longed for a fuller experience and felt deeply hollow inside. Amar Das was well-versed in the Vedas and the rituals that distinguish a well-trained and educated man. And though he performed those rituals flawlessly, they became increasingly meaningless for him.

When he was returning from his twentieth pilgrimage, Amar Das met a friendly swami who was impressed with his style. The swami and Amar Das struck up an intimate friendship very quickly and continued to travel together. They discoursed with each other on the Vedas, the merits of fasting and celibacy, the practice of austerities, and the value of pilgrimage to the sacred places. Amar Das enjoyed the company of the swami and they became so close that they cooked for each other.

Now, Brahmins were very serious about their cooking and in those days Hindus observed strict compliance with the caste system. Brahmins were especially unwilling to keep the company of lower castes and perhaps nothing was more sacred to a Brahmin than how and by whom his food was prepared. There was an elaborate ritual to the preparation of food for a Brahmin.

First, a large circle was inscribed on the ground within which the food was to be prepared. A person of lesser caste, one who was considered to be unclean, could not enter the circle. If such a thing occurred, all the food was considered to be contaminated and inedible. All the utensils had to be blessed and kept in a particular way and even if all was right with the preparation of the food, if either the food or the cooking utensils were touched by a lower caste person, all was considered to be contaminated.

The swami was impressed by the piety and wisdom of Amar Das and especially enjoyed his cooking.

"You have learned very well." The swami regarded Amar Das favorably one evening after their meal. They had cleaned and blessed all the utensils and sat with relaxed contentment under the stars. "You must have a great guru to have imparted to you such wisdom and devotion. May I know his name?"

In the evening light Amar Das paled like the rising moon. "My guru? Uhh . . . well . . . I, uhh, I have learned from many good men."

"I understand. Such a pious man as yourself must have had the great good fortune to have been in the company of many men of God. Clearly, they have helped you to perfect your disciplines. But your guru? Who initiated you? It looks as though your hair has not been cut, so he must be living."

"He . . . uhh . . . yes, yes, as you say."

The swami eyed Amar Das by the light of their small fire. "So, ji, may I know his good name?"

"Forgive me, Swamiji, but I have no guru," Amar Das replied softly, his voice full of shame.

The swami laughed lightly. "Oh, so you want to keep your guru secret? No, my friend, you must share his good name with me. A man should be proud to be associated with his guru!"

"Swamiji, I am ashamed to tell you truly that I have no guru. I have prayed and fasted, performed puja and pilgrimage, but I have yet to find my true guru."

The swami jumped to his feet and stepped back several paces.

"What is this? You have no guru?"

"I am sorry, Swamiji," Amar Das said with a sigh. His head hung low between his shoulders, his chin and beard resting on his chest.

"Heh, Ram! I have committed a great sin!" cried the swami. "Shame on you! My pilgrimage has been wasted. Have I contaminated myself by eating with one who has no guru? What have I done?"

Amar Das was silent and nearly motionless. More than shame, he felt deep regret that he did not have a guru. For twenty years he had faithfully made his pilgrimage to the Ganga and prayed that he would find a guru. For all of that, was this his reward?

The swami began to gather his things. He separated his cooking utensils rewashed and blessed them, rolled them up and put them in his travel bag, watching poor Amar Das the whole time. He was stunned that one who was seemingly so pious and well-trained, was without a guru.

Most unfortunate, he thought to himself. "Oh, Amru, don't you know that one without a guru has no life? Even the great deities of the past Ages had gurus. Sukhdev himself had Raja Janak as his guru. I have become defiled and my cooking utensils have been contaminated. How can you bear to live with no guru? This is sad indeed. Now I can only be purified by returning to the Ganga and bathing in her again."

With that the swami made his way noisily into the night, lamenting to the Heavens about those so unfortunate as not to have a guru.

Amar Das felt deeply humiliated by that experience. His desolation over not having a guru grew. Each day he prayed that I, out of My mercy, would lead him to his guru and end his suffering. In those days there were many gurus around and Amar Das thought that he had visited them all. He took them gifts of food and money and they had all blessed him and offered him initiation with their secret mantras, but Amar Das never felt a binding soul connection with any of them.

Early one morning, sometime after his night of humiliation with the swami, Amar Das was sitting on the roof of his house in Basarke engaged in his morning meditation and prayers. Now in his early sixties, his frustrations were distracting him from his devotional practice and he was beginning to feel that he could die without ever finding his guru. And in that state of mind, he drifted into a prayer.

"Eh, Ram," he prayed, "Listen, I am an old man now. I have lived an honorable life, I have been sincere and consistent with my devotions, and I have longed and prayed to find a guru. How much longer will You make me wait? I know that You hear this prayer. At least acknowledge that You hear me. You always listen, You just don't say much. You created me, You have sustained me through life, You have made me to walk all those pilgrimages and bathe in the Ganga. Now, You should come through for me . . ."

I always loved the prayers of Amar Das. They were so sincere and humble, with unlimited devotion, and they never failed to move Me. So, on that morning things changed. He was deep into his prayer when the dulcet sounds of a woman's voice penetrated the depths of his mind.

He recognized the voice of Bibi Amro, the young wife of his nephew. She was reciting a hymn of Guru Nanak with sincere devotion. Much as the sweetness and vibratory impact of those sounds had affected Bhai Lehna, now they began to transform Amar Das. The totality of her devotion as she recited and the impact of the words of the hymn shook Amar Das from his reverie. In the half light of predawn, as he sat and listened, a slight smile formed under his beard.

"I think you heard me this time." Well, I had heard him every time, but this was the morning that the energy moved.

When she had finished her recitation, Amar Das called to her, "Oh, Bibi, from where did you learn something so lovely?"

"*Chachaji,* my father, the guru at Khadur, has taught me."

"Guru?" he answered breathlessly, "at Khadur? What guru is that"

"He is Guru Angad, Chachaji."

Climbing down from his roof, Amar Das approached Bibi Amro and asked that she recite the hymn again. He sat in front of her like a child watching someone perform a magic trick. When she had finished, he asked her to teach it to him, which she did with great joy. He committed the hymn to memory in a matter of days and recited it constantly. If he missed a passage, he went back to Amro and asked her to recite it for him again. She was lovingly patient with him and very happy to share what she had learned from her father.

When his niece first told him about Guru Angad, the hair stood up on the back of his neck and he got chills along his spine. Each day his heart beat a little faster. He began to have dreams of the guru. He went to bed each night excited about getting up the next morning so he could recite the hymns of the guru again. After a week, Amar Das could stand it no longer. He had to meet the guru in Khadur. So, he requested that his nephew allow Bibi Amro to accompany him to Khadur that he might find the fulfillment of his longing. The next day they took to the road for the half-day journey to Khadur and arrived in the early afternoon.

And there, under the acacia and pipal trees, with his heart pounding, Amar Das found his guru.

TEN

It was in the Treta Yuga that We held the first great convocation and meditated, creating the beam that formed the sacred pool. From the time that the water rose to the surface, it became a place of healing. It was discovered first by nature herself, and animals went there for healing and safe refuge. Later, humans with great spiritual strength went there to bathe in the water and meditate beside it. We did the second meditation in the Kali Yuga when I set My great plan into motion.

Nanak had come and linked the Golden Chain to the Earth. The plan was that the light of Nanak would be passed on to ensure that this path, this *dharma*, would have a solid foundation. Bhai Lehna had received the light of Nanak as the flame of one candle lights the wick of another, and he was carrying the mission forward. Now, the time had come for the Guru of Miracles. So as the Vedi Guru had foretold, in early October 1534 in the city of Lahore, Sodhi Rai was reborn as Jetha.

His mother, Mata Daya Vati, did not recover from childbirth. His father Har Das, a Kashatrya who had fallen on difficult times, worked long and hard to support himself and his infant son. Doing his best to care for the young child, he cooked simple foods and tried to keep Jetha warm and comfortable.

As Jetha neared the age of seven, Pitta Har Das' health also began to fail. Lahore in the sixteenth century was not a healthy place to be, and the hard work, unsanitary conditions, and privations of their poverty all conspired against the basic constitutional weakness of Har Das. Knowing that he was in a decline from which he was unlikely to recover, he grew increasingly concerned for his boy. To prepare him for the worst, Har Das taught Jetha to support himself on his own.

He taught Jetha to prepare *pulses*, a spicy mixture of mung beans and wheat berries, and sent him into the streets to sell them. The world was a frightening place for a motherless seven-year-old who had never ventured far from the opening of their single room hut, but Jetha dragged the heavy iron bucket of pulses to the bazaar with courageous determination. Dragging his bucket between the stalls, he listened to the cacophonous singsong call of the vendors; the haggling of the buyers and sellers, a near sacred tradition of the bazaar; the cries and laughter of children; and the constant shuffle of feet all set against the continuous drone of voices, broken by the sounds of drums, pipes, and strings of street musicians. Sadhus roamed the bazaar performing their tricks, swamis and rishis strolled leisurely with their begging bowls in their hands, and beggars of all kinds worked the aisles.

"Heh, boy!" It was an old beggar, nearly naked, wearing only the ragged remnants of a dhoti. A filthy and severely stained turban covered his face and head, except for his eyes. His right hand was wrapped in an equally dirty grey cloth that had once been white. He held out his dark left hand, stained by dirt and the filth of Lahore, which was missing the pinky and ring fingers.

Jetha and his father were poor and not well-fed. They lived in the slums of Lahore, which was populated by poor and malnourished people, so Jetha was accustomed to seeing people who were hungry, but never in his brief life had he seen anyone as emaciated and hungry-looking as the wraith on the ground before him. He was not aware of it at the time, but that was Me in disguise.

"Please, boy, help this old man." His raspy voice was low against the cacophony of the bazaar.

Dragging his bucket of pulses closer, Jetha looked into the eyes of the beggar, and I swear to Me that he recognized Me! Jetha smiled slightly and spooned a palmful into the unsanitary and slightly shaking hand. He expected it to go immediately into the beggar's mouth. Instead he raised it to his forehead, the juices running down his arm to his elbows.

"Heh, Ram, thank you for this boy, through whose compassion this noisy belly will be stilled." I like when people remember Me and thank Me, but I also like to acknowledge Myself. It cheers Me up.

Jetha smiled brightly as the dirty old beggar inhaled the pulses in one big slurp. The wet hand, now yellow with spices and ghee, rose again, and Jetha refilled it again and again. Finally, Jetha gave the entire bucket to the poor man, who ate it all.

As Jetha collected his bucket and ladle, the beggar reached up with his wet and gooey hand, grabbed Jetha by the wrist, and pulled him down to his level.

"You will be known for your compassion, boy! Never turn from it." And Jetha never did. He depended on selling the pulses to help sustain himself and his father, so he couldn't afford to give away the whole lot on other days. Yet he never refused those who asked and were in need.

Pitta Har Das grew weaker, and sometime after Jetha's seventh birthday, Har Das joined his wife, leaving Jetha another orphan of the streets. With help from his neighbors, Jetha was able to arrange for his father to be cremated at the common cremation ground, and he disposed of the ashes in the River Ravi.

Alone and on his own, he was able to support himself by selling his pulses in the bazaars. Living on the mean streets of Lahore, haggling in the bazaars for his food and the ingredients for his pulses, was a severe life for a seven-year-old. Jetha's closest living relative was his maternal grandmother who lived in Basarke, the village of Amar Das. So in time, arrangements were made for Jetha to go to Basarke and live with her. When Jetha arrived he was full of energy. He had learned a trade from his father and understood the value and necessity of work. In Basarke he continued to mix and sell his pulses in the village streets and bazaars, helping to support himself and his grandmother.

* * *

From the moment Amar Das met Guru Angad, his life changed. After a lifetime of pilgrimages and prayer, he had found his true guru. His frustration and doubt left him, and he was at peace. Amar Das became so deeply enamored of the guru that he could not bear to be away from him, and he daily made the trek from Basarke to Khadur to be with Guru Angad. As the days became years, the devotion of Amar Das never wavered.

Amar Das had four children. His two sons, Mohri and Mohan, were born shortly after he married. His two daughters, Dani and Bani, were born much later in his life. Bani was the youngest and the closest to Amar Das' heart. She was born when Amar Das was in his fifties, and now, as he neared seventy, she had matured into an attractive young woman, with the deep spirituality of her father. She was eighteen and past the traditional age of marriage.

Mata Mansa complained to him that he had done nothing to arrange for the marriage of Bibi Bani. He was spending too much time with his guru and had overlooked his obligations to his own family. Amar Das was in an especially cheerful mood that day and enjoyed the banter with his lifetime companion.

"Bani has passed the age where she should be married," Mansa Devi said sharply. "I have seen the boys of the village noticing her when she walks through the streets. People are talking about her and wondering what is wrong with her that she is not yet married."

"Yes, Mata," replied Amar Das, "you have given the world a most beautiful and wonderful child."

"Don't try to distract me!" snapped Mata Mansa. "You should have advertised for a husband long ago. If I weren't bringing it up now, you would have never thought about it."

"You misjudge me, my moon," Amar Das laughed, "I have been thinking about it for some time."

"You keep too much to yourself. After all these years together you don't share your mind with me."

"You are right, Mata, I should have mentioned to you that it was on my mind. I have some reluctance to advertise for a husband, though. There is something special about Bani that must be protected. I don't know if these village boys are of her caliber. What kind of boy do you think would be suitable for her?"

"He must have a spirituality equal to that of Bani."

"Without question," replied Amar Das.

"He will have to be humble and industrious and respectful of her, as well as someone who will honor her grace and divinity," she paused. She gazed out of the window, seemingly lost in her own thoughts, then added forcefully, "And he must be a nice-looking young man, with sound prospects."

Amar Das asked with a serious tone, "Do you have someone in mind?"

"Of course not," she said sharply, turning to face her husband, "you are her father and should be the one to see to these things. But . . ." She paused as she turned back and gazed idly out the window and onto the active street. "It should be a boy like him, in features and in temperament." She was pointing to Jetha, now sixteen, who was selling his pulses out on the street.

Amar Das looked out and smiled behind his white beard, "Then why not him? Ramu!" he called to his servant, "Bring that boy in here, quickly."

"Wait!" replied Mansa. "He is so poor and he is younger than Bani. I didn't mean *him*, just someone *like* him."

"Why accept an imitation when the real thing is right here? Look at him! If you searched this world and the next you would never find another like him. He has no equal here or hereafter. He *is* the one. Ramu! Bring him in!"

Ramu went down to the street and told Jetha that Amar Das would like to speak to him. Jetha's heart leapt to his throat. He had seen Amar Das almost daily and had sold him pulses on a few occasions. Jetha had developed deepest respect for Amar Das and felt something of a tacit relationship with him.

Now, much that was not clear but deep within him came to his throat. He felt as though he had swallowed a glowing coal, and though he tried valiantly, he could not hold back his tears. Concerned that he may have offended Amar Das, Jetha left his pot of pulses at the door with his shoes, and walked into the presence of Amar Das and Mata Mansa. With his vision blurred because of his tears, he touched the feet of Amar Das, then Mansa Devi, and sat on the floor.

"Why are you crying?" asked Mataji. "Have you injured yourself?"

"No, Mata, please forgive me."

Amar Das regarded Jetha with a smile and placed his hand on Jetha's forehead. His eyes were closed, and the tracks of his tears flowed to the refuge of his sprouting beard. Jetha grew still and then quieted. With his sleeve, he dried his eyes and gazed into the face of Amar Das. It is not possible to describe what took place between them. Jetha did not see the face of an old man. Rather, he saw the light of his life. All his pain and sorrow and longing left him. He felt deep peace, awe, and reverence. Amar Das did not see a young man or his future son-in-law. He saw the answer to the prayers of the Ages and, in his eyes, the miracle of the water.

When Amar Das spoke, his voice was surprising to Jetha, sounding very earthy and matter-of-fact.

"My son," he began, "Mata Mansa Devi and I believe that you would make a suitable husband for our daughter, Bani."

Mataji inhaled sharply and opened her mouth, but held her tongue and said nothing.

"I have nothing to offer her," Jetha said quietly. "I am an orphan and can barely sustain myself and my grandmother."

"Isn't your God infinite?" answered Amar Das.

"Yes."

"Did He not create you?"

"Yes."

"Has God ever abandoned anyone?"

"No."

"Then how can you be an orphan?"

Jetha wiped his tears with his sleeve.

"Does He not provide all things?"

"Yes."

"I have seen that you recite His name each day."

"I do," whispered Jetha.

"One who knows Him by Name will never be abandoned by Him. If He can rotate the Earth and hold the moon in the sky, why can't he take care of you? Join this family," he said warmly, "you will no longer be an orphan. Rather, you will become the protector of all orphans."

Jetha was quiet for some time while Mata Mansa fidgeted, looking at her husband, then at the teenager sitting on the floor before her. She wanted to interrogate Jetha, but placed her trust in her husband and remained silent. Jetha's gaze remained fixed at a point on the carpet upon which he sat, losing himself in the intricate designs and color contrasts woven into it. Then he bent and with reverence, touched the feet of Amar Das.

"It will be my honor to join your family," he said softly.

Amar Das embraced him with a surprising grip for such an old man. Mata Mansa went to find Bani, and Jetha was taken to wash himself. He was given a new white kurta and dhoti and a maroon vest with yellow embroidery. When he had washed and dressed, he looked like a young prince. There was no trace of the orphan who, only an hour before, had been selling pulses on the streets of Basarke.

Mata Mansa Devi brought her daughter into the room to meet her fiancé. Bani had seen Jetha in the village before, selling his pulses and interacting with the other boys of Basarke. Now though, he appeared regal and dignified. To Bani, the sound of Jetha's voice reminded her of her father's voice. The agreement was sealed, and on that morning the course of Jetha's life changed. Within a few days and according to custom, the arrangements were finalized and Bhai Jetha and Bibi Bani were married to a wedding hymn that Jetha had composed himself.

ELEVEN

Guru Angad continued with his mission. He organized his congregations into more tightly and interdependent communities, holding education and the development of commerce as his high priorities. The teachings of Guru Nanak and the daily practices and casteless social structure of the Sikhs were a radical departure from the rigid Hindu and ruling Muslim societies. Guru Angad wanted to ensure that his Sikhs did not get reabsorbed into those traditions; therefore, it was a priority for the guru to establish their independence and unique identity. He held the torch of Guru Nanak high, splitting the darkness of the Kali Yuga. I was very happy with his work.

A Sikh named Goinda had been involved with an unfortunate legal situation with other members of his family. He vowed that if the guru would protect him from defeat in court, he would found a city in his honor. Guru Angad blessed him, and by a considerable margin, the court ruled in his favor. So Goinda, with sincere gratitude, began to establish the city, which was laid out on an open plot of fertile land on the banks of the River Beas. It was an excellent location, situated where the east-west highway crossed the Beas. The road was active with traffic, and a busy ferry carried travelers across the river, presenting excellent opportunities for commerce and growth.

The construction of the city began with prayers, blessings, and great ceremony. The land was cleared, the foundations were dug, and the frames of the first structures were erected. Then strange things began to happen. The work which had been done by day was undone by night. Structures came apart, foundations crumbled overnight, and surveyed plots were skewed and disrupted.

Many blamed the demons. Some blamed the relations of Goinda who had been involved in the litigation against him. No one knew for sure, although it may have been the work of both. Naturally, the demons enjoyed being given much of the credit, but in usual demonic style, they remained hidden. However, the workers were afraid to arrive too early or to stay too late, lest they be there during hours of darkness. And eventually, many workers refused to show up at all. The truth is that it was all My mischief.

Goinda went to Khadur to discuss the problem with Guru Angad, who sent for Amar Das.

"Take this," he said, handing Amar Das his long walking staff, "and accompany Goinda to the village he is constructing. Find out what is going on and correct it so that the work is completed. This"—and he tapped the end of the stick on a stone—"will protect you and all the work."

Amar Das took the staff reverently and touched the guru's feet.

Guru Angad addressed Goinda, "Take Amar Das with you. Show him the damage. His presence will protect you, your workers, and the work. I assure you, Goinda, the work will be completed and you will not be forgotten."

Amar Das and Goinda made their way to the site of the new village the next day. Amar Das walked around the area where the construction was taking place and touched each foundation, structure, brick, and timber with the staff of Guru Angad. As the construction progressed through the day, Amar Das found a shady spot to sit, watch the work, and meditate. Again just before dark he rose and touched the day's work at each site with the guru's staff. He had Goinda make sleeping arrangements for him and stayed the night. In the morning all the previous day's work was intact.

Amar Das faithfully stayed at the site and the construction proceeded uninterrupted. Eventually, the initial construction phase was completed with no further destruction or complication. Sitting on fertile ground on the west bank of the River Beas, the new village was lovely. Amar Das started calling it Goindwal in honor of Goinda, but Guru Angad had not officially named it.

Out of his sincere gratitude to Amar Das for rescuing the project when it looked doomed, Goinda built him a house in the village. Sitting toward the top of a hill with a clear view of the Beas, the house was attractive and large enough to accommodate the family of Amar Das, which included his sons and daughters and their growing families.

When all was suitable to Amar Das, he and Goinda made the trip to Khadur to give the report to Guru Angad.

"The work is finished, ji." Goinda beamed it rather than said it.

"And what have you been calling this new village?" asked the guru.

"Guruji, I have been calling it Goindwal in honor of Goinda." Despite his years, the voice of Amar Das always sounded youthful.

"Goindwal? Well, Goinda, I told you that you would be remembered. Goindwal it shall be!" Goinda touched the feet of Guru Angad, thanking him profusely.

"Oh, Amru."

"Ji?"

"Goinda built you a house there?"

"He did, Guruji. It is lovely. It sits on a hill with its own well overlooking the Beas."

"Your entire family can live in it?"

"With room to grow."

"Very good, then. Take your family and move to that house. See to the development of the village and to the well-being of the people. Make it a commercial center with an independent economy so that it will prevail through the times."

"I have never disobeyed you, Guruji, but I believe that I should be near you." "You should be, Amru. Come to Khadur each morning, but reside in Goindwal."

Though Amar Das was seventy by this time, he happily made the walk to Khadur each morning. Rising three hours before dawn, he went to the clear flowing Beas and took water for the guru's bath. Then he made the walk to Khadur in the dark, reciting the verses of Guru Nanak and Guru Angad. All day he served the guru in the most menial way: fetching water and wood for the kitchen, scrubbing the pots and utensils, and cleaning after the congregation had eaten. In the evening he listened to the evening prayer, then prepared the guru for sleep and put him to rest. When that was done, Amar Das made the walk back to Goindwal, again in the dark. So as not to turn his back to his guru, whom he cherished more than life, he walked backwards all the way.

Guru Angad had developed a severe abscess on his foot, which oozed and caused him extreme discomfort. Amar Das treated it repeatedly, but it would not heal. None of the common remedies worked for more than a day. Amar Das went from healer to healer searching for a remedy that would work. He applied *ghee* mixed with various herbs, different compounds of minerals and precious metals, and combinations of essential oils and tinctures. Some brought temporary relief, but none healed the wound, and it continued to fester. Red streaks crept up the leg of the guru, as the infection spread.

Each morning as Amar Das walked to Khadur, he searched his mind for a remedy. And one morning he remembered the sacred pool and realized that the herbs that grew there would heal the wound. The next day he went to that special place and collected the healing herbs. He filled an urn with water from the pool and sealed it. Then quietly as he had arrived, he mounted his mare and returned to Goindwal.

When he arrived home, he laid the herbs out to dry in the sun and carried the water to his room. When he arose the next morning, along with the water from the Beas for the guru's bath, he took the water from the pool and the dried herbs he had collected to Khadur. When he arrived, he ground a portion of the herbs, mixed them with *ghee* to form a poultice, and tenderly applied it to the guru's wound. With the water of the pond and the remainder of the herbs, he made an infusion, which Guru Angad sipped throughout the day. By the next morning the wound had healed, leaving no scar.

It was at this time that Hymayun, the son of Babur who ascended the throne of India after his father, was overthrown by the Afghan invader Sher Shah. Hymayun hesitated when he should have acted, was soundly beaten in battle, and retreated to the north. Seeking the help of holy men and saints, Hymayun was counseled to visit Guru Angad. When he arrived at Khadur, the guru was in deep meditation while his musicians played the hymns of Guru Nanak. Hymayun was required to wait and was left standing and unattended. In time he became extremely offended, but Guru Angad would not leave the bliss of his meditation. Seething with anger, Hymayun decided to kill the guru for what he considered to be a display of severe disrespect. He gripped the hilt of his sword but was unable to draw it from the scabbard.

It was then that Guru Angad looked up at him. "Oh, king, where was your sword when you faced Sher Shah? Now that you have come among spiritual people, instead of honoring them, you want to draw your sword on them? Had you drawn your sword against Sher Shah, you would have defeated him, but you chose to flee in a cowardly manner. Yet you come here now, posing as a hero and demanding respect?"

Guru Angad looked deep into the eyes of the defeated emperor. "Learn something today. Had you simply been patient and sat with us and enjoyed the *kirtan*, you would have quickly regained your kingdom. Now, however, by placing your hand on the hilt of your sword intending to do harm to those who are engaged in the singing of God's praises, you have cut off that flow. You must retreat to Persia for a while and fight your way back. You will regain your throne, but not until late in your life."

* * *

The Punjabi winter came with its deep fog and chilling rains. Amar Das, ever faithful to his guru, continued to make his trek from Goindwal to Khadur each morning long before the sunrise and dissipation of the fog. Then at night he walked the course in reverse, always keeping his face toward his guru. One stormy night, Amar Das remained in Khadur at the urging of Guru Angad. It was cold, lightning split the sky, and rain seemed imminent. Guru Angad was concerned for Amar Das and did not want his old and faithful disciple out at night in such weather. Amar Das was grateful to have the shelter of the guru's house, and the sounds of the storm caused him to sail into sound slumber.

Well after midnight, Guru Angad called into the darkened house for water, but against the thunder and the wind no one heard him. He called a second time and still there was no response. Finally he got up and shook Datu, his eldest son, and told him to go and bring water.

"It's raining and cold outside, have someone else do it. We have servants, send one of them."

"I have asked you, my son. Now get up and bring me water."

"No, ji, I won't." Datu pulled the blankets over his head, turning his back to his father.

The movement through the house and the sound of the voices woke Amar Das.

"I'll go, Guruji," he said, turning out from under his blankets, his white beard luminous in the darkness of the house.

"No, Amru, no. I don't want you out in this storm. Datu should go as I have asked."

Amar Das had already pulled his old brown woolen shawl around himself and had shouldered an iron urn.

"Then who am I, Baba? Don't I belong to you, too?" he said flatly so that the guru knew there would be no argument.

He stepped out into the night as lightning split the Heavens and the rain poured down. He made his way to the nearest well, but because of the rain, the well water had become muddy and was unsuitable for the guru. The Beas normally flowed clear, even during a storm, so Amar Das decided to go down to the river. The wind drove the cold, hard rain relentlessly, soaking the skin of the elderly disciple. Lightning illuminated his way through the darkness, while the drone of the rain against the iron urn kept him company. Despite the cold and damp, Amar Das was in a cheerful mood, and he reached the Beas quickly. The water of the river was running fast but had not muddied from the storm, so Amar Das waded out into the river where the water flowed fresh and filled the urn. As he walked against the rain back to the village, he began to recite his morning prayers, for it was now the hour when he usually made his trek from Goindwal to Khadur.

As he entered the village and struggled through the muddy streets toward the guru's house, he passed the enclave of weavers, where the holes for their spindles had become filled with water. Losing his balance, he slipped and his foot became stuck in a spindle hole, striking the peg within forcefully. Amar Das fell to one knee, but somehow managed to keep the iron jar upright and only a surprisingly small portion of the water spilled on his already-drenched face and shoulders. The weavers were roused from their sleep by the noise and came running, thinking that a thief was prowling.

Through the sound of the rain they heard Amar Das' strong voice reciting his prayers, which had continued unbroken despite his predicament.

"Heh," laughed a woman, "what kind of thief is that?"

"Oh, Amru," taunted another, "what low-caste job do you perform now?"

"Who is it?" asked a man running out from his house.

"It's crazy, Amru," laughed a woman, "and he has managed to get himself stuck in the mud with a jar on his head. Worse than a hapless *sudra!*"

The weavers stood around Amar Das and laughed and taunted him, but not one stooped to help the aged disciple, who calmly continued to recite his prayer. The suction of the mud-filled hole would not release his foot however much he tried to maneuver it. By this time most of Khadur had been wakened by the commotion, and eventually Guru Angad himself came to the scene. He bent and took the urn from Amar Das' shoulder, set it aside, and helped him to stand with his own hands.

"You think he is just some lowly servant?" The guru was angry. His strong voice and the strength of his words stung more sharply than the rain. "Well, my dear ones, you can mark what I say as truth. He shall be known as the home of the homeless, the honor of the honorless, the strength of the weak, support of the unsupported, shelter of the shelterless, protector of the unprotected, the restorer of what is lost, and the emancipator of the captive!"

The only sound was the falling rain and the slurping of mud against shifting feet.

"Shame on you all!" His voice filled the air like thunder. "Not one of you would bend to help him, yet he shall bend to help all humanity. Not one of you could offer him shelter or support, yet simply by calling his name the shelterless, and the weak shall find comfort and relief. Now out of my sight, all of you!"

The guru covered Amar Das with his own shawl and escorted him to his house. He called some of his trusted Sikhs to come and assist him. He also sent for five copper coins and a coconut.

"Take him, bathe him, and wash his hair. When you are finished, let me know." The guru went to his room to meditate.

When he had been bathed and dried, Guru Angad dressed Amar Das in one of his own long white tunics and tied a white turban on his head. Then, in a simple and solemn ceremony, Guru Angad passed the light of Nanak to Amar Das, as Guru Nanak had passed it to him. Amar Das was now the third guru and the next link in the Golden Chain.

Within a short time, as Guru Nanak had done after passing his light to Bhai Lehna, Guru Angad left his body, leaving Guru Amar Das to carry the flame of Nanak forward.

* * *

Guru Amar Das longed for his guru. For twelve years he had served with unconditional devotion, and everything had been secondary to that. Now the light of Nanak radiated from him. Though Amar Das was now guru, he was also the guru's disciple. He secluded himself in the house that Goinda had built for him in Goindwal and meditated. He recognized, as Guru Angad had before him, that if he did not take measures to make his Sikhs unique in their devotional practices, social behavior, as well as their daily lives, there was the danger that they would fade back into the Hindu and Muslim societies from which they came.

Guru Amar Das, whose greatest joy had been to serve in the guru's kitchen, chose that as his place to start his new mission. He remembered his time spent with the swami after his pilgrimage to the Ganges and understood the necessity of breaking those superstitions regarding caste and the perception that food can be contaminated simply by the presence of the wrong person. Guru Nanak taught that I Am in all things and that anyone has the privilege of calling on Me directly and to ultimately achieve union with Me. Breaking the vise grip of the caste system was a priority for Guru Amar Das.

He understood that if he could not break that custom, the chances of the Sikhs resuming the social practices of Hinduism and losing their distinct identity were considerable. The guru was concerned that if that were to happen, the secure anchor of the Golden Chain could be lost. So he put major focus on the kitchen and established the *langar*, the community kitchen of the guru, where the entire congregation sat equally and dined together. Free and open to all, it became an integral element of Sikh life. In fact, no one was permitted to have an audience with the guru unless first sitting in the dining hall and eating with the community.

In this way Guru Amar Das established unity and commonality within the congregation and developed trust among the Sikhs. Further, there was no discrimination or privilege in the langar hall. Everyone sat in lines on the floor, leveling all caste distinctions. The guru continued to live in Goindwal and served his congregation devotedly. I was very happy. It is nice to be remembered consistently.

In Khadur, however, things were different. Datu could not bear that his father had given his seat to someone whom Datu considered to be nothing more than a servant of his household. Traditionally, a father passed all of his estate to the eldest son. While Guru Angad didn't give Guru Amar Das money or treasure, he did give him the light of the guru. Datu failed to recognize that light and considered it to be a title of privilege, to which he was the rightful heir. He was very bitter that it had been passed to someone whom he considered to be nothing other than an elderly household servant.

"Amru is old," he proclaimed. "He was a mere servant of my family and now he proclaims himself to be successor to my father. I am the prince of the guru's line, and his throne is rightfully mine."

The Sikhs of Khadur, however, knew that the only true guru was the one appointed by Guru Angad himself. Moreover, they considered the behavior of Datu to be dishonorable to his father. Many packed their families and relocated to Goindwal. There they and the village around them flourished with a large and devoted congregation in the guru's durbar.

Datu sent spies to Goindwal to keep him informed of the activities there. And daily, his jealousy grew.

GOINDWAL

Where the land lies green on fertile ground
At the bend of the river, Goindwal is found.
In this humble village lived three Gurus:
Amar Das and Ram Das, and Arjan, too.

TWELVE

In Khadur, Datu's jealousy of Guru Amar Das and resentment toward his father grew unchecked. With Guru Amar Das in Goindwal Datu, with great pomp and panache, placed himself under the canopy of Guru Angad in Khadur and conducted himself as if he were now the guru. Yet daily people steadily streamed to Goindwal to eat in the community kitchen and receive the darshan of Guru Amar Das. Datu chafed at this.

A few self-serving people, recognizing an opportunity, catered darkly to the towering ego of Datu and kept him puffed up. While their words were full of Datu's praises, they did not satisfy his appetite and ambition. He wanted Guru Amar Das to publicly bow to him and openly recognize that he, Datu son of Guru Angad, was rightfully the guru. In his opinion, Guru Amar Das was nothing more than a doddering old fool. Unable to recognize the absolute devotion and selfless service of Amar Das to his father, Datu's bitterness had seeped into his every cell, metastasized into his tissues, coursed through his arteries and veins, and oozed from his every pore. Like a terminal disease, it consumed him body, heart, mind, and soul. He was not only disappointed, but enraged beyond reason and far beyond his capacity to control himself.

Amru? Whom Datu had taunted and abused under his father's own roof? Amru? Who carried water, chopped wood, worked in the kitchen, cleaned the floors, and washed the hair of Datu's father? Amru? Who wore twelve turbans at the same time and who always mumbled the guru's verses to himself? How could it be that old Amru now sat upon the dais of the guru in Goindwal? If he were truly the guru, why didn't he sit at Khadur in Datu's presence? Why did he choose to hide himself in that useless village of Goindwal? Datu was deeply offended that this aged wisp of a man, who to him was no more than a sudra to be kicked and abused, was now sitting in his father's place. No, not his father's place, *his* place!

Datu's rage erupted and became destructively uncontrollable when a group of pilgrims, who were unaware that the true guru was now in Goindwal, came to Khadur. As all pilgrims, they came to the guru to receive his blessings, to hear his words, and to have him hear their prayers and give his guidance for their lives. Their anticipation was great, but when they learned that Datu sat upon the dais and that the true guru appointed by Guru Angad was now in Goindwal, they gathered themselves and the offerings they brought and departed. Upon seeing this, the anger and jealousy of Datu intensified into rage. And that rage blinded him.

I love that I gave mankind free will. This has allowed people to transcend the circumstances of time and space and achieve greatness in the face of overwhelming opposition. Whenever that has happened, it has caused Me to light up the Heavens. Sometimes, though, people have applied their free will in most unfortunate ways, which can be amusing for me. Naturally, Datu chose that course.

Datu's counselor, not wanting to miss a golden opportunity, decided that Datu needed his opinion. "How can you endure this insult, sir? Daily the streets of Goindwal are filled with people who go to meet old Amru. They bring him gifts and offerings while you sit here looking foolish. How can you live while this sweeper of your house sits in your place? Is this humiliation bearable to one so great as you? Should I tell you, ji, that it is unbearable to one such as I, who loves you sincerely and only wants to sing your praises? You, who should be master, are now the servant of your own servant? This is shameful. Nay, intolerable! It is not only a disgrace to you, but also a disgrace to all who, much like myself, revere you and hold you in such great esteem."

Datu regarded his aide sullenly. "What do you suggest I do?"

"Go to Goindwal and see for yourself how he is worshiped and praised. Go and see what rich gifts are brought each day to this cleaner of latrines. Then, perhaps you will find the spine to take manly action yourself and show him and all who worship him who is the rightful guru."

"Do you doubt that I am the rightful Guru! What is there to show?"

"Well, ji, you may not have the stomach for such a thing. After all, if you truly *know* that you are the guru, then you must be on your way without another moment's hesitation. Perhaps you doubt it yourself. If you are simply pretending, then it is understandable why you would hide yourself here. In which case, simply tell us the truth and we will make our way to Goindwal as well. We want only to serve the one true guru."

Datu ground his teeth, tightened his jaw muscles, and capitulated to his overwhelming rage, which finally took refuge in utter insanity. The cobra of madness had struck his brains, and that venom killed all reason, all humility, and all dignity and honor. So early the next morning after a sleepless night, Datu, in his divinely exquisite madness, got up and made his way to Goindwal. As he traveled the distance from Khadur to Goindwal, he remembered that Amar Das would make that walk every morning with an iron jar of water on his shoulders, and then return at night walking backwards. Datu muttered to himself about senile old men and their stupidity.

Not once did it occur to the unfortunate Datu that it was humble, selfless service and unwavering devotion that earned Amar Das the seat of the guru. Amar Das had humbled himself before his guru, and in so doing, his psyche had become soft like wax and the thread of the guru had passed through him. And like the wick of a candle, it had been ignited by the light of Guru Angad. I can create great mischief, but what humans can achieve often surprises even Me.

Poor Datu just never understood it. He arrived in Goindwal and went directly to the durbar without removing his shoes. And pushing people aside, he stood in front of Guru Amar Das.

"Hey, old man! Only yesterday you were nothing but a water carrier in our house: just a servant, a houseboy." He spoke rudely to the guru with a loud and arrogant voice, full of venom and disgust, as though he were speaking to a sudra or lowborn servant. "Yet today," he continued while his amusing madness raged, "you have the audacity to sit on my father's throne as guru? Perhaps you can fool these people, but you fail to fool me!"

Anger and the blindness of his rage then led Datu to take a most foolish action. With a single swift stroke, he lifted his leg and kicked Guru Amar Das off the dais. The septuagenarian guru fell to the ground in great pain. Datu's kick had been forceful, and the guru's old body, though sound for his age, bore the full impact of that kick. The congregation gasped, and some of those attending to the guru jumped forward and seized Datu, but the guru motioned them away.

Now on the ground and in great discomfort, Guru Amar Das could only respond with compassion. He crawled on the ground toward Datu and touched his feet.

"Oh, great king," he said in a breathless voice, "please forgive me. These old bones have become quite hard and must have hurt your foot." He then drew himself up waving away any assistance from those that came to his aid and retired unassisted to the private apartments in his house. He locked the door behind him, sat in solitude, and meditated.

The durbar was stunned. No one spoke or moved. A few shed quiet tears, having witnessed their guru disrespected and humiliated in such an abusive way. Many felt ashamed that they had not stood up and stopped Datu, who now arrogantly sat himself upon the dais of Guru Amar Das and declared himself guru. Belatedly, the Sikhs in the durbar began to grow angry with Datu and started to shout at him. Unwilling to sit before an impostor, the entire congregation left the durbar.

In an amazingly brief time, Datu found himself sitting alone on the seat of the guru. Yet this guru had no Sikhs. All had left and they refused to return. Word of what had occurred spread quickly, and people stopped coming to the durbar. No one was willing to attend to Datu, to bring him water, or to serve him in any way. When he went to the langar, people moved aside and refused to talk to him. He demanded that people return to the durbar and recognize him as guru, but no one responded. He was alone. Not even his parasitic, self-serving advisors could be found.

Datu had expected the Sikhs to continue making offerings and bringing gifts, as they had to his father and Guru Amar Das. He considered all the gifts and wealth that had been brought to Guru Amar Das, which the guru considered as belonging to the Sikhs, to be his own. Daily people brought the guru gifts and offerings of money, gold, cloth, gems, kitchen supplies, and other treasures. These were placed before Guru Amar Das when they were offered, then in the evening they were removed and accounted for. The value of the gifts was considerable, and the guru used them to fund his mission, pay for the langar, and carry out the administration. He took care of his personal obligations through his ongoing enterprises with agriculture and trade.

Now, however, people placed no offerings before Datu, who recognized that he was not likely to fare well in Goindwal. He had humiliated Guru Amar Das and offended the people of the village. Yet in his mind, Datu was satisfied that he had accomplished what he had set out to do.

"At least I put old Amru in his place," he mumbled to himself. "They all saw how he bowed to me. That should stop all this nonsense." He looked around the village and no one stirred. *In time*, he thought, *they'll recognize the truth.*

They already had.

Datu decided that he would do better back in Khadur. At least there he had his father's house and people still came to Khadur unaware that Guru Angad had passed and had appointed Amar Das as Guru. He believed that Guru Amar Das was unlikely to resume his role as guru after he was kicked from his dais. To his final breath, Datu believed that eventually the Sikhs would come back to Khadur and recognize him as guru.

Datu managed to get himself a camel and loaded what offerings from the durbar he could collect onto the temperamental quadruped and set out rather noisily for Khadur. Now the law of karma is such that for every action there is an opposite reaction. Sometimes the reaction is equal, sometimes it is less, and sometimes it returns tenfold. There are those who believe that Datu was a little shortchanged. On the way back to Khadur, the karma of Datu moved faster than his heavily laden camel and soon overtook him. And I only had a little something to do with what followed.

The road from Goindwal to Khadur was as deserted as Datu's heart. This was odd because it was normally a heavily traveled passage, but on that day, at that hour it was deserted—except for a ruthless band of dacoits who sprung on him from the side of the road and knocked him to the ground. Then without mercy they fell upon him and beat him viciously. No part of his body was untouched. He had a severe concussion to the head, his nose was broken, and his entire body was bloody and bruised. His arms, which he used to shield himself from the blows of the dacoits, were fractured and swollen and turned multiple shades of purple. Interestingly, he received a severely crushing blow to the same foot that had kicked Guru Amar Das to the ground. It swelled up to more than twice its size and caused him excruciating pain for the rest of his life. The dacoits took the camel and the treasures of the guru and disappeared, leaving Datu a broken and bloody heap lying on the road. Still, Datu remained unrepentant for the rest of his life.

And as Datu had predicted, the Sikhs recognized the truth. He was never acknowledged as guru, even by mistake.

THIRTEEN

Guru Amar Das meditated long and deep. In silent solitude he sat, his breathing long and slow as he silently recited *Har Har Har*. He searched for answers, and he prayed. He was deeply disturbed by what had happened. This incident with Datu only amplified his pain and desolation over his separation from Guru Angad. Practically, he was concerned that Datu would return and become even more disruptive to his Sikhs. He considered what would be his best course of action and reasoned that as long as he remained in Goindwal, there could be no peace.

I must leave this place, he thought. *A period of separation will be good for everyone. This episode will pass, perhaps Datu's wrath will diminish, and I can get a clear perspective on all of this.*

He resolved to return to Basarke. So early the next morning, he rose at his usual time, three hours before sunrise. In the darkness he slipped out of his house undetected and walked to the village of his birth.

That walk in the predawn hours reminded him of the days when he served Guru Angad. Those mornings when he carried the guru's water on his shoulders were very precious to him. How simple life was at that time! He only had to devote himself to serving his guru and to reciting My sacred names. Now, he was the guru, and the full weight of that responsibility was on him, just as the light of Guru Nanak was in him.

"The water was lighter and easier to carry," he mused to himself.

The sun was well up when he reached the outskirts of Basarke, illuminating a day that looked to be quite lovely. The fragrant smoke from the morning fires hung ever so lightly in the morning air. The smell of masala and chapattis blended invitingly with the smell of the plowed and fertilized earth and the animals that lived upon it. Being near his ancestral home with those smells from his early days made the guru feel happy and relaxed. He was sore from the impact of Datu's foot and his fall to the ground, but the fresh morning ambiance soothed his discomfort.

A local farmer was working his land and recognized the guru, whom he had known since his youth. Guru Amar Das hailed him, and he came across the field to greet the guru.

"Amru! My dear Am . . . My God! You are now the guru! Is it true?" he asked.

"I was blessed by Guru Angad," he smiled for the first time in two days. "He passed the flame of Guru Nanak to this old man."

The old farmer fell to the ground and placed his forehead upon the feet of Guru Amar Das. He would not let go of the guru's ankles, nor would he raise his head, despite the guru's pleadings for him rise. Eventually, and rather reluctantly, the grizzled old farmer slowly got up.

"How is that you are here, alone?" he said, suddenly realizing that the guru was, in fact, by himself.

"Neither the guru nor his Sikhs are ever alone," Guru Amar Das replied quietly, "but sometimes there is a need for solitude, contemplation, and reflection. This is the place of my birth, and a good place for me to sit and reflect on God and my mission. Meditating here will help me to gain clarity and find peace."

"Oh, Guruji, I am just a farmer, but I remember your service and devotion to Guru Angad. I never believed that you were crazy. Uh . . . I mean . . . I admired your devotion, it seemed sincere, not for show, but from the heart. I regret that I never had the courage to walk with you. But now, on this sunny morning you are here!"

He carried a tiffin, which had his day's meal in it consisting of black *channas* cooked with a spicy masala, and a half dozen chapattis. He squatted on the ground and, taking a chapatti, scooped up the black garbanzos. He sprinkled pieces of chopped onion on top and offered it to the guru.

"Today, I have the good fortune to meet you. I have little to offer, but please accept this: it comes from the heart."

Guru Amar Das accepted it gratefully. He squatted next to the farmer and chewed. He looked around at the plowed fields, the new crops making their way toward the morning sun and the cows and mudges calmly grazing, while the ever-present ravens cawed and flapped above and below. The taste of the food was comforting. The oil and spices felt good on his tongue and in his stomach. His heart lightened, and he was content being on the plowed earth near his ancestral home, eating this simple food.

"Guruji, is there some way that I can be of service to you?"

The guru put his hand on the shoulder of the farmer. "My friend," he spoke quietly, "any service to the guru is accepted with gratitude and rewarded with honor. We have known each other for many years, and now I ask for your help. I need some time to be alone and meditate."

The farmer looked at Guru Amar Das expectantly, but the guru was silent for several minutes, gazing far into the distance.

"Do you know of some place where I can sit undisturbed, where no one can find me so that I might assuage this pain in my heart? Is there someplace simple and remote?"

"I have such a place very nearby. Come with me and I'll show you." The farmer spoke softly. He extended his hand to the guru and helped him to his feet. They walked together in silence across the farmer's field. Not far away was an old mud hut, which seemed to have been sitting there since before Guru Amar Das was born.

"I'll fix it up for you, *ji,*" the farmer said matter-of-factly. "I know it is old, but I'll repair it quickly. Please rest yourself, this won't take long."

Guru Amar Das smiled at him. "You make me happy," he said kindly.

The old farmer quickly set to work. He began repairing the little mud hut while the guru sat in the shade and meditated. The farmer worked vigorously, rethatching the roof, supporting the crumbling walls with wood and fresh mud, and rebuilding the door. By the evening, as the sun was setting and the smoke of the evening fires drifted across the fields, the hut was ready. The kind old farmer went to Guru Amar Das and stood beside him quietly.

He admired the guru. He had known the family of Guru Amar Das for many years and always respected his piety and sincere devotion. When Amar Das began serving Guru Angad, it appeared that he was acting irresponsibly. As the twelve years that Amar Das served Guru Angad passed, this gentle farmer had seen the changes in him. Something was different since Amar Das moved his family to the new village. The old farmer noticed a brightness in Amru that he had not see before

Without a word, Guru Amar Das opened his eyes and looked up at the farmer.

The day was late and darkness was gathering. He extended his hand, and the farmer helped him to his feet. When the guru was stable, the farmer led him to the hut. In the cozy little hut there was a place for the guru to sit and meditate where the farmer had laid down straw and covered it with an old horse blanket. A copper pot from which he could draw water stood in one corner, and against the far wall was a place, also covered with straw and an old shawl, where the he could lie down to rest.

Guru Amar Das was happy with the arrangements and sat himself upon the meditation rug. "Seal the door, my friend, and please bring me paper and stylus, quickly."

After some time the man returned with a stylus, parchment, and a lamp. Taking the stylus, the guru wrote upon the parchment, "*Whoever should open this door is no Sikh of mine, nor am I his Guru.*" He handed it to the farmer.

"Put this upon the door securely. See to it that it stays on the door. Check it daily. If it falls off, replace it. Now please seal the door. Thank you for your help, my friend. You have been most kind. I assure you, you will be rewarded here, hereafter, and beyond."

The farmer duly sealed the door and placed the notice upon it, leaving Guru Amar Das to his solitude. In silence and sealed off from the world outside him, the guru meditated.

He penetrated the depths of his heart and mind. And as though he were submerging himself in a deep pool of water, he merged with Me. Guru Nanak and Guru Angad greeted Guru Amar Das. The entire Universe was revealed to him. Ever deeper and higher he went, beholding all that was placed before him.

"There is one who serves you as selflessly as you served Guru Angad," I said to him, "and upon the head of that Sodhi shall be bestowed the crown you now wear. Teach him well, for as you are the honor of the honorless, home of the homeless, and hope of the hopeless, so he shall be the protector of all, the *Raj Yog*, and the Guru of Miracles."

*   *   *

Though his foot ached, Datu felt great satisfaction knowing that Guru Amar Das was missing. Yet in Goindwal the Sikhs were in deep distress. They searched the jungle around Goindwal and all along the banks of the Beas, but nowhere could they find any sign or trace of their guru. Weeks had passed, and no one knew where the guru was. They were desperate and on the verge of panic.

One wise Sikh, however, remained calm and seemingly unperturbed by the events. When he was a very young boy he had met Guru Nanak, having sought him out on his own. Holding the feet of Guru Nanak, he begged the guru to teach him and give him spiritual guidance.

Smiling, Guru Nanak asked him, "Why do you ask this of me, little one? You are very young to be asking for such a thing."

With a gravely serious voice the young child answered, "Guruji, once Babur's troops came onto my father's land and cut down all the young crops to feed their horses. When I insisted that my father defend the land, he told me he was powerless against the emperor's troops. So, we watched my father's crops be cut and fed to the horses of the army. When they started burning the field, I saw how the small branches were the first to burn. I suddenly became very afraid because I realized that if my father was powerless against the emperor, then I would have no chance against death. I became deeply afraid that this world would consume me quickly. So I decided that I must come and learn from you the way to prepare myself for death."

Guru Nanak, still smiling replied, "You are very wise to be so young." He closed his eyes and reflected. "Yes," he said distantly, "you are wise far beyond your years, like the Buddha." Then, looking into the eyes of the child, he said, "I will call you Baba Buddha, for you speak like a wise old man." Guru Nanak placed his hand on Baba Buddha's head and looked deep into his young eyes, "Now, Baba Buddhaji, from this time forward your incarnations and transmigrations shall end."

Baba Buddha matured under the guidance of Guru Nanak, and he became the most respected and revered Sikh in Guru Nanak's court. However, he had no interest in the guruship, though Guru Nanak offered it to him. When it was passed to Angad, Baba Buddha officiated at the simple ceremony and secured the next link in the Golden Chain. When that light was passed to Amar Das, again Baba Buddha officiated.

Though Baba Buddha was not the guru, there was no separation between his spirit and that of the guru. He understood the dilemma of Guru Amar Das and calmly waited for his return. However, the other Sikhs were unraveling and couldn't contain themselves. Finally, out of desperation and with some fear, they went to Baba Buddha for help.

Baba Buddha arose the next morning and meditated. He prayed that Guru Amar Das would guide his Sikhs to him, appealing to the guru through prayer to come out of his seclusion and be with his congregation once again. After his meditation, he called for the Sikhs who had come to him. He directed them to saddle the guru's mare and bring her to him. The Sikhs were so desperate to find the guru that no suggestion seemed too outrageous. Their longing for the guru was so intense, and their desolation over his disappearance so severe, that they were prepared to do anything to be reunited with him, even if it meant following a horse across the Punjab.

They brought the mare before Baba Buddha. He took her bridle in his hands and put his forehead to her soft nose. He whispered to her as she stood patiently, twitching her tail and shifting her weight from side to side. Baba Buddha stood back and looked at her. She neighed and nodded her head up and down, fluffing her mane as she did so. Holding her reins in his right hand, Baba Buddha led her to the main road, then he looped the reins over her neck and let her loose. She walked slowly on the road for about half a furlong, and then quickened her step in the direction of Basarke. She picked up her pace to a trot and sustained that steadily, with the little band of Sikhs trotting along behind her and Baba Buddha walking briskly in the rear.

When she got to the vicinity of Basarke, she slowed to a walk, continuing until she came to the field of the farmer. For some time, she stood in the road, her head turned toward a field. An old mud hut sat in the distance. The Sikhs stood around her, coughing and catching their breath. Baba Buddha stroked her mane as she nodded her head up and down, her long, white tail swishing back and forth. Suddenly she perked up and set off at a canter across the field of the farmer, toward the little mud hut. When the Sikhs caught up with her, she was standing before the door, shaking her head from side to side. She snorted and blew between her lips. When she saw Baba Buddha, she nodded her head up and down and pawed the ground with her left front hoof.

When the excited Sikhs read the inscription that had been placed upon the door, *"Whoever should open this door is no Sikh of mine, nor am I his Guru,"* their hope collapsed. They didn't know what to do. The guru's mare stepped back and released a long stream from between her back legs that trickled into the plowed field, as if to tell the Sikhs that they were being quite foolish. Baba Buddha laughed at this and told the Sikhs to take heart, that no Sikh should be so easily discouraged.

"The Sikhs are with the guru, and the guru is with his Sikhs. For those who are true there is no separation," he told them.

"But look," said Mahan Lal pointing to the sign on the door, "Guru has cut us off."

"No," said Baba Buddha, "Guru has challenged you. If you are truly Sikhs of the Guru, you will find a way to him. And if he is truly your guru, he will show you that there *is* a way to him."

"Babaji," implored Gopal, "please help us here. You are wise but we are not. You have served every guru since you were a child. We have not been blessed with your wisdom or understanding. Can't you give us a hint?"

"Well," mused Baba Buddha, "the inscription reads 'Whoever should open this door . . .' There is nothing to prohibit finding another entrance. If there is no other door, then we will have to make one."

They surveyed the little hut and decided that the only way in was to open a hole in the wall. They searched the area and found a few tools leaning against a nearby tree and began scraping and hammering on the wall. Dust and crumbles of dried mud flew as the ancient wall began to give way. In a short time they had knocked a hole through the lower part of the wall. Quickly, Gopal dropped to his hands and knees, stuck his head through the hole, and joyfully beheld the guru.

By this time, of course, Guru Amar Das had been aroused from his ecstasy. His Sikhs stumbled in, falling over each other. Baba Buddha stuck his head in last.

"What is the meaning of this?" demanded the guru. "My instructions were explicit that no one was to enter here."

"Guruji," answered a Sikh, "we have not violated your directions. The door is intact."

Baba Buddha then spoke to the guru. "Guru Angad attached us to your feet. Yet you have deserted us and concealed yourself here. How are we to survive and find true consolation without you?"

The guru smiled, but remained silent. He held out his hand and the Sikhs helped him slowly to his feet. Everyone, including the guru, left on hands and knees through the hole in the wall. Guru Amar Das laughed as he crawled into the afternoon sun.

Together they recited a prayer. Then the guru mounted his mare and, with much laughter, returned with his Sikhs to Goindwal.

FOURTEEN

Word spread quickly that the true guru had returned to Goindwal and in a very short time the streets were filled with throngs of devoted Sikhs. Many came only to have a sight of their guru, while many others relocated to Goindwal to be near him all the time. Like Guru Angad before him, Guru Amar Das encouraged commerce and Goindwal began to thrive. As the teachings of Guru Nanak and his successors spread, thousands found spiritual and social refuge in a casteless culture where spiritual knowledge was openly and equally shared.

Many lower-caste Hindus, who for generation after generation had been denied spiritual teachings, found fulfillment and prosperity at Goindwal. Many disenchanted Muslims, tired of the oppression and fanaticism of their culture, also found refuge with the guru. It was a comfortable environment, for the guru's teachings emphasized the monotheism of Islam (after all, there is only one Me) with the broader spirituality and deeper cosmology of Hinduism, which I've always appreciated. Yet it pleased Me that the *dharma* of the gurus became unique to itself, rather than simply a blend of Hinduism and Islam. At Goindwal, as at Kartarpur and Khadur, all were welcome and no religion was discounted.

Guru Amar Das applied himself to his responsibilities as guru with considerable energy and enthusiasm. He was happy to be with his Sikhs again and they were overjoyed to be with their guru. The guru paid special attention to his community kitchen. This was central to his administration, for it was there that all class and caste distinction vanished. He knew that without the eradication of the caste system, his Sikhs would not last and people would remain subject to caste tyranny.

The mechanics of running the kitchen were considerable, and the administration of it was rather complex. It was Jetha's responsibly to manage it. Many people came to Goindwal with offerings of raw materials for the guru's kitchen, including various kinds of dal, flour for chapattis, salt and spices, rice, milk, sugar, ghee, and vegetables. All of this had to be inventoried and stored so that it could be preserved without scavengers or insects getting into it. In addition, there needed to be piles of wood to keep the fires going and gallons of oil and ghee for cooking.

While I love all My creation, there are certain places that are special to Me. The ancients discovered some of those places and over time built shrines and temples on them so they could feel closer to Me, forgetting that the heart is My temple of preference. People were drawn there and pilgrimages to sacred places became especially important to the Hindus as in time, pilgrimages to Mecca became integral to Islam. Guru Amar Das wanted to establish holidays, celebrations, and sacred places of pilgrimage for his Sikhs so that their unique identity and culture would flourish. In India the month of Baisakhi, the first month of spring, was traditionally a time of celebration.

A Sikh named Paro lived in the nearby village of Dhalle and had met Guru Nanak when he was a young man. He became devoted to the guru and after Nanak's time he faithfully served Guru Angad. He was highly revered by the Sikhs and was widely known for his wisdom and devotion. He was referred to as Bhai Paro, meaning "Respected Brother" Paro. He often organized the residents of Dhalle and took them to Goindwal to visit the guru, work on the development of the village, and serve in the kitchen. During one of those visits, Bhai Paro made a suggestion to Guru Amar Das.

"Guruji," he began, "we have been blessed to see our congregations grow since the time of Guru Nanak."

"Yes, Paroji," said the guru, "I think you have a suggestion?"

"Well, ji, it occurred to me that we should have a time each year when all congregations can gather together and celebrate our unity. Everyone would have the opportunity to see you as well as meet other Sikhs from different areas. This would improve our society, lead to expansion of trade and commerce, promote marriages between Sikh families, provide help and inspiration to—"

"Perfect!" interrupted the guru. "Now go and organize it."

"Ehh, but, Guruji . . . I was just making a suggestion."

"And a fine suggestion it is, my dear one. So please apply yourself to it and see that it gets organized. It will become our most important celebration of the year. You are a good man, so please don't stand around here talking with me. Go and get it done!"

Bhai Paro did organize it with great enthusiasm and soon had a very strong plan for the occasion. He sent out notification to all the Sikh congregations, not only inviting them to come, but urging them to be there for unity, commerce, and celebration. Guru Amar Das therefore decreed that each year at the time of Baisakhi all Sikhs should make the pilgrimage to Goindwal to be with the guru and the unified congregations.

With the enthusiastic work of Bhai Paro, Baisakhi became an eagerly anticipated event, which people planned for throughout the year. Thousands attended the Baisakhi celebration each year and this annual celebration went far toward fusing the scattered congregations into an increasingly powerful and unified body. As a result, trade and commerce spread between the communities. Marriages were arranged, children and then grandchildren were born, which brought greater unity and tighter bonds between the people. The various congregations became mutually supportive, formed partnerships, made business deals, and grew proud in their unity and prosperous in their endeavors.

In the India of that time, each village was like a different culture. People tended to stick to the villages of their birth and seldom left them. In an individual's lifetime, it was unusual if he ever ventured further than a few furlongs from his ancestral home. The exception, of course, was when people traveled for commerce or made a pilgrimage for spiritual gain. Even so, they always returned to their homes where they lived out their days tightly woven into their families and communities.

Village life was integral to the life of the individual and the survival of the society. India was invaded more than sixty times between the twelfth and eighteenth centuries, and people survived because of the social structure and village unity. They sheltered together and shared what they had with each other. Frequently, entire families all slept in the same bed. So when Guru Amar Das made the call for his Sikhs to come to Goindwal at the time of Baisakhi, it had an impact on the basic foundation of the society of his time.

The requirements of the guru's kitchen as well as the rapid growth of the village, especially during the annual Baisakhi celebrations, placed a huge demand on the wells and water resources of Goindwal. When water was in short supply and the wells were low, it was brought from the River Beas, but it was a laborious process to bring water up from the Beas to the community kitchen.

To solve this problem, Guru Amar Das directed his sons-in-law, Jetha and Rama, to dig a large central well so there would be a source of pure, clean water for bathing and cooking. They recruited other willing men and women of Goindwal and began the long project of digging the guru's well. Each morning, they arrived with their tools and excavation engines and dug deep into the earth.

The location of the well was in the lower part of Goindwal near the banks of the Beas. Guru Amar Das explained that they would find very pure, sweet water if they dug deep enough. Yet, being near the river, the first water that came up was not suitably fresh, so they continued to dig. As they dug, the water rose and much of the digging was in mud and sloppy soil, making the conditions slippery, strenuous, and dangerous.

Jetha and Rama worked side by side as the days became weeks, then months, then years. They not only supervised the project from the top, but went down into the muddy pit themselves on a daily basis to dig and lift and haul. Work began each morning after their morning meditations and prayers and continued until evening when the community gathered for the *Sodar,* the evening prayer. The project began with only Jetha and Rama and a few others willing to assist. As the work went on and the news of it spread, more people joined in the effort. Whole families came. Then villages organized groups to go to Goindwal and participate in the project. As the large open well or *baoli,* as it became known, went deeper and the project grew larger, it became a source of identity and pride for the Sikhs.

The construction of the well took five years. It was extremely deep, and as they dug closer to the water level, the work of bringing up the mud was strenuous and slow. As they neared the deeper water level, the progress was impeded by solid bedrock. Work slowed considerably, as they did not have sufficient tools or the engineering resources to penetrate the bedrock. With Jetha and Rama driving the efforts forward, they chipped away at the bedrock with the tools and skills they had.

This occurred at a time when Akbar, the Mughul emperor and son of Hymayun, made his periodic visit to Lahore. Certain factors had prompted Guru Amar Das to decide on the construction of the well. Chief among them were complaints from some of the Hindus of nearby villages that the langar kitchen was taking their water. The Hindus submitted a written complaint to the emperor in Agra, who accordingly sent for the guru to answer the charges. Guru Amar Das, though, was much too old for such a long and strenuous journey, so he deputized Jetha to represent him before the emperor.

When brought before Akbar, Jetha answered every charge, quoting the words of Guru Nanak, Guru Angad, and Guru Amar Das. Akbar was truly impressed with Jetha and declared all charges to be invalid and dismissed them. Akbar had a special interest in spirituality, loved the company of spiritual men, and at one point sought to start his own religion. Unlike his later descendants, he was extremely tolerant of religions other than Islam and enjoyed learning about different philosophies and schools of thought. Few things made Akbar happier than long hours of spiritual discourse. He engaged Jetha in spiritual discussions for hours and was profoundly moved.

"How do you know so much?" Akbar asked Jetha in awe.

"Oh, Shah, I have learned from my guru."

"Then, my son, we must meet your guru. When we make our annual state visit to Lahore, we will stop at Goindwal and spend time with your guru."

"The Shah and all his entourage will be made welcome any time."

A year later, when the emperor's entourage reached Goindwal, he dismounted and walked barefooted in the direction of the guru's house, showing the greatest respect for the guru. However, he was intercepted by one of the guru's aides.

It was not appropriate to address the emperor directly, so the aide addressed him by speaking to a courtier who then responded on the emperor's behalf.

"Oh, great Shah, it is our honor to have you in this sacred place," said the attendant respectfully.

"The Shah wishes to have an audience with the guru and has little time for waiting," responded the courtier, sharply.

"Guru Amar Das will be pleased to see the Shah after he and his entourage have shared the hospitality of his kitchen."

There was a brief consultation between the emperor and his courtier.

"As we said, the Shah is on a mission of State and has little time for such things. Please announce his royal presence to the guru and escort us to him straightaway."

"Please forgive my inadequate manners and sense of protocol, but I must advise the Shah that by the guru's order, no one is to have an audience with him without first sitting in the langar and dining in the company of the congregation. You must be hungry and thirsty from your travels."

The Sikh was a little apprehensive, but was firm in his resolve to direct Akbar to the kitchen. Akbar and his courtier conferred in quiet tones. The courtier turned to address the guru's aide when Akbar interrupted.

"How does the food taste?"

"Like heaven, great king," was the reply.

Akbar, being a man of honor, though fully cognizant of his place, humbly went to the langar hall with all his entourage. He enjoyed the food and in due time he was led before the guru. Akbar was enchanted with the guru's company. In the presence of the guru, Akbar spoke like a disciple rather than as a king.

"Guruji, I am the ruler of this land, but it is you who rules the heart. I wish to make a grant to you of whatever land you desire and will give whatever other assistance my office can render."

"The great Akal Purkh has given to me all the lands I could want, for it is He who cherishes all levels of existence. By His tender mercies, He has shared His kindness with me. My Sikhs, through their devotion and hard labor, keep my kitchen supplied and running. Whatever comes daily is spent daily. I trust in God for tomorrow."

"Please permit me to give you a few villages to expand your domain," replied Akbar.

"I have no need and no desire. Whatever God wills me to have, He gives me. What He has given you, have it with gratitude and the understanding that all things belong to Him and shall ultimately return to Him."

"My dear Guruji." Akbar smiled. "I clearly understand that you have no need to receive, but I have a great need to give. From your treasury and your kitchen, countless beings receive great bounties. Please count me among those who have benefited by your generosity and kind compassion. Allah has given you all you need and has fulfilled all your longings. Should he be less kind to me? If you will not accept my offering, please allow me to grant those villages and land to someone close to you, so that my own longings shall be fulfilled."

At that moment, Bibi Bani entered the room to serve the guru, and Akbar was taken by her beauty, her grace, and her spiritual presence. The guru introduced his daughter to the emperor as the wife of Jetha.

Remembering how much he enjoyed his time with Jetha and how meaningful their conversations had been, he addressed Bibi Bani.

"Oh, Bibi," he began, "I have been told that anyone who comes to the house of the guru shall not leave unfulfilled. Is it true that all desires are fulfilled in the guru's house?"

She cast her dark almond eyes to the floor and spoke sweetly. "Oh, great king, have you not experienced for yourself the hospitality of the guru? Here in his presence, do you have any desire or concern?"

"Well, there is one desire I have that the guru has not yet fulfilled. I pray that in his presence you might grant that wish yourself."

Bibi Bani pulled her *chuni*, tighter across her right cheek and bowed her head slightly. "In the name of the guru I am at you service."

"I wish to make a grant of land to the guru's house. However, the guru has need of nothing and will not accept it. I have told him that I have a need to give. Will you please do me the honor of accepting it in his name?"

"Like my father, I have need of nothing. My husband is a great man and my children are a comfort to me. From the guru's kitchen I find my sustenance, and in the guru's house I find my life and hope. Yet as daughter of the guru, I cannot allow one as noble or as humble as you to leave this house unfulfilled. Therefore, in the guru's name I accept your offer. However, I will place it in trust with the guru." With that she touched the guru's feet, bowed her head toward Akbar, and exited the room, leaving her fragrance and unforgettable presence behind her.

On the spot Akbar had his agents draw up the documents and signed the land grant. The grant included a large sweep of the Punjab, which included villages and fields, and a large plot of land upon which was a special pool of water. Though the place was known to many spiritual people, the deed belonged to Akbar, who handed it to the guru in trust.

"Guruji, you have made us very happy and have brought peace to our heart and mind. However, we still have a longing to give something to *you*, something that you will accept, and we think we know what that might be," he said.

The guru smiled at Akbar, nodding his head slightly from side to side.

"As we came from the kitchen, we noticed there were those hard at work excavating a new well. They appear to have hit bedrock, and their progress has been arrested. Allow us to send our engineers to assist."

"This well is a labor of love and the work must be completed by my Sikhs, but your assistance with penetrating the bedrock would be received with gratitude, and you will be blessed for your kindness. Send your engineers. They will be well-received and treated with honor."

The guru then blessed Akbar with a robe of honor, and in a short time, Akbar and his entourage left for Lahore. After several weeks, a team of imperial engineers arrived in Goindwal. They surveyed the bedrock and applied their drills and explosives to help Jetha and Rama and their crews to clear away most of the bedrock. Still, the guru wanted the remainder of the work to be completed by the Sikhs themselves. He treated the engineers with great honor and bestowed many gifts and blessings upon them.

Eventually, the Sikhs opened the bedrock, and pure, clear water gushed into the well, filling the reservoir quickly. Now, the finishing touches were put on the baoli. Eighty-four steps were carved into the ramp that led down to the water, representing the 8.4 million incarnations through all the myriad life-forms. The steps and walls were lined with red bricks, and a red-brick kiosk was erected over the opening. Sitting on the top of the kiosk, the Sikhs could look out across the Beas and contemplate the flow of the Infinite. Finally, after five years of hard labor and sacrifice, the baoli was consecrated with a big ceremony at the Baisakhi celebration.

Guru Amar Das blessed all who had worked on the project, saying they had earned freedom from the cycle of birth and death and all their karma had been washed clean. Then he declared the baoli as a place of pilgrimage for the Sikhs. With the creation of the baoli and its identification as a place of pilgrimage, Guru Amar Das established the Sikhs as unique and sovereign to themselves, clearly distinct from the Hindus and Muslims. Further, he established the precedent for the bigger projects that followed.

* * *

The guru was very pleased with the service of both his sons-in-law, and many people in Goindwal were beginning to speculate on who would succeed the guru when the time came. Jetha's devotion to the guru was unquestioned, and although he rendered tireless and devoted service, he was not considered very capable. By the time the baoli was completed,

Bhai Jetha was close to forty and the father of three sons, Prithi Chand, Maha Dev, and Arjan Mal. He held no property except what Akbar had bestowed upon his wife in the guru's name. He had no savings and lived in the guru's house on his kindness, as they had since they were married, contrary to Indian custom. Traditionally, the marriage took place at the home of the bride, but the man was then expected to take her from her family. People often asked the guru when Jetha was going to find a real job, support his family in a proper way, and stop living off the guru.

Jetha had worked very hard on the baoli and in the community kitchen. His hands, feet, arms, legs, torso, and face were covered with calluses, bruises, burns, cuts, scabs and stains. Though he was often physically exhausted and sore, he never stopped working and was always in a cheerful mood. His presence in the kitchen brought laughter and renewed enthusiasm, and his tireless efforts on the baoli kept the project moving forward.

Guru Amar Das did not want people to think badly of Jetha, so it was important that Jetha establish himself in his own right. Further, it was important to the guru that the domain of the Sikhs be extended. So he sent for his son-in-law.

"As long as you have been with me, Goindwal has been your home, and so it will ever be. Even so, you need to establish yourself on your own so that in the future your domain will be confirmed."

"I like it here with you," Jetha protested. "I am happy serving you, so is Bani. Arjan is especially happy here and is learning so much from you. Why should we leave?"

"My son," the guru continued quietly, "though you may not yet realize it, the future rests upon your shoulders. I cannot let that future time come and not have you prepared for it. Further, I want our domain to be expanded, and I need you to take care of that for me."

Jetha brightened somewhat. A job for the guru was something he could understand and was happy to do. It made sense to him.

"As you wish, ji," he replied. "Where would you like this place to be established?"

"The lands that were granted to Bani by Akbar. Go there, procure the surrounding land, and establish a city. See Baba Buddha about the payments and expenses. He will take care of it for you. Occupy your own land and build a house for yourself. Then to the east of your residence where that pool of water waits, begin to excavate a tank where all who come can be cleansed of every stain. It is for this that you were born and shall be remembered. Go now and with a light heart apply yourself to this. I will send for you in time, but this is your priority. As you work, awareness and understanding will flow into you and the great mission and destiny before you will be revealed. The time has come for the promise that was made to you in the Treta Yuga to be fulfilled."

Something resonated in Jetha's soul with the guru's words. And with his heart fluttering, he made arrangements to leave his family and his guru.

FIFTEEN

I HAD KEPT HER WITH ME playing in My lap for more than one-hundred Earth years. Now, the time had come. I had to let her go to her destiny and take her earthly name. I sent for Rishi Mahan Akal and placed her in his charge. And as I did so, I kissed her softly, passing the breath of life into her.

"All the Heavens are behind you. All of humanity is praying for you. The time has now come to heal their wounds and bring them hope."

Rishi Mahan Akal took her and held her gently. It amused Me to see this formidable rishi, whom the demons feared and all the Heavens revered, hold something so small with such tenderness.

"Take her to Earth now. I will watch over her Myself. You have done a great job."

Rishi Mahan Akal bowed before Me, and in less than a heartbeat, he was gone.

* * *

As the land of the five rivers descends from the Himalayas, it opens up into a very broad and flat plain. The land is fertile and, being low and flat, holds water well so that crops can flourish during the long growing season. Even winter crops grow well there, and the green winter fields are topped with yellow as mustard greens blossom and mature. To the southwest of Goindwal and to the northwest of where the rivers Beas and Satluj merge, the land rises. High is relative in that flat terrain, but from there one can have a good look into the distance. Upon that elevated place was founded the village of Patti.

At the northern end of the village, the land rises to its highest point where, surrounded by pipal and banyan trees, stood the palace of the Raja of Patti. From the large red sandstone and marble estate, the entire region could be surveyed and the domain of the Raja controlled. It was in that palace that Rishi Mahan Akal's fine craftsmanship took human form.

In the womb of her mother, exactly one hundred twenty days after conception, the fetus quickened when that radiant soul entered. Her mother felt it and cherished it. Though it was her seventh child, she sensed something different about this one: something more profound, more divine, and somehow more urgent than the others. Mataji nurtured the new life that grew in her, read to her from the Vedas, sang to her the *sutras* of My praises, and told her the stories of the *Mahabharta*, the *Ramayana*, and the *Bagavad Gita*. And five months after the quickening, she gave birth to a beautiful baby girl, her seventh daughter. The little girl was named Rajni, which means "essence of night." It was in the tenth year of the guruship of Guru Amar Das.

Rajni's father was Duni Chand, the Raja of Patti. A wealthy and powerful man, he served the Shah as tax collector for that region. He was a devout Hindu and carried the overbearing pride of a Brahmin. Of course, Duni Chand was unaware of his pride. Since birth he had been taught and believed sincerely that as a Brahmin, all people of lesser caste were secondary to him. And since he was the Raja of Patti, all others, including Brahmins, were secondary to him and his family.

He and his family observed all of the traditions and practices dictated by Vedic scripture. Yet he defied some of the grimmer customs of his time. He was the father of seven beautiful daughters, and in those days, it was considered a great misfortune if the firstborn child was not a son and an even greater misfortune to have no son at all. Often, newborn girls, especially if they were the firstborn, were put to death. Yet Duni Chand loved all of his daughters and took pride in their grace and beauty.

Though he was a raja, he felt no shame that he had no son. They were a wealthy family with many servants on a large estate. Each daughter had her own apartment, her own servants, and was treated as a princess. He loved his family, and each of his daughters was special to him. He delighted in spoiling and pampering them and enjoyed going out in public with his daughters beautifully dressed and decorated and his wife bangled and bejeweled.

When Rajni was born, Duni Chand put on a big celebration as he had done for each of his daughters. He distributed money and food to the poor and engaged seven pundits to come and do puja for Rajni. The pundits read her astrological chart, her palms and the soles of her feet, did her numerology, and felt the shape of her skull. All agreed that she had a great destiny, that she would bring healing to the world through faith, and that she would set the highest example of devotion and sacrifice.

Two of the pundits told Duni Chand that she would lead him to spiritual awareness and that she would inspire millions. Only one pundit, who was a little more truthful, told Duni Chand that because of his pride he would force his daughter into circumstances of extreme suffering, and that his personal salvation lay with her husband, who would be extremely ill and deformed. He further counseled that Rajni had been placed in this situation so she could bring hope and healing for humanity. Duni Chand had that pundit beaten with a shoe and thrown outside.

"Goes with the job," mused the pundit, who then went and did an additional puja for Rajni and her father, free of charge.

The girls truly were beautiful. Each daughter felt that she was special and her father's favorite. Duni Chand was clever in that way. He had a way of paying attention to each daughter individually that drew them in to his personality, and each daughter loved him sincerely. They were always dressed in the most beautifully stitched clothes made of fine silks, pashmina, and linens, all with detailed embroidery that took the local craftsmen months to complete.

As a seriously devout Hindu, Duni Chand felt that the proper education of his daughters was a priority and hired a personal pundit to tutor each daughter individually. They learned Persian, Sanskrit, Arabic, and Urdu as well as mathematics, astrology, astronomy, philosophy, calligraphy, and literature. They were individually taught to read and recite the Vedas and learned the proper procedures for all ceremonies and pujas. In addition, they learned to cook according to Brahmin customs as well as how to manage servants and run a household. Above all else, their place and role as Brahmins in the society was defined and reinforced.

Essentially, every girl was raised to be a wife and mother. She was trained to believe that her husband was Me in her home and that he should be served as if she were serving Me personally. Because each girl had a different pundit, they each learned slight variations of this, but for at least six of them, the theme was the same.

Of course, their teachers were men.

In Duni Chand's house, there was strict observance of the Vedas, and each daughter was familiar with them. Brahmin cooks worked in the kitchen and each meal was prepared in strict accordance with the Vedic customs. Whenever any of the girls were ill, they were treated with the most effective medicines of the ancient Ayurvedic tradition. For this reason, the members of Duni Chand's family were seldom ill, and when they were, they recovered quickly.

Every morning, each daughter's personal servant awakened her by gently massaging her feet. The servant helped the girl out of bed, helped her wash and clean herself, oiled and braided her hair, and dressed her. Each night after the *Arti* or evening prayer, the girls were massaged with fragrant oils, bathed with perfumed water, and then told a bedtime story from the Vedas.

Duni Chand loved to get his daughters together and play with them. Proud as he was, his softness for his daughters and his susceptibility to their beauty and charm was widely known. Few things in his life gave him greater joy or pride than to have all his daughters around him laughing and playing. They climbed on his huge back, slid down over his considerable belly, pulled at him, and teased him. He loved to roll around with them laughing his grizzly laugh, looking more like an oversized child than a raja. Often he disrupted their lessons just to have their attention.

While the raja loved them equally, he seemed to have the greatest weakness for his first and last daughters, who were nearly nine years apart. Although Gita was not a son, she was still his firstborn, and he treated her in much the same way as he would have a firstborn son. Rajni, being the baby, was adored by everyone, and Duni Chand could never resist her. There was something in her eyes and the serenity of her face that stopped his heart.

He felt some remorse after he beat up the pundit who predicted Rajni's hard times, possibly due to the pundit's own prayers. So when Rajni was six, the age when her formal education was to begin, Duni Chand invited the old man back, gave him money, put on a large feast for the entire village as a peace offering, and made him Rajni's personal teacher. He taught her well, with a depth and understanding that the others didn't get. Rather than just teach her about the rules of society according to the Vedas, he taught her the reasons behind the teachings and why they were written. In this way, Rajni learned about life.

"My dear Rajni," the pundit once asked her, "what are the only two things that men and women have in common?"

She pondered and racked her brain, giving him a variety of answers. "They are both created by God?"

"As are all things," Punditji replied.

"They share karma," she answered.

"We all share karma. So do your horses and elephants." He paused to let her think a little, and then answered his own question. "The only thing men and women have in common is that they walk upright and breathe air," he finally told her, laughing. "Men are not women, women are not men, but neither is complete without the other. Never expect a man to think or behave as you would. The mechanism for even the process of thinking is different for men and women."

Rajni was fascinated. Since her infancy, she wanted to know about the world. Why is this that way? Why is that this way?

"Woman," Punditji continued with a twinkle in his eye, "has the advantage of using both halves of her brain. Man only uses the left half. That is how a woman is able to do many things at once. Woman is sixteen times more powerful than any man, sixteen times more reverent and devoted, and sixteen times more intimate with God. This is why a truly spiritual man is a rare thing."

"Punditji," she said with a look of wonder on her little face, bright eyes shining, "God doesn't create useless things. What are men for?"

"Dear girl, you are too wise for this old man," he paused. "I will tell you what I have learned. Everything in this Universe that God has created is vibrating. There is a frequency to all things, and it all vibrates in harmony. There are high tones, low tones, quarter tones, half tones, and even third tones. To make this beautiful raga of the Universe, God strokes the strings of His creation and we all vibrate. Like the strings of the sitar, there are primary strings and sympathetic strings. The primary strings carry the melody, but the sympathetic strings, by creating overtones, give the primary tones depth, richness, and that penetrating quality which touches the psyche and soul of the listener. One without the other is incomplete. You, my dear princess, carry the melody of life. Man's job is to bring depth and to penetrate the environment. If you can understand this, your man will worship you."

Rajni laughed. "Punditji," she began again, "if everything vibrates, does God Himself vibrate?"

Punditji looked at her. Few people challenged him the way she did.

"The vibration of the whole is the vibration of God. When you stroke a string on the rebab, all of the strings vibrate, the air inside the gourd vibrates, and the instrument itself vibrates, though only one string is struck. In the same way, throughout the Universe every action affects every other part of the Universe. When one is harmed, all are harmed, and one is healed, all are healed. After all, God is vibration."

"Then . . ." she mused to herself, her voice drifting off, ". . . can we change our vibration, like tuning the strings of the sitar?"

"Yes," he stated his affirmation, rather than saying it. "That is what mantra and recitation of the sacred scriptures are for. By doing that, we can change how we vibrate."

"Then . . ." she was at it again," . . . we should be able to vibrate to the same frequency of God and . . ."

He stared at her. Who is this girl? "You are correct," he said authoritatively, "that is why we take the incarnation."

"Punditji, you are different. I am glad you are my teacher. My sisters only learn to recite without understanding. They would never believe what you just told me. Why do you know so much? How did you get to be so wise?"

"Because someone very wise recognized the extent of my ignorance and had mercy on me. I used to recite with the best of them, loud, melodic, and hollow. Someone touched me, made me understand, and made me experience the Truth."

"Who was he?" eyes big again.

"He was known as Guru Nanak, and he sent me to teach you," he whispered.

Rajni looked at Punditji for a long time, her oval eyes big and intensely penetrating, a look of wonder on her face.

What a jewel, he thought to himself. She looked pretty sitting on the silk carpet, her midnight-blue sari wrapped around her like she was a precious carving. Her dark hair was pulled tight and braided down her back. Braided into her hair were *parandees* of gold ribbon. Her ears were laden with gold and diamonds that glistened in the morning sun. Around her small neck was a necklace of emeralds and diamonds set in gold, and on each small wrist were four gold bangles. She was sitting on a big red embroidered carpet, which contrasted with the deep blue of her sari, making her appear to be pulsating.

They could hear the gravelly voice of her father rolling off the marble of the halls. He was calling for his daughters.

"Punditji." She had that look again. "Teach me well," she said. Then she jumped up and ran down the hall to her father.

"What have you learned today?" Duni Chand roared to his daughters.

"We are Brahmins," Punditji heard Rajni say. He smiled to himself.

"We are *Brahmins!*" Duni Chand thundered. "We are the closest to God. Turning to a servant, he ordered, "Bring us sweets and tea!" and laughed. The servant scurried away.

"We are Brahmins," he said again. "And we rule this domain. Who cares for you, my precious ones, and gives you everything.

"You do, Papa!" six of the girls shouted. Rajni just smiled, her eyes far away.

Duni Chand eyed her intently. "Rajni!" he thundered.

"And we are grateful for all that we have," she said quickly, and before he could utter another sound, she jumped on him, and he rolled to the floor. Her six sisters followed Rajni's attack, and the palace was filled with little girls' giggles and Duni Chand's laughter.

SIXTEEN

Early one November afternoon, Duni Chand and his wife called their daughters together. The thick morning fog had lifted, and the late autumn sun shined in warmly. The girls sat around their parents in a semicircle on a massive, intricately embroidered silk carpet and leaned against large tubular pillows. A house lizard running across the wall in search of food or a place to hide stopped and canted his head toward the family as though to eavesdrop on what was being discussed. The girls anticipated something exciting and were giggling and whispering to each other.

"God, they are pretty," Duni Chand whispered to his wife, as he looked at them lovingly. "I hate to lose any of them. I wish they would never leave me." *But,* he thought further, *they are growing so fast, something that even I can't stop. It is a good arrangement.*

"It must be done," whispered Mataji reassuringly.

The girls were looking up at him, waiting to hear what he had to tell them, but Duni Chand was lost in his thoughts. He didn't want to break the news to them. His wife prodded him with her elbow, forcing him from his reverie. He smiled to himself thinking, *At least they will give me grandchildren that I can play with. That will bring me great joy. Many, many grandchildren! Yes, yes, I have to do this.*

He motioned to his oldest daughter, who by this time was fifteen.

"Gita, you are my firstborn," he said, "and I have loved you from your very first day. Who has cared for you and given you everything?"

"You have, Papa," she smiled.

"And now," he spoke nervously, fast and loud, "I will give you a husband! You have been engaged!"

One thing about Raja Duni Chand was that he could not be subtle. It was easier for him to get it out if he thundered it at the top of his lungs. All the girls giggled and screamed except for his firstborn. She stood there, trembling, tears forming in her eyes.

It pleased Duni Chand that she seemed to be unhappy. "What is this? He is a good boy, from a good family. Don't be concerned. I have given you everything; don't you think that I will give you a good husband? He will provide for you, uhh, almost as well as I have."

"Yes, Papa," she choked, "but it will not be the same. I will not be living here with you and my sisters. I will be in a strange house, living with strange people. Please don't make me do this."

"Listen to me, Gita," he said somewhat sternly, "you are my first daughter. As your father, I have the obligation to find you a good boy. I have found such a boy. He is from a good family, he will take good care of you. You and he will give me beautiful grandchildren." Duni Chand paused and reflected. "True, he can't take as good care of you as I have, but you can come to this house anytime, and I will see to it that he does what is required. In return, you must also do what is required."

"Does he know the Vedas?" she asked weakly.

"Almost as well as me!" Duni Chand laughed. "You can discuss this with him yourself. He and his family will be here the day after tomorrow. We will seal the engagement then."

"Will we have a sacred household and do puja every morning?"

"I'll see to it personally," he assured her. "It is not only a sacred household, but a most prominent family!"

"What about his mother? Will she treat me kindly? I know girls who have been very badly treated by their mothers-in-law." Gita trembled, imagining all the horror her mind could conjure.

"She is a noble woman and will welcome you as her daughter," said Mataji.

Rajni went to her first sister, put her arms around her, and hugged her for a long time. Her sister stopped trembling. She felt calm and secure. Rajni's touch lingered with Gita for some time, and she never forgot it.

Naturally, the wedding was a big to-do. The preparations required a week of cooking for the sweets alone. People came from as far away as Kabul and Delhi. Tents were erected over the surrounding fields to accommodate all the guests. Hundreds of horses and elephants needed to be cared for, and the saddles, harnesses, and *howdahs* needed to be properly stored. There were musicians and magicians, snake charmers and dancers. The poor were fed, and all guests received gifts from both families. And in true Punjabi fashion, the guests mingled and did business with each other, selling, trading, and dealing.

Gita's nose was pierced, and a nose ring, the mark of a married woman, was inserted. Of course, as the daughter of Raja Duni Chand, her nose ring was pure gold and encrusted with diamonds. Three golden chains connected the nose ring to the earring of her left ear. Her hands were decorated with *mendhi,* beautiful and intricate artistic designs drawn with henna on the hands, arms, legs, and feet of brides and their bridesmaids.

The night of the wedding, the boy and his family arrived with great show and noise. The boy came mounted on a prancing white horse, while the rest of his immediate family were carried by elephants. There were about twenty elephants, an equal number of riders on horses, eight carriages drawn by two horses each, six carts filled with gifts and pulled by teams of oxen, and four heavily laden camels. At the front of the train were sixteen musicians beating drums, blowing horns, clashing cymbals and stirring the people of the region to follow. Behind the musicians came the groom mounted on his white horse, his face veiled in the Punjabi tradition. Behind him came the long train with his large extended family and all the gifts and trappings for a spectacular marriage. Fifteen men carrying torches to light the way and draw attention to the procession surrounded the train. It was clear that this family was equal to the family of Duni Chand and that the boy was worthy of Duni Chand's eldest daughter.

Gita's pundit performed the marriage, and though she was still frightened, she looked beautiful and very regal in her red and gold sari as she circled the fire behind her husband. The herbs and minerals the pundit threw into the fire made it flare. The flames rose and then gave way to fragrant smoke. Her pundit had determined that the appropriate hour for the wedding, according to the stars, was shortly after two in the morning, long before sunrise. The ceremony itself was only for family, some relatives, and close friends, but the following party lasted for the rest of the morning, all afternoon, and late into the following night.

In true Punjabi tradition, Rajni and her sisters conspired to steal the shoes of the groom during the reception, while he and Gita sat together before the huge crowd. The guests and well-wishers came to the couple and gave them money and blessings. Meanwhile Rajni, the designated thief, managed to locate the boy's shoes. He had hidden them under the dais and assigned one of his friends to stand watch over them. Ravi, Rajni's third sister, stunningly beautiful in all her wedding finery, was able to distract the boy so Rajni could crawl under the dais and take the shoes. Then, as part of the tradition, the groom had to buy them back. Rajni and her other five sisters were ruthless in the haggling, but finally agreed to give them back for 108 rupees.

Once the couple retired for the night after a long and tiring day, the entire throng waited outside below Gita's window for the remainder of the night. All the way down the hill and into the village of Patti, people stood and speculated, singing lusty wedding songs while the many musicians played their instruments and banged their drums. The next morning, as the rising sun shone against the red sandstone of the palace, Duni Chand himself poked his red-turbaned head through the bridal window and displayed the white bedsheet with the red stain. The ends of his moustache were still waxed and turned up from the previous night, and his gold and ruby earrings glistened in the morning sun. The roar of the cheering carried across the fields, almost to the River Satluj. Rajni turned and buried her head in her second sister's skirts.

* * *

"Punditji," Rajni asked one day.

She has that look, and that voice, he thought to himself. "Yes, little one," he answered aloud. They were speaking in Arabic.

"What makes a good wife?"

By this time the wedding festivities had occurred four times and four of Rajni's sisters were getting on with their lives. Rajni had nieces and nephews, and Duni Chand had grandchildren. He was still obsessed with his daughters at home and interfered regularly with the lives of his married daughters. Rajni's two unmarried sisters looked after her and still enjoyed spending long hours talking with her, but Rajni was, maturing and with that maturity came changes in her appearance and personality.

She was a startlingly beautiful girl of twelve. Her sisters were in awe of her, and her parents were somewhat afraid of her. She showed all the signs that her days as a girl would be brief and her life as a woman would commence soon. The dark thick braid of her hair, always laced with bright parandees with little bells at the end, hung to her knees. When she sat, she would coil her braid around her waist and hold it in her lap. When she walked or rocked her head from side to side in affirmation when someone was speaking, it was as though she were floating. She was immovably serene and commanded a penetrating gaze from eyes that seemed to see through to the soul. Her voice was rich and melodic and sounded less like that of a young girl and more like a woman. In her serenity she was self-contained, confident, and secure, with more than a bit of arrogance.

Duni Chand did not fully trust Punditji, but any time he tried to replace him, Rajni pitched such a howl and asserted her will so forcefully that Duni Chand had him back in the house within hours. Duni Chand always believed that Punditji was teaching Rajni strange things, though he could not identify what they were. Yet he could not deny that she could recite the Vedas more correctly than her sisters, that her academics were superior to theirs, and her chapattis rounder.

Still, she was not like the other six girls, though Duni Chand could not clearly identify what that difference was. There was a certain air of disdain about her, a kind of solitary arrogance that unnerved Duni Chand. It seemed as though she was always listening to another voice that no one else could hear, which gave the perception that she was privy to some secret. When she entered a room, it was more like she appeared than actually entered, giving people the sense that she had stepped through from another dimension. But she enjoyed socializing and playing with her sisters and friends, loved to cook, and could nearly beat Duni Chand at chess. His greatest doubt about his youngest daughter was that Rajni's answers were always somewhat vague and never seemed to satisfy him. He reminded himself to pay closer attention to her responses in the future.

"A good wife," said Punditji, "is one who brings sacredness to the home."

Rajni looked at him, her mind computing the answer and the next question simultaneously.

"And what is a good husband?" she demanded.

"A good husband is one who honors and protects that sacredness," said Punditji, somewhat relieved. He was happy with his answers. Sometimes Rajni's questions and answers to him had a slight edge as though he were on trial. Sometimes he felt that she was humoring him, but today she seemed to be fully engaged.

"But what if a wife has a bad husband who fails to honor the sacredness of the home?"

"Then she must honor her own sacredness and pray for her husband to come around."

"That's all? She has no other recourse? Then what should a husband do with a bad wife?" she asked, her slightly rocking head mesmerizing Punditji.

Punditji squirmed, but he could not get out of it now. He closed his eyes and drew a long, deep breath through his nostrils then exhaled quickly, his chest falling with the release.

"First, a woman must know and believe in her own grace. She must maintain herself with dignity at all times. The power of her very presence can influence a man to behave with dignity himself. If a woman wants to change a man, she can do so through the power of her projection, radiance, and prayer. Men are thick and slow to respond. They are not women and don't think like women. But men have a marked vulnerability to women because every man is born of a woman. A wise woman will bring her man to her without him ever realizing it."

"But, Punditji, the Vedas say that a woman should treat her husband as though he were God in her home. What if he is a mindless idiot? Such passive behavior will accomplish nothing."

Punditji was somewhat startled by the directness of her question and the authoritarian quality of her tone. He laughed, but knew that Rajni would not let him out of the answer.

God, how she has matured, he thought. Then switching to Sanskrit, he said, "You did not understand the meaning, then. What that means is make your man *believe* that he is God in his home and that you respect him as such. Then he will bend over backwards to make you happy and will die trying to make himself worthy as a living god in the home. Doesn't God do that for us?"

"But I have seen many men who abuse that trust given to them by their wives. Not only that, they abuse their wives as well. My sisters have married friends whose husbands have been very cruel to them. Is a woman just to accept that and be grateful?" Her Sanskrit was impeccable.

"Let me tell you a story," Punditji was sweating. The air was thick and through the open window the drone of cicadas rose and fell in anticipation of the coming monsoon thunderstorm. Lizards scurried across the walls. A monkey climbed through the window into Rajni's room, up to some mischief. Punditji took his walking staff and banged the marble floor forcefully, scaring the monkey, and it jumped out of the window. Punditji never changed his expression. He switched to Urdu, the common tongue.

"Once I knew a woman whose husband used to beat her. She always accepted it and never complained or mentioned it to anyone. Finally, she could no longer bear it and asked for my help. So I suggested that she tell her three sisters and her closest friends. One day they all came to tea while the husband was home, and they told the young woman to leave the house. There were eleven ladies in the company of this gorilla of a husband. They began talking to the husband and serving him tea into which they had put *bhang* and opium."

"After some time the husband began to feel stupid from the tea as he succumbed to its influence. They began to ask him how the marriage was going, how he liked their sister, how they were getting along. As they talked to him, they drew closer and closer until they had surrounded the poor man. Then in unison, they all took their shoes and beat him within a channa of his life. They were unmoved by his cries and he was so helpless from the bhang that he could not defend himself. Anyway, he could not act with violence on these women. They beat him so badly that he couldn't move for two weeks. He told his wife that he had been attacked by dacoits, had fought them off valiantly, and then barely escaped with his life."

"Each day one of the sisters came to his bed with great demonstration of kindness and concern for him, yet quietly told him that any further violence on his part toward their sister would result in his untimely departure from this earth. Thereafter, he was only loving and kind to his wife and never once mentioned the incident to her. The point is, there is strength in numbers, and there are always resources if you can recognize them."

Rajni laughed, her body shook, her red sari fluttered in the air. The gold bangles around her wrists jangled musically, and her dark eyes radiated joy.

"One thing to remember, dear girl," said Punditji. "A good man will always know his duty. A good wife will never try to deter him from his duty, even though she may not like what the man believes in his heart he must do. Men are mission-oriented and are very basic. Actually, they only require simple maintenance. If you serve your man in this way, he will come through for you. Remember, a man is incomplete by himself, as is a woman. It takes both to make each other complete. A man who understands his karma and knows his duty is very rare. Pray that you find such a man."

Rajni switched to the sweeter Persian. "Punditji, you are so wise. I pray that God will bless me to be as wise as you."

"Precious Rajni, you have been blessed with that wisdom. I am not teaching you anything that you don't already know. I am only teaching you how to access it."

A servant appeared at the door, and with a single graceful movement of her eyes and the slight rise of her right index finger, Rajni acknowledged the servant's presence. The afternoon's first raindrops splattered against the sandstone.

"I must take my leave before the downpour." And in what seemed to be a single motion Punditji rose, took his staff, slipped on his shoes, and left.

SEVENTEEN

JETHA WORKED HARD IN THE summer sun. It was hot now. The monsoon season was fast approaching, and the pace of the work slowed. He had learned a lot from the construction of the baoli, and he applied that knowledge here. Bhai Jetha was not inclined to simply direct the workers in their efforts. Guru Amar Das had told him to construct the tank, so he went to work with pick and shovel, carrying baskets of earth on his head, and coordinating the overall effort. Many people came to help, and as with the construction of the baoli, their efforts had to be organized so that the comprehensive plan for the excavation was followed.

He stood on top of a large boulder that had stalled the excavation and swung a heavy maul against a steel rod, driving it deeper into the stone. This was the fifth rod, strategically placed so that eventually the rock would split evenly. Thereafter it could be moved, broken up, and hauled away. He regarded the earthworks around him and the pool of water at the center. The pond was situated at the lowest point of the wide Punjabi plain that ascended ever so slightly around it.

Jetha swung his maul again, and with a loud crack, the boulder split. He studied the boulder, recalling the techniques used by the engineers of Akbar when they assisted with the baoli. He jumped down and taking a pick began to dig behind and under the large halves. He directed that large timbers be brought, which were driven into the ground where Jetha had dug. He climbed back up onto the rock and directed a drover to hitch his big white oxen to each timber. The oxen were driven forward under their deep lowing protest.

As the bulls strained against the timbers and stone, men continued digging below the two pieces opposite the timbers. The drover continued to drive the oxen and under Jetha's direction the earth's grip on the great stones loosened. In a short time the two halves dislodged and fell away. With drills, rods, wedges, and heavy mauls, the workers attacked both halves of the boulder simultaneously until they had been broken into pieces and the area cleared.

Jetha's body clearly showed the strain and abuse he had subjected it to. The hereditary constitutional weakness that had claimed his mother and father was working against him and the five years working on the baoli had been especially hard on his health. Now, breathing the dust of this region and putting his back into the work each hot day, he looked worn. His hands were hard, callused and cracked in places, and the dirt seemed to be permanently under his fingernails and pressed into the pores of his skin. His feet had deep cracks in the heels and sides of the soles, and his eyes were red and irritated. Just as when he was working on the baoli, his body was full of bruises and cuts attesting to the difficult, strenuous, and somewhat dangerous nature of his work.

Bhai Jetha continued to work on the tank, but something deep in him, a different awareness, was blossoming. He worked as though in another world, while fully cognizant of the one he was in. The excavations progressed as Jetha daily directed the work, while putting his own back into it. Every morning before sunrise and every night until very late, Bhai Jetha sat under the beri tree and meditated as Guru Amar Das had taught him. As the months passed, he missed his Guru and his family. One evening as they were preparing to stop work for the day, a courier arrived from Goindwal.

"Bhai Jetha ji," the messenger spoke with great reverence to the mud-covered man before him holding a large pick in his hardened hands. The caked mud on Jetha was dusted with sand that had been blown by the wind.

"Do you bring me news of my Guru?" Jetha said with anticipation.

"I do, my brother," replied the courier as he dismounted. "Guruji wants you in Goindwal. This work is to cease for a while, and you are to return to Goindwal right away."

Jetha dropped his pick and called to the foreman. "Bhai Sahlo," his voice was remarkably loud and authoritative for such a gentle man. Bhai Sahlo came running.

"*Han ji?*" Bhai Sahlo asked.

"Bhai Sahlo, my brother, you and your crew have done a great job."

"Thank you, sir!" he smiled.

"However, the work must stop for now. Collect your people and your tools and leave this project for a while. The monsoons are coming soon anyway. Take the necessary precautions so that your hard work won't be washed away by the rains. Establish your homes around the area and protect what we have accomplished, but leave any further excavation until my return." He smiled behind his long, mud-caked beard. "My Guru calls me and I must see him in Goindwal. Take care of your clan, and I will call for you when it is time to resume."

"But, sir," Bhai Sahlo exclaimed, "the work is going so well! Can't we continue?"

"We will continue, but not now. I have to go and the time for this work must pause. We will resume, Bhai Sahloji, and you won't believe what we create here. Now though, my Guru calls. I must go! But, Bhai Sahlo, please be available when I need you."

"Oh, Bhai Jetha." Bhai Sahlo could not look Jetha in the eye. "Whenever you need us, we will be here."

"Satish!" he called for one of his attendants, "saddle my horse. I am going to Goindwal!"

* * *

The hour was late when they arrived in Goindwal. They washed themselves and had langar. The people in the kitchen were happy to see Jetha again after his long absence. After a brief and joyous reunion he went home, to the house of the guru. Guru Amar Das was awake and wanted to see Jetha right then. He entered the guru's apartment and touched his feet.

"How are you, my son?"

"I am well, sir."

"Tell me the progress."

"We have been digging for almost three months, now. The basic perimeter of the *sarovar* has been defined, and we've been excavating from the perimeter line toward the pool itself. The work progresses slowly, but steadily. We've been calling it Guru's Chaak."

"You have done well. Now, I need you to be with me here for a while. Return to your previous responsibility of looking after my finances, serve in the kitchen, and be around whenever I need you. There are some finishing touches that need to be put on the baoli as well. Please see to them."

Jetha smiled, "As you like, sir. I am just happy to be here."

"Let me ask you, my son, you are in your fortieth year, and I see strands of gray weaving their way through your long beard. What do you have in mind for your future and the future of my daughter?"

"My future is in your hands. I have no other reason to live than to serve you and your mission."

"I am grateful for that, but you have responsibilities in life than I cannot deliver on your behalf. What will you do after my time?"

Jetha closed his eyes. He could not conceive of life without his Guru. "I will serve whoever sits in your place," he said flatly.

"What about your wife and children, how will they be maintained?"

"What do they need? Arjan is so very close to you. Prithia will manage. He is a worldly boy, I'm afraid, and he will always look out for himself first. Mahadev is deeply meditative. He will find his way. They are all grandchildren of the guru, what more do they need?"

"My son," said the guru, "people talk about you. They challenge me repeatedly that my own son-in-law has no future. Bani was given that land grant by Akbar, so you will always have a place to live, but is this what you want to do the rest of your life? You have great ability to lead and inspire millions. Do you think that will be accomplished from my kitchen?"

Jetha felt confused and, as tired as he was, a little emotional. The words he was hearing sounded so strange to him. He had always served the guru's house. He wanted nothing else, and the guru had never told him to do anything else. Why now, after twenty-two years, was the guru challenging him in this way. Excavating the new tank was changing him, and he could not get a grip on what was happening. Now, he felt the hand of God upon his shoulder and could not understand why his Guru was unhappy with him. He coughed violently.

"Jetha, Rama serves me as well as you, yet he maintains his family and is appreciated in the community. Everything for you is secondary to my service. You have served me well, but other people think you are irresponsible. Even your own relatives have confronted you. Doesn't that disturb you?"

"Guruji," Jetha spoke with a pleading tone in his voice, "there is nothing else for me. You married me to your daughter, and she will be maintained as she always has. Why should it disturb me that I am content to serve you and the Sikhs who come for your darshan? What else is there? However, if for Bani's sake you want me to get a proper job

129

and pursue something else, just tell me. I have no life without you and I want nothing more than what I have. If I should lose that, so be the will of God. Yet, if I should lose my connection with you, I will have nothing. If I have dishonored you or my own family, then please forgive me. I want to bring only honor to your house. If you prefer, tomorrow I will find some commercial activity and begin to pursue that." He coughed again, and the guru saw that tears were streaming down his face.

Guru Amar Das looked deep into Jetha, studying his aura. "You are not well, my son."

"I'm fine, just the dust of the Punjab."

"Dearest Jetha, I must soon choose a successor. I am getting old and may be unable to carry this body much longer. Who should sit upon my place?"

"Well, you have two capable sons who could both claim your seat as their birthright. However, Rama has provided the greatest service to your mission. He worked with me on the baoli everyday. He ministers to the poor and sick and has exemplified all that you have taught. I think you should consider him."

"What about you?" asked the guru.

"Guruji, I am just a simple man, an orphan with nothing of my own. It is only by your grace that I have a roof over my head and the family that I have. My reputation and all that I am are because of your mercy. I have always served you and want nothing else. You just said that people consider me to be irresponsible. However, they do hold Rama in very high esteem, and he would represent you well. Besides, I don't want your job. I am happy with my life."

"Well," said the guru, "tomorrow join Rama at the baoli. Help him to finish it up. I will meet with you in the evening."

Jetha touched the guru's feet and made his way to his own apartments. For the first time in months, he lay down next to his wife and fell asleep instantly. Bibi Bani turned, and in her half-awakened state looked at her husband in the faint light of the darkness. She studied his tired face, feeling her love for him swell in her heart. There in the darkness she could see the deep crow's feet at the corners of his eyes. His unlimited kindness and unconditional compassion seemed to shine from his face, as though he were sleeping under a full moon. Even in sleep she felt power and heat radiating from him. She took his long beard between her palms and, holding it softly, drifted into sleep again.

* * *

A few mornings later, Jetha and Rama were working at the baoli when the guru came and called them both out. In front of the baoli on the inland side was a large open area that was raked and landscaped with a raised platform covered by a canopy where the guru sat and presided over the durbar.

"I have a job for each of you," the guru said, irritation in his voice. "I need a platform built here, on either side of the baoli so I can speak to the *sangat*. I am disappointed that you haven't erected it already. You both must have known that I needed this done. It must be elevated so that I can be easily seen by the congregation. It should have a proper support for my back and a support for my arm. Decorate it and make it worthy of the guru's presence. Have them finished by this evening. I will return to inspect them and sit upon the one that most pleases me. Thereafter, I will sit upon one in the morning and the other in the evening. Now move!"

Jetha and Rama scrambled. They each hurried through Goindwal gathering the tools and materials they needed to do the job. They focused on their work throughout the day as they sweated and puffed, hurrying to be finished before Guru Amar Das returned. It was now mid-July, and the weather was very hot and humid. Jetha and Rama worked with fixed attention, barely aware of each other or of the curious people around them. They sawed and sanded, fitted and hammered, polished and painted their platforms as the sun pitched down. Before the evening kirtan, they were finished. The two platforms stood side by side, shining under the setting sun.

Guru Amar Das came down to the baoli and surveyed the work.

He held Jetha by the back of his neck and said in a harsh voice, "This is not what I asked for! Why can't you do something right? Tear it down and rebuild it properly. I've no tolerance for this sloppy work. Worst of all, I am disappointed that you failed to comply with my instructions."

Jetha bowed before the guru, touched his feet, and said nothing.

The guru turned to Rama. "Are you trying to make a fool of an old man? Do you think I've gone senile and will overlook your failure? Tear this down. It is not fitting for a crow to sit on. How could you have been so blind? Do you think I will live forever? What hope is there for the future if my two most trusted sons fail to comply with a simple directive? Who will carry this mission forward now that you have both failed so miserably? There is no room for this lack of awareness from both of you. Now, get to work!"

The people of Goindwal were as stunned as if lightning had struck the platforms in the midst of the two sons-in-law. Guru Amar Das normally displayed open affection for both of these men, and people were very concerned about this display of his temper. The guru was known for always speaking his mind. And whenever he spoke, people were deeply affected, because his words always came true.

They recalled the time the Raja of Haripur came to visit the guru with all his ministers and *ranis*. One of the young queens who was recently married to the raja refused to remove her veil in the presence of the guru. In his ongoing quest for social reform, promoting the equality of women was one of his primary causes. The guru was adamant about prohibiting the Hindu practice of sati as well as the less lethal but what he considered to be the still demeaning Muslim custom of *purdah,* which required women to cover their faces. When the guru asked the rani to remove her veil, the girl, barely sixteen, laughed at him and made a haughty remark about her veil protecting her from the unpleasant sights around her.

"Oh, insane lady"—his eyes and voice penetrated her veil—"if you are not pleased with the guru's face, then why have you come before us?"

With that, the poor young woman tore off her veil, then her clothes, and ran naked into the jungle along the Beas, screaming hysterically and babbling nonsense. She lived in the jungle for months and was completely out of her mind. Occasionally she could be seen darting around the edge of the village, but the people of Goindwal, still superstitious despite the teachings of the guru, were afraid of her and kept their distance. Sometimes late at night she could be seen picking through the discarded langar that had been put out for the animals and birds. Many people associated seeing her with all kinds of evil omens and bad luck.

At that time, whenever the guru went out, there was always a large entourage that followed him. Some of the people actually had specific functions in service to the guru, but most were simply people who enjoyed his company and made it their responsibility to be with him.

Among those who liked to be with the guru's entourage was a kind and gentle man of limited mental ability. His only possession was a tattered old shawl, which he used to cover himself. Anytime the guru spoke, this simple man listened intently to his every word. Whenever the guru paused, with great authority the man pronounced, "*Sach, Sach,*" meaning *true, true.* He always said it with great ceremony as though encouraging the guru to continue because he was on the right track with his discourse. Consequently, the man became known as Bhai Sachansach. Although he was considered to be an idiot, people enjoyed having him around because he had a kind heart, was willing to do anything for anyone, and always made people laugh with the innocence of his behavior. I loved Bhai Sachansach. He was most dear to Me.

Sachansach went to the jungle each morning and afternoon to collect firewood for the guru's kitchen. He enjoyed the outdoors and constantly mumbled to himself whatever he could remember of the guru's hymns. He often got the lines mixed up, but it never mattered to him. It didn't matter to Me either, because he recited the passages out of true devotion.

One morning he had finished gathering his load of wood and was negotiating his way back to Goindwal. There was wood stacked on his back, and he held another bundle in his arms. As he walked, bent from the weight on his back, he recited to himself a hymn of the guru, which in actuality was a mixture of lines from various passages, but to the mind of Sachansach it made great sense. Sachansach felt movement to his right and stopped to peer into the jungle, still chanting to himself.

The sound of footsteps on jungle floor caused his simple heart to race. Could it be a tiger or a lion? A sloth bear? Perhaps a jackal! He moved forward cautiously, fumbling the lines he had been reciting to himself, his breath quickening with his heartbeat.

Suddenly, like a cheetah on the hunt, a naked woman sprung from the jungle and attacked him screaming and thrashing. She fought viciously, kicking, clawing, scratching, and biting the poor man. He dropped the firewood that he held in his arms on his own feet, then fell on top of it, and the load on his back knocked against his head, pinning his head and shoulders to the firewood beneath him. The insane queen of the Raja of Haripur picked up a piece of wood and pounded poor Sachansach with it, then dropped it and ran back into the darkness of the jungle, screaming like an angry raven. Crawling out from under his firewood on hands and knees, blood streaming from all over his body, he found his feet and ran back to Goindwal.

Bhai Sachansach was a sad sight stumbling into the village. The mad rani had clawed his face, chest, and arms with her fingernails. She had kicked him repeatedly in the shins and groin, and he had welts and knots on his ribs, arms, and head where his own firewood had clobbered him. There were gashes across his forehead, his left eye was severely swollen, and there were bite marks all over his body. Sachansach staggered to the baoli, stumbled down the eighty-four steps, and with a big splash fell into the cistern at the bottom.

Several people there helped him up and dressed his wounds for him. His only possession, his old tattered shawl, was bloodstained and now more tattered than ever. He was taken to the guru where he told the story of how a wild witch had leapt from the trees and attacked him. She wanted to eat him and steal his soul, but the hymns of the guru had saved him, although he barely escaped with his life.

Guru Amar Das smiled at him. He had one of his wooden sandals brought and handed it to Sachansach.

"This afternoon, when you go back for your firewood . . ."

"Forgive me, my lord, but Sachansach will not go back! Sachansach could have been killed. Sach Ji! It's very true! Sachansach can't go back, it isn't safe. Sach sir! This witch means to have the soul of Sachansach, and then eat his flesh!"

"My dear Sachansach, please go on my behalf, and when this unfortunate woman approaches you again, simply touch her with my shoe. Her demeanor will change and she will become compliant . . ."

"Sach Ji! So true!"

"Try not to injure her, but bring her to me."

"Sach sir! Sachansach will bring her to you."

Bhai Sachansach took the shoe of the guru, and after a brief rest and food from the guru's kitchen, cautiously went back into the jungle. He began to gather his firewood, mumbling the disjointed lines of the guru's hymns and stopping every half minute to look and listen. He was trembling so much that he could barely hold the wood, but he continued to collect it as the guru had instructed him to.

He heard movement above him and looked up just as the crazed rani, snarling like a tiger dropped from a tree onto his back. Sachansach had tied the guru's shoe to his hand so he would be ready if he was attacked again, and as the young woman, whose body was bruised, scratched, and emaciated from her months in the jungle, leapt at him, Sachansach, in a natural defensive movement, touched her with the shoe.

Upon contact with the shoe of the guru, the teenage girl fell to the ground and began to cry uncontrollably. Her thin body shook with sobs.

Tears streamed down her face and left tracks in the dirt and filth that had accumulated there over the months. Her long dark hair, which once had been perfumed and braided daily, was now filthy and matted, making her appear more as a wild, primitive animal than a queen. Realizing that she was naked and fearing that poor Bhai Sachansach intended her dishonor, she began to scream and tried to cover herself as she backed into the jungle. Bhai Sachansach, though a simple man, understood her humiliation and discomfort. Taking his only possession, he covered her with his tattered shawl, making sure that she was not exposed through the holes of the fabric.

The poor rani was more frightened and distraught than Sachansach had been. The simple and kindhearted old man soothed her and, reassuring her, picked her up and carried her on his back to Goindwal and the house of the guru. She fell before Guru Amar Das and begged his forgiveness for her arrogance. Guru blessed her and had his own physicians tend to her. Eventually she was well enough to travel and was escorted back to the Raja of Haripur. The guru publicly honored Bhai Sachansach and bestowed a sturdy new shawl upon him, which he cherished to his death. Guru Amar Das told him that he was not only honored in this world, but in all other worlds as well.

While My mischief *may* have been afoot here, I was most pleased with Bhai Sachansach. The rani turned her mind to reflect on Me for the rest of her life and achieved a very elevated and intimate union with Me. Sometimes, to get someone's attention, I have to be something of a scoundrel and shake them up a bit. It is interesting that when people are in hardship, they pray to Me, do pujas, light candles, and make promises to Me. But when they are happy and prospering, I am easily forgotten.

That story was clearly in the minds of the people of Goindwal as they stood before the two platforms that late afternoon, regarding the sons-in-law of the guru in their humiliation before him. To all present, the platforms were beautiful. They had been exquisitely crafted with the greatest care, and no one could decide which one was the better.

The words of the guru were powerful, and both Jetha and Rama were popular among the members of the congregation. No one wanted to see either son-in-law of the guru cursed, for none had ever heard the guru speak as harshly as he had to his sons-in-law that day. Throughout the next day, the two men sweated over their respective platforms. All day they worked and reworked, and as the sun began to set, two magnificent platforms again waited for the guru's inspection.

They could hear the guru yelling even before they saw him, and each man knew that he was in trouble. Again the guru was dissatisfied with the results. He went to Rama's platform and criticized it extensively.

He turned to Jetha's platform. "What is this?" he asked quietly. "Has your time away made you inattentive? I gave you clear instructions as to how this is to be constructed. One who cannot understand the instructions of the guru can never follow those instructions. One who cannot follow the instructions of the guru can never find favor in his house, and one without a guru has no hope. Rebuild this mess and don't annoy me further with your incompetence. Do you understand?" The guru's voice was soft, but electric with intensity.

"Yes, my lord," said Jetha quietly, and he bowed and touched the guru's feet.

Another day passed, marked in the afternoon by monsoon rains. Jetha and Rama worked through the storm, and after it passed, the guru arrived to inspect the work.

When Guru Amar Das inspected Rama's platform, he only shook his head. In a quiet voice he said, "This fails to please me, remove it from my sight."

"Guruji," said Rama with some restrained irritation in his voice, "I built it as you instructed. I have worked very hard to make it right."

"I know that you have worked long and hard, but what is the point of your efforts if they fail to please? This is not as I want it. Tear it down and rebuild it to my satisfaction and this time do not fail!"

"Look!" said Rama, "you said to make it approximately so high. Well, measure it! You said to give it a support for your back. Place your back against it! You said to give it a support for your arm. What is that sticking up, a weathervane? I have built it thrice according to your specifications. Can't you see the work and care that has gone into this?"

"I see what you have done. Now tear it down immediately. I no longer want to look at it!"

In a rage Rama smashed the platform, muttering that the guru's age had made him senile and that he no longer knew what he was doing. When the platform lay in a heap, Rama turned to the guru.

"Are you happy now?"

"Not as happy as I will be when you have rebuilt it to my satisfaction," the guru said calmly.

"No!" said Rama, adamantly, "I won't rebuild it. I have done my best, and if it fails to please your aged temperament, I will pursue it no further. You will never be pleased, and I will do no more."

Rama turned and directed his personal servant to pick up his tools, then went to his house with his head down. Guru Amar Das was silent for some time, and no one present dared to move or speak. Many were afraid to breathe and did so slowly. The guru had his eyes closed and seemed not to be present.

Turning to Jetha, he said, "Because of your previous failures and the damage from the rain, this wood is no longer acceptable. I cannot sit on a recycled platform. Tear it down and rebuild it with new wood. Son, you have not come through as I had hoped. Do this job properly or give it up as Rama has."

And so it went. Jetha worked day and night now, trying to build a platform to please the guru. Each evening Guru Amar Das came to inspect his work and without exception he found fault with it. Day after day he was more abusive toward Jetha, finding fault with the minutest detail of the platform. Inconsistencies with the wood, a joint off by a fraction, the way it sounded when the guru tapped it with his walking stick, or how the sunlight did not look right upon it.

The seventh sunrise came, and Jetha, extremely tired and apprehensive, worked on his seventh platform. He had worked through the night and now paused as the sky grew light. He remembered once when he had been with the guru and a group of new Sikhs approached him.

"Guruji," they asked, "previously we would always consult the astrologers to find the auspicious time to begin a project. What should we do now?"

"I love the astrologers," said the guru. "They are always very entertaining. My problem is that we have never found two astrologers who can agree. So which one should we listen to? The one who wants to make us happy and get paid the most? Or the one who is not afraid to speak the truth?"

"But, sir," they pushed further, "is there a way to guarantee the success of a project?"

"Can your astrologer guarantee your success?"

"No, ji."

"Success and failure are held only in the hands of God. If you have a problem, take it to Him. Make God solve it. He gave you the problem in the first place."

"How can we do that?" the startled Sikhs asked in unison.

"I'll tell you what, my dear ones. Invoke the name of God before you begin any undertaking. Say a prayer and ask God to come through for you. Then, leave it up to Him. If things don't work out, tell Him that He is not doing His job." Guru Amar Das laughed. "Just ask God to come through for you. Do so with devotion and humility and see what happens."

Jetha thought about that moment and in the early morning light prayed to the guru to help him, to work though him and construct the platform to his satisfaction. Jetha worked very hard. The day was exceptionally hot and humid. The sweat streamed off him, soaking his clothes and turban, running down his face and under his long beard. Jetha placed a cloth under himself so his perspiration would not touch the platform.

Across the plaza from the baoli, in the guru's kitchen, Rama watched Jetha in silence. Since his confrontation with Guru Amar Das, he felt deepest shame and regret. He was confused and depressed, but mostly unbearably disappointed with himself. He went to the guru and humbly begged for his forgiveness, which Guru Amar Das readily gave him. But Rama still felt uneasy, unable to reconcile his behavior with himself.

Jetha continued working nonstop, oblivious to everyone and everything around him. He never stopped to eat. Occasionally he laid down his tools and walked down the cool, moist steps of the baoli and took water from the well, then climbed back up and resumed his labor.

Jetha had commissioned a canopy to cover the platform, and late in the day he collected it from the weaver and mounted it. On this day his seventh platform was by far his best. All of Goindwal had seen how much Jetha had toiled on the seven platforms. They had seen how the guru had challenged and, to some points of view, abused Jetha at the end of each day. Many could not believe that he continued to do as the guru had directed him, and most agreed that they would have joined Rama by now.

It was a beautiful platform decorated with cushions for the guru's back, and the newly woven canopy was spectacular against the sunset.

When Guru Amar Das arrived for the daily inspection, he paused and was silent. He regarded its every detail in silence.

Then Guru Amar Das turned to Jetha, his white beard flowing in the evening breeze, "This does not please me," he said quietly, "tear it down and build another one."

Jetha drew in his breath and fell at the feet of the guru, holding them as if he were a drowning man grasping a lifeline.

"Oh, my guru," he pleaded, "I am a fool and can't do anything right! I can't comprehend your simple directions, yet you accepted me as your Sikh. Please have mercy on me now and do your duty as my guru and my father. You have all knowledge and all understanding, while I know nothing. Instruct me. Show me what to do. I am so ashamed that I have failed you. Please, I can do nothing more without your help."

Guru Amar Das reached down for Jetha's arm and, lifting his son-in-law, looked through his eyes and into his soul.

"Seven times you obeyed my order and built and rebuilt the guru's platform. Now, my son, for seven generations your line shall sit upon it." Then turning to the amazed people standing in the evening light, he said, "Siblings of destiny, see this man! I have tested him and found his heart to be true and pure. Understand that it is only through the heart that God enters.

"You have all seen the results of this test and you all must understand why Jetha is so very dear to me. Humility and devotion are all that matter to God; everything else is false. Jetha, through his own efforts and by the power of his own devotion and humility, has achieved perfection. He incarnated to bring hope and healing to the world. Those who follow him shall be saved from the darkness of this Kali Yuga. So hear me now: from this day forward he shall be known as Ram Das, God's servant."

The people were astonished. After such exertion on Jetha's part, such humble devotion and sacrifice, the guru had blessed him. All had seen it, and his worthiness could not be challenged.

Rama stood at a distance and observed all that had happened in silence. The words of the guru touched him, and he understood that he had been tested and had failed. *Ram Das, God's humble servant. How appropriate*, thought Rama. *This is what I have lost by my arrogance and anger. He is truly the better man!*

EIGHTEEN

It was becoming evident that Jetha, now known as Ram Das, would succeed Guru Amar Das. Yet he continued to work in the kitchen, serve the guru, carry his water, gather his wood, and clean his dishes. Despite the praise Guru Amar Das bestowed on him after the challenge of the platforms, Ram Das made no pretense and never assumed that he was guru or that he spoke for the guru. His service and devotion to Guru Amar Das recalled the guru's service to Guru Angad.

Daily Ram Das spent long hours with Guru Amar Das, who talked to him about the future and emphasized the growth, development, and administration of the Sikhs. These were precious hours for him. He cherished each moment with his guru as though it would be his last. He continued his hard labor in the guru's service, and his body showed the wear. His heredity, which claimed his mother and father, now pursued him relentlessly.

Bibi Bani served her father as selflessly and devotedly as Jetha. From her earliest years, she was devoted to her father, and for this reason accepted the frequent, extended absences of Bhai Jetha. She was with her father daily, which brought her great satisfaction and fulfillment. She prepared his food, served him, and tended to his various needs, received his many visitors, and still worked in the community kitchen. Often, the only time she spent with her husband during the course of a day was the few hours at night when they slept.

One morning Guru Amar Das sent for Bibi Bani. When she came before her father, she sensed that he had something serious on his mind. She was accustomed to the guru's ways. He was known for his blunt and direct way of confronting and communicating with people, so she was prepared for anything.

When she arrived the guru was sitting on his couch meditating silently. So she sat quietly on the floor in front of him and regarded her elderly father with unconditional love as he sat in the ecstasy of his meditation, his breathing long, slow, and deep. As she studied her father, she noticed that one leg of his couch was broken, destabilizing the couch and threatening to overturn and launch the guru onto the floor. Bani shifted her position and placed her bare hand under the broken leg. Immediately excruciating pain penetrated deep into her hand and arm as blood oozed from her palm. Ever mindful, with her free hand she placed her *dupatta* under the support hand to catch the drops of blood as they flowed from her.

The guru sat silently for some time in deep meditation. When he opened his eyes, he looked at his youngest child, regarding her sweetness, soothing himself in the comfortable depth of her eyes. She was now over forty and the mother of three children. For the first time Guru Amar Das noticed strands of gray in her hair and the signs of aging in her face. She was a lovely woman with a timelessness in her eyes that uplifted him. As Guru Amar Das regarded his daughter, her innocence touched his heart as though she were still an infant, yet pain was clearly on her face.

"Bani! What have you done?" he said as he realized what had happened.

With surprising speed and agility, Guru Amar Das got off his couch and comforted his daughter, calling for help. Quickly help came and Bani's wound was treated and bandaged.

"Why did you do such a thing, my daughter? There was no need."

"You are my father and my guru. If I cannot make such a sacrifice for you, what value do I have? I am neither qualified to be your daughter nor your Sikh."

The guru held her tightly in his arms as though she were a child, surrounding her with his infinite love and compassion.

"Ask anything of me," he said softly, "I will grant any request of yours."

"Guruji it is not my place to ask anything of you except your darshan."

"Ask anyway, and I will grant it."

Bibi Bani closed her eyes and searched her heart and soul. When she opened them, her eyes were as bright as sunlight reflecting off water. It was clear that she had thought of something significant. She looked into her father's eyes with the burning intensity of her own.

"It is not my place to ask anything of you. You are my father and my guru and have given me everything. You married me to a great man who is of the Sodhi line, and now so am I and our three children. Yet if it is true that you are meant to grant me a request, it would be this: that all future gurus are descended from our Sodhi line."

He spoke softly. "This is a serious thing that you ask. The free-flowing stream of the Sat Sangal Dhara will now be made to flow exclusively through the Sodhis. This will bring great suffering to your descendants and require the sacrifice of many. Are you sure you want this?"

"Pittaji, such things must be borne anyway. Let it fall on the Sodhis and spare the others."

They sat together in silence for some time.

"This world is transitory. Everything comes to go. We are not born to reside on this Earth, simply to pass through it. We are spiritual beings here to have the human experience. We are allowed only so much time and so many breaths. You must know now that the time allowed for Ram Das has been consumed and his days will soon end."

Bibi Bani did not speak. She looked at the blurred image of her father through the tears forming in her eyes.

"What will you do after your husband is gone?" His voice, though soft and soothing, penetrated. His words went to her heart. She thought of herself as a widow left with three sons, and though she did not feel fear nor dread, she felt a painful longing for her husband. She looked silently into the eyes of Guru Amar Das for many minutes. The sounds from the streets of Goindwal and from the activities of the guru's household blended with the thoughts racing through her mind.

Then, without speaking, she rose to her feet and left the room. After some time she returned. She was barefooted and wearing an old and well-worn *kameez* and *salwaars*. She had removed all her makeup and jewelry, including her nose ring and wrist bangles. She held these things in her hands, wrapped in her dupatta. She approached her father and placed it all at his feet.

"Guruji," she said unemotionally to her father, her voice even and strong, "you have forbidden the practice of sati. Therefore, my life must go on after my husband has left. Nothing matters to me except to serve you and the house of the guru in his memory. It will be a great loss to me and to your Sikhs, but the hand of God is the hand of God. It cannot and should not be altered. If I am truly your daughter, then I must accept His will as sweet and bear it with honor."

Guru Amar Das embraced his precious daughter. She had touched the power of her own nobility and passed the guru's test. He smiled at her brightly.

"Sometimes, things happen because they must. Sometimes though, when you have a guru, things can happen as a gift. The beautiful Akal Purkh has granted me one hundred years of life. However, I owe Ram Dasji a great debt from previous incarnations. With the permission of the Almighty, I will pass the balance of my time to Ram Das and he shall sit upon my dais. I am ready to pass the guruship as Guru Angad passed the light of Nanak to me. I have tested Ram Das, and there is no other like him. He shall have the rest of my days and you shall continue to enjoy your marriage for that time. Understand, though, that I can give him no more. Further, as guru he will be different; not the man you know now. Once he receives that light, life as you both have known it will end. Your married life will change. His relationship with you and your sons will change. The person you are must also change. Can you accept that?"

"Pittaji, I can accept whatever comes from the guru. Especially, whatever you grant."

"Then from this time forward the Sat Sangal Dhara shall pass through the Sodhi line. It is time for this shift. Since Guru Nanak it has been with the Bedis, but now the time has come for the Sodhis to hold it, as it was prescribed in the Treta Yuga."

"I don't want to lose you either."

"Let me go, my love, it will be your gift to me."

"As my guru, you are my life. As a wife, my husband is my life. Now, you are granting me everything, for my husband shall also be my guru and so my generations to follow." Tears flowed freely from her eyes. Guru Amar Das had tested her, and her true nature had surfaced through that test. Now her emotions as a daughter, as a wife, and as a great woman surfaced.

Guru Amar Das comforted her. *"How noble she looks even with her tears,"* he thought. He put his long arm around her and embraced his daughter, holding her next to his heart. She sobbed into his beard for some time, and then grew still in his embrace.

"I am a Bedi and a Sodhi, Pittaji," she smiled at him, "and it is upon us now to turn the tide of the times." There was the resolve of a warrior in her voice and Guru Amar Das regarded her, his eyes shining.

"You are a lion!" he laughed. "A lion!"

The next morning, the durbar was crowded. There was a sense of excitement in the air and the anticipation grew as the sacred hymns were sung. The musicians played with such vitality and intense reverence that no heart was untouched. As the time neared for the guru to deliver his morning discourse he had a table, slightly higher than his dais and covered with a white sheet, placed next to the dais. Guru Amar Das then stood up and directed Ram Das to stand up. Placing his hands on the shoulders of his son-in-law, he moved him so that he was standing in front of the table. Pushing down on his shoulders, he made Ram Das to sit upon it. Guru Amar Das then circled the table clockwise four times and placed five copper coins and a coconut before Ram Das, as Guru Angad had before him and as Guru Nanak had before Guru Angad.

Smiling with serene joy on his face, he turned to the congregation.

"Oh siblings of destiny, the eternal light of Nanak has now been passed to Ram Das. My time has gratefully passed and now the same flame burns upon a new wick. From this time forward Guru Ram Das is your guru. Look to him for your guidance and give him the respect due the guru."

With that, Guru Amar Das returned to his original seat. As the musicians played the next *shabd,* Guru Ram Das sat silently, his big bright eyes shining. Mohari, the second son of Guru Amar Das, rose and bowed before Guru Ram Das.

"How will you treat the new guru, my son?"

Mohari rose again and with folded hands faced first his father, then turned to Guru Ram Das. "The light of Nanak has been passed by you as it was passed to you. You have chosen to pass it to Ram Das, who is now the guru. I will treat him as the guru with full respect and honor due him."

"You make me very happy," said Guru Amar Das. "Normally, twenty-one generations of a saint get liberated. Yet, in your case, forty-two generations shall be liberated!"

Guru Ram Das had not spoken since he had been placed upon the table. "You are still my guru, sir. Please grant the guruship to Mohari and allow me simply to remain a humble Sikh."

"No, my son. You are the guru and guru is in you. Be clear about this now."

Mohari gasped and only shook his head.

"*You* are Guru Ram Das," said Guru Amar Das firmly, "and it is your destiny to carry the Golden Chain of the guruship. This was the promise made to you in the Treta Yuga. Whatever has been destined for Mohari shall be given to him, but you have been destined to be the guru, and that destiny can only be fulfilled by you."

Baba Buddha stood and bowed before Guru Ram Das, and the rest of the congregation followed him. Guru Ram Das meditated deeper and deeper, oblivious to the people bowing before him.

*   *   *

As I had done three times before, I now came before Guru Ram Das and offered him the cup of nectar. He took it gratefully and drank deeply. I blessed him, whispering in his ear, giving him the key that I had given to Nanak, and Angad, and Amar Das. All the saints and deities, gods and goddesses, and even a few demons (I do love their panache) appeared before him and showed him reverence and honor. He saw what lay ahead: the excavation of the sacred pool and confirmation of the healing powers of the water by a slender young girl. Then looking further into the future, he saw streams and streams of people flowing into the water, emerging healed and their longings fulfilled.

*   *   *

As Guru Ram Das experienced the revelations of his meditation, a festive atmosphere grew in the durbar. The entire congregation got up and bowed before the new Guru as the musicians played with great heart and joy. One by one, they stood in line then bowed before Guru Ram Das with sincere reverence and devotion. There were smiles and quiet laughter, for everyone had seen clearly how the one known as Bhai Jetha had earned the name Ram Das, the servant of God. It was appropriate that now, upon the head of Ram Das, the crown of spirituality had been bestowed.

There was one exception. In spite of the festive atmosphere and warm feelings in the durbar, Mohan, the first son of Guru Amar Das, brooded and kept to himself. He said nothing and retreated sullenly into his shawl. He considered that as the first son of Guru Amar Das, the guruship was rightfully his, and he could not bear the thought that it had been bestowed upon the orphan whom he still called Jetha.

Guru Amar Das sensed Mohan's mind and spoke to him. "Mohanji," he said quietly, "you are not happy with these developments?"

"Why be happy?" muttered Mohan, "you have given my birthright to an orphan."

"The guruship, my dear boy, is not a birthright but a trust. It was given to me in trust and in trust I have passed it to the one to whom it belongs."

"Nonsense," said Mohan. "You could have given it to anyone you wanted. Mohari I could understand, or Rama; at least he is responsible and doesn't forget about himself and his family. But to an orphan with no prospects?"

"Listen," said Guru Amar Das, talking in a powerful whisper, "this trust was given to me by my guru who had it bestowed upon him by Guru Nanak himself. He also bypassed his own sons. You were there the day that Datu kicked me in the durbar."

"I understand him better now," muttered Mohan.

"Let me be specific, my son. You rested while he worked. He sacrificed while you made assumptions. Have you achieved no understanding? It is a trust and one can only be happy when that trust rests with the rightful owner. It is not yours, neither is it mine. I cannot give you what I don't possess."

Guru Amar Das paused, closed his eyes, and in a melodic voice, in harmony with the musicians, he composed the following on the spot and recited it lovingly to his first born:

"One should pass on another's trust to the one to whom it belongs; in this is utter joy."

Guru Amar Das opened his eyes and regarded his firstborn child. Mohan looked into his father's eyes, gradually comprehending the scope and depth of the guru. And in that moment he understood that he lacked that depth, the power of penetration, or the extensive understanding and absolute devotion required of the guru. It was a bittersweet relief for him. It was very hard for him to accept that he was not the one to receive the guruship; that it was not his destiny or his trust. Yet in that understanding came a sense of relief, and he lost his will to resist. Mohan relaxed and silently got up and paid his respects to Guru Ram Das as the musicians completed the shabd.

"Oh Guru Ram Das," called Guru Amar Das, softly, "all the sangat have made obeisance to you. You should open your eyes, dry your tears, and join us."

Guru Ram Das was deep in ecstasy. Now, the voice of his Guru penetrated to the core of his meditation and pulled him to the present. He drew a deep breath and slowly exhaled. He opened his eyes reluctantly and was rather startled to find himself sitting on a table, higher than the rest of the congregation, including Guru Amar Das.

"Guruji," Guru Amar Das said with a smile, "we are still waiting for thy hukam."

He wiped his eyes with the *hazuria* around his neck and with a startlingly clear and melodic voice delivered his first hukamnama.

> "In my mind is Thy desire, oh Lord, how am I to see Thee?
> They alone who love Thee know how much is my desire for Thee.
> I am a sacrifice unto the Guru who united me, the separated one, to Thee, my Creator."

All, including Mohan, recognized that Guru Amar Das had made a wise choice in passing the light of Guru Nanak to Guru Ram Das. It was now mid-September, 1574 CE.

* * *

That evening Guru Amar Das sat quietly in his house. All his family were around him: his two sons with their wives, his two daughters with their husbands, including the new guru, and his wife and grandchildren.

"My dear ones," Guru Amar Das spoke softly, sounding his full ninety-three years, "I am happy to tell you that the time has come for me to go home. Few people have had the honor that has been bestowed upon me. Fewer still have had the blessing to leave such an honorable legacy. I ask that each of you carry on the mission that was started by Guru Nanak and which we have furthered together here. In two days is the full moon. My soul will drop this old body and I will join my guru." He paused to let the impact of what he was saying sink in. The tears in the eyes of his daughters and his sons openly displayed their grief.

"Listen to me," he continued, "there shall be no mourning at the time of my death and no useless ceremonies and rituals." His voice was firm.

"I have directed that a proper bed be constructed for me. I will rest upon it and enjoy the company of the congregation until the correct time when I will leave my body. After my death," he said, looking at Guru Ram Das, "you will erect the funeral pyre and place this brittle body upon it. It should burn quickly for it is dry now. Recite the hymns of the guru, speak with each other about them, and let there be no mourning. I am not unhappy, so why should you be? For seventeen days after my passing, let there be continuous chanting of *Sat Nam Wahe Guru* along with the hymns of the gurus, which Mohan has recorded." He paused again, regarding his family.

"Rama, Mohan, Mohari, see that a magnificent langar is prepared. It should be more rich and varied than the langar for a wedding. Let everyone be fed to their capacity, then whatever is left, have them take it home. Any other leftovers should be put out for the birds and animals. Will you promise me this?"

Mohan, Mohari, and Rama nodded silently.

He looked again at Guru Ram Das. "You will miss me," he said. "Believe me, I know this pain. It will strike you deep, like a lance through your heart. You must not give in to it. Your Sikhs need you and you cannot desert them. Keep your grief private and remain with the congregation. They will comfort you. You will want to hide yourself away. Trust me, Guruji, the congregation will be your comfort and salvation during your grief, and it is in the congregation that you will find me." Guru Ram Das nodded, but did not speak. He already felt the loss of his guru.

"Now go and prepare," he said, "and remember, you are preparing for a celebration! I have done a good job and that should be celebrated. No more tears! No mourning! Mohan! See to the langar, it must be perfect. You have two days!" He looked at Guru Ram Das, "You stay with me awhile, I'd like to talk with you."

Everyone left and there was silence in the room. Guru Amar Das sat with his protégé for a long time, talking with him about the future and his role as guru.

"After I am gone, you must return to Guru's Chaak. Complete the work you started there. For this you will be remembered and for this, the world will worship you. It is for this purpose that you were born and the guruship bestowed upon you."

Two days later, the entire congregation gathered in front of the baoli before sunrise. The bed that had been prepared for Guru Amar Das was placed in front. He came down from his house, escorted by Guru Ram Das and his two sons. He sat cross-legged upon it, smiling while the congregation recited the guru's hymns. He then began to chant, his voice strong and steady. Word had spread quickly of the guru's imminent passing, and thousands of people were in the congregation that day. Guru Ram Das stood beside his guru, slowly fanning him as he had done for the past twenty-two years. People approached the guru to touch his feet, and he blessed all who came. Many were crying.

"Do not mourn for me," he directed, "for I am happy and so you should be. As I was, Guru Ram Das is. You have lost nothing."

Still, there were tears. The chanting continued, and despite the sadness of many, it was a deeply peaceful and comfortable environment. Eventually, Guru Amar Das turned to Guru Ram Das. "My time has come," he said.

He sat up, facing the congregation, and raised his hands in a final benediction. His face was radiant, his eyes full of love and wet with tears. He turned toward Guru Ram Das and extended his long arms in the direction of the guru's feet. Smiling serenely, he lay back on the bed and covered himself with a sheet. Within a few moments, his breathing stopped and his divine soul sprung from the body that had held it for so many years.

I was very happy to have him with Me once again. It always makes Me happy when a soul returns to Me, and it brings special joy when that soul has accomplished something extraordinary. All souls have a purpose. All souls are equal. Yet some souls evolve over time and remind Me of My own beauty. They help to ease My loneliness.

That night, the guru's body was taken and bathed in yogurt then wrapped in a white sheet. The next morning a large pyre of sandalwood was constructed, and Guru Ram Das, Mohan, Mohari, and Rama reverently placed the guru's body upon it. Together, they each took a torch and touched it to the kindling. The pyre quickly caught flame and burned hot and bright.

As Guru Amar Das had directed, the enormous langar was served for the next three days. The remains were put out for the birds and animals. The chanting continued and the sense of sadness gave way to a sense of festivity, and before long, people were smiling and laughing.

NINETEEN

THE CHANTING CONTINUED UNBROKEN FOR the next seventeen days, according to the instructions of Guru Amar Das. On the seventeenth day, there was a final memorial ceremony, then life in Goindwal settled down to a kind of normalcy, though many missed the cheerful presence of the white-bearded guru.

Guru Ram Das was inconsolable with grief, yet he attended the durbar daily, received visitors and those seeking his assistance, and each night he wrote his own hymns and explanations about the realm of consciousness. Eventually though, the pain and shock of separation from his guru overtook him, and he locked himself in his chambers to meditate. He did not disobey his guru's instructions, for each morning he came down and presided at the durbar, though he never uttered a word other than the daily hukamnama. Then in silence he would return to his seclusion. After seven days, Baba Buddha and Mohan grew concerned.

"I am getting too old to track down another guru," said Baba Buddha. "Today he is here in Goindwal, but I don't want to take a chance on tomorrow."

Baba Buddha asked the guru if he and Mohan could speak with him. Though Guru Ram Das did not answer, they followed him to his apartments and closed the door.

"Oh, Guruji," said Baba Buddha tenderly, yet firmly, "you are the fourth guru I have served, the next link in the Golden Chain." He paused to let his words sink in.

"I have deep compassion for you. This is not a simple transition and you have no one that you can confide in." Guru Ram Das remained silent, considering Baba Buddha's words. "However, the Akal Purkh has bestowed the guruship upon your humble head. I know that you never wanted it, but it is your destiny and is upon you now. You have a great responsibility, and thousands of people are looking to you for guidance, for inspiration and," he paused and inhaled deeply, clearly showing his own grief, "and . . . for solace." Though he didn't speak, the face of Guru Ram Das showed that he understood the message.

Baba Buddha stood before the guru with folded hands and bowed his head. "Please, Guruji, don't surrender to your grief. Instead, embrace your duty. Fill that emptiness in your heart with the prayers of your Sikhs. Guru Amar Das attached us to you, as Guru Angad attached us to him. We need you here and now. Let go of your grief. It has no place here. Please, find your consolation and joy in the congregation."

Baba Buddha's arguments were irrefutable, and Guru Ram Das was comforted and reassured by the presence of Mohan.

"Thank you, Babaji," he said quietly. "You are wise and your kind words and persuasive arguments make us happy. The time has come for us all to release our grief."

Baba Buddha was relieved and felt grateful that he didn't have to organize a search for another guru. The next day Guru Ram Das spoke in the durbar and appeared to be his usual cheerful self.

He contemplated the directive given by Guru Amar Das to return to Guru's Chaak and establish a city there. He discussed the idea with Baba Buddha, Mohan, and Mohari, and they encouraged him to return, believing that the change would do them all good. A return mission was organized, and Guru Ram Das, along with his brothers-in-law and Baba Buddha, returned to the earthworks. The monsoons had come during his absence, and some of the foundations were eroded, causing the adjacent excavation work to collapse. Yet the original pond was intact and shimmered in the sunlight under the branches of the beri tree.

It was clear to him that masses of people would come to Guru's Chaak to work on the excavation as they had on the baoli. He knew that as the project proceeded and word spread that the guru was now at this place and no longer at Goindwal, thousands would come to bathe in the healing water and have his blessings and guidance.

Accordingly, his first priority was to establish a kitchen and rest houses so the workers and pilgrims could be fed and have a place to rest. Along with this, work began on a residence for the guru and his family. In his life as Bhai Jetha, he was responsible for the guru's kitchen and his visitors. Now as Guru Ram Das he considered those responsibilities to still be his. It never occurred to him that sitting upon the seat of the guru relieved him of any of his previous responsibilities. Eventually he sent for his family and assigned his eldest son, Prithi Chand, the responsibility of looking after the visitors and the kitchen. When he was satisfied that those priorities were covered, Guru Ram Das turned his attention to excavating the tank.

Bhai Jetha had come from the most humble of beginnings, and Guru Ram Das never lost touch with that. He made no pretense, recalling his life on the dirty and dangerous streets of Lahore. He loved his Sikhs and understood their longings and distresses intimately. Often he went to the kitchen and helped with the food preparation or served the langar himself. Then late at night, as the star-filled hemisphere of the sky rotated overhead, he retired to his rooms where he meditated and wrote his hymns until the early morning hours.

Guru Ram Das was most excited about the excavation of the new tank. It was a colossal project, requiring that massive amounts of earth be excavated and moved. The original pond that We created in the Treta Yuga was to be enlarged to create an enormous tank, which would be fed by the vibrant waters of that sacred spring. Every day the guru went to the site himself and, as with the baoli, swung pick and shovel and carried baskets of mud and rocks on his head. When other responsibilities called for his attention, he sat in the shade of the beri tree and managed the accounts and administrative aspects of the guruship, all while supervising the excavation. Being back at the place he loved and in the water of the pool every day strengthened his constitution.

In a relatively brief period of time, an active village grew up around Guru Ram Das, and people began calling it Ram Das Pur. Word spread that the guru of the Sikhs presided at the new village and hundreds of pilgrims came daily to have his blessing and, as the news spread, to bathe in the water of the expanding pool.

Every night a kind and simple man went to the different rest houses to wash the feet of the arriving pilgrims and see to their needs. The next morning people were surprised when they discovered that Guru Ram Das was the same man who had washed their feet and cared for them the night before. Even as guru he got down into the dirt and mud of the excavation and the soot of the kitchen to ensure that his Sikhs were taken care of.

After Guru Amar Das had been appointed guru, he made a pilgrimage to the village of Barath to ask the blessings of Baba Siri Chand, the firstborn son of Guru Nanak. This greatest of yogis was now well past one hundred years old, and Guru Ram Das longed to see him.

He sent a courier to Barath advising that he would like to visit the son of Nanak and gave an approximate date when he would arrive. The response was positive, so the guru organized his entourage and they made the trek to Barath.

Baba Siri Chand was truly his father's son. He had such power that his body had not aged beyond sixteen years, though at this time he was more than one hundred. While the baba was alive, no practitioner of black tantra or black magic could use that power and because he lived to 142 years, he outlived those dark masters. He was so revered for his compassion and wisdom that even the gurus went to him for advice.

The meditations of Baba Siri Chand were powerful and often lasted for days, sometimes for weeks, and at those times all activity around him was suspended. The devotees who served him, or those who came to him for his darshan, waited reverently at a respectable distance until he was again present in his body.

When Guru Ram Das arrived at Barath, Baba Siri Chand was in such a deep meditation that he didn't come out of it for two and a half days. So the party waited patiently. They were in high spirits and laughed and told stories. Even the guru pulled out a few jokes.

After he had recovered from his ecstasy, the great yogi came himself to greet Guru Ram Das. When he saw Baba Siri Chand approaching, the guru rose and went to meet him. As they approached each other, the baba evaluated Guru Ram Das and was very pleased with what he saw. He opened his arms and they embraced affectionately. He held Guru Ram Das at arm's length, hands on his shoulders, and regarded his face for a long time.

"You remind me of my father!" the baba exclaimed. "You have his light. You have his fire in your eyes. Even your touch is the same as his." He studied Guru Ram Das up and down, smiling with the greatest pleasure. His smile and laugh were infectious. "The only difference, Guruji, is that you have grown such a long beard. Why is that?"

"For no other reason than to wipe the dust from the feet of one so great as you." Then Guru Ram Das knelt down and, taking his long beard in hand, began to wipe the feet of Baba Siri Chand, who took the arm of the guru and made him to stand up.

"In every way you are the image of my father!" His smile was radiant, beaming. "When I see the reflection of Guru Nanak in your face and witness the deep and sincere humility you have demonstrated, it makes me very proud and most happy that you sit in his place."

"I and my Sikhs shall always be at your service," the guru said with a broad smile.

Throughout the day, they sat together and talked at length about the mission that was begun by Guru Nanak, all that had been accomplished by Guru Angad and Guru Amar Das, and what lay ahead for Guru Ram Das.

"As you know we are excavating a sarovar that will be filled with the sacred water."

"I have heard," said Baba Siri Chand reflectively. "I know the place. The water waits for you. Do you understand it?"

"Yes," the guru replied directly.

"She'll come soon." His voice was soft but absolute as thunder.

"We will be ready for her."

They were silent in mutual contemplation for some time, then Guru Ram Das spoke, "A village is growing up there and it will thrive. Many people are coming, building homes and establishing commerce."

"How is it known?"

"We have been calling it Guru Ka Chaak, though many people refer to it as Ram Das Pur. It is not my place and I prefer that it not carry my name. Do you have a suggestion, Babaji?"

Baba Siri Chand closed his eyes and listened to the sound current. "Amritsar," he said matter-of-factly, "call it Amritsar."

"Amritsar," whispered the guru. "The tank of nectar."

Guru Ram Das and Baba Siri Chand enjoyed each other's company several days more, but the duties of the guru were pressing. When it could be put off no longer, Guru Ram Das organized the return to Amritsar. The guru and Baba Siri Chand embraced one final time. He thanked Babaji for seeing him, for inspiring him, and for giving the name of the new city. Then the guru and his staff joyfully returned to Amritsar.

Upon his return, he set about the work of the city and of the excavation of the tank with renewed vigor. In April at the Baisakhi celebration in Goindwal, Guru Ram Das made an announcement.

"My siblings of destiny," he said smiling, "I have the honor to invite you to join me in two months time for the dedication of the holy city of Amritsar. This will be a joyful and historic celebration. Then next year, we will hold the Baisakhi celebration there. Please spread the word to all you meet. Bring your families and friends, but most especially, bring your enemies that they may become your friends."

TWENTY

"Punditji," Rajni asked one day, "why do bad things happen to people?"

"Bad from whose perspective?" he replied.

"Well, from the person who is suffering."

"Why do they suffer?" Punditji asked.

"Because something bad happened to them."

"Like what?"

"Well, like a broken heart, or disappointment, starvation, or torture or . . ." She paused a long time. "Like leprosy."

Punditji stared at Rajni without speaking. He drew his long deep breath then sighed through his nose.

"Dearest Rajni, there is no good or bad, only thinking makes it so. If all things come from God and all things go to God, then so it is with suffering. Whatever causes you pain comes from God, so give it back to Him."

"How, Punditji? I see the people in the streets, crawling around with no arms or legs, I see them begging. They don't appear to be happy. When there is no food in your stomach and you are cold and sick, how can you think that away? How do you give your pain or hunger to God?" Her voice was demanding with that tinge of arrogance creeping in.

When Hymayun was overthrown as emperor by Sher Shah in 1540, he waged a fifteen-year campaign to regain his throne. Still a young man, Punditji served Hymayun's cause as a spy. He was captured by Sher Shah's agents and imprisoned and tortured regularly for two years. He escaped by killing one of his torturers and crippling the other for life. The fighting was ruthless on both sides, but Hymayun prevailed and shortly before his death regained the throne. Akbar, his thirteen-year-old son, was installed as emperor.

During the time that Punditji was in prison, he thought that I had abandoned him. He was still a young man then, and the brutal torture almost killed him. Yet he remembered something that Guru Nanak had told him: if you are not satisfied with your life, then complain to Me. After all, I gave you the problem and only I can remove it. Punditji meditated on that and understood that all things come from Me. While the torture did not end right away, his state of mind changed and the torture became somehow less painful and debilitating. Eventually, he developed a powerful mental resolve to survive, and when the opportunity presented itself, he made his move and was able to escape. He made a pilgrimage to the Ganges at Hardwar where he remained for eleven years, meditating, chanting, and praying until that memory was gone from his tissues.

Because people don't understand Me, it is impossible to understand what I do or the purpose and intent of it, especially where human suffering is concerned. I don't punish, I don't condemn, and I bear no malice. After all, I created everything and every soul. Each soul is precious to Me, but only I know why I created that soul and what each soul's purpose is. When it is only viewed from the human perspective, which is exceedingly limited, it is impossible to understand. I love My vastness. I love that all things, the known and unknown, are found in Me. I feel all pain. I hear all cries. I answer all prayers, though not everyone understands My answers.

"Precious one, God sends us problems to challenge us and make us grow. When we are in pain, when things aren't going the way we want, we always remember God and call on Him to help us, or complain to Him that He is not doing His job. Yet when we are in pleasure, it is easy to forget God because the ego has room to inflate. Under the pressure of God's tests, however, the ego has to submit consciously to His will. When we use difficult situations to grow, then the need for the difficulty ends and circumstances change. When people believe that they are victims and that things will never change for them, they don't."

"But," asked Rajni, "do bad things happen because of bad karma or bad thoughts?"

"Remember, God is neutral and doesn't understand words. He only understands the attention you pay to him. You can curse God or pray to Him: either way you are giving Him attention and recognizing His presence. When we fail to recognize God's presence in whatever happens or whatever comes to us, then it is bad for us because we will continue to relive those experiences until we learn to recognize that Akal Purkh is the doer of all. But sometimes," said Punditji reflectively, "circumstances occur so that a sacrifice can be made for the betterment of all things.

"Karma is neither good nor bad, it is only the reaction of the Universe to the actions we have taken. There is no emotion behind karma, for we create it ourselves by the thought and intent behind our actions. That determines what karma will be incurred.

"Karma is the reaction to one's actions, right? Well, thoughts are actions, and those actions can become your reality. It is not the karma that we want to avoid, because there are ways to find protection from it. What has to change are the *sanskaras*, the habit patterns in the psyche of the soul that cause the soul to repeat the same actions and make the same mistakes lifetime after lifetime."

Punditji paused and Rajni reflected on what he had said. "But when things . . . ."

"Look," said Punditji, "we want to give a value to everything. The mind generates thousands of thoughts per wink of the eye. Our conscious mind tries to catch those thoughts and give them an identity, then value them as good or bad. Once the mind has identified and valued a concept, it is stuck there in the psyche and the psyche will find a way to make that concept the reality. Listen, little jewel, the course of life is never straight. There are twists and turns, highs and lows, and they cannot be avoided. The only thing we truly have control over is our own mind and our own behavior. God gave us our minds so that we can know Him and feel connected to Him."

He paused again and gazed at Rajni for a long time. "Listen to me," he said to her, looking deep into her eyes, "you have a great destiny ahead of you with enormous challenge and great triumph. The challenges help us to remember God. The triumphs are so we can feel gratitude. Whatever comes for you, accept it with gratitude and know that it has come from God, not from your father or circumstances. Tragedy can become triumph if we cut through it with gratitude and surrender to His will. Whatever comes for you," he closed his eyes, "know that it will pass and you will be victorious."

"How can we be protected from our karma?" asked Rajni.

"Through dharma, the path of spiritual duty," laughed Punditji.

"And how can we change our sanskaras and the psyche of the soul?"

"The best and most effective way," Punditji looked at Rajni and paused for a long time then inhaled deeply and let it out slowly through his nose, "is to recite the beautiful names of God. That will change the frequency of your vibration, which will in turn change your habits of behavior."

"There are many Names of God. You have taught me *Rama, Hari, Aum, Om Nama Narayana, Om Nama Shivaya,* and all the others. Is there one that is best? I am just a young girl, but I feel that there is a great weight on me, Punditji. Is there a mantra I can chant or a name I can recite to make that feeling go away?"

Punditji stared at Rajni. "You have never told me this before. Why haven't you spoken of it?"

"Well, it is a feeling that has been growing in me. I can't explain it, but it won't leave me. Sometimes I wake up at night crying and I don't know why. I mean, I don't feel sad. My life is good. But you know," she paused, "when I go out or look out the window and see people suffering, I feel like crying. I mean, I don't want to bear their suffering on my own back so they can be relieved, but I don't like to see people suffer. I don't know how to explain it, I just feel that I should be able to ease their pain, yet I feel helpless because I also feel repulsed by them. They are so dirty and lowborn. Do you know what I mean?"

Punditji placed his hand under her chin and lifted her face to his. He looked deep into her dark, oval eyes, and her breathing slowed.

"Blessed girl, listen to me now," he whispered to her, "I was sent here to teach you. You will ease the suffering of the world. In fact, you will carry it on your own back."

Rajni jerked away from Punditji, but his voice was firm and steady. He placed his hand on her shoulder and she dropped her head, but remained with her back turned to her pundit.

"I have taught you what your father wanted me to teach you, but mostly I have taught you what you need to know to fulfill your destiny. Now listen to me carefully." And he bent down and whispered in her left ear, "*Wahe Guru, Wahe Guru, Wahe Guru, Wahe Guru, Wahe Guru, Wahe Guru, Wahe Guru, Wahe Guru.*" He paused and looked at her. "Recite that, it will bring you to the lotus feet of God. Remember it when you are in need."

Rajni turned slowly toward Punditji. "How should I do it?"

Punditji took her hands and placed the palms together at the center of her chest in a position of prayer. "With your hands in this *mudra*, inhale through your nose and with a full breath, recite *Wahe Guru* eight times. It will change you and protect you and bring you to your destiny. You won't find it in the Vedas, yet believe that what I tell you now is true."

"Punditji, why do I feel afraid?"

"Because you fear the unknown and do not know what God wants to give you. Remember, child, God gives the greatest tests to the ones he loves the most. When it comes for you, thank him for it."

"When I get married, will you still be my pundit?" she asked sweetly.

"Dearest Rajni, you are grown up, more than you realize. We'll see what happens after you are married. Know this though: God Himself is bound by the power of love and must answer to the prayer of anyone who prays to Him from their heart."

* * *

Rajni was now the only unmarried daughter of Duni Chand. She was fourteen and knew that her time was approaching. She thought about what married life would be like, life without her Punditji around. Already Duni Chand had reduced the amount of time he allowed Rajni to spend with Punditji, claiming that she had learned all that she needed to know.

She was lonely and restless in the big house with only her parents and the servants around. The presence of her overbearing father was irritating her, not only with how he obtrusively interacted with her, but also in the way that he went about the business of being the raja. She had seen him forcing people to pay their taxes and was ruthless and brutal in his methods, which distressed Rajni. He seemed obsessed with making more money and elevating his status even higher. He was relentlessly aggressive and forceful in his business dealings and seemed to be angry much of the time. He often pressed her about what she had learned from Punditji, or asked her other silly questions in the same way that he interrogated tax evaders. She continually felt that she was under his relentless scrutiny. Rebelliousness and anger grew inside her.

On two occasions he had arranged for families of eligible boys to come and meet Rajni. Each time Rajni's behavior was insulting to the families, and they withdrew their interest, causing Duni Chand considerable embarrassment and Mataji considerable concern. Had they raised a daughter so arrogant that no family would find her acceptable?

Duni Chand's favorite past time was playing chess. He was sometimes obsessed with it and could carry on a game for days. He loved the strategy, the lure, and the attack, but most of all he loved to win. Winning for Duni Chand was everything, and though he never cheated, he was a very aggressive and ruthless player. If the game wasn't going well for him, or on the rare occasion when he did lose, he could be in a foul mood for days, relentlessly seeking a rematch with the victor. Sometimes, Rajni felt that he played with people the way he played chess; that he viewed those around him as pieces on the chessboard, to move or capture at will. Lately, she felt like the opposing queen who had lost her pawns, knights, and rooks. Her only protection was her bishop, Punditji, and Duni Chand was making it increasingly difficult for him to be near Rajni.

She was grateful that for some time he had not challenged her with the question of who took care of her and gave her everything. Since she no longer had her sisters around to cover her, she was concerned about a direct confrontation with Duni Chand. She had an escalating disdain for Duni Chand and the life she was living, yet she also felt a similar disdain for the people of Patti. She was maturing quickly now, and in her adolescent angst, she found little satisfaction with her life.

She had hopes for the future and always imagined herself in beautiful surroundings. However, her deep spiritual nature always pulled her focus away from the idea of an ordinary married life, like that of her sisters. She thought that each of her sisters had wonderful husbands, but that kind of life somehow did not seem to be a reality for her. In fact, it concerned her. While she believed it to be unavoidable, she did not relish the idea of marriage. She did not care much for the eligible boys she knew and did not want to be forced into marriage, especially with someone who was unlikely to be her equal intellectually or spiritually.

Like many teens throughout time, she struggled in the doldrums between being a girl and being a woman. Hormonal fireworks and the process of maturing worked on her in deep and mysterious ways. She had days of depression and days of optimism, but nothing stable. Her mind and body were changing and she struggled to find balance. Increasingly she felt isolated and dissatisfied with most things in her life. She associated with other girls in the village, but Duni Chand preferred that she only associate with girls from those families of which he approved. She took walks around the gardens of her ancestral estate, and spent long hours alone at Duni Chand's formal gardens, lost in her daydreams and deep contemplation.

Sitting under the mango trees in one of Duni Chand's gardens, Rajni had spent the afternoon with Punditji. It had been nearly a month since their last meeting. Rajni had pouted and complained to Duni Chand for ten days until he finally relented and allowed Punditji to come for an afternoon.

"I've missed you, Punditji. Promise you will never leave me."

"All things will leave you, dear one. The only thing that remains is your meditation. Keep it with you always as I taught you, *Wahe Guru, Wahe Guru, Wahe Guru.* Then . . ." He paused. "You won't need me. I wish I had learned that when I was your age. Fortunately, I learned from my mistakes. Now I pray that I have taught you well enough that you won't make those same mistakes yourself. Learn from me and your path will become clear."

They were silent as a peacock called *aweeoo, aweeoo, aweeoo.* It was a warm afternoon, and the shade of the mango trees was soothing.

"But I don't like that meditation. It is boring."

"Tell me what you feel when you do it."

"I feel angry and frustrated. I feel like my mind is digesting itself."

Punditji laughed his hearty laugh, which confused Rajni. "Then, dearest Rajni, it is working beautifully."

Rajni smiled quizzically at him.

"Just continue to practice it," he laughed. "You will see for yourself what happens."

"Punditji, at Raveena's wedding,"—Raveena was her next eldest sister—"some people came who follow the dharma of Jesu. They told me that there is the lord of the demons called Satan, who tries to get control of our souls so that we can't reincarnate. Jesu is their avatar, but I think he must be an incarnation of Vishnu. He lets his devotees drink his blood and when they do, it makes them more powerful and frightens the demon Satan when he sees them drinking it."

"I have heard of this Jesu," said Punditji reflectively. "He is buried in Kashmir. Islam is related to this dharma."

"They invited me to drink blood with them, but I refused. Are they telling the truth?"

Punditji laughed again. He was in an especially cheerful mood. "Dearest Rajni, there are as many paths to the Akal Purkh as there are souls to walk them. There is no right or wrong way. The Universe is infinite. God gives us many ways to go so that we can enjoy free will. We move according to the will of God, and it is only by our own actions that we draw near Him or drift away from him. I know little of this dharma, but I do know that any dharma you follow, if you do so with a sincere heart and true devotion, will bring you to the heart of the One who created you. When you recite His name with love and devotion, He must respond and take you into His arms."

"I love you, Punditji," and she hugged him.

TWENTY-ONE

Each year after the monsoons, the daughters of Duni Chand came to their ancestral home and spent a month together without their husbands. It was a mostly happy time for all because the husbands did not especially like Duni Chand and much preferred that their wives go home rather than have Duni Chand come for a visit. The sisters liked it because it was a break from their home lives and gave them the opportunity to be together again.

Duni Chand especially liked it because it gave him and his wife more opportunity to meddle in the lives of their daughters. He missed the noise and the attention that came with his daughters. The truth is, Duni Chand was also feeling lonely. He had built his whole life around his daughters and was a devoted family man. Now that all but Rajni were married, he felt as empty as his beautiful palace. Yet he could not leave his daughters alone. He was always meddling in their lives or berating the husbands for not taking proper care of his precious daughters.

He used any excuse to get involved with them because he missed them severely. Even more than Rajni, Duni Chand looked forward to the time when they came home each year. He wanted things to be like they were when his daughters were young girls, but it would never be like that again, and old Duni Chand could not accept it.

Duni Chand was a proud man, mostly because he was raised to be so, but partially because he could not fully understand how he could have risen so high in the world and have so much wealth and power. Whenever that question came into his mind, which wasn't often, he justified himself to himself by declaring that he was a Brahmin and it was his birthright. That usually satisfied him, and he was never interested in looking deeper. As far as he was concerned, it was a mystery without clues that was better left unsolved.

After all, he often mused to himself, *I wouldn't be here if it wasn't my karma to be here, and since I am here and have all this power and money and seven beautiful daughters, I must be a great man. People respect me, many are afraid of me, and my daughters praise me because I, Sri Duni Chand, give them everything! I am a Brahmin and a devout Hindu, and my good karma has brought all this to me.*

The monsoons came and passed, and as summer neared its end, Duni Chand's daughters came home. He hugged each of them and complained about their useless husbands while his wife complained that they were not producing babies fast enough. And they both complained that their daughters looked undernourished and overworked. Of course, the parents then had their daughters wait on them hand and foot, claiming that they had cared for them when they were young and now they should care for them in their old age.

The girls went about it all with amusement. They divided themselves between their parents and massaged them, cooked for them, served them tea, and took their turns losing to Duni Chand at chess. That usually kept Duni Chand and Mataji quiet for a while. Then the girls would get together to gossip and giggle, which they did at every opportunity. They saved their serious conversations for when they went to Duni Chand's formal gardens to bathe and enjoy the shade and colors of the trees and flowers.

Some distance from the village, near the River Satluj, Duni Chand had built enclosed formal gardens with bathing pools and fountains fed from the river. It was an engineering and horticultural accomplishment. Water was diverted from the Satluj along a channel to Duni Chand's gardens. It irrigated the gardens and flowed into several fountains through the bathing pools into several other fountains and then back into the channel, which then flowed back to the Satluj. This was where the girls spent the long humid afternoons of August and September. Pipal, banyan, mango, locust, and jacaranda trees provided deep shade, and the gardens were alive with colors and fragrances from the flowers and aromatic plants that grew there. During these languid afternoons where they were attended to by their servants, the seven sisters talked and sang, played chess, teased each other, and laughed until their sides hurt. These were some of Rajni's happiest times.

At those times, the sisters talked about their husbands or their babies or their parents. Rajni learned from her sisters about the challenges of married life. Her sisters talked about their husbands and the demands they placed on them, about the pain of childbirth, and the joy and challenge of being mothers. They exchanged stories about how they dealt with the various emotional issues of their husbands and how they tried to get their husbands to respond to them in the ways they wanted. Rajni sat and listened, rapt with wonder and confusion. The words of Punditji rang in her head as she imagined herself faced with similar situations.

They talked about intimacy with their husbands, which caused them all to giggle and tease each other. That talk made Rajni feel somewhat out of place and embarrassed since she had no experience in such matters. It was the one thing that Punditji was reluctant to discuss with her and told Rajni that it would be inappropriate for him to teach her about such things.

He simply told her, "You are sacred and your body is the temple where that sacredness is worshipped. Let no one enter in who will not honor and protect that sacredness with absolute devotion."

The subject never came up again. Normally, such matters were reserved for mothers to teach their daughters before their weddings. Now with six married sisters, Rajni was learning more than her mother and Punditji combined could have taught her.

"Did Mataji and your pundits teach you how to do all those things?" she shyly asked her sisters when they were in the safety of the bathing pool.

They laughed, "No, baby sister, we learned out of necessity. We learned by doing and constantly working at it. Remember, it is also a challenge for our husbands. They are learning too. That is what makes it interesting."

Rajni hoped that the day of her marriage was still far off.

Rajni's sisters were happy with their marriages and mostly thought their husbands were good men who cared for them well. They talked about the difficulties they had in the beginning and how their relationships with their husbands evolved. Rajni was now an aunt with six nieces and eight nephews. Duni Chand and Mataji spent the time when their daughters were out to dote on their grandchildren with more lavish treatment than they ever gave their own daughters.

"How are they doing?" Ravi, Rajni's third sister asked as they sat together in the bathing pool, listening to the water flow through it.

"He is more irritable now that the house is empty. He misses you and doesn't like living in an empty house. He always asks me silly questions and wants to know what Punditji is teaching me."

"How is your Punditji?" asked Navleen, her fifth sister.

"He is wonderful!" she said with adoration in her voice. "Unfortunately, Papaji doesn't permit me to spend much time with him anymore. He says that I have learned all I need to know from him. I still see him a few times a month but not every day like before. I think he is a little jealous of my admiration for Punditji."

"What has he taught you?" Saraswati, her fourth sister asked.

"The usual things from the Vedas and how to participate in a puja and the protocol of the kitchen," she said somewhat nonchalantly. "What I like most, though, is the way he engages me in debate and pushes me to reason. He is very smart and knows everything."

"Hey, little sister," her first sister said. After six years of marriage and three children, Gita had gained weight and was beginning to resemble her mother at the tender age of twenty-one. "Be careful. He is going to marry you off this year, and you will be separated from your pundit. Papaji doesn't like him and thinks he has taught you inappropriate things. I don't know what he taught you, but one thing I do know is that you are different from the rest of us. You think differently, and I believe that your life will be different."

Her second sister, Suryia, joined in, "Papaji has complained to me that he thinks you have no gratitude for all he has done for us. He is never satisfied with your answers when he asks us that stupid question. Someday, he is going to confront you directly, and you won't be able to escape with a vague answer. What will you do then?"

Rajni looked at her sisters. "I believe that all things come from God, and back to Him all things return. Parents, husbands, and children are only vehicles to fulfill whatever the will of God is. Papaji has been a channel for God's blessings to us and God has been merciful to him and to us. But"—she paused and seemed very far away while the sound of running water filled the air—"it is God who is the Doer. Don't get me wrong, I love our parents, and I am deeply grateful for all that we have, but God has given it to us. In fact, it is God who gave us our parents. Why can't he accept that? I don't deny his goodness, but I can't give him the credit for something he hasn't done."

"Baby sister," Raveena said pleadingly, "please try to humor him. If you don't, he will become very upset and take it out on you. You know he doesn't have a lot of depth, but he is a good man. Can't you just make him happy?"

"His happiness or sadness is not up to me, it is in his own heart and mind. If he chooses to be unhappy, what can I do? Should I not tell the truth?"

"Can't you just bend the truth a little, be a little less arrogant and a little less blunt?"

"But I know I am right and he needs to hear it," she said flatly as her mind drifted with the sounds of the water and the birds.

"It will make no difference," said Gita. "Why is being right so important? You won't change his ways. All you will do is make him angry."

All the sisters were quiet for some time, lost in their own reflections. Silently, a signal passed between them, and they stepped from the water, dried themselves, and prepared for the walk home. It had been an enjoyable time in the warm sun of late summer. The bond between the sisters grew stronger as they grew older, and days like this were precious to them. They felt concern for Rajni, like she was standing on a precipice about to fall and they were too far away to catch her.

Rajni was feeling very far away and rather oddly detached from her sisters, her parents, and her life as she knew it. She knew a confrontation with her father was coming, and she debated with herself whether to humor him or speak her mind. The idea of defying her father and telling him that God provides everything and parents are only the channel was exhilarating, believing from her teenage perspective that such a retort would change her father for the better.

She remembered an incident that occurred when she was ten. Duni Chand had taken his family on a pilgrimage to Hardwar to have his name inscribed on the family rolls that are kept there. They also went to Rishikesh, and Rajni went with her sisters to a place in the Ganges to bathe in the river. Nearby were high rocks, and a group of boys were jumping from them into the water, which got Rajni excited. When the boys left, she persuaded Ravi to go with her to the rocks. She stood at the edge of the highest rock, holding Ravi's hand as she looked down at the water nearly four meters below her. Then without a word, she let go of her sister's hand and leapt out into the air.

Such a rush of freedom and excitement! The screams of her sisters were muted by the rushing river below and by the exhilaration in her mind. When she hit the water, she let herself go deep, all the way to the bottom, then pushed herself to the surface with her feet. She was oblivious to everything and everyone around her, though her terrified sisters were screaming hysterically. She let the current carry her to some rocks a little further downstream, where she pulled herself out of the water and lay in the sun on the warm rocks.

Her poor sisters thought she was dead or unconscious because she just lay there and didn't move for more than ten minutes, which was the amount of time it took six panicked and hysterical girls to run to the rocks and dog-paddle across the Ganges to where she was. One look at the serene smile on her radiant face told them that Rajni was safe. That moment was very special to her. She felt that she had placed herself in My hands and leapt out on the faith that I would catch her. And I did catch her in My big, wet river. I love all beings, all My creations, equally. Still, there was something about this girl that elevated and comforted Me.

Now, Rajni felt like she was standing on that rock again. She had a sense that everything in her life had brought her to this moment. She felt giddy and excited for no apparent reason. Accompanying her sense of excitement was also a deep fear of the unknown. Something in her stirred. Something in her looked down from those rocks into the eternally flowing Ganges of her soul, and she knew that the time had come for her to let go and take the plunge.

The truth was that I had caught her in My eternal river, had surrounded her with the waters of My love, and she was seeking comfort and refuge upon Me. While in her heart she believed that I would catch her again, in her head was the undefined fear that made her reluctant to let go. Yet she knew there was only one response she could give her father, and she fully understood that it would bring his wrath. In anticipation of that moment, Rajni felt elation and giggled to herself quietly.

She walked with her sisters, and they began to sing a traditional Punjabi song that girls sing in anticipation of their wedding, one about the intricate mendhi designs etched with henna on the hands of the bride. The early afternoon was beautiful, still temperate before the heat of the late afternoon set in. It was always a joy for the seven sisters to be together, but this time seemed especially precious. Gita put her arm around Rajni as they walked and chanted. The blue parandees Rajni had braided into her hair had tiny bells at the end, which tinkled as she walked. It was a blissfully happy moment for her that passed much too quickly. In the months ahead, she would look back on that day and long for that moment.

The seven beautiful sisters continued to sing as they walked through with their long, dark braids flowing over their shoulders and down their backs. They wore their chunis over their heads with the ends thrown back over their shoulders. Their servants, three bodyguards, and a large carriage in case they preferred to ride, followed them as they walked.

As they neared the red sandstone palace of Duni Chand, Rajni heard voices singing. The sound of the music caught her attention, and she stopped her own singing to listen. Without realizing it, she drifted away from her sisters and slowly gravitated toward a group of people she did not recognize. Sitting in a small garden under a cluster of banyan trees, two men were playing *sarangis*, stringed instruments played with a bow. One man was playing *tablas,* the tunable hand drums that keep the rhythm to classical Indian music. A fourth was singing. There was a small group around them listening in deep meditative worship.

Getting closer, she could understand the words they were singing:

"Oh Nanak, He who created the creatures takes care of them all.
The Creator who created the Creation also takes care of it."

And there, sitting with this group of saintly people, was Rajni's Punditji.

"Little sister!" Saraswati called to her. "Come, it is getting late, and Papaji will be angry."

Rajni did not respond but moved closer to the group, as though in a trance.

"Baby sister!" called Gita. "Come now!"

Rajni slowly faced her sisters as though turned by the some invisible force. The look on her face was startling. She was radiant but seemed to be without identity, like she was no longer in her body. She smiled sweetly with her eyes half closed, and all of her seemed to be aglow, as though sunlight was reflected from a mirror behind her. Her sisters stopped and said nothing for a full minute, stunned by the vision of their little sister before them.

"Rajni!" Suryia broke the spell. "Let's go home."

Rajni stared at her for more than a minute, saying nothing. Then in a perfectly normal voice, she said, "Go ahead without me. I want to stay and talk with Punditji," pointing to her pundit sitting with the group.

Her sisters, seeming to be in a trance themselves, nodded in unison and, without a word, continued on their way.

She was happy to see her pundit and, in the joy of that moment, ran to him. Punditji saw her approach and rose to meet her.

"Blessings, dear girl," he smiled at her. "You are enjoying this time with your sisters?"

"Yes, Punditji. I am so happy to be with them. We've been bathing at my father's gardens."

"So I can see," observed Punditji. "Come, I want you to meet these friends of mine." He took Rajni by the hand and led her to the small group under the trees. Punditji introduced her to the men as his best student. He introduced the strangers and told Rajni that they were Sikhs who had come to tell him about the new village of Amritsar and the sacred tank that was under excavation there. They urged him to come for the upcoming Baisakhi celebration.

She sat with them the rest of the afternoon and listened to them sing the hymns of Guru Nanak, Guru Angad, and Guru Amar Das. They told her stories about Guru Ram Das and the story of the seven platforms. They told her stories that explained the teachings of Guru Nanak, both his social reforms and his revolutionary spiritual teachings. After praying with her for her parents and sisters, they invited her to Amritsar for next year's Baisakhi celebration and said they would personally introduce her to Guru Ram Das.

"Are you going there to see him?" she asked.

"Yes, we leave shortly."

Quickly and without a word, Rajni removed her diamond encrusted earrings; a gold, pearl, and amber necklace from around her neck; a ruby ring set in gold from the ring finger of her left hand; a yellow sapphire ring set in gold from the index finger of her right hand, and six gold bangles, three from each wrist. She wrapped them in her chuni and held them out to the lead singer.

"Please give these to your guru," she said softly, that same look on her face. "He has made me very happy."

Punditji reached out his hand and began to protest.

"No, Punditji!" she said firmly and with authority, "I have to do this. I want to do this. It is important."

"So it is," said Punditji quietly and dropped his hand. "And so it must be."

The leader of the group, a kind old man with compassionate eyes and a white beard, looked at Rajni, taking in her intense beauty, small stature, and divine nature. He accepted her offering with both hands. He placed the jewels in his lap then took her hands in his and looked into her eyes.

"In the name of Guru Ram Das, I accept this," he said to her tenderly. "Know that if at any time you need help, simply pray to Guru Ram Das and he will come through for you."

Rajni looked into his kind eyes and slowly bowed her head. Punditji took her hand then and stood her up. "Come, it grows late now, and your father will be upset."

Taking leave of the others, they walked toward Duni Chand's gate. They were both silent the entire distance, Rajni lost in a blissful ecstasy and Punditji contemplating her. At her gate, Rajni touched Punditji's feet. He took her folded hands between his and looked deeply into her eyes.

"It is your time," he whispered and then let her go.

She entered her house and ran to find her sisters.

RAJNI

At that point where doubt condenses into fear,
Before the chime of mourning tolls loudly in my ear
And the tears of grief and sorrow roll streaming down my face;
Before I cross that line between honor and disgrace
Where many before have fallen and many more may slip,
Where many lives drift empty, like a plague upon a ship;
At that point where fear begins to roll into despair,
Yet fails to yield to desperation, as hope takes to the air,
There you are My Beloved, to let the Truth appear!

TWENTY-TWO

There are airborne microbacteria that carry one of the world's most horrifying diseases. Understand that from My perspective. It was necessary that I introduce certain elements into My creation to help maintain the balance and rhythm of the Universe. These things are necessary and important for the overall harmonic balance of all things and to keep the polarities equal. It is not a cruel or unfair thing; it is simply something that is necessary for the maintenance of the cosmos. That may be a difficult concept to comprehend, especially from the perspective that life on earth is all there is. From My point of view, however, it has a value. In the fifteenth and sixteenth centuries, those bacteria flourished.

Strangely, and some may believe cruelly, the disease is not immediately fatal, but is progressive over years. While victims of this disease may pray for their death, it can be a long time coming. It is not contagious by contact, for the bacteria are airborne and the older a person becomes, the less vulnerable to it one is. While adults can still contract it, the bacteria are mostly fond of children. The disease is called leprosy.

In those long-ago days, little was known about leprosy, so virtually nothing was done to treat it. The appearance of a leper was so frightening to the uninfected population that lepers were shunned and forced to keep to themselves. Their movements were restricted, and they normally were not allowed into the villages. In their hopeless isolation and quiet desperation, lepers begged for food and cared for their own as best they could while their disease progressed and their bodies dissolved. It was always exhilarating when those souls dropped their bodies and came back to Me.

In the flatland below the village of Patti was a small colony of lepers who survived mostly by the kindness of the people of Patti. Once a week, the villagers left food and old clothes at a location near the edge of the village, something that Duni Chand had organized, thinking that such an act reflected well on him as a Brahmin and raja. On those nights, while the villagers slept, the lepers crept into Patti like clouds before the moon and collected what had been left for them. The condition was that they had to come in well after dark and be gone well before sunrise.

A young man who had contracted the disease when he was a small child lived in that colony of lepers. Born a cripple, he was disadvantaged from birth. For seventeen years, the leprosy had steadily dissolved his young body, weakening his already frail frame. His legs were as shriveled as the branches of a willow tree. The thumb and first two fingers of his left hand were badly deformed and gnarled. His body was covered with ulcers and alive with maggots and other insects.

His parents had abandoned him when he was five years old, leaving him near a leper camp late one night while he slept. When he awoke alone, hungry, and terrified, his cries attracted the attention of the occupants of the camp, and they took him in. Over time, he learned to care for himself as best he could, though never that well. He could not remember his parents or his birth name and so was simply referred to as Bhai.

Since Bhai could not walk, he lived in a basket, which itself was frighteningly hideous as it hosted worms, spiders, and other insects. Fortunately, he still had use of his hands and arms and was able to propel himself forward by placing his hands on the ground and dragging his basket the length of his arms. He was pretty good at moving through the dirt and grass and got along fairly well as long as his endurance held out. He protected his hands by keeping them wrapped with old turban cloth.

Bhai accepted his condition stoically. It was all that he had ever known. Caste was never a factor in a leper colony, so he had no prejudices regarding caste or faith. In fact, he didn't know into which caste he had been born. It was irrelevant since his disease made him untouchable. Yet he had a strong sense of soul and held to the belief that this incarnation was to clear his karma and that in his next incarnation, his circumstances would improve. Getting through this incarnation in anticipation of the next was always a comfort to Bhai.

On the day that Rajni sat with the Sikhs from Amritsar, Bhai and some of the others from the camp of lepers shuffled, limped, or dragged their way toward Patti. They could not enter the village until after dark but came to the edge of the village in the late afternoon and waited until nightfall. They wanted to get as close to the village as possible so they could be close to the leavings when darkness came. There was stiff competition between the lepers, the village dogs, the monkeys from the surrounding jungle, and the birds. Whoever got there first made out the best.

On that particular day, Bhai dragged himself steadily forward. Breathing had become a challenge for him and his endurance was low. Moving on the streets and roads was not easy. He was often yelled at, whipped by drivers of passing carts and carriages, and frequently pummeled with rocks or other missiles from passersby. The refuse of the road often clung to his basket and interfered with his smooth passage.

Birds enjoyed the company of Bhai since he was host to many of their favorite foods. So as he dragged himself along the road to Patti, the birds dived and picked the worms, maggots, and insects off his body, often taking a little tissue with them.

"Karma," he muttered to himself.

He made it to the entrance of the village earlier than he had expected. The sun was still up and would not set for a couple of hours. He was tired and hungry and decided to take his chances going into Patti while it was still light. It would take some time for him to reach the location of the leavings, and he knew that if he did not continue, he would arrive too late and there would be nothing left.

He was hot and needed rest, shade, and water. Also, he wanted to get off the main road so that fewer people would see him. So he turned onto a shady passage that went up to the highest point in Patti. There he could rest under the cool shade of the banyan trees. Through his blurred vision, he noticed that at the top of the hill was a large red sandstone palace, apparently surrounded by lovely gardens. There, in the shade near the gate to that palace, Bhai rested.

Rajni's sisters were all gathered in the room of their first sister, drinking lassi and talking in whispers. Rajni couldn't wait to tell them about her experience with the Sikhs from Amritsar. She understood that she had been touched by a great power, something beyond her experience in any temple or place of pilgrimage. She had fallen in love with something or someone that she could neither see nor touch but could feel in her every cell, and she knew that life as she had known it would never be the same. It had been such a powerful and special experience! She couldn't wait to talk to her father and get him to organize a trip to Amritsar, hopefully with Punditji, so that she could meet the guru of the

Sikhs. In her excitement and exuberance, she overlooked the concerned faces of her sisters.

She began talking very fast in a rush of girlish emotion and excitement. Gita put her hand upon Rajni's wrist.

"You were gone a long time. Papaji and Mataji have been asking about you. We told them that you were with your pundit."

Rajni slowed a bit, but the luster around her and the light on her face never dimmed.

"That's true! I was with Punditji, and he introduced me to those Sikhs. Did you hear them singing? Oh my God, it was so beautiful!"

Her first sister looked concerned. "Rajni! What have you done? Where is your jewelry?"

"I gave it all to those saintly men," beamed Rajni. "They will to give it to their guru in Amritsar!"

In all their time together, they had never seen Rajni so happy, so brilliantly radiant. Tears welled up in twelve eyes.

"Oh, baby sister," said Navleen, "Papa will be very mad. How do you know they will give your jewelry to their guru?"

"Because they promised. Why should Papa be mad? It was my jewelry. Besides, he should be happy that I gave it as an offering. It is what we've been taught."

"He won't be. Besides, nobody really does things like that."

"Oh, sweet sister, this will be a problem. Can't we get your jewelry back?" said Ravi anxiously.

"I don't want it back! I gave it to them. The words of their guru made me so happy! I want him to have my jewelry. Why can't I give it to him?"

Her eyes were brighter than the reflection of the late afternoon sun on the windowpanes.

Saraswati said, "You know how possessive he is. He will react as if you have given away something of his."

"Well, the jewelry was given to me! And since it was mine, I had the right to give it away. I can only gain from such an action and so can Papaji since he gave the jewelry to me in the first place. In fact, our whole family and each of your families will be blessed. I prayed with them for all of us and each of your families and all of your babies!"

She was positively radiant, like the full moon on a clear October night against the deep blue of the midnight sky.

Her sisters were in tears now. They loved their little sister dearly and their hearts were touched by her sweetness and innocence. They had always admired Rajni's spirituality. But now, they were afraid of Duni Chand and his wrath.

"Perhaps we should ask Mataji for advice," said Suriya.

"Advice for what?" asked Rajni innocently. "What wrong have I done?"

Raveena took Rajni's face between her hands. "Listen, baby sister, Papaji will get very angry when he sees that you have given away his jewelry . . ."

"He gave it to me, so it was mine to do with as I wanted!" Her tone was arrogant.

Still holding her face, Raveena said, "He won't see it that way. He already believes that you have no appreciation for what he has given us. He is lonely and misses us, and he will get angry. These days, he could do anything. Baby sister, this is not a good situation. We better talk to Mataji before he finds out. She might be able to soften him first."

The sisters discussed what they should say to their mother. Finally, they agreed that Gita should go alone and tell her the story while the rest of them waited in her room.

They could hear their mother yelling within a few minutes. Shortly, they heard her fat feet on the marble floor while her voice grew stronger as she neared the room.

"What have you done to me?" she demanded as she entered the room.

"I've done nothing to you, Mataji," said Rajni innocently. "My heart has been opened by the song of the guru. You should have been there, Mata! I prayed for you and Papaji, that you should live long and always be together."

"Can you pray your bangles back on your wrists?"

"No, I don't want to."

"Do you know what your father will do now? He will blame me for this."

"Mataji, I've committed no crime. Why should there be blame? Blame for what? What I did was right."

"Right?" demanded their mother. "Right for whom? I won't endure his wrath for your foolish actions. We have to try and get those things back. If you don't want them, it's fine, we'll put them in the vault. But this is an insult to your father, and he will be very angry. God only knows what he will do to me."

"Why should he do anything to you? It was my decision. I prayed for us, what I did was out of love. My only regret now is that you are upset with me."

"Of course I'm upset! He'll blame me for raising such a foolish child. Wait . . ." Their mother paused and, in a conspiratorial voice, whispered, "It's the influence of that pundit. Yes, it's not my fault, it's all those strange ideas he has put into your innocent little head. We'll arrange to have him beaten and driven from the village . . ."

"No!" shouted Rajni. "This was my decision, my action, and my karma. Punditji had nothing to do with it. In fact, he tried to stop me, but I wouldn't let him. Leave him alone!"

"If he had only taught you properly, like your sisters were taught, I wouldn't be in this mess. How could you have done this to me? That pundit will pay. This is entirely his fault. Entirely his fault!"

Rajni was in tears now. How could something so beautiful and deeply meaningful have gone so wrong? She was confused and becoming frightened. She knew she was right. But if she were right, why would this be happening? Rajni was crying freely, but her mother, unable to comfort her own daughter, was caught up with concerns for her own welfare before the wrath of her husband.

"We must find those men and get that jewelry back," she said with absolute resolve. "Where are they?"

"They have left," sobbed Rajni. "They have left for Amritsar and they *will* give the jewelry to Guru Ram Das. Please Mataji, let them go. I know that their guru will bless us all. Please."

She was crying uncontrollably now. Each sister had a hand on her, patting her back, stroking her hair, holding her hand. Their mother, however, was unmoved.

"So they are gone then?" she asked forcefully.

"Yes, Mataji."

"And the jewelry can't be recovered."

"Mataji, the Vedas teach us to be charitable toward saintly people. I did what was right."

"It's lost," said their mother flatly. "It's lost. Wait until your father hears about this."

Rajni shook with sobs. She tasted the salt of her own tears, which wet her sister's pillows. She could not be consoled. This was not what the sisters had expected from their mother and now they were really afraid for their little sister.

"I'm going to tell your father," said Mataji. "All of you wait here."

All seven sisters sat glumly. The silence was only spiked by the sounds of their sobs. They all were crying and holding on to each other, unable to comfort the one they loved the most.

"Oh, baby sister," Gita sobbed. "I am so sorry. I never meant this to happen."

Rajni could not respond. Her whole body shook as she cried. The pillows, the sheets, and all the chunis were wet from the tears of the seven sisters. The inevitable came rather quickly.

Duni Chand had been playing chess with the headman of his village and was not winning when Mataji came to give him the news. As she launched into the story and the tirade against Punditji, the headman quietly backed out of the room and left the house. At first, Duni Chand did not fully comprehend what she told him, so he made her repeat the story. She did so with her own embellishments, making sure to place heavy blame on Punditji and putting it as far away from herself as possible.

Duni Chand called for one of the servants and had him go out into Patti to find Punditji. Then he sent for his daughters.

"We should have gotten rid of that pundit," said Mataji. "He interfered with all of my motherly influence. How could a holy man permit himself to come between a mother and her daughter?"

Duni Chand was silent.

"She is such a sweet girl, but he has put strange ideas in her head. She thinks differently. I told you we didn't need him anymore, that she had learned enough. He should never be allowed into this house again. All of my good influence on Rajni has been ruined by that old fool."

The girls entered the room slowly. Rajni had managed to calm herself, and her sisters had regained their composure. Gita had her right arm around Rajni's shoulders and held Rajni's right hand in her left.

"Well," said Duni Chand, "my beautiful daughters." He sounded like he was talking to someone who owed considerable taxes and had been evading payment for years. "Who cares for you and gives you everything, my darlings?"

"You do, Papa" was the mumbled reply.

"Who?" he demanded, truly sounding like he was conducting an interrogation.

Catching and interrogating tax evaders was Duni Chand's favorite part of his job. He liked the hunt, but he especially liked when he had the suspect in his presence. He became like a cat toying with a lizard, enjoying the power he wielded. He enjoyed putting the offender through the torture of the interrogation, then passing the judgment and the sentence. It filled him with a sense of power and importance to dominate another person. He applied this same behavior to his business dealings, always ensuring that he took every rupee from a venture, regardless of how it impacted the people he did business with. Now although it was his seven daughters whom he loved so dearly before him, he could neither help his attitude nor the way he applied himself to the situation. It was in his cells and could not be changed.

"What did you say?"

Fourteen eyes stared at the floor and four mouths mumbled, "You do, Papa."

"Look at me!" demanded Duni Chand.

Six heads snapped up. Rajni's remained bowed, her eyes fixed on a matrix in the marble floor.

"Who cares for you and gives you everything!" It was not a question but a demand.

"You do, Papa," said the six flatly. Rajni remained silent.

"I do?"

Silence.

"I *do*?" he roared.

"Yes, Papa" in whispers.

"*I* do!" His voice echoed around the room and down the marbled hallways.

"Rajni!"

Slowly, Rajni raised her head. Her eyes, though she had been crying before, were clear and bright, burning like the eyes of a tiger. She felt surprisingly calm and strangely detached. She remembered how she had felt earlier when she sat with the holy men of Amritsar. She remembered when Punditji whispered those words, *Wahe Guru, Wahe Guru, Wahe Guru*, in her ear, and as she stood now before her father, they echoed in her brain.

Duni Chand was taken aback when he saw his daughter's face. There was no indication of her earlier hysteria. Rather, the depth of her serenity and the penetrating light of her eyes stopped him. He regarded her for a long time, struggling between his love for her and his rage. Eventually though, his predatory instincts and the familiar experience of interrogating thousands of wretched and poor people dominated, inflamed by his insane pride.

"Who cares for *you* and gives *you* everything?" He asked it with intensity, as though Rajni was an escaped criminal who had been found after a desperate manhunt.

"Papaji," she said, her voice beginning to quiver, "know that I love you. Please don't do this. Not today, not ever again."

"Rajni!" The sound of his echo faded down the hallway. "Who—cares for you—and who—gives you—EVERYTHING?" He screamed it, his voice thundering across his estate, causing the big black ravens scavenging on the lawn to jump and take flight.

"Papa, I must tell the truth. God gives us . . . everything. All things come from Him and . . . it is His sweet mercy that cares for us. Parents . . . are only . . . a channel for the flow of . . . His mercy. God has been merciful to us. He . . . has given you wealth which . . . you . . . have shared with us, but it has all been due to His kindness. By His will, everything. . . could disappear. . . in the twinkling . . . of an eye." She was sobbing again, her voice quivering, her small body shaking.

"It *shall* disappear in the twinkling of an eye," growled Duni Chand. "Then we'll see how well God cares for you."

He called the low caste sweeping woman who passed in the hall. "Give her your clothes and you take hers."

"Papa!" cried the sisters. "Papa, don't!"

"Silence, all of you. Anyone who speaks shall join her."

Raveena and Suryia began to run from the room.

"Stop!" shouted Duni Chand. "You are all responsible for this. You will all stay here and keep quiet."

Rajni left the room with the sweeper. She was still dressed in her clothes from the gardens, but they were far better than the filthy old rags of the sweeper. The clothes of the sweeper, a faded red kameez and yellow salwaars, swallowed Rajni and their smell made her feel sick.

Rajni reentered the room to find Punditji facing her father.

"You are the cause of this whole thing!" shouted Duni Chand.

"My dear Duni Chand," said Punditji kindly, "are you unable to recognize your own daughter? It was your devotion and piety that brought you these seven daughters. Their souls were crafted in the Heavens and a soul such as Rajni . . ."

"Silence, *bainchote*!" hissed Duni Chand. The girls paled, unable to comprehend that their father had hurled one of the most crude and offensive Punjabi insults in their presence, and to a holy man. "My first mistake was allowing you back into this house after I had you beaten and thrown out. My next mistake was allowing you to continue to return and bend her mind. You are responsible for this! I should have you beaten and your skin pulled off in strips."

"You are making a mistake, my friend."

"I am not your friend!" shouted Duni Chand, his face red with rage.

"Listen to me," pleaded Punditji. "Rajni is special. She was given to the Earth by the Heavens . . ."

"Enough! You have said enough. I know what happened to you at the time of Hymayun. I know that you can bear physical torture. I have had you beaten before and still you were unrepentant and undeterred. I have a better torture in mind for you though."

Punditji was silent, his face passive.

"You shall perform her marriage . . ."

"I'll be happy to . . ."

". . . with the next man who passes my gate!"

All the sisters gasped and clung to Rajni, instinctively trying to protect her. Mataji sat silently, afraid of her husband. She knew his anger but could not have anticipated such a reaction.

Duni Chand called to his personal servant. "Mokhum! Go down to the gate and bring me the next man who passes. I don't care if he is a beggar or a thief, a Brahmin, or a sudra. Bring him to me quickly!"

It was at that moment that Bhai, who had been making steady progress down the street, came before Duni Chand's gate and stopped to rest in the shade. When the gate opened, Mokhum Das froze. He could not imagine that Duni Chand would marry his daughter to a leper, certainly not one who smelled so foul. He looked up and down the street, but it was oddly deserted. He stared down at Bhai, who was trying to ask for water with his gurgly, unintelligible voice. Mokhum Das didn't know what to do.

"Mokhum!" Duni Chand bellowed through the window. He could not see Mokhum, but Duni Chand could tell that someone was there. Mokhum Das looked toward the house.

"Someone is there?" shouted Duni Chand.

"Well, sir," Mokhum Das hesitated, "not exactly." The stench arising from Bhai was debilitating.

"What do you mean? Someone is there or not?" yelled Duni Chand. "Is he alive?"

"He's alive, sir."

"Then bring him in immediately."

Mokhum Das removed his turban and, tying one end to Bhai's basket, dragged him up the hill and into the courtyard. When Duni Chand saw what Mokhum was bringing in, he inhaled hard but would not soften his resolve. However, he did not want a leper in his house.

"Stop!" he yelled. "Leave him there. Quickly, bring a chamber for the fire, there's going to be a wedding." Duni Chand chuckled out loud. He quickly turned to Punditji. "You will perform this marriage, old man, or I will have your skin pulled off strip by strip. If you refuse, I will find someone else who will do it while you are begging for your death. Do you understand me?"

Rajni made her way quickly to Punditji and grabbed his arm.

"Please, Punditji, I want you to do it. Please, do it for me." Tears were streaming down her face but her voice was firm.

Punditji placed his hands on Rajni's shoulders and looked down into her still shining eyes. "I will do it," he said quietly. "I will do it."

Rajni's mother, who had been silent to this point, looked out the window and screamed. She turned to Duni Chand, "Don't do this to our baby!"

"Be quiet!" shouted Duni Chand and struck Mataji across the face, knocking her to the floor with the palm of his right hand. "Say no more!"

Mataji lay on the floor out of breath and crying while Duni Chand fumed.

"You have six other babies. Forget this one, she is neither of you nor of me. In fact, she no longer exists!"

All six of Rajni's sisters were crying hysterically now, pleading with Duni Chand. Suryia and Raveena were pummeling Duni Chand with their fists, but he pushed them forcefully to the floor and they lay there with their mother.

"Leave this nonsense, or you all will join her!" After years of placing already poor people in hopeless situations, he had perfected the ability to harden his heart. He only felt anger and the thrill of dominance now. His chilled and hardened heart was unmoved by the sobs of his wife and daughters.

Rajni became curiously calm. After an afternoon of crying, she had reached a moment of quiet stability. She went to her mother, who was crying harder than any of them. Her shoulders shook, her entire body crumpled on itself. Rajni put her comforting arm around the shaking shoulders of her mother.

"Mataji," she said bravely, "it is my wedding day. You should be happy. Please, tell me the way to be a good wife."

Her mother lost all control of herself. All of her fat shook like khir in an ox cart while her tears soaked her cheeks.

"Oh, my baby," she babbled, "my baby. I didn't mean for this to happen." Then she was lost in her sobs again.

Rajni's sisters came to her and their mother. All were sobbing hysterically, except for Rajni. They hugged her and apologized to her. Looks of terror and anguish were on their faces. Yet, Rajni's calm prevailed.

Punditji spoke to Duni Chand. "As the pundit who is to perform this wedding, I have the right to counsel the couple."

"By all means," sneered Duni Chand, "they may benefit from your counsel. We can all see how Rajni has benefited from your counsel thus far."

Punditji went to Rajni and took her hand. "Come with me," he said. And he led her out to the courtyard where Bhai, not fully comprehending what was happening, waited in his basket.

"Rajni!" yelled Duni Chand.

She turned and faced him, that look still in her eyes, that radiance still on her face.

"Those shoes belong to me. Leave them at my door. And from this moment forward, you will never enter this house again!" Then he turned his back to her. "Hear me," he yelled to his wife and six daughters, "any among you who gives her aid of any kind will never enter this house again either! Trust what I say." Then he left the room.

As soon as they stepped out of the door, they could smell the stench of Bhai's putrefied body and the dung that clung to his basket. It was a pathetic and horrifying sight. Rajni, despite her calm appearance, began to panic. She gripped Punditji's hand as though she was drowning and her old pundit's hand was her only lifeline.

Punditji pulled the tail of his kurta to his face, revealing a scarred belly above his dhoti. He bent in the direction of Bhai. "Do you have a name?" he asked.

"BBhhaaii," he gurgled, sounding somewhat like a goat.

"Bhai," said Punditji, "today you are getting married."

It was difficult for Bhai to hold his head up, but he moved his head in the direction of Rajni. He could determine that there was a young girl standing before him, though he could not make out the details of her features.

Rajni, however, could easily make out Bhai's features, or the lack of them. It was as though she was looking at the face of a pig. Bhai had a severely damaged nose. His eyes were glazed; the right eye was milky white. Open sores covered his body, and his hands, with their missing fingers and the filthy turban wrapped around them, terrified her. She had never seen a leper so close and her whole body began to tremble uncontrollably. She turned her face against Punditji's chest and sobbed, her slender body shaking. She buried her face against Punditji to muffle the cries of anguish and terror rushing unchecked from her heart. Punditji put his arms around her and tried to hold her and comfort her without breaking into sobs himself.

Slowly, Rajni turned her head back toward Bhai, who was sitting uncomfortably in the afternoon sun. It was the end of the monsoon season and there were few clouds on the horizon. It was unlikely to rain. Suddenly, Rajni pushed away from Punditji and ran toward a corner of the palace. She stumbled over the bottoms of the salwaars that were much too long for her and fell. She continued moving away from Bhai and Punditji, crawling on her hands and knees. She began vomiting until there was nothing left in her. Still she wretched, dry-heaving between sobs, every part of her body shaking.

Finally, she collapsed on the earth with nothing left in her: no more tears, no more food, no more emotions. She lay shivering, and Punditji sat beside her, his hand tenderly on her head.

"Om Shanti, Shanti, Shanti," he chanted repeatedly, his deep, rich voice soft and melodic. Rajni grew still and quiet.

"Punditji," she whispered softly, "please take me to meet my husband."

Without a word, Punditji helped her to stand and brushed her off. He cleaned her face using the hem of his kurta. Taking her by the hand, he walked her slowly back to Bhai. As they walked, Punditji called for water. Still holding her hand, he stood with her in front of Bhai.

"My dear boy, this is Rajni. She is to be your wife."

"Why?" he gurgled.

"Because it is the will of God," said Punditji kindly. "The same God who gave you this terrible condition. She is a sweet and divine girl, and she will take good care of you. Please don't be afraid."

"Afraid?" he uttered in his thick voice. "What do I have to fear?"

"He is wise," said Punditji. He spoke quietly, "Now understand this, whatever are the circumstances, this marriage is the will of God, and you must respect it as such. Never let a day pass that you don't begin by remembering God and giving thanks for what He has given you."

He turned to Rajni who had not let go of his hand. "As your teacher, I should be happy, for all that I have taught you is about to be put to the test. Yet I see your fear and the challenge that lies ahead for you. You are strong, and you will prevail through this with dignity. God abandons no one, He has not abandoned you nor him," indicating Bhai with a thrust of his chin. "Remember above all else, do not compromise your grace. Understand that this is not punishment for you, it is only a test. Know that God gives the greatest tests to those He holds the dearest to His heart. Do you remember the story of Pralad?"

"Yes," she whispered, her face turned against Punditji's chest, afraid to speak out loud.

"You are no different and no less dear to God than he." Punditji pointed to Bhai sitting in his basket. "That is your red hot pillar." He pointed to an ant crawling on Bhai's neck. "See, brave girl," he smiled at her, "embrace it. God has sent this to you for a reason. Carry him upon your young and innocent back. This is the suffering of the world, which you were sent to relieve. It is the crucible out of which will pour sacred healing and hope for mankind in this Kali Yuga. Remember you told me that you wanted to relieve the suffering of the world?"

Rajni nodded, her face still turned to Punditji's chest, saying nothing.

"God has given you what you wanted. Don't relate to him as a man, relate to him as suffering Mankind, which you were born to carry on your back for the good of all."

The preparations had been made for the wedding fire. All the elements needed to perform the wedding ceremony were brought out and set by the fire. No one, however, wanted to be near Bhai. They felt they were witnessing a gruesome execution, and the servants retreated into the house.

Punditji took the water that had been brought and kneeled down next to Bhai.

"You must be thirsty," he said softly and offered him water. Bhai received it gratefully. He was very thirsty. "You have suffered all your life." Punditji sounded like the wise pundit that he was. "But the end of your suffering is not far off."

Duni Chand bellowed from an upstairs window, "Get started, old man. It grows late. I want this filth off my land by nightfall."

Punditji turned to Rajni, pulling her close to him. "Take him to the water. Wash him, keep him clean, and keep the vermin off his body. By washing him, his skin will heal somewhat." Rajni nodded, still keeping silent.

"Now!" shouted Duni Chand.

Facing Rajni, Punditji picked up the end of Mokum's turban, which was still tied to Bhai's basket, and placed it in her hand.

"Are you ready?" he asked softly.

Rajni bent down, trying not to wretch as she faced Bhai. "They call you Bhai?" she asked.

"Yes," he choked.

"You are to be my husband," she said softly, gaining strength and confidence. "It is not proper for me to call you Bhai. I will call you Piare—my beloved."

Rajni rose and faced Punditji. She inhaled deeply through her nose, then exhaled slowly as she had seen Punditji do many times before.

"Let us begin." She smiled her beautiful, radiant smile.

Punditji sat before the fire and firmly began the incantations for the wedding ceremony, throwing the herbs and minerals onto the fire. At the appropriate times, Rajni dragged Bhai, now Piare, in his basket around the fire.

Inside the house, her sisters were sobbing hysterically along with their mother. Duni Chand, standing at an upper window by himself, was impassive. When Punditji had completed the marriage ritual, Duni Chand yelled, "Now get off my land, all of you. Pundit, if I ever see your face again, I will have you killed."

"Kill me now," said Punditji, calmly. "Why wait?"

"Leave!" shouted Duni Chand.

Suddenly, Gita stood up, ran outside, and placed her chuni over the head of Piare. She was quickly followed by her other sisters against Duni Chand's protests.

"I will never set foot in this house again!" Gita shouted.

"Never again!" was repeated five times.

Word traveled fast in the villages of the Punjab, and by now, many villagers were gathered at the gate. They cursed Duni Chand loudly. They offered to host the sisters until they could make arrangements to return to their husbands. Yet Duni Chand was unmoved, his heart hard as granite.

The sun was now a yellow wafer suspended above the wine red horizon. Night was gaining the eastern sky and would soon conquer it all. The first stars were twinkling against the deepening purple of the evening in sharp contrast to the bright red and yellow sunset. The effect of the colors and the light enhanced the surrealistic quality of the moment. Smoke from the evening fires rose, bringing the smells of cooking. The sound of bells announcing the evening prayer ascended with the smoke and aromas of the gathering twilight.

Punditji calmly looked up at Duni Chand as he gazed down from the window of his palace in the fading light. In a steady voice, full of authority Punditji spoke, "Hear me now, Duni Chand Raja of Patti. That day will come when you beg your daughters to return to your home. That day will come when your remorse over what you have done today consumes you. And the day will come when, despite your heartless cruelty, Rajni will forgive you. Yet until that moment, you will find no solace, no comfort, and no joy in your life. Your palace will become as dark and cold as your heart and as devoid of life as you are of compassion. Your suffering commences once your daughters have passed through your gate. It will not be assuaged until Rajni has forgiven you of your cruelty."

"No one is to aid her," Duni Chand proclaimed loudly. "As the raja of Patti, I forbid it, and anyone found giving them any succor will pray for their death before I am finished with them. Now get off my land! All of you!"

Punditji put his arm around Rajni's shoulders. "Go now," he said, "and never look back. Trust yourself to God and remember the advice of my friends. If you need help, call on their guru. He will come through for you." Punditji paused poignantly. "My job is finished."

And for the first time in her life Rajni saw her normally stoic pundit, ever consistent with his behavior, weep quietly.

She gathered Mokum's turban and pulled it over her shoulder. In all her fourteen years she had never lifted anything heavier than her own pillow. It would take all her strength now to pull her husband behind her.

"Come, my beloved," she whispered. "It is our wedding night."

She walked through the gate, dragging the basket with her suffering husband. The people who had gathered there parted silently to let them pass. Her feet, which had always walked upon silk carpets and polished marble, touched the warm dirt of the road. She turned south toward the Satluj, moving very, very slowly as she made her way down toward the plain. The sun had lingered on the edge of the horizon as though waiting patiently for this moment. Now, overcome by the darkness, it surrendered quietly to the night.

The darkness obscured her from Duni Chand's sight.

TWENTY-THREE

It was a spectacularly clear night as Rajni, with Piare in tow, made her way toward the Satluj. It was only that morning that she had walked so cheerfully and innocently with her sisters, singing and laughing on their way to Duni Chand's formal gardens. Tonight, she would pass those gardens in the darkness. The walk to the gardens usually took about an hour, and the Satluj was another half hour past the gardens. Tonight, it would take her well over four hours to reach the banks of the Satluj.

Rajni was a small girl who had lived a pampered and privileged life. She was unaccustomed to the circumstances of the common people, and she had never had to work. Pulling Piare behind her now was the most difficult thing she had ever done. Her bare feet seemed to know the location of every stone and thorn along the way, and in a short time, her feet hurt and bled. To compound the problem, she consistently stepped in the mud and animal droppings that seemed to be everywhere.

She did not stop though. Her only focus was to make it to the Satluj with her husband. She felt a sense of compassion toward Piare and could not imagine the horrors of his life. Whatever they were, she realized soberly that they were now hers to share.

She continued to move forward step by step. When they first set out, the road had been lined with people, but after a furlong, the road was empty and she and Piare were left alone with the night. It was the dark time of the moon and there was little light, yet having travelled it in the early mornings with her sisters so they could be at the gardens before sunrise, she knew the way intimately. This was a heavily traveled road and, as such, was well defined.

Pulling the basket with her unfortunate husband in it was hard work, and in a short time, she weakened and began to tire. She had not eaten since before leaving the gardens and realized idly that she had no idea where her next meal would come from. There was no one on the road, though an occasional dog interrupted her passage. She knew there were aggressively mischievous monkeys in the jungle that lined the road, and though she heard them, they left her alone. She was concerned about other animals, dacoits, or the homeless people who lived along the roadside, but after a few furlongs from Patti, she saw no one. The Punjab was a dangerous place to travel, especially after dark.

Outside of Patti, as Rajni struggled to drag Piare toward the Satluj, they passed the cremation ground. In the deepening darkness, the smell of smoke and burned flesh and hair was overwhelming. In the distance, she could see embers glowing against the night. She saw a human form, like an apparition raised from the dead, moving across the cremation ground. It was an *aghora*. The aghoris were ascetic sadhus who lived in the cremation grounds, covered themselves with the ashes of the dead, performed rituals with corpses, and took their food and drink from the top of a skull to help them gain occult powers.

Rajni stopped and watched in the darkness as the aghora moved among the funeral pyres. There had been two cremations that day, and the aghora was picking through the remains of the burned corpses. The sight and smell of the dead and the strange movements of the aghora made her feel sick and dizzy. She bent over to vomit but only heaved, having lost everything that was in her earlier in the afternoon. She fell to her knees, her heart beating fast and her breathing quick and shallow.

She placed her hands on the ground in front of her, trying to steady herself, and as she did so, a rise in the breeze blew smoke from the pyres over her. She shook but was unable to cry. She heaved again then collapsed in the dirt.

"I have nothing left," she whispered to herself, "nothing left."

Rajni lay there with her eyes closed, unable to move, unable to find the strength or the stability to sit up. She felt as if she was floating. She had no sense of Piare, still sitting on the road in his basket. Her life passed before her with surprising detail: her times with her sisters, her times with Punditji, her life as a princess. She tried to see the life ahead of her, but it was lost in the darkness, like the road that lay before her now. In the darkness, Rajni raised her head and looked out toward the cremation ground, then turned and looked back at Piare sitting in his vermin-ridden basket with his hands wrapped in those disgustingly filthy rags. His head was still covered with the chunis of her sisters, and she imagined his body dissolving under them. The young princess turned her face toward the night sky.

"I have married death!" she screamed into the night. Her body shook, her voice a high-pitched drone sustained softly for the duration of a breath.

"Rajni, the princess, has died," she whispered, burying her face in her hands. "Only Rajni the leper's wife lives."

"Rajni who bears the suffering of the Kali Yuga shall live!"

The whisper was not her voice, and a hand on her back caused her to raise her head slowly. It was the aghora. His thin, dark, ash-covered body and long matted hair under normal circumstances would have terrified her, but she had run out of fear for the night. He smelled of smoke and ash and was naked except for a small wooden cup that covered his groin, tied tightly in place with coarse rope. A string of human molars was strung like prayer beads around his neck.

"Take our suffering to the water." He was smiling, and his teeth and eyes shone in the darkness. "Eh Rajni, who bears the suffering of the Kali Yuga, we know who you are!"

Rajni turned her head to push herself up, and when she raised it again, the aghora was gone. She looked out across the cremation ground but couldn't see him.

"Rajni who bears the suffering of the Kali Yuga shall live!" She heard the voice but could not see the speaker.

"Rajni who bears the suffering of the Kali Yuga shall live!" she whispered it to herself. The words gave her strength. She stood up and looked across at the dying embers of the funeral pyre.

"Rajni the princess has died," she spoke with a strong voice as a sense of confidence arose in her. "Rajni who bears the suffering of the Kali Yuga shall live!" She called it toward the cremation ground, not defying death, but embracing it.

She felt purged and empty, waiting to be filled with her new self. She would remember this night as the defining moment when her life as a girl ended and her life as a woman began. After all, now she was married, and when a girl marries, she leaves the house of the father and moves to the house of the husband, and the house of Piare was on the ground and under the sky. She picked up Mokum's turban and continued to drag Piare toward the Satluj.

As she trudged forward, the only sounds were her labored breathing, the sliding of her feet through the dirt, the scraping sound of Piare's basket, and the faint tinkling of the tiny bells tied to the parandees in her hair. The air was warm and humid, and she saw lightning in the distance. Her feet hurt and bled, while perspiration soaked the oversized kameez on her back. Her shoulders and arms ached from pulling the basket, and her thigh and calf muscles burned. After three hours, she was in agony. Yet she continued moving forward, away from Duni Chand.

She was having a difficult time moving in the oversized clothes of the sweeping woman, and she stopped occasionally to tighten the drawstring around her waist or roll the bottoms of the salwaars above her ankles so she wouldn't step on them. The heavy smell of Piare surrounded her, and she laughed aloud at one point as she imagined herself trying to get away from the smell while she pulled it behind her. That was her only display of emotion.

On the ground, Piare sat in his basket. He tried to comprehend what had happened, tried to grasp how he was now being pulled behind this beautiful girl, and how she was now his wife. He considered the words of the old pundit: that this had happened because it was the will of God, the same God who had given him his disease. He thought he remembered that the pundit had also said something about his suffering ending soon. Right now he was grateful for the chunis that the sisters had draped over him, for the water the pundit had given him, and for the fact that he was being pulled and did not have to propel himself along the road.

He had no idea where they were going, but he felt safe with this girl. The old pundit had told him that she would take care of him. In all his life, he had only experienced occasional acts of kindness. He was accustomed to being abused and mistreated, to having stones, excrement, and rotten food thrown at him, and to having no one to care for him. Yet he understood that Rajni would care for him, though he could not understand why.

He could barely make out her image ahead of him, and as they moved forward in the darkness, he tried to recall how she had looked in the afternoon. His poor vision only hindered his perception of Rajni, yet his sense was that she was elegantly beautiful. He felt a kindness and compassion in her that he had never found in another person.

He wasn't sure how to be a husband. He had no hope of supporting her, of giving her children, or any semblance of a life that was worth living. From his earliest recollection, he had believed that his karma had put him in this condition. His previous incarnations seemed no further away than his infancy, so far removed was he from both. Piare had always prayed that whatever he had to suffer to clear his karma would be in this incarnation so that in the next incarnation he could do something of value. He considered this incarnation as something to be endured until it was over.

Now, everything had changed. In one afternoon, his entire perspective about himself, his life, and his relationship with the world had been overturned. If it was true that he was married, that the girl in front of him pulling his basket was his wife, then it meant that he had something to live for and that he was responsible for someone other than himself.

He felt that he should do something to help Rajni and prove that he could make a contribution and let her know in some small way that he was a man and that they were partners. He reached up and rearranged the chunis so that they still covered his face but left his eyes exposed. He put out his arms and, placing his hands on the ground, began to pull the basket forward as he had done daily for the past twelve years. With Rajni pulling from the front, it was easier to move. Without missing a step, Rajni turned and looked at him, and together they made their way along the road toward the river.

They passed the walls of Duni Chand's formal gardens, and in the darkness, Rajni heard the water running through the canal. That morning with her sisters seemed like another lifetime. She was tempted to stop there and spend the night in the gardens. There were two cottages stocked with shawls, blankets, and cushions. The cottages opened onto a large marble and pink sandstone pavilion that led down to the gardens. There was a well-stocked kitchen, plus five different kinds of mango trees. She knew the night watchmen would not have heard about what happened and would let her in despite Piare. She could rest, they could eat, and she could think about what to do next.

Though Rajni was in pain, she didn't stop and continued walking with her husband in tow. The farther away from Duni Chand she got, the more relieved she felt. She could not believe his cruelty. The look in his face was unforgettably disturbing, for she had seen a side of her father that she never knew existed. It upset her, not because of what he had done to her, but because of what she realized he was capable of doing to anyone. She was revolted by the pretense that he was a pious and devoted Brahmin when in reality he was nothing more than a cruel and bigoted man. She had seen a deep darkness in his heart that seemed to her to be impenetrable and without limit.

She thought about the hymn she had heard that morning:

*"Oh Nanak, He who created the creatures takes care of them all.
The Creator who created the Creation also takes care of it."*

She remembered the sweet melody and let the sound resound in her mind. It helped to uplift her and keep her going.

As they drew closer to the Satluj, Rajni saw one of Duni Chand's villages ahead, near the banks of the river. The village was small and dark and she wanted to avoid being noticed. She followed a path that she often took with her sisters when they went to the river to bathe. It wound down to the north bank, which was where she and Piare would rest for the night. Around midnight, she heard the comforting sounds of the river, and the ground felt moist under her feet. Eventually, she saw the flowing water shining in the darkness. She stopped a short distance from the riverbank and removed two of the chunis from Piare's head. She walked to the river and soaked them in the cool running water, then carried them dripping to Piare.

"Suck on this," she said, her breathing labored. "You must be thirsty."

Piare held the chunis between his hands and sucked the water from them gratefully. He was extremely thirsty, and the water soothed and refreshed him. It tasted slightly of the combined perfumes of Rajni's sisters and stimulated what remained of his senses. He reached out and touched Rajni's hand shyly. She gazed at him without expression, her eyes shining in the darkness.

Rajni made her way back to the river. She drank deeply, standing in the water up to her knees. The water and the soft sand of the river were soothing to her feet while the sound of the river comforted her. She looked up at the sky taking in the light of the stars. Despite her ordeal, she felt a sense of peace. She had stood firm before her father, had held up to his humiliation, and she had made it to the river with her husband in tow.

"Infinite God," she whispered in prayer, "this is all Your will and only You can get me through this. I don't know why this has come on me, but it comes from You so I am happy to receive it. This is only the beginning, and I think that I must have a long way to go. Grant me the strength to bear it gracefully. You have created all things, including me and that poor man in the basket. You have not abandoned either of us. Now I understand what Punditji meant when he told me that pain and strife bring us closer to You. You are my only refuge now, I have nowhere else to turn. If it is Your will that we die, then receive us with open arms. If it is Your will that we survive, then grant that we do so with grace. Whatever happens, just cover me, uphold my honor, and let me not fail to do my duty. Thank you for trusting me with this test."

I listened silently to Rajni's prayer. Its sincerity and devotion penetrated My solitary presence and moved Me. A tear formed then fell from My great eye. As it fell from the Heavens, it appeared in the night as a bright falling star streaking slowly across the sky. Rajni watched it flash then burn into the darkness.

She walked back to Piare.

"Do you sleep in your basket?" she asked him.

"No," he gurgled, feeling helpless and ashamed, "I sleep on the ground."

The time has come, she thought to herself.

She bent down and slipped her arms under his shoulders and lifted him from the basket, laying him down in the soft, dry sand away from the water. The physical contact was difficult for her with his stench amplified by the exertion of the walk. She tried to hold her breath, but the exertion of lifting him forced her to breathe, which turned her stomach. Rajni wasn't sure if she would contract the disease now that she had touched him, and the thought that she might have made her cringe. Still, she could not just leave him in the basket. Despite the circumstances, she was his wife and was determined to do her duty as Punditji had taught her.

The mosquitoes and flying insects had discovered them, and Rajni constantly swatted the air and slapped herself. She took two of her sister's dry chunis and draped them over Piare to shield him from the insects. She lay down next to him and covered herself with Mokum's turban.

"Tomorrow, I am going to wash you in the river," she said somewhat cheerfully. "Remember this night, my beloved," she whispered, "it is our wedding night." And on an impulse, she bent toward Piare's withered and covered body and kissed him on the head, her lips touching the chunis of her sisters.

* * *

Rajni awoke at first light. The mosquitoes had bitten her through the thin turban, and welts covered her face and arms. She had not really slept, just drifted in and out of consciousness until she couldn't stand the discomfort any longer.

"Piare," she said matter-of-factly, "are you awake?" The muffled gurgle told her that he was. "I am going to wash you."

She got up and carefully peeled the chunis off his body. She took Mokum's turban and looped it under one arm, across his chest, and under the other arm. Then pulling the turban over her shoulder as she had the night before when pulling the basket, she dragged Piare to the edge of the river.

"This may be uncomfortable for you," she told him, sounding rather clinical. "But I think you will benefit from it. Punditji said it would be good for you too. So my apologies in advance for any discomfort." Her voice sounded confident, and Piare trusted her.

Rajni looked at him in the presunrise light. He wore a horrifically dirty kurta that was more holes than fabric. It had once been white, but now was transitioning to a dark gray. His dhoti may have been the most disgustingly filthy object Rajni had ever seen. It barely covered him and was encrusted with dirt, dried excrement, and mud from the road, squashed insects, and various bodily fluids. The little hair that he had was crawling with lice, and indeed, there was no part of him that did not have ants, worms, or other insects crawling around. She started to remove the rags from his body and hesitated. Except for the occasional sadhu, she had never seen a naked man before.

He's my husband, she thought, *no better time than now.*

Rajni bent down and carefully removed what he was wearing, fighting the urge to scream when she saw the tragedy that was his body. Rajni shivered at the sight. She almost lost control of her bowels as her colon constricted and would not relax. Tears streamed from her eyes, and she was seized with an overwhelming desire to run back to her father's house screaming. Instead, Rajni turned and ran to the Satluj and immersed herself in it. They were just below where the Beas and Satluj meet, and the current was swift there. Rajni wanted simply to lie on her back and float downstream with the current, wherever it would take her.

She sat in the water up to her armpits, nauseous with fear as her long dark braid trailed downstream beside her. It crossed her mind that all she had to do was walk away. She knew that her father would receive her with open arms and she could have her old life back. Duni Chand would probably throw a big party for her, invite the whole of Patti, and all of his surrounding villages. She could force her father to feed the poor, even set out a special place for the lepers. *Perhaps that would serve more people*, she thought to herself. *Just go home, give Papa his due, and then use him and the family wealth to help others.*

She pondered this. All she had to do was walk home, apologize to her father, tell him that he provided for her, and everything would be fine. She would not have to deal with this tragedy of a man up on the bank. She would not have to beg for food. In fact, she had no idea how to beg. All her life, she had been pampered. The people of Patti adored her, and Rajni had no sense of what life would be like without her father's protection or the status of her family.

This thought frightened her. She could not comprehend it. How difficult would it be to go back and apologize to Duni Chand? She shivered as the fear surged in her. Her tears ran down her cheeks and into the water, losing their individual identity in the vastness of the river.

I cannot bear this, she thought to herself. "He is so disgusting!" she screamed. "Who is *he* to be with *me*? And as my husband? Oh God! Oh God! Oh God! Please help me!" she cried hysterically.

She visualized going back and approaching her father. She tried to formulate in her mind what she would say to him, but the words wouldn't come. She saw his face from yesterday and the impenetrable darkness of his heart that he had revealed to her. She could not imagine herself telling Duni Chand that he was the one who provided for her and gave her everything.

"Then who will care for me?" she sobbed out loud.

She sat in the water crying, her tears falling into the ever-flowing river, her despair dominating her. She remembered Punditji and the way she felt yesterday when she sat with the Sikhs from Amritsar.

"Wahe Guru, Wahe Guru, Wahe Guru, Wahe Guru, Wahe Guru, Wahe Guru, Wahe Guru, Wahe Guru" she recited to herself the way Punditji had taught her, eight times to the breath. After the first few hysterical attempts, her breath grew stronger and the sacred sounds calmed her. She closed her eyes and squeezed out her tears. She continued to recite and eventually stopped crying.

Rajni inhaled deeply and began to recite the couplet that stuck in her mind from the hymn the she heard the Sikhs singing the day before:

> *"Oh Nanak, He who created the creatures takes care of them all.*
> *The Creator who created the Creation also takes care of it."*

Forming the sounds with her tongue comforted her. She recited it over and over again and her trembling began to diminish. After some time, she was still, sitting quietly in the water. Rajni visualized the face of Punditji smiling at her and remembered his words, that she was like Pralad, and Piare was her glowing hot pillar.

She stood up and waded out of the Satluj toward Piare.

"Punditji says that God gives the difficult tests to those he loves the most." She smiled at him, "Beloved Piare, God must be deeply in love with us both."

Rajni dragged Piare into the river and waded with him in tow out to some large rocks near midstream. Bits of flesh began to float downstream along with the maggots, worms, and insects that had been attached to Piare. She propped him against a rock so he wouldn't be washed away, yet where the river could flow over him with some velocity. She took the now wet turban and began gently to wipe his face and eyes.

"Listen to me," she said somewhat sternly. "I was raised as a princess. Even though we are in a difficult situation, we don't have to live like vermin. I will wash you every day, and I will find you new clothes. My life has changed and so will yours. We are together now, and I will help you all I can. But you must do your part and help. Does the water hurt you?"

The cold water on his open sores did sting, but Piare liked the feeling of getting clean and not having bugs on him. For the first time in many, many years, Piare smiled.

Rajni left him in the water for a while and then pulled him up on the rock, and they sat under the rising sun. She opened the wet turban and covered him with it.

"I want you to learn the couplet I learned yesterday." Rajni closed her eyes and began reciting:

> *"Oh Nanak, He who created the creatures takes care of them all.*
> *The Creator who created the Creation also takes care of it."*

After a few minutes, Rajni noticed that Piare was mumbling the words. Although it was not melodic, his voice sounded somewhat more human. The water seemed to have helped. She shuddered to think how long it had been since he had washed.

Rajni stood up, knee-deep in the water. "You rest here in the sun. I will go and find us food."

TWENTY-FOUR

Rajni waded the distance to the shore wondering how she would find food. In all her life, she had never asked for anything. Growing up in Duni Chand's house with servants everywhere waiting to do her bidding, she only had to tell them what she wanted, and it was brought to her. Now, she had to go to the house of strangers and beg them to give her food.

Covering her head with one of her sisters' chunis, she set out along the path from the river, stepping cautiously as she went. Her feet were sore and tender from last night's walk, and each step brought more discomfort. She tried not to think about her situation. She didn't want to give in to her fear because she knew that if she did, she would run for Patti as fast as she could.

As she walked, she thought about her sisters and wondered if they were actually arranging to return to their husbands. She cried a little, thinking about their tender concern for her. She cried a little more thinking about her mother who, through her own fear of Duni Chand, precipitated yesterday's events.

"Oh Merciful God," she prayed, "have mercy on my father. Not that he should take me back, but that he can be in Your grace in this lifetime."

It always makes Me happy when people talk to Me. Whether in prayer or in curse, it is all the same to Me because they acknowledge My presence and I love that connection. Her tears stopped. The prayer made Rajni feel better and more at ease.

She was on the main road toward Patti. There was a farmhouse ahead, one she had passed many times between her house and the river. It was a Muslim family. She could see over the wall as the morning sun illuminated the scene before her. Three women were around the oven outside the house, clearly a mother and her daughter, then standing rather sullenly to the side, her daughter-in-law. Rajni followed the wall to the gate then paused, trembling as something in her genetic programming came to the surface with a rush.

She was a Brahmin, the daughter of a powerful man with wide-reaching influence, and she was about to beg for food from a Muslim family, meat eaters with no caste who did not respect the sacredness of the cooking circle. Were they clean? Would this food contaminate her and her soul? She choked back her fear, trying to find justification outside of her Brahmin training and programming.

She squatted down on the side of the road to think. Punditji had taught her about food preparation and the importance of cooking consciously. However, unlike her sister's teachers or Duni Chand himself, Punditji never put a lot of emphasis on keeping the wrong people out. In fact, Punditji never really emphasized caste, though he dutifully taught her about it. She sat in the morning sun, her young heart racing, still reeling from the events of the past twenty-four hours. Her life had literally changed overnight.

She watched the clouds pass overhead and the crows and vultures circling beneath them, then she lowered her gaze to contemplate the gate across the road. She felt a sense of grief and humiliation, mixed with her ever-escalating fear. She doodled in the dirt and tried to both reconcile to herself the issue of taking food prepared by the wrong people and to find the courage to go and ask for it.

"I think these are good people," she said out loud, regarding a large beetle crawling in the dirt, pushing its dung ball. "What could make them unclean?" Never in her life had she taken food that had not been prepared in accordance with strict Vedic guidelines.

She brightened slightly. "Purity or impurity," she said to the beetle, "doesn't come from outside of me." She drew in her breath hard and let it out slowly through her nose as Punditji had taught her to do.

She regarded the beetle as though expecting him to confirm or dispute her theory. She looked up at the vultures for rebuttal.

"What I take into my body might make me sick, but it won't contaminate my soul. Yet if I act cruelly, if I fail to remember God or"—she paused, again addressing the beetle who had stopped—"fail to respect another and their worship of God," she reasoned to herself, "*then*, I contaminate my soul. If others give to me out of kindness and in the Name of God, then I am blessed and so are they."

She remembered a recent afternoon sitting with Punditji in one of Duni Chand's mango groves. "What is a sin, Punditji?"

"Sin?" he spoke from far back in his mind, as though recalling distant memories. "Sin is any action that breaks the heart of another, that compromises the reputation of another, that compromises your own reputation, or that causes your own self-esteem to be diminished. Simply, it is acting without recognizing that God is the doer."

Rajni was surprised by his answer. "So is there no absolute right or wrong?"

"Sins simply create karma, and karma has to be cleared. Recite God's Name and refrain from those actions in the future, then leave the rest to God. He put you in the situation, make Him get you out of it. If you make it God's problem and keep yourself out of the equation, then He is forced to resolve it.

"Remember the story of Daropadi? Her honor was about to be compromised because she was forced to remove her sari. She prayed to Lord Krishna and what happened?"

"Krishna saved her by extending her sari so that it never ran out."

"Blessed Rajni, do you think God loves you less?"

Sitting there in the morning light with the warm smell of food and livestock comforting her, Rajni smiled to herself. She loved her Punditji and felt as though he were talking to her.

"Now," she whispered to herself, the sound of her own voice giving her courage, "I have no one but God to care for me, to feed me and that poor man who is my husband. God gave this to me?" Her voice rose to a high-pitched whisper and she fell silent, her mind racing. "Then," she continued aloud, "He *must* take care of me. And for Him to do that . . . I have to ask for help. Food won't appear in my hand, I have to ask for it. They are Muslims, but they must believe in God, the same God who has brought me to their gate." She paused again. "It was my father's pride as a Brahmin that has put me in this situation. Perhaps God has put me here to break that pride."

Finding the beetle nonresponsive, she now addressed a raven that had landed on the wall across the road, "So what I feel is that same foolish pride. God was with me yesterday," she whispered. "He is with me now and so must be with me tomorrow." That thought delighted her. "Blessed Rajni," she said aloud, remembering Punditji, "do you think that God loves you less?"

She stood and crossed the road and entered the gate.

The air was fragrant with the morning's cooking. Bound to the aroma of food and fire was the thick smell of livestock. To one side of the mud and thatch house were three mudges, chewing their cud and twitching their tails. Flies buzzed around them as they swayed slightly, shifting their weight. The morning milking had been done, and the ground around the mudges was still wet where the women had put water down to hold the flies back. The odors and aromas comforted her and gave her courage.

"*Asalam alikam*," she said shyly.

"*Alikam asalam*," they said in unison.

The ladies looked up and recognition dawned. They had seen Rajni many times. They knew who she was and who her father was, but they could not understand why she was dressed so shabbily. Rajni had never considered her appearance. She had always been a princess, always dressed in the finest clothes, even when going to bathe in the river. Now she entered the gate dressed in the still wet clothes of a sweeper, with no shoes. Her hair, which every day of her fourteen years had been combed, oiled, and braided twice a day, was disheveled, with her wet braid in the process of unraveling.

"Aren't you the daughter of Raja Duni Chand?" the daughter of the house asked, her eyes wide in disbelief.

"Yes, sister . . . I, I mean I was his daughter."

"You *were* his daughter? Has he died then? Are you in mourning?"

"Uhh, well, . . . no, he hasn't died but . . . uhh . . . yes, I am in a kind of mourning." Rajni felt very nervous and vulnerable. She had never been unsure of her place before.

The women looked confused, and Rajni was reluctant to tell the story. She knew Duni Chand had threatened the people of Patti, vowing to punish them if they helped her. She didn't think that these people knew yet what had happened, but she did not want to take a risk. She was very hungry.

"What is it then?" the begum half asked, half demanded.

"Please, madam," pleaded Rajni, "I mean no dishonor upon your home. Have mercy on me at this time of need. I prefer not to speak of the circumstances that have brought me here. Suffice it to say that I need your help desperately. I am here because God in His sweet mercy brought me through my tears to your gate."

No one spoke for more than a minute. All three women regarded Rajni. Such a beautiful girl! Though she was dressed like a sweeper and looked sad and desperate, she still carried herself in a noble way. Her presence overpowered her appearance. None of this made sense.

"How can we help you, child?" The begum was stern but seemed charitable.

"I only ask for a little food. Enough for two people," she added quickly. "Also, I know this might seem unusual, but if you have a spare kurta, I would be most grateful, and I believe that God will show His gratitude to you. I simply ask this in His name."

"Little daughter," said the older woman, "I don't know what has happened that would put you in this position. Yet I can see from your face and the light in your eyes that you have not dishonored yourself. This is most unusual. You have asked in the name of Allah, we cannot refuse you. Please wait here."

The begum went into the house, and Rajni could hear her talking, yelling actually, to the men inside; probably her husband and son. She heard the clanging of metal and the scraping of wood, the woman talking all the while. Outside, the daughter-in-law, just a couple of years older than Rajni, brought her boiled milk, sweetened with crystallized cane juice. She never spoke to Rajni but could not take her eyes off her.

Eventually, the old woman came from the house with a bundle and gave it to Rajni. She then took several chapattis from the oven, wrapped them in a cloth, and gave those to her.

"Whatever it is, my child, Allah's mercy be with you."

Rajni accepted the bundle and held it to her forehead in gratitude. She turned and passed through the gate. As she started the walk back toward the river, she could hear the old woman yelling to her son to get up and go into Patti and find out what was going on. Rajni did not look in the bundle but uttered a brief prayer of thanks. She always remembered Me, even in those trying circumstances.

The chapattis were warm against her skin as she walked quickly back to the river. Her feet were suffering, but she was encouraged that her first attempt at begging had gone rather well. When Rajni reached the river, she could see Piare still sprawled out on the rock, the turban covering him. He hadn't moved. She waded out to him and set her bundle down on the rock.

"How do you feel?" she asked. The fragrant aroma of the food nearly overwhelmed them both.

"Beetterrr," he said.

"Back into the water, then I'll feed you." She did not give Piare the opportunity to protest. She quickly looped the turban around him and lowered him back into the river and let him soak. While he was in the water, Rajni looked through the bundle. Wrapped in an old but reasonably clean kurta and turban were small tiffins of black garbanzos and fresh yogurt, and there was a wooden comb. Rajni was grateful that there was no meat and smiled at the sight of the wooden comb. She took the bundle of chapattis and laid them on the rock to keep them warm. She fished Piare out of the water, covered him with the turban, and propped him against the rock.

She took a chapatti, placed a portion of the garbanzos in the middle, and poured a little yogurt over it. She handed it to Piare. He took it in both hands and held it to his forehead with closed eyes, then tearing a piece of the chapatti, scooped up the garbanzos and began to eat gratefully.

The day passed slowly, and they remained on the rocks in the river. Rajni dunked Piare in the water several more times throughout the day. The water stung him, but the cleansing made him feel better. At least all the insects and worms were off his body, and Rajni was determined to keep it that way. She could not tell if there were insect eggs in Piare's flesh, but she thought that if she bathed him regularly, they would either wash off or be drowned.

Rajni gratefully took the comb and combed and rebraided her hair, tying the parandees in. She looked at Piare. He hardly had hair, so she didn't need to worry for him. That was a relief since she wasn't sure if she would have shared the comb with him.

The sun passed its zenith and pitched down toward the horizon. Rajni thought that it was curious that no one had come to the river all day. Usually, it was an active place where ladies came to bathe and to pound their laundry on the rocks. It eventually dawned on her that no one had come because it was known that she and Piare were there, making it clear to her that they would get no more help from anyone in the vicinity of Patti. The reach of Duni Chand was far, and she and Piare would have to leave the area to avoid it.

* * *

Duni Chand had not softened overnight. Over the pleadings of his distraught wife, his anger prevailed. His other six daughters had sent their servants to collect their things and prepared to return to their husbands. They made no attempt to speak to him or their mother, which only angered Duni Chand further and pained their mother more.

As his anger magnified, he sent his agents throughout Patti and the surrounding villages to warn and intimidate the people. No one was to render any aid whatsoever to Rajni, and by late in the day, everyone knew it. While the people despised Duni Chand for what he had done, they were also afraid of him and what he could do to make their lives miserable. Their fear outweighed their hatred, and Rajni understood this.

Duni Chand was a proud man who had never been in a situation he did not control. From early childhood, he had demanded and received obedience from everyone around him. So the defiance of his daughters fanned the flames of his rage. Not only did they not have gratitude for all that he had done for them, they also defied him publicly. This was unforgivable in his estimation. He didn't care if he never saw any of them again. No one was going to defy him, especially not his daughters!

He anticipated that any time now Rajni and her sisters would come to him in tears and apologize. Throughout the day, he listened for the familiar sound of Rajni's footsteps or the lyrical timbre of her voice. Yet the house remained deafeningly silent, broken only by the sobs and lamentations of Mataji.

"Even if she doesn't come today," reasoned Duni Chand, "it won't be a very long wait. If the leper doesn't die, she can just leave him by the road. She is so fragile. She won't be able to endure the torture I have put on her." He smiled to himself, feeling proud of his scheme. "As soon as I hear her apology, I'll put on a big party, and the whole of Patti will celebrate."

Duni Chand was so convinced that the situation would pass and all would be forgiven and forgotten that he started making plans for the celebration.

He would have a long wait.

*   *   *

As the sun neared the horizon, Rajni's stomach reminded her that she had eaten very little in the past two days, and with some anxiety, she realized that this was to be her life. Part of her did not believe that these circumstances would last, but it was very clear to her that they would not pass quickly. She closed her eyes and recited the hymn of Guru Nanak to herself.

Rajni moved to the shore and did her best to prepare a place for them to sleep. She gathered thatch from the jungle floor and laid it down on the soft sand. As she was doing so, the smell from Piare's basket, which was where she had left it the night before, was unbearable. She had piled his tattered old kurta and dhoti in it that morning. She didn't want to touch it or look inside it, so she found a long stick and pushed it into the river.

Piare was watching her from the rocks and panicked when he saw what she was doing. He waved his arms, trying to get Rajni's attention. That basket was his home, his only place of refuge. He had lived in that particular basket for close to five years, perhaps the five most unbearable years of his already miserable life, but it gave him the security of a mother's womb. Now as he watched it float downstream he felt as though his whole life was being washed away.

"Those are my only possessions!" He was in a panic. "Where will I live? Now I have no place of refuge, no home, no comfort." He hung his head and placed his calloused and stubby hands against his forehead. *My life has changed,* he thought, *what will happen now? Oh Lord Rama, give me courage.* He sat with his forehead against his hands, listening to the flowing of the water and thinking back through his life.

Not such a bad thing, he thought to himself, *I need a change.*

Piare surrendered to the realization that now, he truly was in My hands. His security was gone downstream, along with the companions his body had hosted for all those years, yet he was no worse off. He felt the kurta that Rajni had been given that morning. Though it swallowed him, it was the first clean thing he had worn in years. In fact, all of him was clean. He was still hungry, but hunger had been his constant companion for most of his life. Yet now, for the first time in his life he had hope.

Rajni waded back out to the rock and dragged him back to the shore.

"Don't worry," she told him. "If I have to carry you on my back, I will. But I won't permit you to live that way ever again. Shame on you for allowing yourself to reach that condition. Your arms are strong, you could have cleaned yourself. You gave up didn't you?"

Piare looked at her and nodded.

"I won't have a husband who gives up. Do you understand me?"

"Neverrr againnn," he spewed.

Rajni smiled at him. She took one of her sister's chunis, tied a kind of loincloth around him, and pulled the kurta over his head and shoulders. Then she sat with him and recited the Arti. She laid him down and covered him with the turban of Mokum. She lay next to him and covered herself with the turban she had been given that morning, hoping that she would be better protected from the mosquitoes. She was very tired and fell asleep quickly.

Rajni awoke with a start. Terrified, her heart was racing, her breathing difficult. At first, she didn't know where she was. When she opened her eyes, all she could see was the velvet blackness of My sky and billions of stars. The sound of the river comforted her, but there was another sound away from the river, toward the Patti road.

Dacoits, she thought. She was terrified and knew that if bandits were there, she would be helpless before them. She could not identify the sound clearly, but it sounded like wheels turning. Then she heard footsteps moving quickly away from her. Her heart pounded as adrenaline surged through her body. The footsteps faded, leaving her alone with the sound of the river and Piare's labored breathing.

She was afraid to move and decided that whatever it was had no interest in them. She drifted back to sleep but woke up every few minutes. At first light, the mosquitoes claimed victory, and she got up. She made her way to the river to clean herself and when she turned back toward the bundle that was her husband, she noticed something familiar further ahead. She stepped around Piare and walked toward it.

A short distance from where they slept was a small gardening wagon with wooden wheels. She recognized it as one of the gardening carts from Duni Chand's formal gardens. A rope was looped through the handle of the little wagon, coiled and placed neatly inside. In the cart were two shawls, which she recognized as among those that were kept in the garden cottage, two clay pots containing dal and yogurt, a half-dozen chapattis wrapped in burlap, five mangoes, one of each variety from Duni Chand's groves, a small curved knife, a fire starting kit, and a pair of shoes.

"Piare," she exclaimed happily, "we're rich!" She got him up and washed him, then sat with him and recited the hymn, holding his mangled hands. They ate, and Rajni forced Piare to talk, wanting to improve his speech. She was relentless in her determination to make him better.

"Listen, my beloved," she said, "this is a message to us that we must leave this area. No one will come to this spot as long as we are here, and no one in the Patti district will help us. We have to move on and see where God leads us. Do you understand?"

"I do," said Piare.

"Very good," said Rajni. She smiled to him, her eyes flashing in the morning sunlight, "You are doing better."

Rajni lined the bottom of the wagon with the shawls, then lifted and pushed until Piare was in a stable position in the little wagon. She covered Piare with four of the chunis, withholding one for herself, then placed the pots with the remaining dal and yogurt in front of him. She rinsed Mokum's turban in the river, then folded it wet, and placed it and the one given her by the begum in the cart over the food. She slipped her sore feet into the shoes, which were too big for her, and stepped forward, pulling the little wagon with her husband behind her.

They made an odd sight as they set out on the road. A beautiful young girl, wearing clothes and shoes that were too big, pulling a gardening cart containing what appeared to be a person draped with chunis. People passed them on the road curiously, but no one spoke to them. Everyone knew.

TWENTY-FIVE

SHE FOLLOWED THE SATLUJ UPSTREAM, going east for no other reason than it gave her the sense that she was getting farther away from Duni Chand. For two days, they lived on the mangoes and dal that she found in the wagon. They went without eating for a day, then finally, Rajni had no choice but to beg for food. Her experience with the begum on that first morning had encouraged her and given her the hope that begging would not be so difficult. She found though that begging was hard work. She hated to do it, hated to face the fear that arose in her each day when she anticipated it, hated how it made her feel to hold out her pots and beg for food, asking for the leavings of others.

It was at these times that her Brahmin programming ran headfirst into the hard and inflexible wall of reality. She could not afford to observe the practices she had grown up with. If she did, they would starve. Whenever they stopped at a village, they always camped near the outskirts where the untouchables and outcastes stayed.

Once, she tried to enter a village with Piare. She pulled the little wagon to the village well and moved in among the people there who were drawing water, as she would have done in any village around Patti. Immediately, people began yelling and pelting her and Piare with shoes, stones, and rotten food.

After that, they camped on the outskirts of the villages. Rajni would leave Piare and go to the wells alone. Initially, she found it difficult to associate with the lowborn who camped outside the villages with them. She had been taught that if she made physical contact with a sudra, she would become contaminated and then would have to bathe and perform puja to cleanse herself. Sudras were never allowed in the dining area or kitchen of Duni Chand's house, nor were they allowed in some temples. Yet now she found herself eating with them frequently or sleeping next to them in their camping places. This was a challenge for her, and she did not take to it comfortably.

Before her wedding day, she had never gone a day in her life without bathing or changing her clothes. Now she grew accustomed to her own smell, which clung firmly to her clothes and body. At night, when they camped with the lowborn, with only one shawl covering her, she would lie awake taking in the strong human odors that arose with the snores of the sleepers.

The human smell, she mused, *comes from everyone the same. I am Brahmin, they are sudra*—she gazed into the darkness of the night—*and we all stink. Does my caste change that? I think that in our core, we are the same.* "God is equal in us all," she whispered to herself in the dark. "I can tell by His smell. Eh Ram," she prayed, "give me understanding. Is this why this has happened to me? So that I can understand that You are equally in us all?"

As she pulled the rope over her shoulder, she constantly tried to make sense out of what had happened to her, tried to assess herself against the life she was living, and sought the truth about herself and her relationship with Me. Yet she found that these were simply people, also created by Me, who had their needs and longings. With the exception of their circumstances, at their core, they were no different than anyone else.

The true measure of a person is what is in the heart, she mused to herself. *These people may not be educated and have never read the Vedas, but they understand the divinity of all things. My father is Brahmin, yet he is so cruel to others. His faith is all show, but their faith, though simple, seems true.*

Rajni remembered Punditji's words to her on her wedding day, "*As your teacher, I should be happy, for all that I have taught you is about to be put to the test now.*"

It was true. All that she had learned from her family and her beloved Punditji was being put to the test. When she started walking east, it was late summer. She was still a Brahmin and the daughter of Raja Duni Chand. It seemed that she was setting out on a great adventure and was optimistic about where it would lead her. Yet by the cold darkness of the month of *Pausa*, the lunar month between December and January, she was an Untouchable, hungry and cold. Every morning Rajni went out and begged for food, and she frequently came back empty-handed. After that first morning, she found that the notion of food being contaminated by people of low caste was a superstition, especially since she realized that now she had become an Untouchable herself. Dressed in the oversized and worn clothes of the sweeper, she was nearly indistinguishable as a Brahmin.

Unable to care for herself properly each day, the smooth fairness of her Aryan skin was darkened by constant exposure to the sun and weather, by the dirt and filth of the road, by insect bites and stings, scratches, cuts, and bruises. She had lost her comb and the radiant, raven blackness of her disheveled hair was streaked with dirt and mud. Bits of leaves and twigs were entangled in it and, what had been her tightly woven braid, was now loose and unraveling.

Yet the elegant refinement of her nose and cheeks, the noble rise of her eyebrows, the almond ovals and bright obsidian darkness of her eyes, and the regal dignity of her mouth and chin could not be obscured. She carried herself with dignified grace, whether she leaned forward pulling Piare in the gardening wagon or stood in the bazaars and villages to beg. The quiet nobility of her heart and mind still endured.

Perhaps, people assumed, she was the result of the indiscretion of some high-born Brahmin or that some other irregularity in her bloodline gave her such distinctive features. She was an Untouchable, though fortunate enough to have the presence of a Brahmin.

She found that the lower castes were more generous and willing to share what little they had. Since they already shared a common suffering, a piece of chapatti or a spoonful of dal was usually willingly shared when available. In fact, many Brahmins refused to give her aid and some tried to take advantage of her.

One morning, she came to the large estate of a Brahmin to ask for help. She spoke to the elder son who at first refused her then seemed to change his mind. He told her to follow him and led her to the back of the estate, toward the stable and manger area. As they walked, she noticed an exquisite shrine to the goddess Durga built around a carved marble statue of the deity astride her lion.

As they walked, Rajni admired the boy, who was about two years older. She was sure that he was someone whom Duni Chand would have considered as a possible match for her. She could not keep from thinking that if she had listened to her sisters and not defied her father, she would be married to a boy like this instead of a crippled leper. He was an attractive boy. His personality vibrant, his body muscular. She found herself longing to be in such a situation, with a good family and attractive husband, away from Piare and the wagon and her desperate circumstances. Her mind drifted to fantasy as they passed toward the back of the estate. Rajni believed that he was taking her to the kitchen or was going to have her work in exchange for food. But the harsh reality of her life shattered that fantasy as his intentions became clear. They were behind a mud wall that contained the livestock feeding at the manger.

In a sudden move that caught Rajni completely by surprise, the boy turned and pushed her against the wall of the manger. He pinned her shoulders and pushed his body against her, his passion growing.

"Before I satisfy your appetite, you must satisfy mine," he whispered in her ear.

Rajni looked at him, her eyes wide, her heart accelerating. "You call yourself a Brahmin? Go ahead, then," said Rajni quietly. "I've been thinking that I should kill myself anyway. After all, my father has disowned me, and I am married to a leper. I have nothing left in this life. If you rape me, you will help me to make the decision to kill my husband, then myself, a decision I have delayed for much too long."

The young Brahmin stared at her, speechless. His hands fell to his side as his passion receded with each heartbeat. "You shouldn't talk that way," he said. "You are young and beautiful, things could change in your life. You must have something to live for."

"My friend, my only assets are my grace and honor. I live only for that. If you do as you intend and take that from me, then you leave me with nothing and I am worse than dead. I have been flirting with death these past months anyway. In fact, I married death itself. So go ahead. Do as you like. My only resource is my honor." She paused reflectively. "Before you take that from me, I would like to ask you one question."

"Ask," his voice was quiet.

"What satisfaction do you get? For one as strong and powerful as you to overcome a small girl such as me is not difficult. You know you can have your way with me. What satisfaction is in it for you? It can't be romantic. It can't be especially pleasurable. I am neither your enemy nor a woman of means. What is the point? Does it satisfy you to violate the honor of one who only has God to uphold it? Is your life so devoid of grace and dignity that you despise all who respect that in themselves? Do you then feel that you are so much more powerful than God that you must violate the honor of one weaker than you? If so," she spread her arms in invitation, "then please try. I can understand facing a respected enemy on the field of battle. But a hungry girl who contemplates her own death with a helpless and dying husband? What satisfaction can there be?"

The truth was, Rajni *had* been contemplating death. She was tired and hungry and Piare's presence in her life was becoming increasingly burdensome. Piare revolted her. Aggravated by her constant hunger and the relentless cold, just being around Piare disgusted her and made her angry with the world. She couldn't bear to look at him and despised her circumstances to the point that she was beginning to believe that the only way out was suicide.

The Brahmin was speechless.

"Eh ji, you are a Brahmin, and I see that you and your family are devoted to Durga. Shame on you! How can you betray the goddess you worship?"

"Uhh, I . . ."

"Well, get on with it, then. I believe in my grace and honor and I believe that she whom you worship will protect me. Let's see if you are more powerful than she. I would like to see if your passion and malignant heart can destroy my grace."

The Brahmin dropped to his knees, his face in his hands. His whole body shook. He fell forward onto his face and gripped Rajni's ankles.

"Please have mercy on me, sister. Oh God, you have touched my heart. Forgive me, forgive me," he whined.

Rajni bent down and placed her hands on his head. She began to recite, *"Aum Aiem Hareem Karem Shri Karam Kareem,"* a most sacred and esoteric mantra that invokes the goddess Durga.

The Brahmin sat up, startled, wiping tears from his eyes. "Where did you learn that?"

"My Punditji taught it to me," she said matter-of-factly. "Why?"

"Your Punditji? How could you have a pundit, and if so, how could he have taught you this . . . unless you? . . . Are you? . . . Eh Ram, what have I done?"

Rajni slapped the back of his head. "Listen to me, oh great Brahmin, any girl of any caste should be respected and protected, not just a Brahmin girl."

"Oh Durga Devi, please forgive me."

A horse shifted in the manger. Another kicked the wall. Mudges shifted and lowed. Flies buzzed around the head of the Brahmin, who was now quite filthy from groveling on the ground. He stood up slowly and looked toward the house.

"Little sister," he said softly, "I will give you food and quilts, but please don't mention this to my family."

Rajni's look was contemptuous, and the bright obsidian shine of her eyes made the arrogant young man feel even more ashamed. He felt as though he was standing before Durga herself. In a way he was, since Rishi Mahan Akal had infused her soul with the essence of that goddess.

"I will do as you ask, but you must do as I ask and never violate a woman or a girl again." Rajni took him by the hand and pulled him before the family shrine. "You vow this now before Durga Devi, and I will let you go."

"Before Durga, I vow it," he said sincerely and prostrated himself before the shrine.

True to his word, he gave her enough food for four days and two thick quilts. Two days later, he left his ancestral home, shaved his head, and retreated to Jawalamukhi, where Lehna had danced for Durga. For three years, he lived as a hermit, serving Durga by cleaning her shrine and serving the pilgrims who went there.

That encounter deeply disturbed Rajni. As she walked away, she thanked Me that she had a teacher as incredible as Punditji. Without his teachings and loving guidance, she would not have been able to confront the Brahmin and walk away unharmed. She was hit hard by the real dangers she faced and her vulnerability to them. That realization nearly paralyzed her.

After the encounter with the Brahmin, Rajni and Piare spoke little. It required all of Rajni's strength to keep moving, and when they rested she was too tired, hungry, and out of breath to talk. Sometimes they would remain outside of a village for several days, but seldom more than that. The course of the Satluj was not easy to follow, and when they were not near the water, Rajni had to find it and carry it back to Piare. And the already slender girl grew thinner.

Piare improved somewhat under Rajni's care, but the reality of his disease was not dismissed. Though his body was no longer host to vermin and a food source for the birds, the progressive nature of leprosy continued unchecked. She kept him covered with the chunis of her sisters so that his ulcerated skin would be protected and so that he would be hidden from sight. She washed him daily, washed his kurta occasionally, and fed him before she ate. A silent communication developed between them since Rajni was usually too tired and annoyed to talk, and speech for Piare was always a challenge. She always knew when he needed something or when he was uncomfortable or in pain. And although she despised him for requiring it and herself for doing it, she would stop and comfort him, find him food, or give him aid. But always in silence.

While Rajni had never known such misery, Piare had never known such kindness, not even in himself. Growing up in the leper camps, the lepers did what they could for each other, but their primary concern was always for themselves, and as he matured, Piare was no different. He remembered snatching food from the hands of another leper who was weaker than him. Another time, he took the shawl of a leper who was dying, reasoning to himself that she would not be cold much longer, but that her shawl would keep him warm for some time. When he thought about that now, he felt unbearable shame and regret.

His gratitude and love for Rajni grew. Despite herself, she was always tender with him. Even when she was tired and hungry, she always made sure that he was warm and comfortable. Yet her silence and emotional distance troubled him. He could not fault her for it, and though he tried to engage her, she seldom responded.

Each morning, she sat off by herself and did the *Wahe Guru* meditation Punditji had taught her. Occasionally, they recited the hymn of Guru Nanak together, and each evening they recited the *Arti*. Whenever they passed a temple, whether to Shiva, Vishnu, or Ganesh, Hanuman, Durga, or Kali, Rajni went in, bowed, and offered whatever she could. She would pray for Piare, pray for her father and mother, pray for her sisters, and pray that she had the strength not to give up.

Though Rajni never revealed her feelings to Piare, she often felt hopeless, afraid, and overcome by panic and despair. Sometimes, she told Piare that she was going out to beg, but as soon as she was out of his sight and range of hearing, she fell to the ground, dropped her head to her hands, and sobbed. Her slender body shook and the tears flowed copiously. Each day was a struggle for her to maintain herself, to keep her balance and dignity, to get up and keep moving. The arrogant young princess, daughter of a powerful and influential man, was now simple and helpless. She tried to push her doubts and desolation deeper into her heart, and though she tried, she could not make sense out of what had happened to her.

Thanks to what she had been taught, to her own resilience, and to her invincible heart, she persevered. Despite all that had happened to her, the brutality and deprivations she encountered, she still maintained her innocence and sweetness. Her life with Piare, a life with only Me to lean on, had become the crucible from which her true essence, the pure and immutable element of her soul, would be distilled. Maturity and understanding grew like a fetus inside of her.

Each day, she got up and pulled the little wagon without a clear destination in mind. Rajni just wanted to keep moving, partially because it gave her a sense of getting away from the situation she was in and partially because it gave her some hope that she was moving toward something better. Welts developed on her slender shoulders from pulling the wagon. Her feet and hands became badly blistered then callused. Deep cracks formed in her heels and along the sides of her feet, making each step painful. Still, Rajni felt a constant pull to keep moving.

TWENTY-SIX

THE EASTERN REGION OF THE Punjab rises toward the foothills of the Himalayas, and as Rajni followed the Satluj east, the terrain became more difficult for her to negotiate. This area was more sparsely populated, there were fewer people on the roads, and the nights were colder and made her feel uneasy. The darkness of the winter nights was extended and made darker by the dense fog that rose during the night and settled like a shroud over the Punjab. Many mornings, it lingered until well past midday when it dissipated reluctantly and, on some days, not at all. The nights were especially uncomfortable for her. They were damp and cold, and a quilt was insufficient to hold her body heat in and keep the cold out. The fog made the darkness seem more uncertain and the future seem more threatening to her.

As the winter progressed, a fog rose steadily from her mind and settled in her heart. Piare seemed to be worsening while her resolve was growing weaker. Some days, when she shouldered the rope and set out on her quest to nowhere, the weight she pulled seemed greater and her strength to pull it seemed less. They went days without speaking, sometimes days without eating, and occasionally, days without moving when Rajni simply didn't have the will to get up and step forward.

When she did speak to Piare, it was with irritation in her voice, the voice of the princess. She was short-tempered with him, disgusted by him actually. Under normal circumstances, her father would have never allowed even the shadow of such a lowborn and filthy wretch to fall across his gate. She could not bear to look at him or hear him speak. She hated that he was so helpless and useless. How he had managed to stay alive was a complete mystery to her. She wondered why he should even be alive. She recognized with some shame that she wished he would die so she could be free of his smell, his weight, and his hopeless dependency on her.

Or she wished that she would die so this nightmare could end. Rajni was especially irritable on days when they did not eat or when they had little food to share. She was repulsed by Piare's presence and resented that she had to share what little she got from begging with him. Yet she felt that she could not leave him, that the rope she held in her calloused and aching hands somehow bound her to this wretched and miserable human being. How insane could she have been when she told Punditji that she wanted to bear the suffering of others on her back?

Then one horrifying day, she lost her will completely as they passed a cremation ground. They had passed many, and Rajni normally tried not to look at them. Yet on this day, there was a large funeral underway, obviously for a wealthy and important Brahmin like Duni Chand. The pyre had been set aflame. Rajni and Piare watched as the flames climbed aggressively over the sandalwood logs and the body wrapped in white upon it. She tried not to look, but the hysterical screams of a young woman stopped her cold and she could not move. As if frozen in place, Rajni stood on the road and watched as unspeakable horror unfolded before her eyes. Standing above the funeral pyre were the family of the deceased, and among them was his wife, who appeared to be approximately the age of Gita, Rajni's eldest sister. The young woman was clearly distraught, and Rajni believed that her screams were those of deepest mourning.

At first, it appeared to Rajni that the family was trying to hold and comfort the young widow, but she quickly recognized that what was actually taking place was a life-or-death struggle. The girl's shrieks were those of terror, desperation, and hopelessness, not from grief, but fear. The family of the deceased, led by his mother, was trying to push the girl into the fire to die in the flames with her husband in the practice of sati. The poor girl was hysterical with fear and grief, struggling for her life, begging for mercy. But there was no mercy, and the hopelessness in the woman's screams tortured Rajni's raw and suffering heart. Rajni, terrified and sickened by what she was witnessing, could not move or turn away.

With a cacophonous, mind-shattering scream of resignation, the girl lost her balance after being pushed by the mother and fell backward onto the burning body of her husband. Immediately, her cries for mercy became the desperately hysterical screams of excruciating pain and anguish. Rajni watched as the girl's sari caught fire and then ignited her hair. The poor woman writhed in agony, begging for help. She tried to pull herself from the flames, but she lacked the strength. Eventually, she was overcome and collapsed, leaving only the sounds of the fire and the stench of burning flesh.

Rajni trembled, her knees weakened, and she fought not to become hysterical herself as the stench overtook her. She dropped to her knees and was violently ill, losing what little she had in her stomach, then continuing to heave in horror. The sounds, the images, and the smell of burning flesh and hair clung like oil to her nostrils and clothes. The foul odor would not leave her and haunted her for days.

Several mornings later, Rajni sat off by herself with her arms across her knees, her head resting heavily on her forearms. She had been unable to sleep. So cold and miserable, she got up before the coming of the light and, taking her begging pots, moved away from Piare to be by herself and take refuge in the fog. She had also removed the rope from Piare's wagon.

She cried and brooded. What if Piare were to die? Would she be forced to jump on his funeral pyre and die with him? That thought made her shiver in the cold. Was such a wretch worth dying for? And if not, she wasn't sure what she would do next. She felt crushed by the weight of her circumstances. Pulling Piare gave her a sense of purpose, and without this hideously deformed soul to care for, what would she do? Would she go home back to Duni Chand after experiencing his heartless cruelty? She could not imagine it. Yet she hated her situation and could not find in herself any spark of warmth toward her husband. Doubt as dense as the fog rose in her. She felt lost and helpless with no one to turn to.

Rajni thought of her mother and wondered tearfully if Mataji would fling herself onto the pyre of Duni Chand. Rajni could not imagine it and equated it to her jumping onto the pyre of Piare. Was a man as heartless and cruel as Duni Chand worth dying in such agony for? She screamed for her mother and cried hysterically.

When she had lived in the house of Duni Chand, when she was well-fed and comfortable, it was easy for her to recognize Me as the provider of everything. Now, she wasn't sure. She wondered, as many humans do, if I had abandoned her. By insulting her father had she caused this karma that she now had to bear? Perhaps if she had only humored him, she would be home in her warm bed now.

"I can't change what has happened," she whispered into the fog, "but I can't continue like this."

Her tears left tracks in the dirt on her face as they rolled down her cheeks. In the stillness of the morning, she cried her soft tears of hopelessness and defeat. She stood up and looked through the fog. Spotting a tall tree, she took the rope and trudged toward it. She climbed up several branches then reached up and tied one end of the rope around a branch above her. She formed a loop with the other end of the rope and secured it firmly around her neck.

Humans have been blessed with the power of free will, and the application of that can alter one's destiny. I am sometimes amazed by the decisions that people make, so I was especially surprised by the decision that this precious soul made. But it was hers to make, and I had to allow her to go through with it. I understood her loneliness. It was something We shared.

Balancing precariously, she closed her eyes and thought of Punditji and her sisters. "Eh Ram, I surrender," she spoke softly, barely able to hear her own voice. Then as she had that day on the rocks at Rishikesh, she jumped. This time I caught her on My firm and solid Earth. She hit the ground hard, twisting both her ankles, skinning her knees and spraining her right wrist. The branch around which the rope had been tied came crashing down and landed painfully across her shoulders and head with a crackling thud and breaking of twigs. She had a severe rope burn around her neck.

Rajni looked up painfully through the fog, dizzy and stunned by what had happened. She lay under the branch, covered her face with her hands and screamed hysterically.

"I can't even kill myself! Is there no escape from this horror? Help me then. Tell me what to do," she screamed into the fog.

"You must become zero!" The voice was firm but comforting.

Rajni raised her head slightly. She was not startled by the voice, simply aware of it as she was aware of the fog and the cold. Opening her eyes, she saw in the faint light of the foggy dawn two bare feet. Crawling out from under the branch, the rope still around her neck, she raised her head and followed the legs to which the feet were attached and saw a naked sadhu standing before her. He was covered with ashes, and his long white hair was coiled high on his head. Three white horizontal lines across his forehead identified him as a Shaivite, a devotee of Lord Shiva. In his right hand, he held a formidable trident, which is the symbol of Shiva. Though it was decorated and a garland of marigolds hung from the broad central prong, it was clearly a weapon and the sadhu appeared to be fully capable of using it. Around his neck hung a large lion's claw and four strands of carved wooden beads. A thick ivory bracelet closed with a large silver clasp around his right wrist.

Rajni was not frightened by his presence, just as she had not been frightened by the aghora on her wedding night. Neither his nakedness nor the stealth of his appearance upset her or seemed out of place to her. In fact, the presence of the sadhu comforted her. He had been in the area meditating in union with Me. My girl was in trouble, and I needed someone to help her. So I asked him to do the job. It was her choice to place the rope around the weakest branch in the tree, but I had created her for a special purpose and I needed someone to comfort her and give her clarity. Even I have My weaknesses.

"First become zero, then you will become one." He spoke in very precise Sanskrit.

Rajni simply stared at him, thinking it curious that behind his white beard and mustache, she could not see his mouth move when he spoke, so it seemed that his voice came out of the fog. The sun broke the plane of the horizon and ascended toward its zenith, illuminating the morning sky. The light of the sun filtered through the fog of the Punjab, causing an ethereal radiance to spread over Rajni and the sadhu.

"We know who you are and we are watching. Reach the *shunnya*," he whispered, "and you will be filled. This *Wahe Guru* mantra that you recite will take you there. Exaggerate the movement of your mouth when you recite it, you will notice the difference."

Shifting the *tershul* to his left hand, the sadhu rubbed the thumb and fingertips of his right hand together, and she saw ashes fall from them. He extended his arm, and the ashes fell copiously upon her head and shoulders. Their fragrance was deep, mysterious and otherworldly, an enchanting mixture of sandalwood and rose, amber and resins, flowers and opium, and Rajni became intoxicated by the smell. Then the old sadhu bent down and placed his right thumb between her eyebrows, rubbing the ashes into her "third eye." The tips of his other fingers pushed down through her lice-infested hair and onto her skull.

"Oh Rajni, who bears the suffering of the Kali Yuga," he still whispered, as the sound of his voice gripped her psyche, "take our suffering to the water. He who rotates the Earth shall protect you."

The smell of the ashes was potent and affected her awareness. The sound of his voice was soothing and mesmerizing. She began to drift, her head began to roll, and she lost consciousness. With the sadhu's hand maintaining gentle contact, her head fell forward onto her arms, and she fell into a deep trancelike sleep, the rope still around her neck.

And she began to dream. She saw Punditji emerge from the fog, smiling. He pointed up, and she raised her head to behold a clear night sky. The seven stars of the Pleiades twinkled against the deep velvet of the night.

From the light of those stars appeared the faces of her sisters, then Rishi Mahan Akal appeared. He reached down and lifted Rajni up in his hands. He held her close to his face and smiled, and Rajni gazed deep into his eyes. In their glow, another face appeared. It was the face of a saintly man with a long, flowing beard and crow's-feet at the corners of his eyes. She found herself standing before him. He was dressed in white and sat on a raised dais. He motioned her to come toward him. She approached, bowed before him, then looked up. She had never seen such a sweetly serene and compassionate face.

"Have no fear. I walk with you always." And Rajni noticed that his feet were as cut and raw as hers. The sound of his voice was like a rebab and brought her serene relief. It was not as though she heard it, but more as if the voice came from within her. "You bear the suffering of the Kali Yuga. Bring it to the water so that it can be washed from this Age."

Rajni awoke, still covered with the fragrant ashes. They were in her hair, on her clothes, forehead, and cheeks, and on the ground around her. The sadhu was gone, and the fog had dissipated. She removed the rope from around her neck and brushed the twigs off her. Sore from her fall, she picked up her begging pots, ready to go find breakfast. Surprised by how heavy and warm they felt, she looked in them. They were filled with dal and rice, yogurt, and chapattis.

*   *   *

Piare was awake when Rajni got up but, as usual, kept to himself. Since that first day at the Satluj when she had bathed him and committed his basket to the river, she had been his lifeline. Though he had managed to survive for the eleven years since he had been abandoned by his parents, his life had been little more than that: a continuous quest for survival, like a jackal. He had stayed alive by scavenging, by taking advantage of those who were weaker, and by an irrepressible determination to live.

Now that determination was slipping. Sitting in silence as he watched Rajni bend under the rope and pull him in the wagon day after day, he began to probe himself and study the circumstances of his life—his motivation and actions—which ultimately led him to reflect on his karma and his relationship with the Universe. He had never had it as good as he did now, and he did not overlook the fact that it was the reverse for Rajni. He could not understand why nor could he understand what dynamic of time and space had caused this to happen to each of them. He didn't feel that either of them deserved the other, but he could not disregard the bond, though unacknowledged, that was growing between them.

He took stock of his body. He was literally eaten up with the leprosy and knew that he would never recover. He would never walk, would never be able to earn his own bread, and would never be able to be productive in any way. In the shrouded light of the morning fog, he held up his hands. He studied his ulcerated flesh and withered fingers. His arms were strong from years of using them to lift and propel him in his basket. His hands, despite their hideous appearance, were strong but limited in how he could use them. He looked down at the wispy tendrils of his legs and shuddered. He had never assessed himself so carefully and so honestly. What had he done in his previous lifetimes to have such karma to bear in this one?

He knew that his condition was worsening. His respiration was more labored, and the deterioration of his flesh was clearly evident, though Rajni never mentioned it. Piare lay back down and looked up through the fog. The early morning light diffusing through the fog gave him a sense that he was neither on the earth nor in the air. He felt that he was floating, lost in the sea of eternity. He was afraid that he would drift like that, lost forever in the infinite flow of time and space: ever a burden, never to be loved.

As he lay there, it seemed that the fog closed in on him, not only surrounding him but also filling him. Because of the ravages of the leprosy he had had hallucinations before, but this experience seemed real. He saw his human incarnations back to the time of the Golden Age. He was a warrior, powerful and fearless, but he fought without mercy and, in so doing, lost his honor and nobility.

He saw another incarnation, again as a warrior and he fought on the side of Raja Kal Rai of Lahore. In the devastating defeat of that battle, he was severely wounded. Weak and bloody and nearly delirious with thirst, he crawled on his stomach trying to find water, and the water he found was the sacred pool. He drank and washed his wounds.

He made poultices with the herbs that grew there and healed quickly. He was restored but because of the defeat of Raja Kal Rai he, like the Raja himself, was forced to leave his home and settle in Sandoh Desh. He returned to the vicinity of the pool and lived a life of seclusion and contemplation.

He incarnated again and learned the healing arts of Ayurveda and became renowned for his diagnoses and treatments. In time, he came under the influence of the Vedi Guru and the teachings of the Vedas. He fell deeply in love with Me. He was highly regarded as a healer and teacher with great power. People came from afar to be healed by him or to hear his teachings. Then one afternoon as he walked along the road to meet the Vedi Guru, he heard a cry for help. He was in a blissful state, deep in contemplation, chanting a sacred refrain, and hesitated to stop. He heard the cry again, and looking at the side of the road, he saw a wretched soul. Dark-skinned, sick and dying, the suffering man held out his hand for help.

"In the Name of God," the poor man cried, "have mercy on me and please help. Just a little water and a little comfort before I slip into that great void." That was Me. I do things like that to test people sometimes, and it was his turn.

The body that Piare's soul inhabited and the conscious mind that drove it were unwilling to leave that blissful state, especially to help someone so lowly and so near death. He turned and continued walking. When he reached the Vedi Guru, he was trembling and feverish. The Vedi Guru called him in.

"My son, you have committed a grave error today."

Piare's soul knew it to be so. He felt it in his every fiber. The old sanskara that had caused him to dishonor himself in the Golden Age had once again surfaced because through all his meditation and spiritual achievement, he had never recognized that I was working through him. Spiritual ego had caused him to betray his own divinity.

The Vedi Guru's voice cut like the executioner's sword, "Today, you turned your back on God Himself. You have performed great service and austerities to achieve the power you have. God in His mercy blessed you, and His healing energy has flowed through you. Yet the one thing that you must have to be a true healer and master you have failed to cultivate. Until you surrender to your compassion and humility, you will never be free. You have lost the human touch and that has cursed you."

The body that housed Piare's soul fell before the Vedi Guru and clung to his feet. "What can I do? How can I purify myself and be freed of this sin?"

"Go home, dedicate yourself to prayer and meditation. Fast and always remember God's Name. This sickness that grows in you now will free you from this body soon. You will die alone and in great pain. In the Kali Yuga, the suffering of humanity will fall upon you, and your illness will be great. Yet when Sodhi Rai incarnates as the Guru of Miracles, he will relieve your suffering. Through your own suffering, you will learn compassion while remembering God. That will humble you, and you will be freed. Go now. You will not see my face again in this life."

The vision faded, and Piare could only see fog. He became aware of his body and the ground beneath him, but something had changed. There was light. He opened his eyes and saw Rajni sitting in the sun next to him, smiling.

"Piare, my love, something has happened."

TWENTY-SEVEN

They rested for sometime near the village of Kiratpur beside the Satluj. There, near the headwaters, the river is narrow and shallow. With Naina Devi, a high peak and Hindu place of pilgrimage in the foothills of the Himalayas rising behind them, they passed their time silently contemplating the depth and meaning of their individual visions.

The water ran cold there, making Piare's daily bath both painful and stimulating, and he seemed to improve a bit. Rajni had hoped that this might be the water she had been told to find, but with each passing day, it became more clear to her that she had further to go. Still, Kiratpur was a pleasant place. Early signs of spring began to reveal themselves, and Rajni's spirits gradually lifted. They enjoyed the time there; the people of the area were generous and they ate daily. Yet as the weeks passed, Rajni grew restless.

"Beloved," she addressed Piare one morning, "I keep thinking about the message of the aghora on our wedding night and now the message of the sadhu. Both told me to find the water. I had hoped that this was the place, but I know in my heart and soul that we have further to go. You have improved here, but now that spring is coming, I feel that we should move on and seek the place of the water."

Piare looked at her and reflected for some time. "Don't . . . be misled. Wh . . . while I may be . . . better-r now than when you . . . found me, due . . . s-solely to your kindness and tender care, this disease . . . that lives in me . . . will not be reversed. Don't believe that wh . . . wherever we go, we are going to a place wh . . . where I . . .will be healed."

"Piar . . ."

He held up his right hand. "You were . . . right our . . . first day together. I ha . . . had given up, but you have ch . . . changed that in me. I want to live . . . I wo . . . would like to be healed, but I have seen things that I pray you neverr see . . . I know wh . . . what this sickness does to a person. I am . . . resigned to wh . . . whatever . . . is God's will. For that reason . . . and from the impact of my vision, I . . . I feel that we should continue. I know mirracles can ha . . . happen in my life. You are proof of that. But for me to be . . . healed and be . . . come a capable person . . . is beyond my capacity to believe. Ye . . . yet, let us . . . continue. I don't know how long I will last . . ."

"Piare! Don't talk that way."

Piare held up his hand again. "You mu . . . must understand . . . the reality of my condition . . . I . . . I know what this . . . disease does. Everyone who . . . has it dies from it. I have sseen many, myself . . . among them, wh . . . who pray for their . . . death to come. You have ch . . . changed that in me, but . . . I . . will worsen in time. Still, perhaps together . . . we . . . ca . . . can find the water . . . and it will create a miracle. That . . . mmiracle may free me fromm . . . this consumed body." Piare paused, nearly out of breath. "And . . . free you from bearing . . . such a burden. S . . . so, let us . . . go and see what is God's will."

Rajni shivered in the cold, gathering darkness of the evening. What Piare told her was chilling, but she knew it to be true. She fed Piare and laid him down for the night, then sat by the Satluj and contemplated the reflection of the sky in the water. It was true that she had felt Piare as a burden many times, but the thought of losing him disturbed and saddened her. There had been a time when she would have felt relief if he died, but if she lost him now, she would be left feeling empty and desperate. She made up her mind that she would find the water and keep her husband alive.

So after another week, Rajni turned back to the northwest and away from the steady flow of the Satluj, the river of her youth. As the spring thaw in the Himalayas set in, the level of the river rose. She descended down into the area between the Satluj and Beas rivers. The land between two rivers was called *doab,* and these were the lowlands of the Jullundur Doab. Here yellow fields of mustard in full blossom, a sure sign that the winter was passing, greeted her. The sight cheered her, and since the terrain of the Punjab slopes away from the Himalayas, the passage became easier for her.

This was an active area. There were more people on the roads: farmers with their harvests of sugar cane or cotton piled twenty feet high in their heavy carts, caravans of trades people moving across the region, and the ubiquitous soldiers serving the Shah and the regional governor. The bustle was energizing for Rajni, but her discomfort in the presence of so many people lingered.

Along the road, she applied her considerable charm to the young boys selling their red carrots and long white radishes to have mercy on her and give her some. They munched on them noisily as Rajni pulled Piare in the wagon.

Being between the Satluj and Beas rivers, she had to rely mostly on wells for water, which usually meant going into the villages and leaving Piare on the outskirts. She had found a clay jar that she used for carrying water and would enter the village, go to the well and fill the jar with water, and then carry it back to Piare. Raised as a princess, she had never learned to balance a jar on her head properly, which was the common way Punjabi women carried everything. So she carried it on her shoulder or held it on her head, which identified her as a stranger to the area and placed her under the constant scrutiny of the locals.

After the encounter with the sadhu, Rajni was changed. Her depression and sense of desperation were lifted. She was still unsure about the future, but she never again thought about abandoning Piare and returning to Duni Chand. She became more conversational and less isolated. Gradually, her crying spells tapered off.

As they steadily moved across the doab, she pondered what the sadhu had told her: that she had to become zero before she could become one. What did that mean? He had said the same words to her that the aghora had said that first night, which now seemed like many incarnations ago.

"We know who you are and we are watching."

What did that mean? They both spoke to her in such familiar terms. How did they know her and who were they who were watching?

But the strangest thing to her was that the aghora and the Shaivite had also said, *"Oh Rajni, who bears the suffering of humankind, take our suffering to the water."*

Then the saint with the long beard and compassionate eyes in her dream had said, *"You bear the suffering of the Kali Yuga. Bring it to the water, that it can be washed from this Age."*

Where was the water? And what suffering did she bear? It was true that she had suffered since the day Duni Chand had confronted her. Life with Piare had been difficult. She was tired and hungry most of the time, cold and damp at night, and her body ached. As she pulled on the rope, the squeak and rumble of the little wagon comforted her and made her feel secure.

Strange, she thought, h*ow transitional life is. Circumstances can change and spin us in the twinkling of an eye.* She recognized how the sound of Piare's cart soothed her, and Rajni smiled to herself. *If we are truly at peace, truly content and surrender to the Will of God, then even the sound of our own labors can reassure us.*

She continued walking, never looking back at Piare. She could tell from the sound of the wheels and the feel of the rope if he was all right or in need of anything.

The sadhu had told her that she had to reach the shunnya. She thought back to another lifetime, when she sat in her father's gardens with Punditji and he explained to her about shunnya. It was early morning. Rajni had slept in one of the rest houses at the gardens, and Punditji had come to meet her. She remembered the plaintive cry of a peacock at the far end of the gardens and the glowing orb of the sun through the morning mist.

"Shunnya is the state of zero."

"There it is!" she stopped walking and turned back toward Piare. "Shunnya is the zero!" Then she turned back, shouldered the rope, and began walking again.

She thought back to her mathematics lessons and remembered that Punditji had taught her that the concept of zero came from the Vedas. He told her that zero had totally changed the concept of mathematics and that from zero had come the concept of infinity.

"Zero is not nothing, it is the totality." She could hear Punditji's voice in her head clearly, as if he were walking next to her. "It is the sacred core of all teachings and all knowledge. When you reach that state, the mind and body are synchronized at the same level of energy so that all thoughts and feelings become neutral or still, and just as a vacuum is instantly filled, the finite mind expands to infinity or a state of zero. Then the mind is completely open. Our individual thoughts and emotions are limited and bind us to this Earth, but zero is infinite and beyond our earthly mind. In the state of the shunnya, both hemispheres of the brain function in perfect harmony, and the flow from the infinite is free and unrestrained."

"Become zero," he said. Rajni's mind was racing, closing in rapidly on a deep understanding. "Touch the shunnya, and you will be filled."

She thought back to that morning with Punditji. "When you touch the shunnya, you have achieved perfect harmony between the sensory input and the elevated awareness. The sixth sense, the intuition, is what prevails, and the balance between the infinite and the finite is perfect, for there is no interference from the physical body or the ruminations of the psyche. In this vibratory state, you are in harmonic communication with all the knowledge of the Universe. You find the infinite self contained in the finite sphere of the human existence."

Punditji paused, listening to the peacock.

"Isn't God beautiful?" he asked. His expression and the tone of his voice were innocent, like a young boy first beholding the wonder and majesty of things.

"Dearest Rajni," Punditji lowered his voice to a whisper, "touch the shunnya, and health, happiness, harmony and fulfillment will come to you."

Then, Punditji taught her a simple meditation, a Sanskrit recitation. But the sadhu had said that the "*Wahe Guru mantra that you recite will take you there.*" And Punditji, in his wisdom, had taught her the *Wahe Guru* meditation, eight recitations to one breath. Could that be what the sadhu meant? And exaggerate the movement of the mouth?

"Yes," she spoke into her knuckles, gripping the rope, "the *Wahe Guru* meditation."

She continued walking and talking to herself. "What about the water?"

Even Punditji had said it.

"But where is the water?"

TWENTY-EIGHT

As Rajni leaned her five-foot three inch, eighty-five-pound frame against the rope and pulled Piare and the little wagon northwest across the Jullundur Doab, her mother looked out of her window from Duni Chand's palace in Patti. Since the night of Rajni's wedding, Mataji had seldom moved from that spot. She spent her days sitting at the window looking for her baby girl to come through the gate and up the hill. She hardly ate, hardly interacted with her servants and household, and never spoke to Duni Chand. She had moved into Rajni's room, slept in Rajni's bed, and looked out Rajni's window daily toward the entrance to the estate.

Her other daughters left Patti the day after that terrible night. They had lodged with other families in the village then sent their servants to collect their belongings the next day. They left Patti unceremoniously, without saying good-bye to Duni Chand or Mataji. They did not correspond or have any other contact with their parents. Each sister made daily offerings and puja to Ganesha, Durga, and Vishnu for Rajni's well-being and protection. They consulted their pundits, who told them that Rajni would not die and that she would survive her ordeal, but that brought them little comfort.

Punditji had resigned himself to Rajni's destiny and spent long hours in prayer and meditation for her. He understood that it was her destiny to go through this, but that understanding did little to ease his concern for her. He agonized daily about her. Had he taught her well enough? Had he prepared her sufficiently for what she would face? Would she remember what he had taught her and use those teachings to keep herself going? While he believed that he had done all that he could, he could not assuage his lingering doubt and prevalent concern. Therefore, he did what he had always done: prayed and meditated and drew from his deep reserve of patience.

Duni Chand continued to wax the ends of his moustache each day, affix his ruby and gold earrings to his ears, and tie his brightly colored turbans. As ever, he especially favored red. He thought that a red turban made him appear to be more authoritarian and intimidating. He still pursued the collection of revenues, but his business dealings were not doing well, and he was falling on hard times.

Outwardly, Duni Chand's hubris and panache seemed to be undiminished. Yet in the tomblike silence of his palace and alone in his room with no one to talk to, Duni Chand questioned what he had done. Not that he was repentant, but an element of doubt had begun to breach his arrogance. Periodically, he sent his men out to try to locate his youngest daughter. He had instructed them that if they found her, they were to kill Piare and bring Rajni back. They never found her, but always came back with reports that people had seen her pulling Piare through the jungle or along the riverbanks.

Each morning and evening, he sent for the family pundit who came and performed puja in supplication to Durga, Vishnu, and Ganesha for Rajni's protection. Since Mataji had isolated herself and refused to have any contact or dialogue with Duni Chand whatsoever, Duni Chand performed his puja as a solitary act with only his family pundit to guide him through the ceremony he knew so well. Yet somehow, the presence of the pundit gave him a sense of hope.

The people of Patti did not forgive Duni Chand. Though they could not be rid of him and had to pay their homage whenever he passed, they did so in such a way that it was clear to him what they thought. As the months passed, some of the more bold villagers jeered at him and on occasion threw their shoes at him. Perhaps most demoralizing of all for Duni Chand was that no one in Patti or the surrounding villages owned by him would play chess with him. Still, he bore it all in his usual arrogant style, with his chin up and apparently in complete disregard for their disdain. But when he got home to his dark and silent palace, he sat for hours in the darkness trying to justify himself to himself. Depression, like the gathering clouds of the monsoon, began to occupy his mind.

One night, he lay in his bed in the darkness. As had been the case since the night of Rajni's wedding and as Punditji had predicted, none of the lamps of the palace had been lighted and the cold was as pervasive as the darkness. Duni Chand lay shivering under his quilts. Since the night of Rajni's wedding, Duni Chand put himself to sleep at night by reliving Rajni's life in his mind and especially his confrontation with her the last day he saw her, the day she refused to acknowledge all that he had done for her.

He questioned why she failed to recognize that he had indeed provided everything for her. He tried to understand what he perceived as her lack of gratitude and her failure to honor him as her father. After all, he had ensured that she was provided for, educated, well-dressed, and bejeweled. She had learned the Vedas and had been raised as a proper Brahmin princess. And what was her answer? That God was the provider of everything? She didn't even reference a deity. Not Vishnu. Not Ganesha. Not even Brahma. No, the word she used was Akal Purkh, a term that was deeply philosophical and advanced for one so young. And a girl at that.

He could blame the pundit for putting such radical thoughts in her head, but somewhere in his escalating remorse, he realized that it wasn't the pundit. Rather, it was simply Rajni. And in a momentary illumination of understanding, he understood the power of her soul. As he trembled and shivered in the darkness, he knew that she had spoken the truth.

He began to drift, floating apart from his body. He found himself standing at his window, looking out onto his estate. Along the passageway up the hill from the gate to the courtyard of the palace, he saw cobras. There were hundreds of them under the light of the full moon. They were coiled with hoods flared and heads raised, lining either side of the passageway and swaying in the moonlight.

The heavy wood and iron gates at the entrance to the estate swung open slowly, and Duni Chand saw Rajni enter. She was leaning forward with a rope over her shoulder, pulling something behind her. His heart soared with delight at the sight of her and then plummeted with disbelief when he saw the leper in the wagon behind her. Then he remembered the snakes. He tried to call to her through the window, but his voice remained in his head. He could not release it into the air to be carried to her in warning. He sickened with panic, desperation, and despair as Rajni slowly began the climb up the hill.

Duni Chand watched in horror as Rajni's movements drew the attention of the cobras. In the moonlight so bright that the distinctive markings on the snakes were clear as the day of the summer solstice, they grew larger so that each one appeared to be at least sixteen feet long. As Rajni made her way up the hill, the cobras rose to their full height, their hoods flared wide ready to strike. To Duni Chand, it appeared that Rajni was blind to them.

As she pulled the little wagon up the hill bent against the weight behind her, her head bowed as though in surrender to the karma she bore, the giant cobras drew their heads back and then bent forward in unison. Duni Chand gasped, but rather than striking her, the mystical serpents touched their noses across the path, forming an arc to cover and honor Rajni as she made her way up the hill. When she reached the top of the hill, the strangest thing happened: the leper arose from the wagon and appeared to be in full health. Lifting Rajni into his arms, he carried her into the palace of Duni Chand.

Duni Chand opened his eyes to the dark silence of his palace. The sounds of his runaway heartbeat and heavy respiration were loud in his ears. He lay under his quilts shivering in the night, unable to move or utter a sound. Eventually, the deep darkness and muffling silence of the night muted the thundering of his heart. The moonlight streamed defiantly through his windows and revealed the glistening tears that streamed in solitude from his eyes.

* * *

Rajni and Piare rested under the trees beside the River Beas. The sound of running water was a comfort to Rajni, something she hadn't heard since they turned from the Satluj, and she delighted in the melody of the river. She helped Piare to settle in the cold running water, which soothed his skin, and left him there for half a day. Rajni washed his kurta and their shawls, slapping them against the rocks until she was satisfied that they were reasonably clean, and then draped them over the tree branches and rocks of the riverbank to dry.

They had stopped near an active crossing and there was a steady flow of people, horses, elephants, camels, mudges, and cows throughout the day. The bells on the livestock and the songs and chants of the mahouts to their elephants and the herdsmen to their animals created an ever-evolving descant against the reassuring drone of the Beas. Kingfishers, crows, and vultures patrolled and scavenged the area. Their pizzicato chirping and cawing supported the daily raga, like tabla under a sitar.

On both sides of the riverbank were food stalls selling dal, chapattis, tea, pulses, pakoras, samosas, and other fare for the passing travelers. The vendors called out long before a caravan or group of travelers approached from either side, each one lauding the superiority of their fare over that of their competitors. Rajni situated herself and Piare far enough away from the main flow of the traffic so that the sight of Piare would not frighten people, and she took advantage of the situation by begging for leftovers from the vendors and the leavings of customers.

When the shawls were dry, she tied them around herself and washed her own clothes, using care against the rocks so as to avoid enlarging the holes that were growing in them. The thin garments dried quickly in the sun and, though they were far from spotless, it refreshed her to wear clean clothes.

The weather was getting warmer and the riverbank was spotted with the furtive colors of winter's passing. She had enjoyed their passage across the doab, where the farmers worked their fields diligently. Their white Brahma cows, with the curious hump between their shoulders and their long, thin, and curved horns pointing to the sky, pulled the plows and cultivating tools. The smells of the plowed earth and livestock and the sounds of the farmers chanting to their animals reminded Rajni of her best days in Patti. A deeper peace and contentment had settled in her and each day was less a matter of putting one foot in front of the other just to make it from morning to sunset.

She had frequently crept into the yellow mustard fields along the way and picked enough of the mustard greens to prepare *saag* for her and Piare, which she cooked in a clay pot that she had scavenged along the way. Saag is one of the special dishes of Punjab, consisting of mustard greens, spices, and large amounts of ghee. Rajni learned to make it when very young. She had successfully begged for ghee, salt, and spices to make the saag flavorful and for enough flour so that they had chapattis every day for a week.

She had begun to think of the future in a way that was more optimistic than hopeless, and she sincerely believed that something meaningful and fulfilling lay ahead for her. With the ashes of the sadhu on her head and visions of Punditji and the long-bearded saint in her mind, that morning in the fog had affected her profoundly. Now she had heard the same message three times and could not ignore it.

She had hoped that the Beas was *"the water"* but knew in short order that wherever it lay, it was farther ahead of her. Still, it made her happy to rest and be in one place for a while, but the serenity of their life by the Beas was disrupted too many times by dacoits and soldiers. Rajni had chosen a point that was also a favorite crossing for the territorial bandits who passed between the Jallundur Doab and the Bari Doab to the west. While the days were busy with traders and travelers crossing the Beas, the nights belonged to the bandits and the soldiers who pursued them.

Rajni and Piare weren't in danger from the dacoits, but the vendors who hawked their wares on either bank were often accosted and intimidated, first by the bandits then by the soldiers. A thin young girl and a leper didn't offer an outlaw much. Occasionally, a passing bandit considered taking advantage of Rajni. Yet once he saw Piare, Rajni was left in peace.

Being low caste themselves and appreciative of her suffering, the dacoits often gave her food. Though by her appearance she was clearly of Brahmin lineage, they recognized that her circumstances were not privileged and, like many others, assumed that she was the discarded result of some Brahmin's indiscretion. Some though had heard the story of the princess whose father had thrown her out of his house and forced her into marriage with a leper. By now, especially with Duni Chand's men making their periodic forays in search of her, she was becoming known by reputation, which enhanced Rajni's standing among the criminals.

Soldiers were often in pursuit of the dacoits, and they frequently stopped and questioned Rajni, usually after they had rousted out the food vendors and forced the frightened and defenseless wretches to feed them. The bandits were usually more civil and respectful of her and her situation and that of the vendors than the soldiers. The soldiers were always arrogant, unpleasant, and often crude. Yet like the dacoits, once the soldiers became aware of Piare, they backed off. Without realizing it or understanding it, Piare protected Rajni simply by the power of his presence.

After two weeks at the Beas, it became clear to Rajni that they could no longer stay there. There was so much coming and going of caravans and traders, livestock and herdsmen, and bandits and soldiers that it was becoming disruptive and dangerous. She had made them a little camp and wanted to stay there for a while. She liked being by the river and the fact that she could safely and successfully beg for food from the vendors and the passing travelers. But late one night, she was awakened by loud voices, then the ringing clash of steel followed by the screams of dying men.

Two rival bands of dacoits had clashed over territorial rights, something sacred to their code, with the result that four men were killed.

The only reason that fight ended was because soldiers had ambushed the bandits who scattered, with Akbar's men in hot pursuit. In the process, the vending stalls had been disrupted, pots had been overturned, and sleeping travelers had been awakened. There was screaming, loud cursing, and the sounds of panicked animals. The livestock had been frightened and ran wildly in all directions. Two wildly terrified mudges and one crazed camel crashed through the brush and trees, nearly trampling Piare in their panic.

Rajni stifled her screams, but once the scrum had moved across the Beas and back toward the east, she collected Piare in her shawl and pulling him onto her back, carried him across to the western bank, careful not to step on the bodies that lay dead against the rocks. She then recrossed the river, piled their shawls and a few other things into the gardening wagon, and carried it on her head across to Piare. Now on the western bank of the river, she loaded Piare into the wagon, shouldered the rope, and moved as quickly as she could until dawn, leaving most of their meager possessions behind.

Rajni recovered surprisingly quickly from that night. By now, she had been through so many disruptive and frightening situations that this was simply another obstacle, like a boulder in the road that she had to cross. It was now the month of *Phalguna*, the lunar month between February and March and the time of Holi. Rajni's spirits could not be repressed.

In the Vedic tradition, Holi is one of the most favorite celebrations. When Harynikash set fire to the countryside and forced Pralad to embrace the red-hot pillar, it was Pralad's sister, Holika, who protected him. Harynikash, being a powerful king, had many wives and by one of his wives produced a daughter whom he named Holika. She was a powerful soul. It was she who persuaded Harynikash to pursue his austerities in worship of Vishnu, which led to his achievement of such great power and Vishnu's blessing upon him. However, he forgot about the power of the female.

Holika tried to persuade Harynikash not to impose his ego on his kingdom and rebuked him when persuasion failed. When he turned his wrath against Pralad, she tried to stop him, but Harynikash was in no mood to listen. Yet Holika had power over fire, and she protected her brother as he made his walk to the glowing hot pillar. She allowed herself to be consumed by the fire to save Pralad and teach her father a lesson in the process.

Hindus remember the occasion and Holika with the annual celebration of Holi. To a nation of farmers, it also represents the coming of spring and the end of the cold season. Holi is a joyful and somewhat raucous celebration, marked by rather chaotic playing in the streets where people throw colored dye powder at each other in recognition of Holika. The mornings and early afternoons were a wild free-for-all in every village, with the villagers throwing the colorful dyes on anyone and everyone, leaving the roads and walls of the villages spotted with color. The evenings were spent feasting and celebrating with families.

Rajni always loved to play Holi, and each year she and her sisters went out into the streets of Patti and bombed the villagers with colors. They applied henna to their hair, put on their white kameez and salwaars, (although Duni Chand preferred that his daughters wear saris) and ran through the streets of Patti, splattering anyone they saw and getting equally splattered themselves. During the time of Holi, the distinctions of caste and privilege were lost in splashes of color, and even Duni Chand liked to get out and run wild through his villages. Over the two-week period of Holi, he made it a point to go to each of his villages and participate with his daughters in the festivities.

This Holi was especially meaningful for Rajni. She turned and looked at Piare in the wagon behind her, remembering her wedding day when Punditji told her that Piare was her "red-hot pillar." He was stained with red, as they had been attacked several times in the past few days, and in the sunlight, he appeared to be glowing. Uttering a brief prayer to Vishnu and to Holika, she smiled at Piare then turned and continued walking.

Holi is a time when people feel generous, and Rajni fared well during this time. Most days, they ate twice. Rajni felt content. She had reached a point where she had surrendered to the fact that this was her karma and there was no other way past it, except to keep up and go through it. Every morning now, she got up before sunrise and practiced the *Wahe Guru* meditation, and as the days passed, she noticed subtle changes in her state of mind. It was becoming like a narcotic for her, something that she had to have daily.

It hadn't been that way when she first started. Often during the process of the meditation feelings of intense anger and other upheavals of emotion erupted in her. She would cry and laugh, squirm and wiggle, yet she never stopped her practice. Now that phase seemed to be behind her, and since the encounter in the fog, she had settled into something deeper, which brought her insight and tranquility. She still had her doubts and her periods of frustration and anxiety, but the spectrum of her emotions was more contained and stable, and her periods of disruption were briefer.

The time of Holi passed, and at the latter part of the month of *Chaitra*, approximately the beginning of April, she found herself along the banks of the River Ravi in the northeastern region of the Bari Doab, not far below Kartarpur where Guru Nanak had lived. With the rope across her shoulders and the comforting weight of Piare and the wagon behind her, she pondered the words of the aghora and the sadhu. She was searching for "the water" as the aghora, the sadhu, and the saint in her dream had told her.

Rajni was obsessed with the concept of "the water." She stretched her mind trying to understand what it was or where it was. It was obvious to her that it had not been the Satluj or the Beas and now, as she walked along the banks of the Ravi, she admitted to herself that the Ravi was not the water either. She wondered if it was actually something real. Perhaps it was nothing more than a concept, something more esoteric than an actual location. But Punditji had told her to take him to the water. Did he mean someplace ethereal? She didn't think so. The aghora had told her the same thing within hours of Punditji telling her. The sadhu had told her, then the saint in her dream had also told her.

Now she had been to three rivers, and none of them seemed to be the place. She wondered if it could be at a holy place of pilgrimage. For Hindus, there are sixty-eight places of pilgrimage, and it occurred to her that perhaps that at one of those she would find "the water."

"Perhaps we should go to Hardwar," she spoke to herself as had become her habit.

She stopped and considered that. To reach the Ganges, she would have to turn back to the East and climb the Shivalik Hills, something she didn't look forward to. And in that moment, as the spring evening began to erase the day, she heard sounds that she could not identify. At this hour, there were few people on the road, most travelers having made their camps for the night. But Rajni had been lost in her thoughts and had continued walking long past the hour when she would have normally stopped.

She stopped and listened. Gradually, she realized that what she was hearing was human voices chanting. She started moving again in the direction of the sound, toward the river Ravi. She came to an open area along the riverbank and saw a group of about twenty bearded men sitting in a semicircle. In front of the group was a young man with a dark beard who was obviously leading them.

Each man sat with his arms folded in front of him at shoulder height and parallel to the ground. With their spines straight and eyes closed, they rotated in a clockwise direction.

As they rotated, they recited, *"Aahh laah hoo"* in a hypnotic monotone.

Rajni recognized them as Sufis, Muslim mystics with devotional practices that often put them into deep, blissful trance. They believed in the universality of humankind and, like Guru Nanak, taught that the way to be close with God was through reciting His Name with devotion. Deeply mystical and compassionate, the Sufis developed such practices as the whirling derveshes, other forms of Sufi dance, and meditation practices that bring the practitioner to an otherworldly awareness.

The scene was peaceful and inviting, so Rajni pulled Piare to the back of the group and helped him out of the wagon, and they sat behind the semicircle. The leader then directed the group to rotate in the opposite direction. Closing her eyes and folding her arms, she began to rotate and chant softly with the others. She drifted. The sound was mesmerizing, and as she chanted and slowly rotated, she fell deeper and deeper into a blissful peace.

She lost all sense of time or space. She was unable to remember where she was or how she got there. In fact, she was unable even to think. As she became lost in her timeless trance with her breath suspended, she experienced absolute stillness, absolute quiet: an eternally fleeting moment of no thought, no mental or emotional movement, nor sense of self. And into that vast nothingness, in the absence of time or space, awareness flooded.

It was the shunnya.

She had no sense of how long the moment had lasted, but as her consciousness returned slowly to the present, she felt that she had reached a deeper understanding of herself and identity, a more profound recognition of herself and the karma that she bore. It was not something that she could quantify or describe, but the awareness was real and her every fiber pulsated with it. The last of the chanting faded and was followed by silence as Rajni sat with her eyes still closed.

Eventually, she heard instruments tuning as musicians plucked their strings, and the tabla player tuned his drum heads with a silver hammer. Then they started singing and clapping their hands in rhythm with the music. The lead singer sang in a very high-pitched voice, which had great power, and the group responded to his call as they clapped and swayed with the music. The songs were about love. But the identity of the beloved was unclear, for in that elevated state God becomes the beloved.

Slowly, Rajni opened her eyes and saw that the youthful leader of the group, the Pir, was sitting patiently in front of her. He had obviously been there for some time but showed no indication of impatience. In fact, he seemed quite content to sit and meditate with her as long as she was inclined to do so.

"You are near the water," he spoke in Persian.

Rajni stared at him. His voice was deep and mellifluous and seemed to hold her in the shunnya state.

"Where is the water?" She whispered it, barely able to hear her own voice over the sounds of the music.

"You will find it without knowing it. He," pointing to Piare, "will reveal it to you."

Rajni closed her eyes and remained silent. Piare gazed intently at the Pir. His mind filled with questions that he did not ask. The Pir studied him in the firelight as the singing rose in pitch and intensity.

"You will be freed of this karma. Your debt from the time of the Vedi Guru will be settled in this lifetime."

"Where is the water?" croaked Piare.

The sound of Piare's voice startled her, and Rajni opened her eyes. She felt as though the Pir was looking into her heart.

"Think back to the day you started on this path." He spoke directly to Rajni, not shifting his gaze or blinking his eyes. "What was it that set you on this course?" The question seemed more rhetorical than direct, and Rajni faltered, unsure if she should answer or simply listen.

"Well . . .," she said in hesitation, ". . . my father got angry when . . ."

The Pir held up his right hand, palm toward Rajni, as the group began another *kawaal*.

"Your father did as he was meant to do, as you are doing what you are meant to do. Follow your bliss. There, you will find the water and the jewels." From the way he looked at her, Rajni knew there was no point in speaking. "You will rest here safely tonight, but a test still lies ahead of you. It will be your most difficult, and through it you will find your power. Remain strong and do what must be done when that time comes. Do not cross this river,"—he gestured toward the Ravi—"but continue in that direction." He gestured toward the southeast.

"May we know your good name?" Piare asked. He seldom spoke to the people they met. However, this man made Piare feel comfortable.

"I am Mian Mir," he said. "Now," he stood up and waved his hand toward the group of men, "let us eat."

TWENTY-NINE

Piare pondered the words of the Pir as Rajni strained against the rope ahead of him. He realized that in all the time that they had been together, he had seen more of her back than her face. He had learned to read her moods and thoughts by how she pulled the wagon. Sometimes she walked with her head up, her body erect against the weight and it seemed to be effortless for her to pull him. Other times, she leaned into the rope with her whole body forward, her head down, and her steps plodding. Constantly she talked to herself, talking into her hands as they held the rope across her shoulders. Her body language always signaled to Piare her mood and what she was thinking.

Leaning into the rope with her head down watching her feet, Rajni was clearly as lost in thought as he was. The Pir had told them that they would find the water without knowing it, and that Piare would reveal it to her. He had no idea what that meant, but there was a ring of truth to it that struck Piare. Then the Pir had told him that he would be freed of this karma. That alone was cause for serious consideration, but the fact that the Pir told him that his debt from the time of the Vedi Guru would be settled in this lifetime shook Piare. It confirmed the truth of his experience that morning in the fog, which meant that those incarnations were real, that the vision was real, and that a powerful energy was moving him forward toward a destiny much different from anything he had considered before.

Yet the Pir had not told them where to find the water. He had only pointed them toward it. They would find it without knowing it, and he would reveal it to her. He felt foolish. How could he reveal the location of the water to Rajni? Was he going to have another vision that would show him where to find it? Would a miracle occur so that he could get up and walk and lead Rajni to the water? Piare didn't think so. He had lived with suffering all his life and had yet to experience a miracle, so he had little faith in that. Yet he wanted to believe the Pir as badly as he wanted to do something for Rajni to ease her suffering.

Perhaps the only way to truly be freed of this karma was to be freed of the body that bore it. He thought about that often. What purpose did his life serve? It was a question he could not answer. Clearly, he had only incarnated to clear his karma. If that debt were to be settled, then what use would he have for his consumed and shriveled body?

"How did I fail before?" He had started talking to himself. "I failed to show compassion," he answered his own question. "I failed to share what I had with one in need. I failed to ease the suffering of another who asked it in the Name of God. And I could have done so easily."

He sat in silence as he and the little wagon rolled on behind his beautiful wife. In his heart and mind stirred a hurricane of emotion and confusion. His vision in the fog was powerful, and the words of the Pir felt so true to him. Was it because he wanted so badly to believe they were true, or was it because, in fact, that they *were* true?

How could he be healed? And even if he were healed, he had no skills or status in life. What would he do, how could he support his wife? What value did he have as a man? He was tired of being a beggar and, yes, a thief. He was tired of being a burden, unable to contribute, unable to be productive, unable to do anything except suffer. He was tired of being a leper.

He studied Rajni's back. The thin and faded kameez clung to her skin. Moist patches of perspiration darkened the fine red muslin in the midday sun. Her braid bounced and swayed against her with each step. It had once been immaculate, with belled blue parandees woven through her braid. They had been lost long ago. He could not remember when the gay tinkle of the tiny bells no longer blended with the rolling of the wooden wheels below him. How many months had it been like this?

Before Rajni, time had meant nothing to Piare. One day ran into the next without distinction, with nothing to mark it except whether or not he ate that day. Now he marked his life from the day of his marriage, and while each day was still a quest for food, that aspect seemed only to be a way of passing the time. Each day was a new memory for him of something Rajni had said or done, of moments they had shared together, or just the way her back looked to him on different days.

Without turning to look, Rajni understood that Piare was lost in contemplation, trying to put the pieces together. She could feel it in the rope, just as if they were talking face to face. So as she trudged toward the southeast, she knew that he was pondering the words of the Pir, just as she was. After all, the Pir told him that he would be freed of this karma. Did that mean that he would be healed?

"How could that be?" she asked her hands.

And for the first time, someone had told them that they were near the water. This put a different perspective on things for her. She wasn't told to take him to the water, she was told that she was near the water; that she would find it without knowing it. The only thing he told her was to *"think back to the day"* when she started on this path.

"Did he mean my wedding day?" She wasn't sure which day he meant, and her hands did not reveal the answer.

The Pir had asked her what was it that had set her on this course. She was becoming frustrated. She knew that the answer was in her, but she was missing it.

"What set me on this course? My father? My mother telling my father about . . ." Rajni stopped and turned to Piare. "The jewels!" She smiled, dropped the rope, and threw her hands into the air, dancing in the staccato steps of bhangra. "The jewels, Piare! I gave those Sikhs my jewels to give to Guru Ram Das because his words touched my soul and put me in such deep bliss!"

She screamed with laughter and continued with her dance steps as though someone were playing the *dhol* next to her. People passing on the road stopped and watched her jubilation.

"Piare, my jewels are with Guru Ram Das! My bliss came from Guru Ram Das. If we can find him, we can find the water!" Picking up the rope, she began to sing:

"Oh Nanak, He who created the creatures takes care of them all.
The Creator who created the Creation also takes care of it."

*   *   *

That night, they camped by a well. As the day faded, Rajni fell quiet after the elation of her moment of revelation. She made their camp but was unsuccessful begging for food. So as they lay down for the night, she was hungry and a little irritable. She had expected some indication that her realization had been right. That had not happened, so as she had done many nights before, she lay down with an empty stomach. The sounds of the night calmed her, and she fell into a light sleep, with images, faces, and sounds passing through her mind.

Suddenly, she sat bolt upright, startling Piare. "The saint in my vision was Guru Ram Das!" she exclaimed to the night. Then just as suddenly, she lay back down and was quiet.

They both had finally drifted off to sleep when a band of dacoits rode upon them, waking them with their noise. Rajni stood up and, in an authoritative voice for such a small girl, demanded to know who they were and what business they were pursuing.

"Who are you people!" It was not a request, but the demand of a princess. "Why are you traipsing around at night like a band of dacoits, disturbing innocent people?"

The men on horseback laughed robustly, but their leader was silent. He stared at Rajni with eyes that had seen too much. Rajni looked at him squarely in the moonlight.

"Are you responsible for these men?" Her voice had softened a bit, but she was speaking as the daughter of a raja, not a destitute girl.

"I am," he said quietly.

"So you are responsible for disturbing me and my suffering husband?"

"I suppose I am." Then in an equally demanding voice, he said, "And who are you to interrogate me?" He spoke a thick regional Urdu with heavy Persian idioms, the language of the Western frontier.

Rajni was somewhat taken aback, her anger beginning to diminish and a slight touch of fear finding its way into her mind. Then softly she spoke. "I am the one who carries the suffering of the Kali Yuga."

"There is much suffering in the Kali Yuga," he replied.

Without shifting his gaze from Rajni, he extended his left arm parallel to the ground and pointed his left index finger down, indicating that he intended to dismount. Immediately, one of his men dismounted and placed himself on all fours beneath the left stirrup of the huge bandit. He dismounted his horse, stepped from the stirrup onto the back of his man, then to the ground.

He looked carefully at Rajni, an intense fire in his eyes, even in the darkness. He moved toward her, "Are you the girl to who pulls the leper?" His voice and accent were heavy and thick.

"Yes."

He looked at this frail little girl, dressed in worn-out clothes that were much too big for her. There was something about her eyes, so intensely shining in the night as though they were a distant constellation.

Suddenly, he rushed toward Rajni. Rajni never moved but closed her eyes, thinking that the inevitable was about to happen. Instead, the huge bandit fell at Rajni's feet and held them with both his hands.

"Forgive me, my little sister," he said sincerely, his voice quivering. "They say there is honor among thieves, but I lost mine long ago. I believe that Allah has led me here tonight to hear your words, that I might still find redemption before Him. Please forgive me and bless me, for I have been guided here to you tonight."

Rajni was in shock. She had hoped for a sign, but this was much more than she expected. She reached her small hands down and placed them on his massive head.

"I forgive you." She paused. "And . . . in . . . the Name of Guru Ram Das . . ." she hesitated, somewhat startled by her own words, "I . . . I bless you."

The dacoit stood, towering over Rajni but feeling as though he were a child standing before his own mother. His men shifted uneasily in their saddles, not knowing what to make of this strange situation.

"I am Mustafa Khan," he said, his tears glistening in the moonlight. He wiped his face with his rough hands. "I control this area. As long as you are here, you are under my protection."

He shouted orders to his men, and they dismounted, beginning a rush of activity.

"We will camp here tonight with you, and you will be safe. Any man who so much as looks at this girl inappropriately," he thundered at his men, "will lose his manhood by my blade!"

All his men bowed and turned away. Mustafa Khan paused. "Is your husband really a leper?" He sounded like a child asking if angels really existed.

"He is."

"Please," Mustafa Khan said gently, "you must tell me your story. But first, we must eat!"

In those days, one of the most popular forms of entertainment was storytelling. All Punjabis, even dacoits, loved a good story, and Mustafa Khan had a feeling that Rajni's story would be a good one. He ordered his men to make the camp quickly, build a fire, and prepare food for his guests. He had immediately assumed the role of host.

Piare sat near Rajni, but remained covered and silent, with only his eyes exposed. It bothered him that as the husband of Rajni, he was unable to do anything for her. He could not care for her or protect her. If these bandits had malicious intent, he would have been unable to do anything to protect her, and that realization pained him. This incident reminded him of the severity of his condition and how much of a burden he was for Rajni. He was happy for the fire and the food and the company, but in his withering heart, he neared a resolution with himself.

When food had been served and all had eaten, Mustafa Khan again asked Rajni to tell him her story. She was an excellent and charming storyteller. She looked out at the faces around the fire. Her months on the road had hardened her. She had seen and experienced things she never knew existed. She had been forced to do things she never believed she would do. She had sucked the dust of the Punjab and spent too many nights wet and cold, her empty stomach and aching heart keeping her awake. Now the girlishness was gone from her face.

Despite all that she had been through and all the truly frightening things she had seen, she had never in her life seen such hard faces as those before her now, made more severe by the dancing of the flames and the mystery of the shadows. She studied them quietly, trying not to think about what these men must have done to people, especially to other women. She could see clearly in their faces that they cared for no one and would not hesitate to act if ordered to do so. It was also clear that they both feared and respected Mustafa Khan. And Mustafa Khan himself seemed to be the most ruthless of the whole group.

They looked at her expectantly, so she began her story. "My name is Rajni. I was born the seventh daughter of Duni Chand, the Raja of Patti. We lived in a beautiful palace, I and my sisters. We were all very close. My father is a very powerful man, a revenue officer of the Shah."

"We are well aware of him and his holdings," stated the bandit.

Rajni spoke, looking him directly in the eye. "He owns several villages and commands many people. He is a good man, a deeply devoted Brahman. It is because of his devotions that my sisters and I learned the Vedas. We each had our own pundit to tutor us, except third sister and second sister shared the same pundit because they were close. Still, I learned from my own Punditji." Rajni paused, remembering her Punditji.

As she told her story, the faces of the villains who surrounded her seemed to soften, and within a short time, they all looked like schoolboys listening to a teacher.

"My beloved Punditji taught me so many things. He is very wise. He was captured and tortured by Sher Shah when Hymayun fought to reclaim his throne."

"I know of that cruelty," said Mustafa Khan. "In fact, I owe my career to that cruelty."

Rajni's penetrating glance silenced him, and he looked sheepishly into the fire.

What a strange man, she thought to herself. The sound of the fire and the shifting of the horses seemed to accent her thoughts.

Mustafa Khan spoke. "Please forgive me, little sister," he said sincerely. "When I was young, my father was also taken by the army of Sher Shah, and I was left alone in this harsh world. Were it not for the dacoits who picked me up and cared for me, I might not be with you tonight. They taught me my craft, dark though it is, and I excelled at it. For many years, I have lived as a ruthless bandit. I have killed many men and taken many women against their will."

Despite the fire, Rajni's blood ran cold. She paled and pulled her chuni around her left cheek, lowered her eyes, and bit into the chuni as she turned her head away from the dacoit.

She did not look up. Mustafa Khan continued as Rajni maintained her gaze upon the dark earth beneath her, which had been her only place of refuge for the past nine months.

"After many years of causing suffering, my anger over my own suffering began to diminish. One night, we raided a village that had been warned to pay us, but which had refused. Mind you, this was a prosperous village and had much to share. Few villages had ever refused Mustafa Khan and none had remained standing to tell the story. Curiously, I felt some respect for these people. They did not cower before Mustafa Khan, they defied me! I was intrigued, but could not fail to act, so I formed up my men and we prepared to assault the village.

"The villagers were prepared and put up a stiff resistance, though they had few weapons. They fought with staffs and hammers, plows, and farm tools. A few had swords and other weapons, and they fought us with surprising courage, if little skill. Even so, I lost men that night, and in the end, we gained little of what we had come for. We killed many of the villagers, but their resolve would not wane. As I charged through the village, I saw a shapely young woman running with a small child in tow."

Rajni lowered her head between her knees, her teeth clenched. Mustafa Khan continued.

"It was my intent to take this woman, but she turned and faced me, looked me directly in the eye as you did, not two hours ago. She pushed her young child behind her and stood more firm than the earth beneath her. I reined my horse and stopped before her, much as I stopped before you earlier. I was heated with the charge and the fire of combat. My sword was wet and red, and the thrill of death was upon me!" Mustafa Khan paused and stared at the fire, his eyes the color of the flames.

Rajni had been wandering the Punjab for more than nine months, during which time she had been frightened many times. There were numerous nights when she awoke with her heart pounding and a scream in her throat. Each time she went to a door to beg, she felt afraid. But in all those dark nights and difficult days, she had never feared for her life or her honor, not even when the young Brahmin with the family devoted to Durga wanted to rape her. Yet now, she shivered with fear.

She dared a long sideways gaze at the powerful and frightening bandit before her. He was more than two meters tall, with shoulders as wide as a bull's and a huge head. He had a thick bushy beard that was still dark below eyes that seemed not to miss anything. He wore a rather dirty and somewhat ragged yellow turban and was clearly capable of the most violent of actions. Rajni knew she was powerless in this situation and could only expect the worst, despite his apparent kindness and hospitality.

Mustafa Khan's face looked wild as a tiger in the jungle. His eyes were distant and the light of the fire burned in them. His fists were clenched tight as though he was in combat and his gaze was intensely fixed upon the fire. Even his own men moved away from him a little. For some time, he was silent, apparently reliving some distant battle, some desperate struggle for survival.

Rajni was curious. What could have happened that night? Was he remembering his violence upon that helpless woman, helpless as she was tonight? Was there much difference between her and the girl of Mustafa's story? He looked up from the fire suddenly, looking directly at Rajni. She cringed. He opened his mouth then closed it. Gradually, his expression softened as he began to realize the impact his story was having on her.

"Don't be afraid, little sister," he said with surprising tenderness. "Please understand that I was raised in violent times among ruthless men. I knew no other way. Life for me was strike first and show no mercy, lest your weaknesses become exposed and someone else take advantage of you. I had killed many men and accumulated great wealth. Many feared me, yet my mind was restless. On that bloody night, everything changed. Will it disturb you if I continue?"

Rajni stared at Mustafa Khan for a long time. His face seemed to change by the light of the fire. His fierce and coldhearted countenance softened. He was no longer a bandit, a slayer of men, and a taker of women. He looked more like the many pilgrims Rajni had seen in her travels: people searching the sacred places to find solace for their souls. She realized that something had transformed this mountain of a bandit and she wanted to hear the rest of the story.

"I am honored that you feel you can trust your story with me," she said softly. "I would like to hear the rest. Continue." She spoke as Rajni, daughter of the Raja of Patti. Her presence seemed to grow larger. She shifted her position and sat straight and regal as a princess.

Mustafa Khan withdrew a bit, again as in awe of her as he was when he dismounted his horse and fell at her feet. He continued his story, speaking with his strong colloquial accent.

"I pulled up before that young woman and dismounted my horse, the very horse I ride tonight! I moved quickly to take her, for I was hot with the passion of killing and angry with the resistance of the villagers. I was less than three paces from her, yet she never flinched. Instead, she held out her hand, palm toward me and, with a voice soft as autumn rain, simply said '*Stop.*' And so I did," he said quietly.

Mustafa Khan's men seemed stunned. Clearly few of them, if any, had heard this story, and few could imagine their leader stopped by the word of a woman.

"I couldn't move as I faced this girl. Time and space seemed to stand still, the chaos and destruction going on around me became as a dream. I could only look in the eyes of the girl. The sounds of the fighting and the screams of death became like wind in the trees. Then she stepped toward me and reaching up, placed her hand on my heart. 'You have killed enough,' she said. 'Now you must find your peace.'

"I couldn't move. She reached behind her and placed her hand on the shoulder of the child. Bringing him around, she told me to look at him. 'Do you remember?' she said. The poor child looked terrified, an expression of absolute helplessness and overwhelming fear was upon him. 'Do you remember when you were this age?' she spoke again. I couldn't take my eyes from that young boy. I was no longer the dacoit leader that I am today,"—he paused—"or that I was on that night. I was a six-year-old child in a village that was being sacked by the army of Sher Shah. I saw people being slaughtered, women raped and beaten. Then I remembered my father being taken away, pressed into Sher Shah's army. I saw the soldiers take my mother and twelve-year-old sister. I could hear their screams and pleas for mercy. But no mercy was forthcoming.

"She looked deeply into my eyes. 'You possess that mercy that was denied your mother and sister so many years ago,' she told me. 'It is yours to give now, in memory of those who loved you.'

"I remembered being left alone in the world, standing in our ruined village, the naked and bloody bodies of my mother and sister before me. I sat with them for two days, unable to move. I watched the crows and vultures come and eat their flesh. Still, I could not move. Then the second night, the dacoits came for the spoils and took me with them.

"To their credit, they helped me to bury my sister and mother. They raised me and took care of me. They trained me in the use of arms and taught me how to sit a horse. And"—he paused, drawing a deep breath through his nose—"they taught me to do the work of a bandit. I was strong and learned fast and eventually took control of those bandits. We expanded our influence to a wider and wider area. Now I control this entire region." He paused then sighed deeply. "The truth is that I have lived a violent life and have inflicted harm upon many people.

"On the night I stood before that woman and young child, my life passed before me. As I looked into the eyes of the boy, I looked deep into the darkness of my own soul. A profound terror struck me as I beheld the man I had become and I was afraid that on the judgment day Allah would have no choice but to turn me away. An impenetrable remorse invaded my heart, just as I had invaded that village. Her hand never left my heart, and an increasing warmth began to fill me. I felt my mother and sister and the love of my father. Her gaze never left mine, and it seemed that a thick mist had settled upon the village. At first, I thought it was the smoke from the huts that were burning, but I realized that the pitch of the battle seemed to be far away and the scent of smoke was remote.

"With the slightest push of her hand, she turned me from her and stood beside me. She waved her hand before me, and again I could see the battle, but it was bloodier and more horrific than any I had seen before. I not only saw the fight, but I could see the souls of the dead and the dark spirits who came for those men of mine who fell. The screams of their souls were more hopeless and cacophonous than the sounds of the worst battle. A dark energy was around them, preventing them from calling God's Name and blocking all prayers for their souls.

"Then out of that darkness appeared a form before me, a form more black than the darkest night, a black deeper than the deepest well. It was the form of a woman, with teeth like those of a tiger and eyes burning hotter than this fire. Around her neck was a necklace of skulls that rattled with the sound of painful death. Her face came close, and she put her fingers around my throat. 'You have one chance,' she said with a hiss. 'Make your choice now!' I fell to the ground, and she placed her foot upon my chest. It was as if an elephant was standing on me. It felt as though all the blood was being squeezed from my heart. I closed my eyes and cried for mercy, but the weight only increased. I cried again, 'Oh God, have mercy upon my soul so that I may show mercy to others!'"

"Kali!" whispered Rajni. The sound of her voice startled everyone. Even the horses snorted and neighed. Mustafa Khan snapped his head up as if they were under sudden attack. He smiled as he looked Rajni in the eye.

"In an instant, the weight was gone, and once again I found myself standing before the young maiden. 'We will meet again,' she said, 'but you must change your ways and purify yourself.' Then the smoke lifted and I found myself standing alone, the fighting still raging as if I had not missed a second of it. I ordered my lieutenants to call in the men and cease the fighting. I called the village elders and told them that from that time forward, they would be under my protection. Then, gathering my men, we rode away as the dawn broke over Mecca.

"I made my way to Lahore alone, asking everyone along the way the name of one I might seek out who could give me spiritual instruction and help me to purify myself and change my ways. The mercy of Allah brought me under the guidance of Mian Mir who had recently come to the area. My life has changed, little sister. Sometimes I forget myself, old habits don't die easily, but something is now different with me. I have heard of you and your suffering. I have sought you out because I believe that it is Allah's will that I help you. The young woman that night told me that we would meet again, and I believe that she has returned to me as you. Allah's mercy has led me to you and, therefore, I am at your service. Please forgive my interruption."

Neither Rajni nor any of Mustafa Khan's men spoke. The fire had been recently stoked and burned brightly, crackling and sparking. The sounds of the horses and the movement of the sentries were beyond the fire, and in the distance, a nightingale was singing. Rajni looked at the face of Mustafa Khan. It appeared to have been transformed by the telling of his tale. He, who had just minutes before caused Rajni to fear for her life, now seemed as gentle as a puppy.

"In many ways, bhai," she spoke quietly, her voice just slightly louder than the sound of the flames, "our stories are not that different. We are both pilgrims on this path called life. We have only the mercy of the Akal Purkh to depend on. And it seems that He is bringing us both closer to His loving presence. I always believed that it was God who cared for me and gave me everything, but only by my experience in these past months do I know that to be true.

"As I told you before, my father is the Raja of Patti and a very powerful and wealthy man. He is in love with the Vedas and the process of learning. Though he can recite with authority, he has very little understanding. Still, he is a sincere man and believes in his birth as a Brahmin. He has been a good husband to my mother and a loving father to my sisters and me. As the Raja of Patti, he has control of the revenues of a large area and has been very successful collecting what is owed. He holds high favor with the governor for his efficiency and the accuracy of his accounting. This has made him both a proud and ruthless man.

"He fathered seven daughters, of which I am the youngest. He doted on each of us, gave us whatever we asked for and much that we didn't. As I told you, he gave each of us our own pundit to teach us the Vedas and the Brahminical ways. That is how I came to meet my Punditji. He tutored me, taught me how to pray and,"—Rajni paused, her eyes sparkling—"how to meditate," she said with a whisper and a radiant smile.

"So," asked Mustafa Khan, "how did such a high-born girl come to be here?" He hesitated and looked past the fire to where Piare lay. Slowly raising his head, he indicated with his chin, "And with him?"

Rajni looked at Mustafa Khan, her dark eyes dancing with the light of the fire. "My father is a proud and arrogant man. Each month or so, he called my sisters and me together and demanded of us, 'Who cares for you and gives you everything?'" Rajni imitated Duni Chand's guttural voice. "Each of my sisters would answer, 'You do, Papa.' Somehow, I was always able to avoid a direct answer because I believed," she reflected briefly, "and now I know, that it is God who cares for us and gives us everything. I sort of outsmarted him. I could get away with it because I was the youngest and, in many ways, also his favorite."

Rajni seemed somehow defiant. As she spoke, her confidence increased and the criminals before her were, to a man, taken in by her presence.

"He would blame my Punditji for putting strange ideas into my impressionable head."

As she spoke, Rajni realized that it had been sometime since she had actually made conversation with anyone. She talked with Piare, but they didn't really converse. She begged for food and sometimes would talk briefly with the kinder people along their way, but one unspoken rule of begging was to take what was offered, then leave as quickly as possible. She was enjoying this evening.

"My sisters were married one at a time, and as each one went to her husband and left my father's house, he became more possessive and demanding. Each year at the time of the monsoons, they returned home, and we would be together for almost two months. That was always a joy and Papa would be more relaxed and normal. But he always got us together and asked us that stupid question.

"One morning last summer, I went to my father's gardens with my sisters and we had a wonderful time. As we were walking home, I saw my Punditji sitting with a saintly looking group of men and he called me over to meet them. They were from Amritsar and played the most beautiful kirtan. I sat with them for several hours, and they told me of their guru, Guru Ram Das. My heart filled with the most wonderful feelings. They taught me a hymn of Guru Nanak." She stared at the fire, her mind back to that precious moment, then reflecting forward through the days since then.

"When I first learned that hymn," she said thoughtfully, "I truly believed it and believed that everything would come for me . . ." She paused again. "Perhaps I am jumping ahead," she said with a smile. "My heart was touched by the love of Guru Ram Das and the devotion of his humble Sikhs. They told me that they were to leave that evening for Amritsar, the guru's home, and invited me to come sometime and meet the guru in person. I removed my jewelry and gave it to the Sikhs and asked that it be given to their guru. The leader of the group assured me that it would be."

Mustafa Khan's men stirred. This was a strange girl indeed. Not only did she apparently insult her father, but also she gave her jewelry to total strangers and asked that it be given to a fakir.

The bandits hung on every word she spoke, and when she stopped, they looked at her expectantly, enraptured by her presence and the power of her story. After some time, Rajni looked up and continued, telling about how concerned her sisters were with what she had done. She told them how her sisters had tried to persuade her to get the jewelry back and the reaction of her mother when she learned that Rajni had given it away.

Then with tears in her eyes, Rajni told of the confrontation with her father, the pleas and sobs of her sisters and mother, and Duni Chand's reaction, pointing to the clothes she was wearing as the clothes of the sweeper. There were shouts of anger and offers from the group to go to Patti and kill her father, but Rajni quieted them, telling them that he was suffering enough. She described their long walk to the Satluj and her reaction when she first saw the extent of Piare's hopeless condition. She recounted her first experience of begging that following morning and then the discovery of the gardening cart on their second morning.

"I understood that the time had come to leave the Patti district and place myself in the hands of the Akal Purkh. It was at that point that I understood the hymn. I have recited it daily, many mornings with an empty stomach, many nights when I was cold and wet. While I am no longer under the protection of my father, I understand clearly that I am now and have always been under the protection of the Creator.

"Quite often, people have been generous, but I must tell you that even now I am not accustomed to the act of begging. One time, I was beaten when I asked for help. Many times we have been passed on the road, only to have stones or excrement thrown at us. Still, I have always followed my Punditji's advice. Each day, I have bathed my husband and have recited the hymn of the guru. In ways that I confess are not fully clear to me, God has cared for us."

Many of the hardened criminals around her were now teary-eyed.

"For His reasons and the reasons of my own destiny, which I don't fully comprehend, I am bound to do this, to travel these roads, pulling this poor soul who depends on me and daily face my own fears and doubts." Rajni gazed at Mustafa Khan, whose face looked hard in the firelight.

"This is how much God has cared for me," she looked at them with a dark expression on her face. "One night, after a long day in which all who we asked for help refused us, we stopped near a well, close to this area. On this night, a powerful dacoit and more than sixty of his men surrounded us. They were all well-armed and their leader was a giant of a man, tall and powerful with a frightening look on his face. In all these months, I have been afraid many times, but on this night, I believed that my honor and our lives were soon to be lost. The dacoit leader dismounted his horse and came straight for me." She paused and looked at the fire, shivering slightly as her voice trailed off.

The anticipation of the men around her was unbearable, and Mustafa Khan seemed to be near a powerful rage. He could not tolerate the thought that other dacoits were moving in his area. Even more, he could not tolerate the thought that someone would endanger this girl.

"You said it was in this area?" he demanded in a powerful voice.

"Yes," Rajni said innocently.

"Were you harmed?" he demanded again. Before Rajni could answer, he called two of his lieutenants to get their men ready to ride. He would not stand for this!

"By God's grace, I was not harmed," Rajni smiled.

"When did this happen, perhaps he is still in the area. Did you learn the name of this dead man?" Mustafa Khan was clearly in a killing mood now.

"He is still in the area," Rajni's shivering became uncontrollable shaking, and Mustafa Khan believed she was shaking with fear. "For it happened only tonight, and I learned his name. He is Mustafa Khan, and he is sitting before me now!"

She could no longer control herself. Her shaking gave way to giggles, then her giggles gave way to such powerful laughter that Rajni could barely breathe. Slowly, Mustafa Khan and all his men realized that they had been had, and as the joke dawned on them, they laughed as uncontrollably as Rajni. She looked at them sweetly and smiled brightly.

By the light of the fire she looked radiant, like the divine princess that she was. She had enchanted every man there.

"I know of this guru in whose name you blessed me," said Mustafa Khan, still smiling. "You have never met him?"

"No, I have only met his Sikhs."

"You must go to Amritsar! It is a new village that this guru is building. I think he can help you. If you like, we will escort you to the outer reach of my territory and put you on the right road to Amritsar."

"You've been very kind to us. I'll discuss it with my husband, and we will let you know in the morning."

"In the morning then!" said Mustafa Khan. He ordered that blankets be brought for Rajni. He watched in amazement as she tenderly laid Piare down and covered him before ever tending to herself.

"Who is this girl?" he said aloud.

THIRTY

Rajni lay down next to Piare. For the first time since she left her father's house, she was lying on a soft pad and covered with a proper blanket. She enjoyed telling her story to the bandits, but at the same time, it was painful for her. Rajni was a strong girl and had found in herself the fortitude to meet every challenge and difficulty that she had been faced with.

Yet as she lay there looking up at the stars, listening to the dying fire, a tidal wave of emotion flowed over her. She had survived these months by keeping her mind focused on surviving and by not thinking about the reality of what she was doing or the severity of her circumstances. Now after telling her story, the horrors of those experiences flooded her mind.

She understood that Piare's condition would never improve. It is true that he was better off than he had been on their wedding day, but the progressive nature of his disease was steadily and literally eating him alive. During their time together, they had spoken little, mostly about the urgent matters of their own survival. It took all her strength to pull him in his cart. What remained of her strength had to be used for begging, bringing water, and bathing and caring for Piare. Although she once thought about returning to her father, she had simply pushed ahead day after day.

Lying there now, she could see how they had been protected and taken care of. She knew in her heart and mind that she would survive and this time would pass. Yet her previous life seemed a very remote memory. She thought about going to Amritsar to meet Guru Ram Das. The idea excited her, and she wondered why she had not thought of it before. She couldn't wait to discuss it with Piare in the morning.

That was one of the truly sweet things about Rajni. Even though her husband was incapable of all but the most minimal actions, she still treated him as though he was a man in every way. Since the morning of her encounter with the sadhu and the resulting dream, she always consulted with Piare, discussed what they should do, and asked his approval for everything in the traditional way of Indian marriages. She was no longer patronizing or condescending toward Piare and always treated and referred to him respectfully. Eventually, her tears watered the seeds of sleep, and peaceful dreams sprouted in her fertile mind.

It was the most peaceful sleep for Rajni since she left her father's house. For Piare, it may have been the most peaceful night of his life. The quiet of the night was accented by the snores of Mustafa Khan and his men, the stirring of the horses, and the movement of the ever-watchful sentries. After all, they were bandits who were wanted and hunted. Rival dacoits also pursued and often attacked them, but not tonight. It was as though Rajni had cast a magic spell over everyone, and they all slept deeply and peacefully.

Piare awoke before Rajni. She was usually awake and up before he ever stirred, but this morning, she slept soundly. Last night was the first time he had heard the details of her story. In all their months together, she had never told him the details, referring occasionally to her sisters or her pundit but little else. She had told him that she was raised as a princess, but he did not fully comprehend how wealthy and privileged her life had been. Yet life for Piare had improved considerably with Rajni. These had been the best months of his life.

He thought about the words of the Pir and the power of his vision. He firmly believed that his leprosy was due to his actions in previous incarnations and that his suffering in this life would help free him from the cycle of birth and death. In fact, he wondered if in some way he bore the suffering of others. As he grew older and it became obvious that he would never recover from his leprosy, he became negligent of himself. Ultimately, he became discouraged and hopeless. Rajni had been right that day at the Satluj. He had given up. It was only since he had come under Rajni's care that he dared to hope. He knew his hope was futile, that he would never fully be a man capable of caring for a wife such as Rajni, and that troubled him.

As he lay quietly in the predawn light, he couldn't understand why Rajni had to suffer with him. So he tried to think of a way that he, and therefore Rajni, could be freed of this karma. He remembered Rajni's realization the previous day. If they could find Guru Ram Das, they would find the water.

He brightened a little. Perhaps they should go to Amritsar and try to meet the guru. Piare loved Rajni and couldn't bear the fact that he was unable to care for her. He saw how hard she worked to keep him alive. Yet sick as he was, he was not blind to the toll it was taking on her. Though her beauty had not diminished, her face had hardened, and her eyes seemed distant. Her all-too-seldom laughter had been infrequent and metallic sounding. Now the fear, the trials of the road, and the hardships she endured for them both all showed in her face.

"Eh Ram," he prayed silently, "let me no longer be a burden to her. Lead us to Guru Ram Das where she can rest and be safe and I can be healed. Otherwise, take me back to You and free her from this weight she bears."

I listened to his simple prayer. Piare was becoming selfless and that pleased Me.

Rajni stirred. Sensing that Piare was awake, she turned. "Piare?" she whispered.

"*Han ji.*"

"What do you think of the idea of going to Amritsar to meet Guru Ram Das? It must be a sacred place because Guru Ram Das is there. Punditji said that if we need help, we should call on him. The Pir said to follow my bliss and the jewels. So let's go there. Perhaps Guru Ram Das can help us. Then we won't need to look further. After all, it was the guru who brought us together. Had I not met those Sikhs, I would have never given my jewelry. I would have gone directly home, you would not have been at my gate at that time. Everything would be different."

"I was just. . . thinking that," he laughed. "Yes," Piare said thoughtfully, "let's go to . . . Amritsar . . . and meet the guru. He. . .will help us."

Rajni's heart quickened. She wondered why they had not thought of it before. She couldn't wait to start, so she got up quickly, went to the well, drew water, and cleaned herself. She filled a bucket and began to drag it back to Piare, but before she had taken three steps, at least eight of Mustafa Khan's men ran to carry the bucket for her.

She removed the chunis from Piare and undressed him. The hardened criminals around her cringed when they saw how badly disfigured Piare was. Though they didn't want to watch, they couldn't help themselves as Rajni methodically went about washing Piare. She did it so tenderly and sweetly that those men—who would not hesitate to cut the heart out of someone simply for the satisfaction of doing so—were touched. Rajni dressed and covered Piare then approached Mustafa Khan.

"Good morning, uncle," she smiled.

Mustafa Khan had been a bandit since he was ten years old. He killed his first man before he was eleven and took his first woman when he was barely twelve. By the time he was sixteen, he had his own band of forty men, and together, they terrorized the territory. There was no lock or door that he could not open and no horse that he could not tame and ride. Now, nearing forty, he had killed almost eighty men and had more than sixteen-hundred men under his immediate control.

Though Mustafa Khan had a reputation as a fierce bandit, he had become a rather sincere Muslim. He had just finished his morning prayers and was feeling somewhat humble and reverent when Rajni approached him.

"Have you agreed to allow me to help you?"

"We have. How far is it to Amritsar from here?"

"By walking, it should take you less than two days from the perimeter of my territory. Could be a bit longer at your pace."

"And how far can you escort us?"

"Another half day to that point."

"Can we begin soon?"

"Whenever you like. I and all that I have are at your service. You have cut through my heart with greater precision than a *falad* blade, and I will never forget you."

Rajni looked at him. Curiously, she remembered a falling star, the tear I shed on her wedding night as she looked up to the infinite sky, standing in the Satluj up to her knees in water.

"We must eat before leaving, this is not Ramadan!" Mustafa Khan said heartily.

Rajni stopped. They had just eaten the night before. Now they were going to eat again? And she was reasonably certain they would eat again before sunset.

"Yes," she said quietly, causing Mustafa Khan to stop and look at her intently. "We must eat before leaving."

Mustafa Khan's men broke the camp and prepared to move. Rajni collected their things and put them in the wagon, then carefully set Piare in it. She gathered the rope, pulled it over her shoulder, and walked toward Mustafa Khan.

"Let my men tie your cart to a horse. The wagon can be pulled, and you can ride."

"It is better that I pull him as I always have," she said. "We share this karma. We will discharge it together. But thank you for your kindness."

"Then at least permit me to help." He ordered that a saddle pad be cut and stitched over the rope to protect Rajni's shoulders.

"You've been very kind to us," she said, her eyes dropping to the ground. "I believe you will be blessed and still find honor before Allah."

"Thank you, little sister, I pray that it will be so. I will remember your name to Him on that glorious day."

Rather than mount his horse, Mustafa Khan walked alongside Rajni, holding the reins in his hands as the whole group set out slowly at Rajni's pace. It was difficult for many of his men to keep their spirited horses under control while moving so slowly, so Mustafa Khan sent a large contingent forward to secure the area as they went.

They walked throughout the morning, talking little. Mustafa Khan, however, could not stop thinking about this strange situation and how powerful his experience the night before had been.

This girl is special, he thought to himself. *She is not an ordinary human. How could the father of any child, but especially a child such as this, inflict such hardship upon his own daughter? Yet, she bears no malice toward anyone. Oh Allah,* he prayed, *only You are merciful. Watch after this divine girl and her suffering husband. By Thy Mercy remember her for her sacrifice.*

He thought about going to Patti and killing Duni Chand himself. It enraged him when he thought about what Duni Chand had done to his own daughter, and he felt compelled to correct it on her behalf. Then he realized that to have lost a child such as Rajni must be unbearable. He thought, as Rajni herself had said when she told her story, that Duni Chand must be in great pain.

Then he had the idea to kill Piare. He could have his men poison Piare's food. He would die peacefully and be relieved of his suffering, and Rajni would be free of that burden. Had it been any other time in Mustafa Khan's life, he would have killed both Duni Chand and Piare. However, it was time for the midday prayer, so they halted in a grove of trees near the intersection of the road they were on and the road that led to Amritsar.

"This is the boundary of my territory. We'll say our prayers here," said Mustafa Khan. "We'll dine together again and then must part company."

Rajni went to Piare and gave him water. "My beloved," Rajni spoke softly, not wanting to be heard by the others, "in these months, I have learned many things, and together we have shared many things. I have never known such hardship, yet you have never known such comfort. This is the blessing God has given us. Believe me when I tell you that you are a good and honorable man. Please don't think of yourself as less than that. You did what you needed to do to survive so that you could come to this point in time and space. Soon we will meet Guru Ram Das who brought us together. This little life that we share and the little suffering we have endured will all pass. What is important is what dwells in the temple of the heart. In you there beats one that is noble and honorable, and somehow, I do believe that the strength that is here"—she reached out and placed her palm over Piare's heart—"will prevail."

Piare's body quivered. How could anyone find anything redeemable in him? *What a strange karma to be dying a long, slow death yet have this angel to watch over me.* His mind reeled.

Mustafa Khan's men prepared a simple meal, and his men pleaded with Rajni to tell her story again. For a second time, she enchanted some of the most hardened criminals of the Punjab, retelling her story with passion. Again, many of the murderers, rapists, thieves, and robbers were in tears from her tale. To them, they were before a living goddess who had come to Earth to bless them.

Rajni suddenly rose and stood before them. "Listen, my uncles and brothers," she said loudly, "you have showed my husband and me only the greatest kindness. It is not my place to ask anything of you now. Yet"—she paused, taking in the faces rapt with her presence—"I know that you have inflicted pain and suffering on many others. I believe that you will all be forgiven by the kindness you have shown to us, but I urge that you no longer take advantage of the weak and never again violate a woman!" Her voice was strong, and forty men shifted uncomfortably.

"You have a special skill," she continued. "Use it to protect the weak. You will find that you lose nothing and gain much. Remember me. Remember this face that you first saw by the fire in the moonlight, and remember it the next time you are compelled to take advantage of a weaker person. They are just simple people like me." She paused, looking up at the sky then down at the ground. Without raising her head, she said, "Forgive my outburst. I meant no ingratitude."

Then turning to Mustafa Khan, she said, "Last night you asked me to bless you. You have also blessed us with your kind generosity. I pray that in the future you will show this same mercy to others. Each day, you pray to Allah, the Merciful. When you yourself show mercy, you become like Him. You are a good and honorable man. When you blend that with Allah's mercy, you become a great man. Please consider what I have said and forgive any offense that I may have committed toward you."

Like a lost child who has been found by his mother, Mustafa Khan the ferocious bandit bowed and touched Rajni's feet. "My little sister, Allah's mercy has brought us here to serve His purposes. I have only fed your body, but you have nourished my soul. Before Allah, I give my word that I will never again harm an innocent or helpless person."

Rajni placed both her hands on his big head. "In the Name of Guru Ram Das," she said strongly, "I bless you . . . again."

Mustafa Khan stood up, and Rajni bowed her head slightly. "Now," she said, "we must set out for Amritsar!"

Mustafa Khan had one of his men bring him a bundle, and he presented it to Rajni.

"Little sister," he said, pointing, "this road will take you to Amritsar. You will find your way. If you reach the Beas, you have gone too far, but you will find the village of Ram Das before that point." He handed her the bundle. "Please accept this."

Rajni opened it. Inside was food and one hundred rupees. She looked at him, and his rough and massive hands covered hers.

"Please," he said again. "In this way you can buy food and sleep at a rest house. You have suffered enough."

Rajni lowered her eyes and bowed her head. "It has been the mercy of Allah that has brought us together. Now it is His mercy that sets us on the road to the guru. I accept this in His name."

He looked into her radiant face and shining eyes. "I will never forget you, my little sister, and I will remember your name to Him on Judgment Day."

"And I will remember your name to the guru!"

With a radiant smile, Rajni picked up the padded rope and pulled it over her shoulders. Without looking back, she set off on the road to Amritsar.

THIRTY-ONE

MUSTAFA KHAN AND HIS MEN watched Rajni and Piare until they were lost from sight, indistinguishable in the colorful blend of people, animals, and wagons moving along the road. They were on a major thoroughfare between Lahore and Delhi, and the passage was clotted with traffic. Rajni and Piare made their way slowly through the melee as the sun began its slow descent to the horizon.

The music of the road, which until recently had intimidated Rajni and made her feel insecure and uneasy, now cheered and encouraged her. The moos, neighs, and hoofbeats of the animals made her feel secure as she walked while the sounds of bells, chants, and the voices of people talking and singing along the way uplifted her. The time spent with Mustafa Khan had renewed her and restored her hope.

She thought about all that had happened the night before with Mustafa Khan when she had blessed him in the name of Guru Ram Das. When she weighed that against the words of the Pir, the sadhu, and the aghora, as well as her realization the day before, things began to make sense to her. She felt that Guru Ram Das had reached out and touched her that day in Patti and that he had been calling her to him since then. Now she found herself on the road to him where she would find the answers she was seeking and the fulfillment of her destiny and longing.

Around tea time, they stopped, taking the shade of a cluster of trees near a well. There were several food stalls nearby where the ever-enterprising Punjabis were selling food, tea, and other refreshments. Other travelers rested nearby, so she moved to the most remote spot and went to the well and drew water. She gave water to Piare and then drank herself as she cooled in the shade. They ate some of the food that Mustafa Khan had given them that morning, not because they were especially hungry, but because they had food and could eat. Rajni was cheerful and sang to herself as she rested and drifted into a light sleep.

After a while, a recently married couple also took rest under the trees, and Rajni, coming out of her light nap, was surprised when they began to strike up a conversation with her. Normally, no one spoke to her, and unless she was begging for food or asking for help, she seldom spoke to others. Yet these people seemed eager to connect with her.

"Forgive me," said the wife, unable to take her eyes off the form of Piare, covered with the now ragged and stained chunis of Rajni's sisters, "but are you the daughter of Raja Duni Chand?" Her Urdu indicated that she was partially educated and from a good family.

Rajni looked at the woman, a girl actually, and understood that she meant no insult. She was young, approximately Rajni's age. Yet there was a wide gap between them. It was not age, but a matter of wisdom and awareness. Rajni's experiences of the past nine months had matured her rather than aged her and had given her wisdom rather than hardened her. In the decorated girl before her, Rajni saw the apparition of the girl that she had once been.

"I was his daughter," she said softly, in a somewhat faraway voice.

"We have heard of you," said the girl, somewhat in awe. "Many people know what happened to you and have been moved by it."

Rajni stared at her in amazement. No one ever spoke to them. People seldom were willing to help. "How could that be?" asked Rajni, truly surprised.

"Forgive me, madam," said the girl, "but everyone in this area is familiar with the cruelty of your father. He gave instructions throughout his domain that no one should aide you. Now he sends his men out weekly to look for you. Word has spread."

The husband, who was seventeen or eighteen, tried to speak with authority. "Please excuse my wife. She is young. However, she does speak the truth, we have heard of you. Please forgive our intrusion, we don't mean to trouble you with a matter that must be unpleasant. Are you going to Amritsar?"

"Yes," there was excitement in her tone. "We are going to Amritsar to meet Guru Ram Das." She was relieved that the subject had changed.

"We are also going to join in the Baisakhi celebration," said the husband.

"Have you met Guru Ram Das?" asked Rajni.

"Being with him is indescribable!" exclaimed the young man. "When you are there, you have no longing, no doubt about anything. Everything changes just with his glance. You will see for yourself."

"Although I have never met the guru, in certain ways he is the reason for my disagreement with my father and my circumstances now. Because of Guru Ram Das, I met my husband and we were married."

"Oh . . . yes," said the young man, studying what he could see of Piare's face through the chunis. He was asleep. "Well, we have enjoyed meeting you, but we must be moving on. People are expecting us in Amritsar. We would invite you to travel with us, but we really must keep a rather brisk pace, you see. Come, Bibi," he said to his wife tersely, "time to move. We're off to see the guru! I Hope we see you in Amritsar."

They quickly headed out to the road and became another brushstroke on the canvas before her, mixed among the horses, ox carts, cows, water buffaloes, and people moving in both directions.

Rajni smiled to herself. She turned to Piare and gently shook him, "Beloved, it is time to move."

He stirred slightly and Rajni loaded him back into the wagon. As they stepped out into the road, Rajni noticed for the first time that people stepped away from them, giving them respectful space.

There was a lot of traffic on the road, much of it going toward Amritsar. Everywhere there were high spirits, and people were chanting and laughing. With all the people on the road, it was hard for Rajni not to go at a faster-than-normal pace. The first stars had already appeared when they came to a village. Rajni remembered the one hundred rupees and the words of Mustafa Khan. She decided to look for a rest house where they could stay for the night. The comfort of the previous night was still in her mind.

There were two rest houses in the village, simple outdoor structures, not really houses. Under a thatched canopy were beds where travelers could sleep, where food was served, and where they could wash. Each was full due to all the people traveling to Amritsar. Room could have been made for them, but no rest house would accept a leper. As she was leaving the second rest house, a small man with a big smile approached her.

"Good evening, little sister."

His Urdu was heavily accented. By his small frame and darker skin, Rajni recognized him as being from the southern provinces. She eyed the strange man who appeared to be in his early fifties. He was bare-chested and wore a saffron-colored dhoti with a saffron-colored cotton shawl around his shoulders. In his right hand, he carried a long wooden staff that was studded with small, flat metal disks. On his forehead, below his shaved scalp, was the U-shaped mark of Vishnu, and around his neck were large wooden beads. He smelled strongly of betel, and his rotten teeth and darkened gums showed that he was addicted to the nut stimulant. Though he appeared to be a swami, something about him did not seem authentic and made Rajni feel uneasy. She kept her distance.

"Do you need something, ji?" Rajni replied.

"Actually, my child, I was thinking that you might need something. My name is Gopi Das, and just at the other end of this village, I have a small place of refuge for those pilgrims who might need aid."

Rajni look at him in the gathering darkness. There was something rather slimy about his voice.

"Why do you think that we need aid?"

"Well," he said smoothly, "you have checked at the two rest houses and found them full."

"Have you been following me?" Rajni snapped suspiciously.

"No, no, no, no, nooo, dear daughter. I have only been on the lookout for those whom I can help—nothing more. I am just a simple man of faith. I think of myself as the Lord's helper, trying to give aid to those in need. Please, do come with me. We have a shrine, which I think will be comforting to you. There is food and a comfortable place for you to sleep. Do come."

"What about my husband?"

"Everyone is welcome," he said slowly, stretching out the words. "I only want to serve God and I must accept whoever He sends to me. Tonight He has sent you. Don't you trust me?"

"How much?"

The truth was that in all her life, Rajni had never handled money. Although her father was rich, she had never had a reason to deal with money. Whenever she went out shopping with her sisters, they would settle the price, which to them was an abstract concept, and later, a servant would bring the payment to the merchant. The one hundred rupees that Mustafa Khan gave them made little sense to her.

"Oh my child, please don't insult me. I ask for nothing except your prayers on my behalf and on behalf of those to whom I can provide comfort. I do this to help those who seek the refuge of the Lord."

"Well," said Rajni, "people are not normally so kind."

"Please, please, it is my blessing." And he reached out to take the rope from Rajni's shoulders.

"Stop!" she said and stepped back.

The swami stopped, his hand outstretched. "I only want to assist you, young princess."

"I will pull him myself," said Rajni sternly.

"As you like, child, as you like. Then follow me."

Cautiously, Rajni followed this strange man to the far end of the village. They came to a simple mud and thatch hut. In front of the hut was a thatch canopy that leaned unsteadily. Under the canopy were six *charpoys*, wooden frames with woven hemp mesh across them used as beds throughout India. She saw aside from the hut a small shrine to an indistinguishable goddess, somewhat in disrepair. There were three other travelers already resting on the beds.

"Welcome," said the swami. He pointed to the two beds closest to the hut. "Please," he said as he made his way into the hut.

Rajni helped Piare onto the inside bed.

"How do you feel?" she asked with concern. His breathing had been difficult all afternoon.

"I'll be fine. There is something about this place though."

"Would you prefer that we leave?" she asked with an edge of anxiety to her voice.

"No, we are here, and we need to rest. We'll start early in the morning."

"I'll get you up early before the sun has come up, and we will be on the road before it gets crowded. Do you want to eat?"

Her concern for Piare had grown, and she worried about him constantly. Once, she had been a princess with jewels, fine clothes, food whenever she wanted, and servants to tend to her. Now all she had was her husband. She realized that if he were to die, she would be truly alone in the world. She pushed that thought out of her mind.

"God give us strength," she whispered to herself.

"In . . . these last few days . . ."—he paused and gasped for breath, his voice gurgling—"we have . . . eaten more than . . . we have in the . . . previous week." It concerned Rajni that his voice was slipping back to its old nature.

"Shhh," whispered Rajni, "don't talk now, just rest. I'll see about food. Or we can eat what is left from Mustafa Khan."

As if on cue, Gopi Das appeared from the hut with a thin chapatti in each hand. On top of each was a little dal.

"Please be my guests. Make yourselves comfortable and eat. You must be tired, and you should sleep soon,' he said, his smile revealing his rotten teeth and gums in all their disrepair.

Rajni accepted the food and helped Piare to get into a position where he could feed himself. While they were eating, Gopi Das went around to the other guests and served them tea. Neither Rajni nor Piare wanted tea despite Gopi Das' slimy insistence. Eventually, he gave up, wished them all good night, and extinguished the lantern.

In the darkness, Rajni prepared herself and Piare for sleeping. She pushed her charpoy closer to his and left the wagon at the foot of their beds. She covered him with one of the blankets that Mustafa Khan's men had placed in the wagon that same morning. As she covered herself, she noticed that all the other guests were already sleeping deeply, so she tried not to disturb them. As an afterthought, she took the bundle of rupees from the cart and placed it next to Piare and fell asleep.

* * *

Rajni awoke with her heart racing. Opening her eyes, she saw the shadowy form of Gopi Das looming at the foot of her charpoy. He held something in his right hand as he quickly climbed onto the charpoy and pressed his body against her, trying to force himself between her legs.

"I'm glad you refused the tea, dear girl," he whispered. "I'll enjoy you more awake because now it's time to pay." His breath was putrid.

The object in his right hand was a large and bloody knife, which he placed against her neck, smearing blood onto her skin.

"Gopi Das will enjoy the young girl before sending her to God."

Rajni stared at him wide-eyed, paralyzed by fear. Gopi Das had her pinned to the bed with the weight of his body, and the slightest movement on her part caused the edge of the knife to push against her flesh. Rajni felt his left hand move to her waist, feeling for the drawstring of her salwaars. She could not scream with the knife blade against her throat. She brought her knees up, trying desperately to stop the swami from raping her, and as she did, the knife cut her neck.

Suddenly, Gopi Das lost his balance, fell on top of Rajni, then crashed down between the charpoys. As he fell, the blade of his knife raked across Rajni's left cheek and chin, leaving a deep gash. She screamed in pain but moved quickly. She rose and kicked Gopi Das hard in the stomach and groin. Nine months of pulling Piare across the Punjab had made her legs very strong. Gopi Das cried out in pain and fell back onto the ground.

Rajni saw that the reason Gopi Das had lost his balance was because Piare had reached out and grabbed the swami's arm, pulling him off the charpoy. After years of pulling himself in his basket, Piare's arms were strong and powerful. With his left hand, he had gripped the arm of Gopi Das and pulled him off balance. It was a heroic act for Piare and taxed most of his strength. Yet he had protected his wife.

Quickly, with blood streaming from her face and neck, Rajni jumped up. She was crying but still sensible. "Piare, you protected me! We must leave this place quickly."

Rajni thought it strange that the other guests were sleeping soundly and had not been awakened by the commotion. Gopi Das moaned on the ground but suddenly sprang to his feet with surprising agility. He forced Rajni to the ground between the charpoys then turned, and with considerable force, knocked Piare from his bed. Piare crashed across Rajni's bed, then rolled across the ground, hitting his head hard on a rock. Gopi Das stepped over Rajni, moving toward Piare, raising his left leg to step over her charpoy.

When Rajni fell to the ground, she found the bloody knife still lying between the charpoys where Gopi Das had dropped it. She gripped it with both hands, and doing what came instinctively, pushed the knife up in the direction of the outstretched leg of the swami. It penetrated the inside of Gopi Das' right thigh, four inches above the knee. She continued to drive the blade upward to the hilt, deep into his thigh, severing the femoral artery.

Gopi Das howled in pain, spraying a fountain of blood as he fell toward the foot of the charpoy. He landed on top of Piare's wagon, smashing it completely and screamed in agony as he lay bleeding on the broken wood. Quickly, Rajni collected Piare by making a sling of her shawl. Pulling him onto her back, she ran barefoot toward the road, leaving behind what little they owned. She was almost bent double with Piare on her back, but Rajni did not stop as her thin legs churned, moving as fast as possible along the road.

Piare was semiconscious from the impact of the rock. Rajni was not sure if he was dead or alive, but she was afraid to stop and check, so she kept moving. The wounds on her neck and cheek were deep and bled copiously. Blood ran down her neck to her chest and dripped steadily on her shoulder, saturating her kameez, which was already sprayed with the blood of Gopi Das.

By the deep darkness and silvery slit of the new moon, she judged that it must be an hour or so after midnight. Rajni had visions of Gopi Das pursuing them or telling the soldiers posted in the village that a young girl had tried to kill him when he had offered his hospitality. She was not aware that she had crippled Gopi Das and that he would eventually bleed to death. Or that Gopi Das, in what proved to be a night of horror, had cut the throats of the other travelers. She wasn't sure what to do, so she just kept moving.

* * *

Gopi Das knew that he had been fatally injured. Blood gushed from his leg with each beat of his heart. When he fell onto Piare's wagon, a sliver of wood about eight inches long and an inch wide had lodged in the base of his spine. For years, he had taken advantage of travelers by offering them refuge then taking their belongings as they slept. On occasion, he cut the throats of his guests so there could be no complaint. He never expected that a thin, young girl would have the power to bring him before the *Dharam Raj,* My Lord of Death.

He lay back, paralyzed from the waist down and bleeding profusely. He knew that he was helpless to save himself and had no chance of surviving the night. He regarded his own knife embedded deep in his thigh. After such a fight, he felt calm, remembering the beautiful young girl with the bright eyes and sparkling radiance. She reminded him of his youth as his life played out before him.

When Gopi Das was quite young, he had sought the path of a swami and was sincerely devout. As he grew older though, he became disillusioned with the life of a renunciate and left the order. He fell in love with a girl who was above his station, a princess like Rajni with similar features and mannerisms. It was an unrequited love, and he was enraged that fate had made him a just a simple swami with few prospects. He resented his station in life, resented that he was not wealthy or powerful, and deeply resented that he was unable to attract the girl with money, power, or status.

To try to forget the girl and elevate himself, he attempted to perform some ritualistic austerities, but he was neither very sincere nor very good at sacrificing and his attempts were only halfhearted. With each austerity, his bitterness increased. The pain in his heart was not assuaged, and the burning anger in his mind was not cooled. He sought to relieve his pain in other ways and was caught with a prostitute, whom he had paid with offerings of the temple. His guru dismissed him.

Gopi Das wandered around India for many years, living off people by begging and making a great show of being a holy man. He posed well as a swami since insincerity was often the trademark of swamis. For a while, he set up his own little ashram near Hardwar. That worked for a few years, and he accumulated some wealth but took to giving very personal counsel to the women in the area. Eventually, the daughter of one of the local magistrates was found to be pregnant after receiving the personal spiritual instruction of Gopi Das. The people beat him with their shoes, drove him from Hardwar, and he crawled away, barely alive. That experience softened him, and he thought that perhaps if he actually did try to help people, his life would improve.

He trudged across the Punjab and set up his humble rest house. And for a while, he was kind to people and gave them refuge. All his years as a swami were not wasted, and he served weary travelers and helped to heal the sick. Unfortunately, the old unresolved bitterness and frustration with his life resurfaced as he realized that now he was aging and very unfulfilled. He also realized how easy it would be to take advantage of his guests, and ultimately, he could not resist that temptation.

He began roaming the streets at night, hiding by the other rest houses to collect the travelers who had been turned away. He took them to his own little rest house and offered them refuge for the night. Since Guru Ram Das had established the village of Amritsar, people with money and valuable gifts for the guru frequently passed through the village. Naturally Gopi Das felt that he, as much as the guru, should benefit from their quest and that his cause was equally just.

His practice was to feed them, give them heavily opiated tea and then, while they were deep in their opium dreams, take their valuables. In the morning, he made a great show of indignance that someone would dare to come to such a humble place and take advantage of the sincere pilgrims who rested there. Sometimes, he decided that instead of meeting the guru, the pilgrims would meet Me, and he would cut their throats.

And as he had intended this night, if a girl attracted him, he took advantage of her while she slept her opiated sleep. Usually, he disposed of the bodies in the surrounding jungle where the jackals and other scavengers ate them. Others he carried to the cremation grounds to dispose of using the leftover wood and coals from the funeral pyres. He set the bodies upon them and lighted the fires himself as he recited the incantations he had learned in his youth.

Now as he lay dying, the memories of his life passed before him. The anger and frustration of his youth finally left him. The hope with which he started this life and the devotion that set him on the spiritual path so many years ago returned to him as he neared death. With calm resignation, Gopi Das understood that he had wasted his life.

My *Dharam Raj* was near. Gopi Das could hear him approach, and he knew that soon he would have to account for himself. With considerable effort, he pulled the sliver of the broken cart from his back. Using it as a stylus, he dipped it in his own blood and wrote upon his dhoti in perfect Sanskrit, *This is my karma, which I brought upon myself. Thank you, little sister, for freeing me.*

Peacefully, Gopi Das surrendered his soul to Me.

THIRTY-TWO

After two hours, Rajni was exhausted. Her legs were unstable, and her back ached from the weight of Piare. Her face, neck, chest, and feet were caked with blood, and as she grew weaker, she fell. She managed to keep Piare on her back, but the impact of his weight nearly crushed her spine when they hit the ground. She looped the shawl under Piare's arms and dragged him to a nearby cluster of trees. The predawn air was cool. There was a slight breeze, and Rajni's sweat-soaked body was chilled.

Piare understood her discomfort and convinced her to cover herself with the shawl, and she did so reluctantly. Her cheek and neck throbbed with pain from the cuts made by the blade of Gopi Das. The bleeding had slowed, and she covered her wounds with her chuni to keep the insects out of them. Though she could not see her face, she believed that she had been scarred for life.

She shivered as much from fear as from cold, breathing fast and shallow. Rajni sat under the trees with the shawl wrapped around her body and over her head. Her arms were wrapped around her shins, and her chin rested on her knees. She stared into the darkness, trying to compose herself. She went over and over the images, and actions seared in her mind. Even with the extreme exertion of carrying Piare for hours, she had not expended the energy generated by her body when Gopi Das attacked her. She was unable to relax or calm herself.

Piare was hurt from the blow of Gopi Das. His whole body ached from the tumble to the ground, and his frail skin was torn and bleeding. He had a large gash on his head where he hit the rock, and his ribs and joints hurt from the impact of the fall. He coughed and daubed at his bloody wounds with a torn shred of a chuni.

Rajni's silence was deep and remote. Piare, deeply concerned for her, reached out his hand and placed it on her forearm. His touch comforted Rajni, though her shaking never stopped. They sat there as the sky grew opaque in anticipation of dawn. Rajni began to recite the shabd of Guru

Nanak, repeating it over and over. Her forehead fell forward to her knees, and she slept for an hour.

She awoke with a start, snapping her head up and gasping for air. It was a minute before she recognized where she was. She placed her head back on her knees and started to cry, sobbing deeply for some time. Her body shook with sobs of pain and deepest grief. Piare lay on his back, semiconscious and feeling useless, unable to give his wife comfort or support.

She reached out and touched Piare. "Do you think that I killed him?" There was an edge of panic in her voice. "Piare, there was so . . . much . . . blood!" she sobbed with her forehead against her knees. Her thin frame shook with grief.

In his breathy, gurgly voice, Piare spoke wisely. "No. You and I . . . and hhe . . . are only mere mortals. We don't . . . hhave power over life or death. If he is . . . dead, it is because it was his time." Piare paused, trying to catch his breath. "You wwere simply . . . the instrument bby . . . whhich . . . his karma . . . was dispatched." He tried to suppress a cough but couldn't. "You did . . . what the Pir . . . told you to do." He sounded like he was choking. "You remained strong . . . and did what you had to do." He wheezed and coughed violently.

Rajni placed her hand on his back, and Piare stilled. "You also remained strong and did what you had to do," she said with a partial smile. "You saved my life and my honor. You are a good man."

Piare took her hand. It had, in fact, been a true act of courage for Piare. He was very weak, and the effort of reaching out and pulling Gopi Das from the bed had been a huge exertion for him, but the act had been cathartic. Something had changed in him, and though he knew he was dying, he felt more in control of his life than he ever had.

"It was the most selfless thing, I . . . I . . . I"—he paused to collect himself and regulate his speech—"hhave everr done." The sincerity and desperation of his voice struck Rajni.

Rajni gripped his hand, "My beloved, you are destined for something great. I know it in my soul. We will make it to Amritsar and meet Guru Ram Das." She got up, stretched, and shook out the shawl.

She arranged the shawl and placed Piare in it and hoisted him up onto her back. The activity and exertion took her attention away from the terror of the night before and the pain from her wounds. In the early morning light, she set out toward the road but hesitated after a few steps.

What if Gopi Das had told the soldiers about her? What if they were patrolling the road looking for her? Panic began to rise in her, and she backed away from the road.

Rajni wasn't sure what to do. "Well," she said to Piare, "if they are looking for me, they will eventually find me. A young girl covered with blood and carrying a leper on her back can't be overlooked. We will be safer on the road." She started out again, but it was slow going.

She stumbled several times as they went but managed to get under Piare's weight in a way that made the going a little easier for her. She had to stop frequently to rest her back and catch her breath. Rajni's feet were bloody and in intense pain, but she would not quit. A power was awake in her now, driving her forward and pushing her to Amritsar.

If anyone along the road tried to talk to Rajni or offer assistance, she quickly ended the conversation, not trusting anyone. Yet in the throng that passed as the day wore on, she picked up snippets of conversation and learned that the unsavory swami at the far end of the last village was dead. No one mourned his loss.

They had not eaten since the night before, yet the prospect of begging for food terrified Rajni. She preferred hunger to begging. Her mind was focused on reaching Amritsar and meeting Guru Ram Das. She pushed herself for another three hours after sunset, sweating in the darkness. She trudged on in silence and passed through a village without stopping for water, afraid of the dogs that barked at her relentlessly. Finally, Rajni stumbled off the road and set Piare down. She covered him with the shawl, and without a word, curled up with her knees against her chest in a tight fetal position and fell asleep.

She awoke an hour before sunrise, desperate for water. She hastily gathered Piare in the shawl and set out again. Her body shook from hunger and overexertion. Her muscles were cramped from dehydration. Infection had spread into her wounds. Her tongue stuck to the roof of her mouth, her eyes were red and irritated, and her lips were cracked and dry. It was excruciating for her to walk with the weight of Piare on her back and the sound of him struggling to breathe in her ear, but the focus of her mind was unwavering, and she pushed herself along the road heroically.

As the sun crested the horizon, they came to a small village with a well at the center. In that early morning light, a few women, laughing and gossiping, had gathered to take the daily water for their families. Their bangles and nose rings tinkled over the splashing of the water. Their multicolored saris and kameez were bright in the morning sun. When they saw Rajni approaching, they became still and silent as midnight. Rajni knew better than to approach the well with Piare, so she set him down against a mud wall some distance away, pulled a chuni from him, and went to the well alone. The women of the village drew back from the well and stared silently at the wounded and bloodstained girl approaching the well.

Rajni drew the water up and poured it over the chuni, which she took to Piare to suck on. Then she returned to the well and drew water for herself. Filling her palms with the cold water, she drank as though her thirst could never be quenched. She wet her own chuni and daubed at the incisions on her face and neck, doing her best to clean the blood from her skin. She detached a bucket from the wheel and poured water over herself repeatedly. She never looked at any of the village women, and her determined expression never changed. She carried the bucket to Piare and poured the water over him.

She was soaked to the skin, her hair stuck to the side of her face, the water stung her wounds, but she was also refreshed. My precious soul dropped to her knees, placed her forehead against the side of the well, and thanked Me for putting it there and for keeping her and Piare moving when their situation seemed so desperate. I felt her prayers deep within Myself. She wrestled Piare up onto her back, and without ever having said a word or acknowledging the other women, she set out again in the direction of Amritsar.

The women watched her in awe, as if she had swooped down from the sky and then taken flight again. They remained silent for some time after the strange pair had disappeared from sight. Then with their bare feet glistening in the morning sun, the women began to gossip in whispers. They knew.

Rajni felt that she could not walk fast enough. Her shoulders and back screamed for relief. Her feet bled, and her legs and arms were cramped. There was no part of her young body that was not in pain now. The sky glowed red, then faded to black as another day ended, and once again Rajni pushed herself forward into the night. Two hours after sunset, she collapsed and fell to the ground, tumbling into a thicket by the road with Piare still on her back. Unable to move another step, she lay on the ground and cried softly, unable to care for Piare or herself. Within minutes, she was asleep.

With considerable effort, Piare untangled himself from the shawl and rolled off Rajni's back. With the little strength he had, he pulled the shawl over Rajni, then lay on his back, looking up at the sky as he listened to the heavy sounds of Rajni's breathing.

Piare lay awake in the darkness, concerned for his wife. She could not go at this pace for another day, perhaps not another hour. He remembered Punditji's advice to Rajni on their wedding day. *"If you need help, call on their Guru, I believe he will come through for you."* Piare reflected on that for some time, realizing that they desperately needed help.

"Guru Ram Das," he prayed silently, "we were told that we could call on you if we need help. Well, we are desperate. My life has little value, but Rajni will die if you don't protect her. Help her at this time of crisis. I am a burden to her. Either heal me soon or kill me, but free her from this suffering. I don't want to live as the stone around her neck. We come only to see you. Get us to Amritsar tomorrow and bless her for her sacrifice." Feeling at peace, Piare slept.

Rajni awoke before dawn. She could not make herself get up and face another day. Her body ached and cramped, her feet were sore and raw. But neither could she stop the drive to keep moving. Gradually, her ears awakened to sounds in the distance. Then drifting like smoke over the flat plain of the Punjab, Rajni heard music.

"Piare!" she said softly, "it's kirtan. We must be close!"

Excited, she situated Piare in the shawl then strained to pull him up over her back. He felt heavier than ever. Already, traffic was active on the road as Rajni set out in the direction of the music. With every step, the weight of Piare seemed to increase. She grew weaker and more desperate, but her drive to reach Amritsar did not diminish. Now that she could hear the sound of the kirtan, she would not stop.

Each step tortured her raw and bloody feet. All her muscles ached and cramped. She was dizzy and shook from hunger and thirst. Her head throbbed with pain. Infection raged in the open cuts on her face and neck. Red streaks ran back along her face as the infection spread. Yet her will overpowered her pain. She moved very slowly while the weight on her back seemed to grow heavier.

* * *

"We must pray for her now!" commanded Rishi Mahan Akal. "She bears the suffering of the Kali Yuga. Pray for her!"

How I loved that rishi!

Everyone prayed. The command of a rishi cannot be disobeyed.

It was understood that as a human she had to make that sacrifice and bear the weight on her own. It was the demand of the Age, a job that had to be done by a human, not by a deity, and I could not interfere. Yet, even the angels shed tears as they watched that girl with such a noble spirit and invincible heart.

They prayed and projected. Rishi Mahan Akal closed his eyes and meditated. He remembered that day when I placed her in his hands after giving her My sweet kiss of life. Now, the answer to so many prayers rested upon her resolve.

Then a most curious thing happened. From the eye of that great rishi who was totally in control of his emotions, whom the entire Universe revered, and whom the demons feared, rolled a great tear.

* * *

Rajni had not only reached her limit, she had passed it, and her body refused to carry on. There were thousands of people around them now, moving and jostling. The air was filled with the smell of food and incense, the sounds of kirtan, people talking and yelling, vendors selling their wares, children playing, and babies crying. There were bazaars with stalls selling goods. Gradually it dawned on Rajni that she was standing in the heart of Amritsar.

Uncomfortable with Piare in such a chaotic environment, she sought a more secluded spot where she could set Piare down so he would be safe and protected from the sun and the crowds. She would find them food, and after they had eaten and rested, they would go and find Guru Ram Das.

Rajni drifted away from the crowds toward a less active area. She was weak and light-headed, nearly delerious, and barely able to stand. As she trudged through the hordes of people, she feared that she might drop Piare. The sounds of the kirtan were everywhere, and despite her exhaustion, her spirits lifted as she listened to it.

"Piare, do you hear it?"

Piare did not respond. He was semiconscious, weakened by hunger and the exertion of the last three days. He had considerable difficulty breathing. His head fell against Rajni's shoulders and did not move.

Threading her way through the chaos of Amritsar, Rajni found her way to an area where an excavation project was underway. She saw that massive amounts of earth had been excavated around a pool of water. Because of the Baisakhi celebration, no one was working, but there were a few people sitting by the water meditating and talking quietly. It seemed like a calm and peaceful place where Piare could rest and be safe.

Rajni made it to the shade of an old beri tree, and she gently set Piare down.

"We are here, my beloved," she whispered. Piare looked at her blankly. "Rest now, I will go and find us food. I'll be back as soon as I am able. Then after we have eaten, we will find Guru Ram Das."

Rajni left Piare under the beri tree and turned back toward the active area of the village, limping and moving unsteadily and very slowly. The people were joyful and friendly, and she felt comfortable enough to ask where she might find food for herself and her husband. She was directed toward the nearest langar tent.

Under the shade of the beri tree, Piare rested.

GURU OF MIRACLES

You gave to the world the Sarovar
To wash away the wounds of the Soul,
Where we who are broken are restored whole,
And those who are defeated start over.

THIRTY-THREE

With Guru Ram Das now living in Amritsar, the small rural village had evolved into an active city. Well-positioned in the vicinity of Lahore, Amritsar became a stopping place for caravans moving east, west, north, and south, as well as a sanctuary for those seeking spiritual and emotional solace. Hundreds of pilgrims came to see the guru and hear his teachings daily. Many who were without hope, lost, and desperate found refuge and renewed life in Amritsar.

After the visit with Baba Siri Chand, Guru Ram Das was excited and returned to his holy city with big plans. The dedication ceremony was a joyous event, and thousands of Sikhs came, some from great distances, to join in the celebration. Baba Buddha laid the cornerstone of the city with great reverence, and as Baba Siri Chand had suggested, the city was officially named Amritsar.

It was awhile before work on the tank could resume. There were many other urgent needs that Guru Ram Das had to supervise, and though he was anxious to resume the excavation, he had to ensure that the essentials were covered first.

As the village rapidly grew, new challenges and crises daily claimed the guru's attention. Houses had to be built, revenues had to be managed, city planning had to be done, roads and infrastructure had to be built, and the administration of both the village and the ever-growing mission of the guru had to be conducted.

The guru especially wanted his Sikhs to become active in commerce. He knew that if the people could not support themselves and live well, the future of Amritsar would be brief. Further, by establishing commerce with other cities and regions, the influence of the Sikhs would spread. So taking advantage of Amritsar's location, he encouraged trade and pushed his Sikhs to start businesses and extend their markets in all directions. In this way, Amritsar became a thriving commercial center. In order to sustain it, an entire support system had to be created. Money houses and other financial resources were established, as well as good roads and an organized market where goods were delivered and sold.

Many people were attracted to Amritsar not only because of the guru, but also for the opportunities they found there. Often the guru counseled people regarding what work, trade, or business to pursue. People who had suffered losses or who had been unsuccessful in other ventures found opportunities for success and prosperity in Amritsar. The activity in Amritsar was so extensive and fast-paced that daily, from several miles away, dust could be seen rising in the air.

Eventually though, out of the chaos, a degree of order was established. The guru then called for Baba Buddha and his old foreman, Bhai Sahlo. He placed Baba Buddha in charge of the excavation project, and the excavation of the tank resumed with intensity.

Each morning, Guru Ram Das sat under the now broad-reaching beri tree and tended to the administrative responsibilities of the guruship while overseeing the excavation. Once those obligations had been discharged, he picked up a tool and started moving dirt himself. Periodically, he would stop and sit under the beri tree to survey the project or deal with an administrative point, then again step back into the mud. In the afternoons, he presided in the durbar.

Some of the earlier work was damaged due to neglect and the effects of the monsoons. Forms and supports which had been previously used for the excavation had been seized for the construction of other projects in Amritsar. Yet under Baba Buddha's direction, they made order out of what was left, salvaged what they could, and resumed with focus. The excavation of this tank was a big project following the specific plan and design given by Guru Amar Das.

The concept of the tank was huge. It was to be seventeen feet deep, covering a large area of nearly four acres. A causeway would be constructed leading to the center of the tank, where a flat foundation would be laid and upon which a mandir would be erected. Moving away from the original pool toward the south, shovel by shovel, the project grew.

In preparation for the upcoming Baisakhi, Amritsar had been a blur of activity since January. The work on the excavation of the tank had stopped once again in mid-March. Now, all attention was shifted to the Baisakhi celebration and the preparations that were needed to care for thousands of people. Additional rest houses and camps had to be constructed, along with additional kitchens to supplement the main one. The main kitchen of Amritsar was on the same scale as the one at Goindwal, which Bhai Jetha had served so faithfully. For Baisakhi additional kitchens were needed to accommodate the masses of people who were on their way. All the kitchens would be cooking and serving nonstop during the week of Baisakhi, and they needed firewood, water, cooking utensils, and the staples for cooking.

Around the beginning of the month of Baisakhi, people began to trickle into Amritsar. By midweek, that trickle had become a flow. The smells of wood smoke, spices, and cooking from the kitchens mixed with the smells of people, horses, cows, elephants, mudges, goats, and burning incense. The sounds of kirtan harmonized with the sounds of laughter, crying and playing children, barking dogs, and the hammer and saw sounds of constant building. The byways were thick with traffic. By the end of that week, the flow had become a gush, which quickly became a flood, and it was into this gushing flood of humanity that Rajni made her way with Piare on her back.

* * *

Piare leaned against the beri tree, dying. He was not only weak from the ordeals of the last few days, the truth was that he was now overcome by his disease. He struggled to breathe and maintain himself without completely losing consciousness. Like Rajni, his wounds had not been treated and infection grew in the broken skin, which his body did not have the resistance to fight. Hunger and thirst made him weaker. Movement was difficult.

He drifted in and out of consciousness, listening to the kirtan and the sounds of Amritsar in the distance. Between those sounds and the weakness of his body, Piare was in a kind of trancelike stupor as he looked out across the pool and the earthworks rising around it. It was midday, and Piare could not remember when they had last eaten or had water.

Piare reflected on Rajni's sacrifices for him. They had been selfless, and she neither asked for nor expected anything in return. He had prayed multiple times to die if he could not be healed and free Rajni of his burden. Now, as he sat in the rising heat of midday, it dawned on him that his prayers might be answered. He drifted into a languid stupor but was awakened by the sounds of birds chattering.

Something splashed in the water and startled him. In the periphery of his blurred vision, he had a glimpse of two dark shapes splashing into the water of the pond. He turned his head and saw the heads of two white birds that he could not identify break the surface of the water and fly away.

Strange, he thought, *it seemed like they were black birds.*

He gazed out across the pond, lost in his reverie. The sounds of the kirtan drifted with his thoughts.

"Guru Ram Das," he prayed, "we have come here because of you, because Rajni believes that you will help us. I am just a pathetic leper trying to clear my karma. I have brought pain to many people. By your mercy, this deity of a girl has cared for me, but now I am beyond care. If I am not worthy to be healed, then let me die today so she can be free. She has suffered too much, as though she has borne the entire suffering of the Kali Yuga . . ." Piare drifted out of consciousness, and his chin fell upon his chest.

The sound of the birds brought him back again. Again, he thought he saw black birds fall into the water and white birds fly out.

Hallucinations, he thought to himself. And he drifted into another prayer.

"Forgive me for falling asleep. If I can't stay awake to pray, what value do I have as a man? Free us both. Set her free today. She gave her jewelry to those men with a pure heart and whether you received it or not, bless her now and set her free. Have mercy on us both . . ." He drifted away again.

Overhead, he heard two ravens arguing. He idly looked up. Having grown up in leper colonies, he had lived with ravens most of his life, fighting with them for food. They were always humorous in their gruff kind of way, and Piare was fond of their company.

Those two particular birds were engaged in a heated discourse, and each one had a strong and opposing opinion about the subject under discussion. They were arguing and dive-bombing each other, unable to reach a resolution to their dispute. They settled in the beri tree, continuing to insult each other and shaking Piare to alertness. The matter for discussion was a chapatti.

"Hey!" Piare said out loud, "you're both black."

The birds tilted their heads and looked at him. They were quiet for at least a minute, but each one wanted to have the last word, so they started up again. One sprang into the air with the chapatti, taunting the other, who followed in hot pursuit. They went at it again in the air, and Piare watched with interest. Although they were having quite an argument, there was something about it that, despite his discomfort and growing hopelessness, made Piare smile.

As Piare watched, the chapatti fell from the grip of both birds and drifted like a heavy leaf into the water below. It floated briefly on the surface of the water and then sank in a slow, laguid descent as the fish living in the water nibbled at it. The ravens dived after it and disappeared below the surface of the water. Piare leaned forward to see the outcome, but there was no movement in the water. Suddenly, two white birds looking strangely like white ravens broke the surface and flew away.

Piare was stunned. Was such a thing possible? The ravages of leprosy had caused him to have delusions and hallucinations before. Was that happening now? He leaned back against the beri tree, looking at the spot in the water where the two white birds had surfaced and flown away.

In a brilliant moment of clarity, he remembered the words of the Pir. *You will find it without knowing it.* Could this be the water? *You will be freed of this karma. Your debt from the time of the Vedi Guru will be settled in this lifetime.*

"Perhaps this is the way to be freed from this karma," he spoke out loud to himself. "If I drown myself in this water, Rajni will be free of me, and I will be free of this karma!"

He thought about that. Would there be additional karma if he drowned himself?

"Well," he looked up at the beri tree spread out over him, its longest branches reaching out over the water, "I'll hold on and go in the water. If my strength fails me, it is the will of God."

Reaching up with the fingers of his right hand, he gripped the lowest branch and eased himself along to the edge of the water. The branch bent with his weight and lowered him into the water with an abrupt splash.

His entire body tingled. He felt as though millions of needles were penetrating his skin, driving deep into his flesh and the tissue below. He tried to force himself to stay under, but his weak lungs could barely hold air. He squirmed, his feet kicked, and he rose quickly. His head broke the surface, and he gulped air.

This time, he thought, *I'll let go.*

He loosed all but the little finger of his right hand from around the thin branch of the beri tree, took a breath, and plunged as deeply into the water as he could. He felt like he was bleeding profusely while being pierced by millions of darts. The sensation was both excruciating and exhilarating. He felt nauseous, as though everything inside him would come out, yet he forced himself to remain under the water. Though his lungs ached and his mind screamed, his pinky never released the branch.

Something strange was happening to him. He broke the surface again and screamed hysterically, like a man being tortured. His body squirmed, his spindly legs kicked, he sobbed like a motherless child, and though he swallowed large volumes of the water, he neither let go of the branch nor tried to get out of the pond. He sucked in another breath and submerged himself a third time. This time, it was easier to remain under the water. His lungs were less painful and the tingling in his body diminished, but the water felt unusually cold. The cold penetrated through his tissues and blood and into his bones. His body grew numb.

Perhaps I'm dying, he thought. *Then let me surrender to this water, let it take me now.*

In his mind, he could not tell if he was above or below the water. He had lost all sense of time and space, all sense of self and identity, and all sensation in his body. He felt deep and peaceful calm, without conflict or desire. He felt the presence of Rajni, felt her healing touch, and from her, through the water surrounding him, he felt life filling him. And in that moment of epiphany, he knew that he wanted to live, that life was still ahead of him.

He opened his eyes, and through the sunlight penetrating the surface of the water, he saw himself walking along the road to the Vedi Guru. His mind was in the deepest bliss, and as he walked, he was lost in the ecstasy of his heart. He heard a cry for help. Just ahead on the side of the road, he saw a wretched and dying pilgrim in great pain. Piare wanted only to continue with his divine song and hold that blissful state in his mind, but from his heart flowed great compassion. He stopped and knelt beside the suffering man. Piare gave him water and comfort as he held his head tenderly. The bright eyes of the stranger were clear against his dark features, and as Piare gazed into them, he saw his own incarnations back through the Ages: all of his trials and failures, his sacrifices and triumphs, and his births and deaths.

Then he saw the time before he incarnated, back through the blue ethers and into the Heavens. He saw himself sitting with the angels and deities in infinitely long lines, chanting the *Wahe Guru* mantra and sending that energy to the water that now surrounded him. He could hear that divine sound vibrating in his every fiber. The whites of the eyes into which he gazed merged with the light that penetrated the water, and its brightness grew so that Piare was surrounded and filled by white light. And in those eyes, he saw himself in this incarnation and the sickness that he had borne through this lifetime. He tilted his head back and looked up through the water. The light penetrating the water also penetrated him, filled him, and pushed the disease out of him. Piare clearly saw it flow out of his pores and become consumed by the light and the water.

You are free. It was the voice of the pilgrim. Piare reverently laid his head to the ground. As he did so, the image of the pilgrim faded into the light.

Piare kicked hard, and his head broke the surface of the water. He sucked in the fresh air of Amritsar and screamed hysterically. He submerged himself once again, screaming into the water. He broke the surface again and looked up at the deep blue afternoon sky. He had never let go of the beri tree.

He pulled himself out of the water, and when his feet touched the mud, he found that his legs supported him. He climbed back up under the beri tree, breathing hard. His entire body felt strangely different, and he studied himself, dumbfounded. His legs, arms, and hands were whole. The little finger and part of his right hand, which he had looped around the branch of the beri tree, still showed evidence of leprosy, but no other part of his body showed any sign of the disease that had eaten away his youth. He pulled off the kurta that he had worn since his first morning with Rajni at the Satluj and stood naked under the tree, studying himself. All of his skin was whole and smooth, and his body was full and strong. His heart and mind reeled against the outter limits of the emotional spectrum. He could not fully comprehend what had just occurred.

Quickly, Piare tied the sleeves of the old kurta around his waist and pulled the tail up between his legs and under the sleeves, forming a kind of loincloth.

"Guru Ram Das," he sobbed, "all the divine powers of the Heavens and of the Earth, thank you for hearing and answering my prayers! Make me worthy of this."

Piare was in a daze, feeling simultaneously overwhelmed with emotion and still and calm. He was no longer hungry, thirsty, or tired. While in the water, he had swallowed several liters, and now felt fully satiated in every way.

He studied his little finger, looking with clinical detachment at the deterioration of the digit. There was little of it left, and he was rather amazed that it had not fallen off while he was holding on to the beri tree. The flesh, which was deeply ulcerated, was peeling off, leaving the tissue under it raw. He could feel the ulceration of the bone beneath the little bit of flesh that covered it.

Tears of joy and gratitude filled his eyes, yet he could neither laugh nor cry. He simply sat serenely in the shade of the beri tree.

THIRTY-FOUR

RAJNI SQUEEZED SLOWLY THROUGH THE celebrating throngs to the main langar kitchen. It was easy to find, she just followed the smells. Tired and aching from the ordeal of the past few days, she moved as though she still carried Piare on her back. Without his weight, she felt incomplete and vulnerable, yet the joyful nature of the throngs around her lifted her and helped her to keep moving.

The langar was full of movement and activity. The noise was on a symphonic scale with the orchestral hum of voices, the percussive clatter of the kitchen, and the woodwind and brass sound of people moving, talking, and laughing. There was a large open area covered by an enormous *fulkari* canopy that was full of colored patches and tiny mirrors. At the far end was the actual kitchen itself, while under the canopy in relatively straight lines sat hundreds of people. Those to the right side of the kitchen were eating, and those to the left were waiting to be served. At the ends of the lines were organizers who directed people where to sit while squads of servers moved quickly up and down the lines carrying buckets of dal, yogurt, spicy vegetables, baskets of warm chapattis, and multiple sweets.

Rajni approached one of the organizers unsteadily, and unable to disguise the fatigue and desperation in her voice, explained her circumstances and asked how she could get food for herself and her husband. Recognizing Rajni's condition, the kind man called for someone to bring a physician to attend her injuries. Then in true Punjabi fashion, several other organizers joined in and a lively and loud discussion followed on how to resolve the problem. They had a difficult time persuading her to wait for the doctor, but the constant throbbing of her now severely infected wounds prevented her from moving. The physician came and cleaned her wounds, disinfecting them with tinctures of neem, tulsi, and camphor. He then placed a poultice of herbs over them, adhering it to her skin with myrrh gum.

The langar organizers tried to get her to eat first and then take food to her husband, but she would not consider it, insisting that her husband was dying, and she had to get back to Piare quickly. So, they stirred around to find her a tiffin to carry the food in and insisted that she take at least a cup of lassi.

At last, as she sipped her lassi from the steel cup, Rajni felt revived and somewhat at ease. She had finally made it to Amritsar, and as she reflected on that, the words of the Pir came to her mind. *Follow your bliss. There, you will find the water and the jewels.* Now that she was in Amritsar, where would she find the water? Would Guru Ram Das tell her?

When the food was brought to her, she asked how she could meet the guru. She was told that he presided in the durbar in the afternoons, at which time people had the opportunity to speak with him. Revived by the lassi, Rajni felt excited. She made her way back toward the excavation site more comfortably. Just holding the warm food in her hands and the hope in her heart eased her fear and pain. She began to cultivate hope for a bath and perhaps some clean clothes.

Poor Piare, she thought to herself. *I just left him there under that tree. I at least should have given him water.* "Oh God," she prayed, overcome by a sudden anxiety, "protect him now. We have come so far. Sustain him so that he can meet Guru Ram Das."

And in that moment, Rajni finally admitted to herself that Piare was close to death. She half expected to find him lying dead under the beri tree when she returned. That thought sobered her because she realized that if he were dead, she would be both free of him and without him. Something deep in her felt relief at that thought, yet also felt shame for thinking that way. Bringing Piare to the water, and therefore now to Amritsar had been her quest. Would it end now that she was here? Would he no longer be a factor in her life? Then what would she do and where would she go? Certainly not back to the palace of Duni Chand. Still, her shame did not keep her from realizing how light she would be if she no longer had Piare as a burden. She hoped that at least seeing the guru before he died would free his soul or perhaps even spare his life.

She moved faster and with more determination through the crowds. Though her feet hurt, she made her way quickly. She turned from the main flow of traffic and eased her way through the wagon ruts and construction equipment toward the excavation site and her husband.

As she approached the beri tree, she saw a half-naked man sitting under it. Where was Piare? Had this man done something to her poor husband? In a rush, her accumulated fear, frustration, desperation, and anxiety flooded her mind in multiples of ten. She dropped the tiffin holding the langar offering and stood shaking with fear, believing that the worst had happened. Her sounds attracted the attention of the young man who turned and jumped up. With a big smile, he rushed toward Rajni, his arms outstretched.

From behind Rajni's navel, a superhuman energy uncoiled and, with the speed and intensity of a cobra, struck her brain. Her lungs filled with more air than they had ever held, which she released through her vocal cords, supported by the upward thrust of her diaphragm. The resulting sound was a loud, bloodcurdling scream that seemed to hang in the air for minutes. People as far away as the langar kitchen—a walk that had taken a weakened Rajni fifteen minutes and would take a healthy, vital man at least five minutes—heard her scream and dropped their ladles and serving pots. Much of Amritsar stopped what it was doing and ran in the direction of the scream. Piare stopped dead still.

"Who are you!" she shouted, her voice roaring like a lioness.

"Rajni," said Piare, completely startled, "it's me!" It had never occurred to Piare that Rajni would not recognize him.

"I don't know who you are! Where is my husband? What have you done with him?"

"Raj . . ."

"You have come to this sacred place to defile it with your cruelty? Have you thrown him into the water . . . Come no closer! What kind of man are you to dispatch a helpless leper and then take advantage of an innocent girl?"

She paused, her eyes wide, her breathing heavy. She studied Piare for a minute or more then drew a sudden breath.

"How do you know my name? Did my father send you? Is *this* the culmination of his cruelty?" Her voice was powerful and cut through the other sounds of Amritsar.

A crowd gathered quickly. People stood around Rajni now, ready to defend her. Others gathered around Piare.

"Rajni, please listen!" To the crowd, he said, "Please listen! Allow me to speak."

"He must have a story to tell," said an older man next to Rajni. "Speak, son."

"Rajni," said Piare, "our prayers have been answered!" He opened his arms. "They've been answered!" he said softly, reverently. "I let myself into the water, and the water healed me. Look!" And he held up his still-diseased pinky. "With this finger, I held on to the branch of the beri tree. I didn't put it in the water because I wanted to show you." Piare turned, and for the first time in his life, he ran. He made it to the edge of the pool and dipped his hand into the water. He pulled it out and held it high above his head, water streaming along his bare arm. The leprosy was gone from his body forever.

Rajni's only response was to lose consciousness. Unable to comprehend what had happened and being far past her limits, she succumbed to her exhaustion. Her breath rushed from her, and her body fell to the ground, her mind far away. The people surrounded her. Although Piare's story seemed credible, they would not let him come close to Rajni. People had seen the miracle of his little finger, but he was very strangely dressed, and the girl was obviously afraid of him.

Someone had the presence of mind to bring Rajni water. They wiped her face with it, being mindful of her wounds and caressed her hands and tattered feet. She began to come around, so they gave her the rest of it to drink. The water revived her quickly, and she sat on the ground, staring at Piare silently. Her dark eyes darted from him to the pond to the sky then back to him. She placed her forehead on her knees and then snapped her head up and stared again at Piare.

Someone pushed his way through the crowd. "Guruji wants to know what all the screaming and commotion is about."

"I've been cured of leprosy by the waters of that pool!" shouted Piare at the top of his lungs. It felt good to fill his lungs with air and to make a lot of noise with his voice. "My poor wife, who was forced into marriage to me by the cruelty of her father and who cared for me selflessly all these months, doesn't believe me." He was speaking very fast.

Rajni looked up. "You seem to know the details," she said. "But I must be sure."

The guru's messenger spoke, "We must go to the guru. He will tell you what is the truth."

Rajni eyed the messenger. "Guru Ram Das?"

"Yes, Guru Ram Das is the guru."

"And he is willing to see us? . . . me? . . . us?" She looked at Piare, eyes wide, eyebrows raised.

"He would like to see you now. Please come."

Rajni slowly got to her feet. She was painfully aware that her clothes were filthy, ragged, and bloodstained. Her beautiful, long black hair was disheveled. There were the remnants of a braid, but most of her hair drifted wherever it cared to go. She was wet and muddy. She suddenly felt very tired and got to her feet slowly.

A man pushed his way through the crowd and presented Piare with a kurta and dhoti. The men formed a circle around him while he dressed himself. Rajni ran her fingers through her hair.

"Is there a comb I might use?"

One was brought, and several ladies helped her to comb and braid her hair. Someone offered her amla oil, which helped to smooth and shine her hair. Someone else brought a shawl that she draped regally over her small frame.

The nine months as a beggar had not diminished her noble bearing. She looked at the people around her, thanking them gracefully. Then she turned to Piare and stared at him intently, contemplating every inch of him.

"Come," she said. It was Rajni the princess who spoke.

Neither Rajni nor Piare spoke a word. Yet as the crowd moved toward the durbar, the rest of the group was lively. For many, this was their first visit to Amritsar, and such a miracle, if it were true, had profound implications for them. Many had recently become Sikhs, converting from the repressive caste and social system of the Hindus or the growing oppression of Islam. A leper being healed in the water that would eventually become a place of pilgrimage where everyone would be blessed equally was auspicious, and they all talked about it.

Rajni and Piare walked at some distance from each other, both lost in their own reflections. It felt odd to Rajni not to pull the weight of Piare. For all those months, she had pushed everything else out of her mind and focused only on getting from one place to the next while keeping them both alive. Piare had become a part of her, and she felt incomplete without the rope over her shoulder or his weight upon her back.

Now she was on her way to meet the guru and it was not as she had visualized it during her days on the road. She reflected back over all the months to that day when her heart and soul had been touched by the guru's words. She remembered her excitement and how she intended to ask her father to take her to Amritsar. The urgency she had felt to get to Amritsar since meeting Mustafa Khan rose up in her, and she quickened her pace. Guru Ram Das would sort this out and make everything right.

What would she say to him? Punditji had trained her well regarding how to meet a holy man, and now she was not prepared to do it properly, being dirty and wearing ragged, bloodstained, and worn-out clothes.

Well, she thought to herself, *this must be the way God wants it.* And she was right. It was indeed how I wanted it.

Without the weight of Piare, her regal carriage was magnified. Despite the bandages on her face and neck, no one in that group noticed what she was wearing. Her presence was the personification of dignity and grace. People were blind to the details.

Rajni raised her head and looked out at the crowd and the growing city around her. There were thousands of people moving, laughing, and celebrating. If this situation proved to be real, she would have much to celebrate as well. A glint of reflected sunlight caught her eye, and she looked up to find its source. Standing on a wall above the moving masses, Rajni saw the Shaivite sadhu who had covered her with ashes holding his tershul in such a way that the sunlight reflected off the broad central prong. Standing next to him was the ash-smeared aghora from the cremation grounds. The sadhu raised his trident high in the air, the sunlight reflecting brightly off it. The aghora brought his palms together at his forehead. Rajni smiled brightly.

Piare could scarcely believe that he was actually walking and breathing easily. A body that was not dissolving away was something new and strange to him, and he delighted in the feeling. Only this morning, he was semiconscious and close to death. Now his body was restored, and he was walking upright, supported by his own two legs. Nowhere on his body was there any sign of disease.

He regarded Rajni as she made her way with the crowd toward the durbar. Now that their ordeal seemed to be ending, what would happen next? She had lovingly cared for him and never asked for or expected anything. He had prayed to be healed so that he could care for her properly. Now would she still consider that they were married? Would he be able to find a way to care for her?

He studied her as she moved ahead of him. She was truly beautiful. Even now, she carried herself like a queen, and all the people wanted to be close to her, to touch her, or to have her look at them. He could not see her face clearly, but she seemed to be deep in thought. She had lost much weight since their wedding day, yet she still retained a spark that set her apart from everyone else.

The hushed tones of the crowd and the devotional sounds of the kirtan told Piare that they were near the durbar where a huge tent capable of holding several thousand people had been erected. Like the fulkari cloth of the langar tent, the tiny mirrors woven into the colorful fabric reflected light onto the congregation. Hundreds of wooden poles supported the canopy and walls, and the ground was covered with white sheets.

A long aisle went up the middle of the durbar to a raised dais upon which Guru Ram Das sat. The women sat on the right of the aisle, and the men sat to the left. There were about five hundred people in the durbar, and before the guru were two men seeking his advice to resolve a business dispute. Rajni looked up shyly at Guru Ram Das. He lifted his head, looked at her, and then turned his attention back to the matter at hand.

Rajni studied Guru Ram Das as he listened to the arguments of the two men before him. He was a beautiful man with a radiant presence. He was wearing a long white tunic and a saffron-colored *hazooria* hung around his neck and draped over his chest. Upon his head was tied a regal white turban, and around his neck was a beautiful necklace made of pearl and gold beads. The necklace was difficult to see because of his long beard which, sitting cross-legged and leaning forward slightly as he was, touched his lap.

In his right hand, he held a sandalwood rosary. He rolled the beads between his thumb and middle finger as he listened to the two men. Standing behind the guru was a young man close to Piare's age, fanning him. Over the guru was a large, deep red canopy, beautifully embroidered with intricate designs.

Rajni and Piare sat at the front on their respective sides and stared at Guru Ram Das. Rajni was enraptured, and her heart raced. She listened to the kirtan and recognized it as the shabd she first heard on her wedding day. The guru looked at her and quickly winked, then turned his attention back to the two men in front of him. Eventually, the matter was concluded, the two men embraced each other, bowed to the guru, and left. Rajni's heart accelerated.

Guru Ram Das wiped his face with a cloth and took a long drink of water. He looked at Rajni and Piare. "Come," he said and motioned with his hand for them to come forward. Shyly, they both came before the guru while a courtier went to the guru to explain the situation.

"I know," he said without looking at his aide, his attention focused on Rajni and Piare.

"My sweet daughter," Guru Ram Das spoke to Rajni, his voice blending with the music, "this is the man you married," pointing to Piare. "You came to this Earth to bear this burden and to show the world the healing powers of that water."

Rajni stared at the guru, speechless. Then at Piare then back to the guru. Tears flooded her eyes and rolled down her cheeks. Piare bowed before Guru Ram Das.

"All I have known is life as a leper. I have only known the company of lepers. Now I am well and by God's grace, I have been married to a deity!"

Guru Ram Das smiled. "My son, you were born with this karma for a reason. You bore the suffering of the Kali Yuga, which took the form of your disease. You, my dear daughter, carried that suffering upon your back for all humanity in this dark age. You were formed by the collective consciousness of the Heavens through the collective power of prayer. Upon you was placed the burden to bring the suffering of the Kali Yuga to that sacred water. And it is sacred! It is the result of the prayers, incantations, meditations, and devotions of all the Ages."

The guru's voice was a mellifluous baritone, and it calmed and reassured Rajni. There was deep compassion in his very presence. Rajni remembered the conversation with the young couple only a few days earlier. *When you are there you have no longing, no doubt about anything. Everything changes just with his glance. You will see for yourself.* Now sitting in the guru's immediate presence, she did see for herself. And at that moment, she had no longing or doubt about anything. She felt fulfilled.

"Beloved daughter," said Guru Ram Das, "your sacrifice and his suffering will change the times. No one other than you could have borne this karma."

At last, Rajni had reached a point of stability and calm. She was very still and content. Piare too reached that safe and tranquil place found only within the refuge of a humble heart.

The kirtan ended, and Guru Ram Das looked out at the sangat. "My siblings of destiny, you must understand one important thing: this beautiful girl is a child of the Heavens. See how she has suffered? See the sacrifices she had to make? This was not because she has 'bad' karma, it is not because anything is wrong with her. She incarnated to relieve the suffering of the Age by bringing it to this sacred water."

The guru looked over the congregation benevolently.

"Many of you suffer from superstition. You believe that if you are faced with hard times or disappointments, then something is wrong with you, that your karma is bad, or that you have done something to displease God. Don't waste your time and energy with such foolishness! Lord Rama was the incarnation of God, and look how he suffered. My own Guru, Guru Amar Das, served Guru Angad with perfection and absolute devotion, yet Datu kicked him off his dais. Was that due to bad karma? Had he caused some offense to the angels?" Guru's voice softened, "No, my dear ones. Understand me, God gives us challenges. When you face these challenges with gratitude, when you go forward believing that God is with you, then what is the concern? All is in His hands. It is only the effort that matters. Don't be concerned about the results, leave that to God. It is all His play. Understand that and forget these superstitions!

"God has no anger, no enmity. He does not punish us. We punish ourselves. Rajni has demonstrated how to bear the challenges that come from God with grace and dignity. God is merciful and what He gives us is His kindness. The problem is that you fail to recognize it, and so you suffer because of it. Accept all that comes as His gift and instruct your mind not to grumble needlessly. After all, this human life is temporary. We are here to experience and to grow, but we belong only to Him." Guru Ram Das again wiped the perspiration from his face.

Then looking back at Rajni, he said, "See clearly the power of Love!"

Guru Ram Das leaned to Rajni and whispered, "There is still an imbalance that must be adjusted."

Rajni and Piare were honored by the guru and presented with gifts and new clothes. Then they were taken and bathed. Rajni's hair was massaged with aromatic oil to remove the lice, then shampooed and combed, restoring it to its original luster. They spent the rest of the day and long into the evening in the company of Guru Ram Das and Bibi Bani.

And that night, under the starry skies, Rajni stepped into the sacred water. She could hear the kirtan playing and the sounds of people celebrating in the distance, but there in the water, it was still and peaceful. She held the branch of the beri tree as Piare had done. The water soothed her feet and aching body. She released the beri tree and submerged herself, letting the silent solace of the water comfort and nurture her.

She lay next to Piare on beds that had been prepared for them and looked up at the stars. She was very happy.

Gently, softly, she drifted to sleep.

THIRTY-FIVE

When the messenger arrived from Guru Ram Das, Duni Chand feared the worst. He and his wife seldom spoke to one another, and Mataji spent most of each day sitting at the window, hoping to see her daughter come through the gate. Mataji was so upset that she seldom ate, the result being that by the time the messenger of Guru Ram Das arrived, she had lost more than twenty-five pounds. Sometimes, there is an advantage to suffering other than calling on Me all the time.

Yet it was Duni Chand who suffered the most. He felt the pain of his wife and the anger of his daughters. He felt the disgust of the people of Patti and his other villages. None of that, however, was equal to the grief and depression that had overtaken him. Duni Chand was a plainly simple man who had sacrificed little and suffered little in his life. His family had been everything to him, but Rajni had been the pearl in the oyster shell. Now that she was gone, he had lost his enthusiasm for living and was forced to play chess by himself.

True to their word, Rajni's sisters never again set foot in the village of Patti or their father's house. Duni Chand had tried to visit his daughters, but when he did, they left their own homes and went to visit a sister, instructing their husbands and servants to advise Duni Chand that their whereabouts were unknown. Neither Duni Chand nor his wife had seen any of their daughters or grandchildren in nine months.

Duni Chand was still Raja of Patti, but the people despised him. They avoided his company, even if it was inconvenient to do so. His holdings and business dealings suffered, and he faced difficult times ahead. He had been forced to sell two of his villages. Even some of his servants sought other work and left his household. For a servant to leave the employment of a family was most unusual. They tended to remain with a family not only for life but for generations. Mokum Das took a job at a house of lesser status in order to be free of Duni Chand.

When the guru's messenger arrived from Amritsar, Duni Chand feared that it was news of her death. The messenger said that the guru was requesting their presence and that he wished to consult with Duni Chand regarding his daughter. Duni Chand tried to bully the Sikh for details, but all that the messenger told him was that Guru Ram Das wanted him to come to Amritsar immediately, that he had information regarding Rajni which was for his ears only. Duni Chand's blood ran cold.

The guru also sent messengers to Rajni's sisters, but they were told the truth, that Rajni was safe in Amritsar and that Guru Ram Das would be grateful if they would come there to meet her. The messenger also told them that they should not tell their father. Since none of them were speaking to Duni Chand anyway, that part was easy. The sisters wasted no time in contacting each other and, with great excitement, made arrangements to travel to Amritsar together.

Meanwhile Duni Chand and his considerably thinner wife forlornly made their plans to travel to Amritsar, expecting to find the crumpled body of their beloved baby girl. Duni Chand collected what remained of his household staff and had them prepare for the journey. By direct route, at the leisurely pace of a raja from Patti to Amritsar would take slightly more than a day. Duni Chand realized he would have to listen to Mataji's sobs the whole distance and ordered separate elephants. At least he could have a little peace and quiet and enjoy his own misery without sharing that of his wife. So it was that Duni Chand's procession set out for Amritsar somberly, with Mataji howling in the back, Duni Chand miserable in the front, and their elephants ignoring the emotional scene on top of them.

In contrast, Rajni's sisters set out for their journey to Amritsar together, and they were in high spirits. They went in two howdahs of three each, and the elephants seemed to sway with their laughter. Their nannies followed in carriages with the various children of the sisters.

At every stop, different sisters changed places so that no one would miss any gossip, occasionally pausing to nurse a child or to comfort one who was crying. They were ecstatically happy to know that Rajni was alive, and although they did not know what to expect when they reached Amritsar, they all sensed that it would be something good. The elephants swayed as the mahouts drove them forward. The babies cried and were nursed and the sisters gossiped and giggled on that beautiful spring morning.

One other person made his way to Amritsar that day. The guru's messenger had also visited Punditji. Since the day he married Rajni to Piare, Punditji had daily recited special prayers and performed regular puja for her welfare. He had contemplated going to Amritsar for the Baisakhi celebration but had decided not to make the trip, considering himself to be too old for the journey. It didn't matter that Punditji was, in fact, quite healthy and each morning and evening effortlessly walked four miles at a pace that would tax a teenager. When the guru's messenger arrived, Punditji knew that he had made the wrong decision and quickly set out for Amritsar on foot.

By the time he arrived, Duni Chand was in a foul mood. He had listened to Mataji's sobbing and howling all the way from Patti, which simply compounded his depression and enhanced his own misery. Because of his personal pain, he did not sit as a regal raja on his elephant, but rather slumped down in the howdah, grieving for Rajni and trying futilely to block out the wailing of Mataji. When they had stopped for the night, Duni Chand had Mataji's tent set up far from his, near to where the elephants were hobbled, but could not sleep.

* * *

The day after the miracle had been a day of rejoicing and celebration. Rajni and Piare walked the streets of Amritsar as crowds gathered around them. People asked for their blessings or healing touch, bowed their heads with their hands folded, or fell to the ground and touched their feet when they passed. Everyone wanted to have contact with the man healed by the miracle of the water and the divine princess who brought him there.

They spent the evening with Guru Ram Das and remained with him and Bibi Bani late into the night. The guru's personal physician tended to them.

"Your scars will be slight," the guru told her. "Just enough to show that Akal Purkh has claimed you as His own and to remind you of the great thing you have done."

Rajni fell at the guru's feet. "I did a horrible thing, Guruji, and have to live with that now. Please tell me, did I kill Gopi Das?" Her voice was apprehensive.

"No, my dear, his days were used up. You simply allowed your hand to be guided so he could meet the Dharam Raj." Rajni shivered. "I know this is an additional burden for you, something you will bear for the rest of your days. But have no remorse. You did what was required, and you did it honorably. By your action you saved many other women from his cruel depravity. You have made the world a better place. Bless you, Rajni," said Guru Ram Das as he placed his big hands on her shoulders. "And thank you for all humanity.

"I was always with you," the compassionate Guru told her. "Look at my feet." He lifted his feet, and Rajni cried when she saw how cut and bruised they were.

"Guruji," said Rajni shyly, "I promised a friend that I would remember his name to you."

"Don't worry, dear," said Guru Ram Das. "Mustafa Khan will be blessed in this world and the next. Mian Mir will be known far and wide, and your friend will learn much from him." Rajni stared at him, her hand to her mouth. The guru truly had been with them, had watched over them every day, every step. He had heard every prayer and seen every tear fall.

"Guruji," she said sweetly, "it was my Punditji who taught me everything. Because of him I met your Sikhs and was inspired by their devotion. I ask your blessings for him as well."

"That has already been done," Guru smiled. "You will see him soon."

Piare talked with the guru about the excavation of the tank, and Guru Ram Das explained the scope and design of the whole project.

"It occurred to me, Guruji, that if you dig steps along the sides, it will be easier for people to bathe in the water."

Guru Ram Das smiled, "I have been waiting for you to arrive so that project can be undertaken. You will supervise it and see that it is completed." He laughed, "You have been restored for this purpose!"

The following day, Guru Ram Das sent for them. They were to come to the durbar immediately. As quickly as possible, they threaded their way through the throngs to the durbar. They entered and bowed before the guru, who had them sit by his side on the dais.

Guru Ram Das turned to one of his aides. "Bring them," he said and smiled at Rajni.

She felt a tingle of excitement. Looking toward the back of the durbar, she saw a stately old man bow then rise and make his way toward the front.

"Punditji!" she screamed excitedly and jumped up. Then realizing she was in the durbar with Guru Ram Das, she sat down quickly and covered her face with her chuni. Punditji bowed to the Guru. Rajni, unable to control herself any longer, jumped up and hugged her Punditji as she had when she was six years old. Guru Ram Das had Punditji sit on the dais with him, Rajni, and Piare. Rajni was beaming.

As Punditji and Rajni were taking their seats, her six sisters and their children made their grand entrance. And it was quite a spectacle, as only those six girls could create. They were smiling and laughing, beautifully dressed, decorated, and perfumed with their children and nannies in parade behind them.

Rajni, sufficiently embarrassed from her display with Punditji, touched the feet of Guru Ram Das in gratitude and smiled at her six sisters. The children were delegated to their nannies, and the sisters joined the others on the guru's dais. Rajni giggled like a schoolgirl and could not refrain from squeezing and hugging her sisters.

A short while later, Duni Chand and Mataji trudged into the durbar, a cloud of hopeless depression hanging over them. Rajni could barely recognize her lighter and thinner mother, but there was no mistaking her father. Duni Chand wore a deep green kurta with yellow paisleys embroidered on it, a white dhoti, and a yellow vest that matched the paisleys. He had tied a red turban, and his moustache was waxed and turned up. He looked supremely annoyed and distressed.

Mataji wore a blue sari with a silver border. Her face was tearstained, and her eyes were red. Rajni had never seen anyone look so defeated and without hope as her mother. Her heart raced as she watched her parents walk slowly up the aisle. It wasn't until Duni Chand and Mataji were seated before the guru that they recognized Rajni.

Though she had been treated by the guru's doctors and had submersed herself in the sacred water, to her parents she appeared as she had the day she arrived in Amritsar. They gasped for breath when they saw Rajni's emaciated body and her beautiful face wounded, infected and oozing, covered with insect bites, cuts, and scratches. Her feet were scarred and raw. They both recognized that the filthy, bloodstained clothes she wore as those of the sweeper. Mataji shrieked and began to cry uncontrollably, nearly unable to breathe. Duni Chand began to sweat and shake, and for the only time in his life, he felt ashamed.

Guru Ram Das directed them to sit in front of him and their children. They studied their youngest daughter sitting on the dais next to the guru. She had walked out of their lives as a frightened and innocent girl, pulling that wretched leper in his basket. Duni Chand had believed with all his heart that she would leave the leper on the side of the road, return to him the next day and beg for his forgiveness.

The person who sat before them now was not the same girl. In fact, to call her a girl was far from truth. Though she looked worn from her ordeal, she was not beaten. A power emanated from her that was perceptible. There was a stronger set to her jaw, a deep knowing and understanding in her eyes, and a noble resolve in her face that neither parent had ever noticed in their daughter before. Not that she appeared to be hardened—her innocence was still there—but it was protected by a seemingly invincible strength that could not be disregarded. Mataji realized remorsefully that Rajni had passed her fifteenth birthday some months back.

"You are Duni Chand, Raja of Patti?" asked the guru calmly.

"I am, ji." He tried to sound like a raja.

"I am told that you are a most devout Hindu and you know the Vedas intimately?" Guru Ram Das raised his eyebrows.

"I have studied them," Duni Chand pronounced.

"Each Veda?" asked Guru Ram Das.

"All of them I have studied, though my intimacy with them has never been sufficient."

"How many sons do you have?" asked the guru, confusing Duni Chand with the change of subject.

"I . . . uhh, err, I-I-I, uh . . . I have no sons."

"Aren't you ashamed that you have no sons?" The guru's voice was incredulous.

"Uhh, well . . . why no, I'm not ashamed. I loved . . . love . . . my, my family."

"So you are a family man?"

"Welll . . . uhh, yes."

"You have children then?"

"Yes, ji, they sit around you now."

"Oh?" said the guru, the pitch of his voice going up a step. "Do you mean these girls here?"

"Yes, those are my daughters."

"All of them?"

"Uhh . . . welll . . . siixx . . . I mean . . . *han ji* they are all my daughters."

"Does this jewelry belong to you?" Confusing Duni Chand again, Guru Ram Das opened a piece of red silk, embroidered with gold and blue paisleys. Inside was Rajni's chuni, which the guru opened, revealing the jewelry that Rajni had given the Sikhs on her wedding day.

The eyes of Duni Chand grew wide, as did Rajni's and her sisters'. Rajni smiled. She had always wondered what had happened to the jewelry. She had clung to the belief that the Sikhs had brought it to the guru in her name, but she had no way of knowing for certain. Now, seeing those pieces that she had entrusted to the Sikhs that afternoon in Patti actually in the guru's hands thrilled her.

"Uhhh . . . welll . . . I, uhhh . . . well it once belonged to my . . . I mean, I guess it belonged once to my . . . to me . . .

"Did it once belong to you and you gave it to your daughter?"

"*Han ji.*"

"Was it given to her as a loan?"

"As a loan?"

"Was the gift of the jewelry to her conditional? Did you advise her that you would eventually take it back from her?" Guru Ram Das sounded annoyed, much the way Duni Chand sounded when he interrogated people who owed taxes.

"No! No! No! Each piece was a gift to her." Duni Chand was soaked with sweat.

"So was she free to do with it as she pleased?"

"Well no! Uhh . . . I . . . I mean . . ." Then he mumbled, "Well, it was hers . . ."

"You are aware that one of these girls here with me sent this to the guru as a gift?"

"Uhhh . . . yes. . . I . . ."

"Which one, ji?"

"Uhhh . . . yes, it . . . uhh . . . it was Ra . . . uhh . . . Rajni." Duni Chand lowered his head.

"Oh?" asked Guru Ram Das. "Is Rajni *your* daughter?"

"Yes . . . I mean she waa . . ." A long pause. He raised his head and looked at Rajni. "Yes. She is my daughter," he said solemnly.

"Rajni is *your* daughter."

Duni Chand lowered his head. *"Han ji,"* he mumbled.

"Look at her!" The guru's voice rang like a gong over the congregation, penetrating the atmosphere, resonating deep in Duni Chand's heart. His head fell lower. Guru Ram Das took Rajni's right foot in his left hand. "Look at her feet! Look at her face! Look at her hands! Look at what you have done to your own child!"

Duni Chand could not look, and Mataji could not control her tears.

The guru whispered, "Yet she still retains her grace and dignity." The sound of the guru's voice struck Duni Chand like lightning.

Duni Chand looked up sheepishly. He could not comprehend what he saw. His own beloved daughter sat before him in her bloody clothes looking worn, abused, and frail, yet as undefeated as a deity.

"Oh Duni Chand, please recite to me from the Vedas where it says that a father should throw his daughter away because her spiritual authority supersedes his."

"I . . . I . . . uhhh . . ." Tears formed in Duni Chand's eyes. Guru Ram Das was penetrating his massive ego and touching his soul.

"Please recite to me from the Vedas where it says that all things come from the parents rather than from the Akal Purkh."

Duni Chand was shaking now, unable to speak.

"Did you once get angry with your youngest daughter?" His voice was softer now.

"Yes."

"What did you do?"

"I . . . I . . . forced her to marry a leper and leave my house."

"Did that satisfy you?" The guru's voice sounded genuinely interested.

"For a short time. I . . . I . . . believed that she would come back and ask forgiveness." He looked at Rajni, tears filling his eyes. He lowered his head and whispered loud enough for the guru to hear, "But she never came back. I stood at my window day after day, yet she never came back."

"What wrong had she done to be forgiven?"

Duni Chand looked at Rajni for a long time without speaking. He studied the deep emaciation of her cut, scratched, and insect-bitten face, the lice in her hair, the open sores on her feet, the cuts and calluses on her hands and arms, and the bloodstains on her clothes.

Duni Chand reluctantly turned his head to address Guru Ram Das. "She gave her jewelry . . . uhh . . . that jewelry, to some whom she considered to be holy men, believing they would bring it to you, ji. When

I confronted her about what seemed to be to be a rash and irresponsible act, shh . . . shhe refused . . . to acknowledge me . . . in . . . the way that . . . I . . . I wanted."

"Have it!" It was the roar of a tiger, and Duni Chand quaked before the guru like a gazelle before the kill.

Guru Ram Das took the bundle of jewelry and threw it forcefully at Duni Chand. It struck him solidly over his heart like a cannonball. His head snapped back, and Duni Chand toppled over backwards. His mind reeled, his heart pounded.

"Does that buy you relief? What kind of father would do such a thing to an innocent child?"

Neither Rajni nor her sisters nor Duni Chand himself had ever heard such a loud voice. And no one, in all Duni Chand's life, had ever spoken to him that way and lived. Yet now, Duni Chand was frozen with fear.

Guru Ram Das normally spoke in a very gentle and kind way. Now, his voice exploded like cannon fire, and Duni Chand took it full in the heart. His body went limp and fell forward, his forehead down on the white sheet beneath him.

"Oh, Guruji." There was deep pain and regret in his voice. Duni Chand's entire body shook, his ego broken. "No man wh, whoo . . . callss himself a fatherrr . . ."—Duni Chand paused, choked by his own tears and sincere remorse—"should ever inflict such a thing on his own child."

Duni Chand composed himself enough to raise his head and look directly at Guru Ram Das. "I was once a proud and powerful man. My influence and power were absolute over my domain. I believed that as a Brahmin, I was above the rest. Yet by my own actions, all that I am and all that I had have lost their value. My family was once my greatest treasure. Yet they have all turned from me." Duni Chand was sobbing uncontrollably. "And now," his voice rose to a falsetto, "no one will even play chess with me!"

And with that, his grief and his shame collided in a spectacular display of remorse. His sobbed copious tears, his entire body shook, and his red turban was lopsided. He sat before the guru, desolate, his ego deflated, consumed by his shame.

Rajni could bear it no longer. She got up, jumped from the dais, and went to her father. She had never seen him humbled before another person. Yet now, before hundreds of people and the holy Guru Ram Das, he was reduced to the point of helpless blubbering. Before her eyes,

Rajni had seen her father transformed. She put her arms around him and comforted him, as she had comforted Piare a thousand times before.

That simple act of compassion brought Duni Chand relief, and he began to calm. Mataji put her arms around Rajni, sobbing over and over, "My baby, my baby!"

Piare rose and stepped from the dais. He sat in front of Duni Chand and touched his feet. "Oh Duni Chand," Piare said with sincerity, "I am so deeply indebted to you. Had you not married me to Rajni, I would have never met the guru and would have died from my disease. Look at me now!"

Duni Chand was startled by these words and raised his head to look at Piare. Since he had not seen a leper anywhere around, he assumed that Piare had died or that Rajni had simply left him on the side of the road, something that he would have done himself. It never occurred to him while he was under scrutiny by Guru Ram Das that Piare was among those beside the guru. He placed his hands on Piare.

"But . . ." He took a deep breath. "You were a rotting corpse! We couldn't stand your smell. I was sure you would die within weeks, if not days."

Piare took Rajni's hand. "It was her love and her prayers that kept me alive and brought me here to be healed." Piare gazed intently into the eyes of Duni Chand. "You can be healed too," he said directly.

Duni Chand looked up at Guru Ram Das. "I think I have been, boy."

Now both parents saw their youngest child as she was, with her wounds healing, the cut on her face treated, her body clean, and in beautiful clothes given to her by Guru Ram Das.

"Oh, Duni Chand, what dowry did you give for your daughter's hand?" the guru asked mischievously.

"Uhhh, I . . . I . . . welll . . . I gave nothing."

"Understand something, my friend. God has two qualities that you can always rely on. One, He is patient. Two, He is merciful, and He will always give us the opportunity to correct our mistakes. Today, because of your devotion, because you raised your daughters properly, and because" —the guru placed his hand on Punditji's arm—"you gave Rajni such a great teacher, God has given you the opportunity to correct the wrong you have done."

"Can that be?" asked Duni Chand sincerely. "I have been so cruel."

Guru Ram Das looked at Rajni and Piare. "See how they forgive you? See how your own daughter, who just as easily could have died, forgives you? She bears you no ill will even after all she has had to endure. It is the compassion of the Akal Purkh that lives in her heart. Do you think God's forgiveness and love for you to be any less?"

"No, ji. Only *my* compassion is . . . uhh, was less."

"Take your daughter now and give her a proper dowry. You married her to a good boy. Teach him administration and finance. He will make a good Raja of Patti someday. And," Guru spoke openly to all the sisters, Duni Chand, and Mataji, "come to see me here once a month. Work as a family in my kitchen, help with the earthworks, and serve those pilgrims who come here to pray." Guru Ram Das took the hand of Punditji. "Punditji, only you could have prepared her for this destiny. Now, see that everything happens right and come with them once a month. I don't want to have to send for you again."

Rajni helped Duni Chand to get up. He reverently replaced the jewelry back in Rajni's chuni and wrapped it again in the red silk. With the greatest reverence, Duni Chand went forward and laid it at the feet of Guru Ram Das. It was the most humble act of his life.

"Rajni has taught me the meaning of giving, and I would be grateful if you will accept this again."

"My friend," said the guru, "she has taught us all the meaning of giving, and I assure you that the sacrifices she has made will keep her name enshrined in this world and the next. And so shall you be remembered."

Duni Chand then turned to Rajni and his other daughters and as Punditji had predicted, folded his hands, bowed his head, and said, "My arrogance and my cruelty led me to do and say things to all of you that I will regret long after my ashes have gone into the Ganga. Although I don't deserve it, I beg your forgiveness and mercy."

Duni Chand dropped to his knees and, with his hands still folded and his head bowed, said, "I beg you, please come home, return to Patti with us, and enter the house you turned your backs on. If not for me, then please do it for your mother who has suffered nearly as much as Rajni."

In unison, as though it had been choreographed, all of Duni Chand's seven daughters went to him and put their arms around him. His tears were unstoppable for some time.

The guru then spoke to the congregation. "Now we need to have a proper wedding. Tomorrow, these two divine souls will be joined with the vows that I wrote for my own wedding!"

And so it happened. The next day, they were married before the Guru of Miracles.

Duni Chand paid for thousands to be fed and worked in the kitchen himself, chopping and stirring. It was a stretch for him to feel comfortable in a situation that was so far outside of the strict Vedic guidelines that he had based his life on. Yet the combination of sincere remorse over what his arrogance as a Brahmin had inflicted on his family and the absolute joy he felt in his heart over reuniting with Rajni simmered with the words of the guru in his mind and helped him to cross the arbitrary confines of the cooking circle. He promised a considerable dowry for Rajni and made a significant annual pledge to the guru's kitchen.

"I am serious," said the guru. "Your entire family must come once a month. And you my son," he said, turning to Piare, "must impart your wisdom to your father-in-law and teach him all that you know."

The guru turned to Duni Chand. "Work with this boy. He will help you find a way out of your financial troubles and reestablish your wealth."

"But what do I know?" protested Piare.

"Meditate, my son, you know everything. Come and dig the steps of the sarovar. They will lead you to God."

Duni Chand pulled Punditji aside. "On that day more than fifteen years ago, you said that Rajni would endure great suffering because of me but that she would lead me to spiritual awareness. You also said that my salvation lay with her husband."

"I remember," said Punditji kindly.

"I had you beaten and thrown out, but time has proven you right. Your words have come true. Please forgive me. I have been a most arrogant and inconsiderate fool. I ask that you return to our home and teach my grandchildren as you taught Rajni."

Punditji took Duni Chand's right hand in both of his. "It will be an honor," he said.

*   *   *

Duni Chand gathered his daughters, his wife, Piare, and Punditji and they all made a joyful procession back to Patti. While she laughed with her sisters and swayed in the howdah next to her husband, Rajni contemplated how she had been transformed. She no longer pulled a rope over her shoulder, but she recognized that she would always bear the mark of what she had done, how she had suffered, and the knowledge that she had killed another human being. As Guru Ram Das predicted, the scar upon her beautiful face was slight. Yet it was enough to alter her features and expressions ever so slightly so that each time she regarded her own reflection, she remembered that night of horror and how it irrevocably changed her. Her gaze always remained sweet and comforting to others, but was ever that of someone who looked from a remote and perhaps unattainable place.

As her body bore the many scars from her ordeal, so would her heart and soul continue to bear some of the weight that I had laid upon her and for which she had incarnated. Her destiny had brought her to that confrontation, had put her in the position to bear such a heavy load upon her young and slender shoulders, and she understood that she would never be completely free of it. She was returning with great joy and gratitude to the place of her birth, but life as she had known it would never be the same. Her compassion and sensitivity increased as she matured, and people found great comfort in her presence. Yet for the rest of her life, she never shed another tear.

She had no regrets. The words of Guru Ram Das and the miracle of the sacred water had made it clear to her that she had achieved something extraordinary, and she understood that she had incarnated to accomplish that remarkable feat. The applied power of her mind to stay with Piare and not give up, to keep going step after step, had transformed her. As she matured and grew into a noble and graceful woman, the feeling of the rope across her shoulder with only Me to depend on never left her, and the intimate relationship she had developed with Me sustained her for the rest of her life and beyond.

Two nights later, Rajni lay with Piare in her own bed in the palace of her father while her six sisters listened mischievously at the door. Duni Chand lay smiling with Mataji, listening with gratitude to the giggles of his daughters.

I and the three hundred thirty million deities and angels were very happy. Shiva, Indra, and Vishnu consumed considerable amounts of soma, and Rishi Mahan Akal meditated in deepest bliss.

That night many stars fell from the sky.

EPILOGUE

SHE HAD DONE ALL THAT I asked of her with nobility, dignity, and grace. The burden she had to bear was a heavy one, and she bore the full weight of it to her last breath. She continued to serve the house of the guru with her husband for all their remaining days. He returned to Me first, and Rajni followed in time. She did her duty and in so doing, she brought sweet relief to My solitude and hope for mankind.

Eventually, Mustafa Khan gave up his life as an outlaw and surrendered fully to the tutelage of Mian Mir. He applied himself to the instructions of his master and was transformed into a deeply spiritual man who helped to elevate the souls of many. He always attributed his transformation to Rajni's influence and never forgot the night he found her. At Mian Mir's urging, Mustafa Khan went to Patti and had a joyful reunion with Rajni and Piare. They maintained their friendship to the ends of their lives and when Mustafa Khan passed, I received him with great joy as well.

The Golden Chain was well-established on the Earth, and the mission of Guru Nanak flourishes in the world. The excavation of the tank was completed, and the sacred water filled it. That charge of the divine from the time the water bubbled to the surface continues to thrive. The son of Guru Ram Das, Guru Arjan, completed the vision of his grandfather and erected a spectacular mandir in the center of the tank. Since the day it was completed, My praises have been continuously sung there. Millions of people have made pilgrimage to bathe in that water and, in so doing, have found solace and serenity. It is one of My favorite places.

I am pleased. But then, I am always pleased. Few understand that. Some people have the idea that I am angry or that I prefer one group over another or that I punish for one thing or another. Perhaps that idea helps some to remember me as they go through the sequence of their lives. I emphasize again that I am without fear or enmity and abandon no one. Neither do I punish anyone because they displease Me. Humankind seems to do a fine job of punishing itself.

Yes people die, people get ill, misfortune comes and goes. It is fine not to like it; after all the human perspective is limited. It is fine not understand it, which few do since the human mind cannot fully understand Me. It is fine to say I don't exist. At least I have been considered.

To truly understand Me is not accomplished with the mind. If you wish to know Me and experience My love, simply come and walk on My street with your head in your hands.

Rajni did.

DISCLAIMER

I, Gurutej Singh Khalsa, the author of this book, am not the Akal Purkh and make no claim to speak on behalf of the Akal Purkh! As a literary device to tell this story, I tried to present it from what my mind perceived could be the perspective of the Akal Purkh if He were to sit with me and tell me this story in person. Neither do I claim to speak for the gurus of the Sikhs or to know firsthand and verbatim what they said. In an effort to make the story live, I gave voice to the gurus, as if I were telling a story in the gurdwara. The only exceptions occur where the guru's words are written in italics, in which case it is taken from their own writings. Consider this not as a word for word translation but rather as an interpretation.

HISTORICAL NOTE

This work is based on a traditional story about a girl, Rajni, who was raised as the daughter of a powerful raja. She defied her father and he forced her into marriage with a crippled leper. Other than that, little is known about her or the life she lived. Central to this tale is the story of the founding of Sikh Dharma and the lives of the first four gurus of the Sikhs.

There were ten gurus who gave the Sikh religion, properly called Sikh Dharma, its foundation, code of conduct, and scripture. This story includes the lives of the first four. It should be understood that the stories of the gurus as related here are based on research and common tradition. I have made every effort to be true the historical facts that apply to the lives of the gurus and the history of India as I understand them. Because I am not fluent in Punjabi, my research has been limited to those texts that are written in English and to what I have learned from my own teacher, Siri Singh Sahib Bhai Sahib Harbhajan Singh Khalsa Yogiji (1929–2004), also known as Yogi Bhajan or affectionately as Yogiji. I have also talked with other Sikh scholars, and the first draft of this work was reviewed for historical accuracy by a group of scholars in India.

Because this is a novel, the characters, including the gurus, speak and interact. Where I have written dialogue involving the gurus, it is based on how I believe they may have spoken and what they may have said in those situations, based on historical research and Sikh tradition. In every instance, I have done my best to remain true to the spirit and teachings of those gurus.

I have tried to capture a sense of the times in India in the fifteenth and sixteenth centuries, but I westernized and modernized it somewhat to make it more accessible to the reader. I went to Patti to try to find a trace of Rajni, but only a little trace was there. There is an old fort there that I was advised was established by Maharaja Ranjit Singh in the early nineteenth century, and I was told that this was erected where Duni

Chand's palace once stood. Whether that is true or not, I used it as the site for Duni Chand's palace in the book.

I have tried to be faithful to the stories and traditions of the gurus. The story of the engagement of Bhai Jetha and Bibi Bani is traditionally set in Goindwal, but in researching it and discussing with people who are considerably more knowledgeable than I am, it seems that this may have actually taken place in Basarke. So I placed it there. The character of Mustafa Khan refers to Mian Mir as his spiritual teacher. The great Sufi saint began his ministry when he was in his early to mid twenties. He became very close friends with the fifth guru, Guru Arjan, the youngest son of Guru Ram Das and was a few years older. It is certainly possible, therefore, that a young Mian Mir could have influenced someone like Mustafa Khan while Guru Ram Das was still alive.

The tradition of the guru or spiritual teacher is long and sacred in India, but is not fully understood outside of Asia and most especially misunderstood in the West. That realtionship is perhaps one of the most intimate as well as confusing relationships one can experience. Awareness or spiritual enlightenment is not something that is learned, but something that is transmitted. Therefore, the channel between the guru and the student must be clear and unobstructed, which means the ego of the student must be removed. It is only then that the guru can transmit the vision of God, or darshan, to the student. I have tried to demonstrate how Bhai Lehna, Amar Das, and Bhai Jetha humbled themselves before their gurus so that light could come in.

India in the fifteenth and sixteenth centuries was physically different than the India of today. The Punjab of that time was much more lush, and portions of it were covered by jungle and alive with wild animals. Today, largely due to extensive deforestation under the British during the nineteenth century and early twentieth century, those lush jungles and the wild animals that populated them are gone.

The story of Rajni as written here is pure conjecture though based on the traditional story and is the result of considerable meditation, contemplation, prayer, and imagination. We know that she was raised as a princess, and we know that her father forced her into marriage with a leper and that she pulled him around the Punjab in a small wagon. I could not find any specific details about her experiences, so I created them. After all, this is a work of fiction. I did find one reference to her husband conceiving of and digging the steps that lead down into the water of the sarovar, so I included that in the story. However, the meditations that Rajni and the Sufis practice are real. Yogi Bhajan taught them to me, and I offer them here.

There are those who say that the story of Rajni is mere fable, while others maintain that she lived and her story is true. There is little documented information, so I will leave that to be decided by those with minds greater than mine. However, if this story touches the heart of the reader as it did mine in the writing of it, then I think that makes for a strong argument in her favor.

ACKNOWLEDGMENTS

THERE ARE VARIOUS SOURCES I referred to for this book, such as Kushwant Singh's *History of the Sikhs* and Patwant Singh's *The Sikhs*. However, I leaned most heavily on the six-volume work of Max Arthur Macauliffe, *The Sikh Religion: its Gurus, Sacred Writings, and Authors*. Naturally, the Internet was also a valuable resource. Also, in the early 1970s, I lived in St. Louis, Missouri, and was appointed librarian for the gurdwara, which at that time consisted of keeping the books with me since there was no physical location for the gurdwara then. There were a number of books in English that I read, although unfortunately I do not remember the titles or authors of most of them. Yet I learned a great deal about Sikh history and the Sikh gurus. Also, because I have always loved history anyway, as my life evolved, I welcomed every opportunity to hear stories and learn from those much more knowledgeable than me about Sikh history and its traditions and culture.

The greatest resource for me, though, was my amazing teacher Siri Singh Sahib Bhai Sahib Harbhajan Singh Khalsa Yogiji, aka Yogi Bhajan (1929–2004). His knowledge and understanding of Sikh history and its teachings is profound. He encouraged me to write this book, and from him, I learned more than can ever be recounted here. Through him, I met a number of Sikh scholars who were great resources as well. As previously mentioned, some of those scholars reviewed an earlier version of the text.

There were also a number of people who gave bits of information, input, or told me stories; a number of people who read various incarnations of the manuscript before this final version, and even a few who listened to me read it to them. For reasons known only to me (and Akal Purkh), I will not mention names, but you know who you are, and to each of you I am grateful beyond words. That being said, however, I would like to thank M.M. (Maude) Adjarian, my editor, who was a huge help and support in getting the manuscript into a readable version. I would also like to thank Ditta Khalsa (Ditta <seldomscene1@gmail.com>) who worked patiently with me to develop the cover art.

CPSIA information can be obtained
at www.ICGtesting.com
Printed in the USA
BVHW07s2124251018
531255BV00001B/30/P